SHADOWS

SHADOWS

ROBIN McKINLEY

Nancy Paulsen Books
An Imprint of Penguin Group (USA) Inc.

NANCY PAULSEN BOOKS
An imprint of Penguin Young Readers Group
Published by The Penguin Group
Penguin Group (USA) Inc., 375 Hudson Street, New York, NY 10014, USA

USA | Canada | UK | Ireland | Australia | New Zealand | India | South Africa | China
Penguin Books Ltd, Registered Offices: 80 Strand, London WC2R 0RL, England
For more information about the Penguin Group, visit penguin.com

Library of Congress Cataloging-in-Publication Data is available upon request.

Published simultaneously in Canada.
Printed in the United States of America.
ISBN 978-0-399-16579-5
1 3 5 7 9 10 8 6 4 2

Design by Marikka Tamura.
Text set in Stempel Garamond.
The publisher does not have any control over and does not assume any
responsibility for author or third-party websites or their content.

to Diana Wynne Jones

CHAPTER 1

THE STORY STARTS LIKE SOMETHING OUT OF A
fairy tale: I hated my stepfather.

It's usually stepmothers in fairy tales. Well, equal time for step-
fathers.

I almost don't know why I hated Val so *much*. He was short and
hairy and didn't know how to wear Newworld clothes and spoke
with a funny accent and used a lot of really dreeping words that
nobody in Newworld had used in two hundred years. Have you
ever heard *anyone* say "ablutions"? I didn't think so. He looked
like the kind of creepazoid you'd cross the street to avoid walking
past too close to. And this guy who looks like a homeless crazy-
dumb who's about to start shouting about the evil magician who
planted electrodes in his brain stands there smiling gently at my
mother . . . and she laughs and puts her arm through his because
she loves him. *Uggh.*

Maybe I hated him because she loved him, although I was
pretty old for that kind of doolally. I'd turned seventeen by the

time they got together, and my brother, Ran (short for Randal not Randolph), who wasn't quite thirteen yet, thought he was wonderful. I don't know what went wrong with me. It was like an evil magician had put electrodes in my brain.

Margaret Alastrina (everyone calls me Maggie, but the full lineup is way more effective if you want to shout), *there's no point in telling this story if you're not going to be honest.* Okay, okay, I do know why I couldn't deal with Val. It was the shadows. But in Newworld, where we're all about science and you stop reading fairy tales about the time you *learn* to read (which always seemed really unfair), being afraid of shadows was silly and pathetic. Even if there were a lot of them and they didn't seem to be the shadow *of* anything. (And if they were, whatever it was had way too many legs.) So I hated him for making me silly and pathetic. That's *scientifically logical,* isn't it?

For a while Mom made a fuss about it and tried to get us—Val and me—to do things together, I guess because she couldn't believe I wouldn't like him if I got to know him better. You know the kind of thing. We did the grocery shopping—with him being as useless as it's humanly possible to be and me having to explain everything; why he hadn't starved to death before he met Mom I have no idea—and when I got my learner's permit Mom was always "Oh, take Val, I haven't got time right now," which was probably true but it was also Mom trying to make us friends. (And honestly, he was a pretty good learner driver's passenger. He never blew about dumb stuff—and he didn't even get upset when I put the tiniest— the *tiniest*—dent in Mom's fender because there was this really unnecessary knob on the side of one of those big metal anti-cobey boxes and I couldn't see it because the front of the car was in the way. We got out and looked at it and I thought, My life is over, but all Val said was, "I can bend that out again. Back into the driveway tonight so it's on the other side and she'll never know.")

Mom probably couldn't believe what had happened to her daughter. I'd been this disgustingly sweet, cooperative kid, always worried about everyone else (this got worse after Ran was born. I am *never* having kids. Moms with new babies have *no* life), which is to say this dreary little dreep. What started giving me my own personality finally was when I got old enough to volunteer at the Orchard Animal Shelter. I was *thrilled* at being allowed to shovel critter crap and scrub bowls. The self-confidence issues of a nine-year-old can be pretty weird.

I'd wanted a dog since forever, but about six months after Dad died, and Mom was still trying to be extra-nice to Ran and me, especially because she was working about twenty-six hours a day and exhausted and miserable and cranky when we saw her at all, I told her I'd found *my dog.* So while she gave me the old "a dog is a big responsibility" lecture and reminded me with lots of Mom gestures and eye contact that she was working twenty-six hours a day and backup from her was a nonstarter, her heart wasn't really in it. I had wanted almost every dog that came into the shelter be-cause whatever it was it was a *dog,* but this time it was one of those your-eyes-meet-and-you-know-you're-made-for-each-other things. (My friend Laura has them about every six months with a new boy.) Clare was saving him for me while I dealt with Mom (and Ran, although Ran is fine about most things including dogs as long as they're not his problem). So we brought Mongo home.

Mongo is short for *mongrel*—we don't know anything about him; one of the Watchguard guys brought him to Clare—but he's totally a border collie.

He was maybe five months old and already crazy, and you could guess that some ordinary family hadn't been able to cope with a hairy attack squad caroming off the walls and trying to fetch pieces of furniture so somebody would throw them for him. Mom, even having folded on the subject of my dog, was a little worried about Mongo but Clare said I'd cope, which made me feel better than anything ever had in my life before, certainly anything since Dad died. Mongo is also really, really happy and cheerful and loving (as well as crazy) and he was totally a good idea and just what we needed.

But the point is, he was my dog. We had him because I wanted a dog. I had to walk him twice a day and feed him and brush him (*way* too much fur. If I'd realized, I might have tried to fall in love with something short-haired) and make sure his water bowl was clean and full and all that. Which in Mongo's case included a *lot* of remedial training, starting with SIT. Sitting to have his lead put on, sitting before he was allowed out the door, sitting before he could jump in the car, sitting before his food bowl was put down— and the accidental swallowing of the hand holding the bowl is not allowed either. Sitting got him used to paying attention to me as something more than the hand that throws the stick and puts the food bowl on the floor. (And pets him. Mongo will *lie still* for as long as someone is petting him.) Then there was convincing him that eating sofa cushions wasn't allowed, or baseboards or shoes or origami figures that happen to fall on the floor—he ate the best dragon I ever made and the fact that Takahiro made me a better one doesn't change anything—and finding a more or less chew-proof dog bed before I spent my entire college fund replacing the ones that weren't chew-proof enough. I thought teaching him the long down was going to kill us both, although possibly my attention span wasn't up to it either.

But I did it. I did it all. He barely even ate newspapers or gloves or (empty) cereal boxes after the first six months with us. I was the kind of kid who *did* walk the dog every day. Twice. Just getting enough exercise was a big thing with Mongo.

Although having to walk the dog became my excuse for not doing stuff with my friends. I kind of stopped having friends after Dad died. Everybody but Jill. Jill hung on like . . . like a really good friend who'd had her parents split up two years before and *was not going to lose* anybody else. She used to come home with me after school and walk Mongo too. I am really lucky to have Jill, although I didn't know it for a while. I didn't feel lucky.

Dad died when I was ten and Ran was six, because this guy who got drunk the first night they let him out of jail for drunk driving came over the median strip on the highway in his double-muscle-macho car and killed him. The guy didn't kill himself until the next time they let him out of jail and he ran into a tree, but that was too late for Dad. I think I was sweet for the next several years, after almost everyone else had turned into a teenager, because I was afraid that if I wasn't really good maybe Mom would die too. I was young enough to believe that kind of thing, although when Ran kept asking me—especially when he hadn't been good—I always said no, it was a stupid accident and Mom was really careful. She was really careful, but Dad had been really careful too; there just wasn't a lot he could do about something the size of an army anti-cobey truck coming over the median strip at eighty miles an hour.

Mom dated a few other guys over the years, but not very many. "I don't have time," she said. Mom always had pictures of us on her desk. This would be cute except that even after she had pictures of us well past the rug-rat stage she kept the really loser baby ones. She worked five and a half days a week as the office manager for an accounting firm, which meant that she should have met lots of interesting men, because every grown-up has to do their taxes, but Tennel & Zeet didn't have the right kind of clients. I know they didn't have the right kind of clients because Val was one of them. Tennel & Zeet had a specialty in immigrants from the Slav Commonwealth so that's probably why Val went to them.

Ran and I didn't think a lot about it at first when she said she was bringing this new guy home. She did occasionally bring guys home—or, better, we'd all go to a restaurant: neutral ground, and somebody else cleaned up after—although she hadn't in nearly a year, so whoever he was would be a little interesting for the novelty. But by the day he came I wanted to hide the salad or lay the tablecloth (yes, a real tablecloth and in the real dining room) face-down or something, just to break the circuit, as she went zinging around the kitchen like she was the most organized person in the world, which she isn't. We had a joke, Ran and Mom and me, that she used up all her organization at work. But the way Mom was behaving was the first clue that Val might be more important than the other (few) guys we'd met, so I was probably already on the wrong channel with him when the doorbell rang.

Also I'd been thinking why were we having him over for dinner for this first meeting? I like having someone else doing the cooking—someone other than Mom (or me. Although quite sane people will come to dinner when I make my spaghetti sauce). Val didn't have much money—Mom didn't quite say this, but I figured it out. And she wanted to show him what a happy little family we were. Well, he could have cooked *us* dinner, couldn't he? At *his* place.

So I was feeling kind of unplugged about Mom pretending we were supposed to believe it was no big deal about this Val person coming over. And when she sang out—and I mean *sang*, it was disgusting—for me to answer the door when the bell went, I think I was going to dislike him even if he was a billionaire with a private island big enough for a wild animal sanctuary and a really cute son who was just my type.

But when I opened the door . . .

It was like there was more than just Val there. As if he was twice the size of a human person, or there were two of him, or something. It was really dark out, in spite of the porch light, and at first I couldn't see his face. I was frightened. I didn't like being frightened. I'd been frightened about almost everything since Dad died.

And there was something *wrong* with Val being too big. In that first shock I don't think I noticed there was something wrong with the darkness—it was February, it still got dark early, it was nearly seven p.m.—that it was *shadows*. If I'd noticed they wiggled I might have just slammed the door on him.

"I am Val," he said in his funny voice, and stepped forward and I got my first eyeful of his clothes sense, which was pretty frightening all by itself. I stepped back like he was a big ugly cobey-unit goon with a zapper and I was a homeless loophead, and now in the light of the hall I could see him plainly, see that he was short and hairy as well as having a funny voice, and I've seen orangutans that wore clothes better. I didn't recognize Val's accent but that wasn't surprising. The Slav Commonwealth is like ninety countries, some of them no bigger than your front yard, and every one of them has its own language.

He was smiling at me. It was a hopeful smile and I didn't like it, because it meant this dinner was important to him too, and I'd already decided I didn't like him. Or his big (wiggly) shadows.

The darkness, or whatever it was, seemed to retreat a little, or maybe press itself down nearer the floor where it wasn't so obvious, as he stepped forward. I actually peered over his shoulder as if I was looking for someone, or maybe something, but I couldn't see anything, although the nearest streetlight seemed farther away than usual. I looked back at him and I thought his smile had changed. He was looking at me too hard behind the smile. I thought of all those fairy tales where once you invite the evil magician over your threshold you'd had it. But I hadn't invited him. He'd just come in, and I'd given way. Did that count?

Probably.

Hey. This is Newworld. We don't have magicians in Newworld, evil or otherwise.

"Mom's in the kitchen," I said ungraciously, but he didn't seem to notice the ungracious. His face lit up at the mention of Mom. As he took another step forward he made a tiny bow and waved me to go ahead of him, which I should have thought was cute but I didn't maybe partly because there was something freaky about the shadow of his arm against the wall—a sudden sharp ragged line along the line of his forearm, and then just as suddenly it collapsed into the proper arm shadow like it had realized I could see it. I tried not to stare but by now I was totally creeped out and couldn't wait to get away from him—but getting away meant leading him farther into my house, farther away from the door. My great-grandmom's quilt hangs on the other, long wall by the front door, and I put my hand on it, either like I was dizzy or like it was going to protect me. Protect us. I had a moment when I thought, I'm not going to let this shadow man near my family: I'm going to tell him to go away.

Too late. The evil magician was already over the threshold. And the quilt was just a quilt.

I don't guess all of this took more than a minute. It was a long minute. It was long enough for Mom to call, "Vaaaaaal?" Yuck. When we went into the kitchen Mom's face was so bright I could hardly stand to look at it. Even Mongo liked him, although Mongo likes everybody. (Also Mongo was so thrilled with himself for staying in the dog bed till I'd released him that *nothing* was going to blow his mood.) Then Ran found out that Val would listen to him about cars—cars were Ran's biggest thing—and that was pretty much it for the rest of the evening. Ran talked and Val and Mom made shiny electric eyes at each other.

Once we were all sitting down and eating (Mom had made her chicken, apples, and cream, which usually only came out on birthdays) I was watching the shadows on the wall behind Val's chair. They were too lively and there were *way* too many of them. One or another of them always seemed about to turn into something I

9

could recognize—a Komodo dragon or an alligator or a ninety-tentacled space alien. No, I was imagining it (especially the space alien. Sixty tentacles, tops). I hoped I was imagining it.

I looked at Mongo, who was fast asleep against the manic wall, paws twitching faintly and looking utterly relaxed. That made one of us.

After Val left Mom came and put her arm around me. "Are you okay, honey? You were awfully quiet at dinner." I didn't say anything and she laughed a little and said, "Well, you can't get a word in when Ran's on full current, can you?"

I could hear her not asking what I'd thought of Val. Before I blurted out something I'd be sorry for later I said, "Where is he from again? Ors—Orsk—"

"Orzaskan," Mom said carefully. "I have to keep looking it up."

"And why'd he leave?" I said as neutrally as possible.

I felt her shrug. "The latest bunch of government gizmoheads don't like academics, and he's a professor of philosophy."

Physwiz—the physics of the worlds—is sometimes called philosophy. I hoped not in this case. "And it doesn't get much more academic than philosophy," I said into Mom's silence. Or as loopheaded as physwiz. But I'd never heard of even the most out-there creepo collecting shadows.

She turned me around to face her. "Maggie . . . I'm sorry he made a bad first impression on you. I don't suppose you want to tell me what went wrong?"

That his shadow is too big for him and there was something out of a bad science-fiction movie on the wall behind his chair at dinner? Not to mention that shirt. I shook my head.

"Well, give him a chance, won't you?" she said.

"Sure," I said.

She stared at me a few seconds longer. I could see the thought bubble forming over her head. It said "teenagers." I smiled, and she relaxed a little and hugged me again, and moved off toward the stairs. "You'll lock up after you take Mongo out," she said, which was Mom-speak for "It's a school night, go to bed."

"Mom," I said. Mongo had appeared at the sound of his name, but I waited till Mom had gone upstairs and I saw the bathroom light go on. Then I put Mongo's lead on like we were going out as normal. Our dining room used to be a garage. Now it's a dining room, Mom's office, and a coat closet. I paused at the dining room door and then flung it open and flicked the light switch on as if I was expecting to catch somebody at something.

There wasn't anything there except a (mostly cleared-off) table and some chairs and the corner cupboards with Mom's china and stuff, and a piece of Ran's parka sticking out through the closed closet door. The space alien(s) had gone home with Val. I guessed that was something.

Mongo and I had a nice little cruise around the block while he examined every inch of the sidewalk, fences, trees, patches of grass, and the Watchguard call box on the corner and chose precisely the right six(teen) spots to pee. I locked the door behind us when we came in again, took his lead off—and went back to check that I had locked the door. I always lock the door. I didn't need to check. I spent a minute staring at the floor, like I was watching for jagged-edged, wiggly shadows to eel under the locked door. For the minute I was watching they didn't. Then I shut Mongo in the kitchen, where the official dog bed was (plus 5,214 dog toys so he didn't have any excuses to eat chair legs), and went to bed myself. And dreamed about alligators and space aliens. But that's my problem, right?

You already know how chapter one has to end: they got married. I told myself he was *not* my stepfather, maybe he was married to my mother but that doesn't make him my *anything* father. (He even tried to adopt us. Ran said yes and I said no. I managed not to say "you must be dreeping kidding, no bugsucking way.")

I was Mom's attendant and I'd like to say I got a great dress out of it but we were broke. Actually it was a pretty good dress because Mom's sister Gwenda brought their own mom and grandmom's party dresses from her attic and told me I could pick one. Gwenda lives in their old family house, way upstate from us in Station. I like vintage as well as the next teenage girl with cash flow problems and wearing dead people's clothes isn't usually a problem but there was something a bit buggie about these. Maybe because I knew Great-grandmom had been a magician. It was Grandmom's generation that got gene-chopped, and they're still checking in case they missed something. You get scanned at birth and then you get another scan and they give you a blood test some time during adolescence—with girls you're supposed to go back when you start menstruating. The scan made me pretty sick the second time, which is supposed to mean that I would have had the gene if it hadn't been chopped. It must have been really, really rough for Great-grandmom and her daughters.

Or maybe I wasn't hot-wired by the dresses because I was dreading the wedding. By heroic self-control I didn't choose the black one with the grey lace and sequins although it was seriously electric, and picked out a pink and maroon one instead that looked a little less like the wicked fairy who's come to curse the princess. Jill was helping me and pulled out a beigey-cream one that would have made me look like I had died (speaking of dead people) but looked terrific against her dark skin.

"Hey, babe, *utsukushii*," I said, which is Japanese for "beautiful." Mostly we insulted each other with the (approximately ten) Japanese words we'd looked up on the webnet to annoy Takahiro with. We only knew a couple of nice ones.

Gwenda laughed. "Okay, you have that one," she said to Jill. Jill by special perk was invited to the wedding to keep me company; other than her it was just Mom's family and friends. (Val didn't seem to have any friends, and if he had any family they were still back in Whatsit-kan.) "And you can keep the black one too," she said to me. "None of this has been out of the attic in thirty years. Nobody's going to miss it."

Gwenda herself was wearing this sharp emerald suit for the wedding, totally looking like the no-nonsense lawyer that she was, even if she was as broke as the rest of the family because she specialized in defending people accused of practicing magic. (I'm not talking about big evil-magician-with-electrodes stuff. Just a charm to cure warts or make hair grow, if it worked, the government would come after you.) She usually got them off (she usually managed to prove it was science really) and almost none of them could afford to pay her.

The problem with the green of her suit was the way the *shadows* seemed to like it. Bugsuck. Also *shimatta*. (Japanese for "damn.") They liked my second aunt, Rhonwyn's, blue dress too, but not as much as the green. Jill was busy twirling and maybe they didn't like cream and beige and taupe. The pink and maroon in my dress was in panels, plus this lacy pink shawl Jill loaned me to hide that my dress didn't quite fit (I'm hopeless with needle and thread) and I was telling myself they liked solid colors, although it was probably just that I couldn't bear thinking of them crawling on me or my best friend. Although I had the feeling there was one particular shadow that was kind of following me around. It *writhed* along the ground after me. *Uggh.* If I'm not imagining you, *Go. Away.*

The shadows were particularly bad that day. I'd figured out by then that the shadows were worse when Val was tensed up about something. He was tense about having dinner at our house that first time. He was majorly tense on his wedding day.

Jill cried. Well, somebody should cry at a wedding, and I wasn't going to. What bothered me the most—besides Val's shadows—was that I was beginning to forget what having Dad around had been like. I remembered the loneliness, how tiny and broken our world felt when there were suddenly only three of us. Sometimes it was like there was only two of us because at first, before Tennel & Zeet hired her, Mom was working three part-time jobs and got home late every night. Our poky little suburban three-bedroom house felt enormous when I was the oldest person in it. I still remembered feeling tiny and broken. But I was forgetting Dad.

And now my world was full of *shadows.*

I was having some of these thoughts for about the six-hundredth time that day when Val turned around and caught my eye and smiled. I wasn't anything like ready at that moment to be nice to my mother's new husband and it must have showed on my face—and then Val's shadows went crazy and I stared straight over his shoulder and I probably twitched or something and I may have taken a step back. Val went so still that that was as eye-catching as the stuff on the wall behind him and I looked back at him and he was staring at me and he wasn't smiling.

And then Jill came up and put her arms around me and her head on my shoulder and bawled, and I could put my arms around her and my cheek against her hair and *not look at Val* although I didn't like turning my back on him (*and the shadows*) either. But what was he going to do with twenty-five other people in the house? Turn me into a space alien or an alligator? Call his creepy minions and have them carry me away to his secret lair?

The woman who said the legal words over them had come to our house and we had the reception there too. It was just food, there wasn't an official wedding cake, but there were several *cakes,* and one of Mom's friends had made a cake in a fancy pan with a hole in the middle and Gwenda put a little vase with some white roses out of Mom's garden in the hole, so that's the one they cut like a wedding cake while almost everybody but me took pictures. Mom did look gorgeous in her gold dress, and Rhonwyn had made her a sort of cap of yellow roses that should have looked totally woopy but was fantastic. (There's a fourth sister—Blanchefleur—but no one's seen her in like twenty years, and a half brother, Darnel, but he's in a cobey unit, and on the wedding day was off being deployed somewhere saving Newworld from gaps in reality.) But Val was there all the time too, wearing a suit that fit him about as well as a horse blanket on a goat (his trouser legs were *rolled up*. He couldn't have got them shortened for his *wedding*?) and he was pretty much glued to Mom's side so that kind of ruined photo ops for me.

Mongo was totally thrilled by all the people (in Mongo's opinion we didn't entertain enough) and since these were nearly all friends of his too no one said anything about getting long black and white hairs on their good clothes. But after I stopped the third person trying to give him a piece of cake—sugar is *so* not a good idea with a dog who's mental to begin with—I hooked my hand through his collar and dragged him out. He was all stiff-legged and resisting on the way to the kitchen door but as soon as I got him over the sill into the back yard he collapsed and turned into a sad hairy forlorn dog blob. I looked at him and laughed. I couldn't remember the last time I'd laughed. He raised his head and thumped his tail hopefully.

"No," I said. "You may *not* go back in there and cruise for handouts." But I did go back indoors myself long enough to grab a handful of dog biscuits and started running him through all of his tricks. He learned stuff really fast if there were biscuits involved but he forgot really fast too so you had to keep reminding him. I heard the kitchen door open as Mongo was dancing on his hind legs. I looked around warily but it was only Jill.

"Your mom says to stop playing with your dog and come in and talk to people," she said. Her eyelids were still swollen from crying. I wanted to know why she was crying at my mom's wedding, but I wasn't ready to ask her yet.

"In a minute," I said. "Go stand in the middle of the lawn and be herded." She rolled her eyes but she went. It would be really useful if I could teach Mongo to fetch critters rather than just balls and sticks and towels with knots in them. Clare's shelter had been a farm in her dad's day before the town ate most of it, but she still owned several acres, and when someone wanted to adopt a wether or a goat or a pony you could guarantee they'd all be at the farthest end of their field. So I was trying to teach Mongo to herd. Jill did what I told her while I semaphored at Mongo. Uggh. Well, we'd get it one day. Maybe. I'd better watch the Teach Your Dog Herding vids again.

Jill walked back to me with Mongo at her heels. He was very likely to follow her around anyway, but when he came to me and sat hopefully, I gave him his last dog biscuit. First rule: If your dog doesn't do what you want, it's *your* fault.

I watched Jill look around our back yard. It was a corner lot, so it was pretty big. It was big enough for both Mongo and Mom's flowers, if nobody was dumb enough to leave Mongo out here by himself for longer than he needed to pee (I'd like *once* asked Ran to put Mongo out when I was going to be home late from a school thing, Ran forgot to bring him in, and Mongo ate a rosebush. I have *no* idea why he didn't cut his mouth to pieces. Special border-collie thorn-proof chromosome). And there was the old shed. It used to be Dad's workshop. Mom had cleared it out really soon after Dad died—the only thing left was the old hammer that now lived under the kitchen sink. Since then it had filled up again and Mom had cleared it out again (Ran's space station with the zillions of drone ships and the cheesy wormhole finally went to the charity shop to make some other family's life miserable) because it was now Val's office. I saw Jill's eyes settle on the shed and stay there.

I turned around to look at it myself. Dad had built it out of a kit so it was pretty buggie, but Mom had planted stuff around it, and some of the vines and things had covered most of it up. Val had started moving his stuff in this week and . . .

. . . there were more of those *kusatta* shadows. Whatever was throwing them out here had just amazing numbers of legs unless it was several of them doing a synchronized team thing *uggggh.* . . .

I looked down at Mongo. He was whuffling through the grass around my feet, hoping for dog biscuit crumbs. Val's shadows had never bothered Mongo. Fat lot of good *you* are, I thought at him. Aren't dogs supposed to be sensitive to the weird and the icky? In the absence of crumbs, Mongo began licking the grass. I took a deep breath and looked over at Jill. She was scowling at the shed but it wasn't a holy-electricity-what-is-that scowl, it was a trying-not-to-cry-any-more scowl. "Does the shed look . . . funny to you?" I said carefully.

Jill stopped scowling and looked blank. "No. Uh. What do you mean, funny? It's a shed."

"Never mind," I said, suddenly very tired. I put my arm around her. "Now tell me what you're crying about."

She gave a drippy sniff. "Aren't you supposed to cry at weddings?"

I didn't say anything and she sighed and said, "I broke up with Eddie."

"You—oh."

"Try not to cheer," she said.

I had never liked Eddie. "I'm sorry," I said.

"No you're not," she said, but she put her head on my shoulder. "Oh, flastic, I bet your dress is silk. If I leave tear marks on it your aunt will kill me."

"Gwenda only kills plaintiffs," I said. "And then only when they've had a chance to withdraw and haven't taken it."

But Jill had stopped paying attention. "You know . . . there *is* something weird about—I think it's the shadows on that shed. Is that what you mean?"

I went cold. Maybe it was better to think you were imagining things.

Jill was still staring at the shed. "Maybe it's just the wind in the vines and stuff. Your mom sure knows how to make things grow."

"Yeah," I said.

My best friend turned her head and stared at me. "Why do you dislike Val so much?"

I shrugged, staring at the shadows snaking over the shed. "He gives me the creeps."

"Oh, Maggie," said Jill, worried. "Not like—"

"Oh, gods' engines," I said. "No. Nothing like Mr. Roberts." Mr. Roberts had taught geometry at our high school till his stepdaughter had told her best friend that he was sleeping with her and she wished he wouldn't. It was about the biggest scandal Station had ever had. Mr. Roberts went to jail and the stepdaughter and her mom left town. I hoped they were okay.

"Like Arnie then," she said, and all the life went out of her voice, and she leaned against me as if she was cold, although the weather was so warm I was only wearing the shawl because my dress didn't fit. (Just by the way, Jill and I looked *amazing*. You'd never know my dress didn't fit, and I'd bought these fabulous pink shoes on sale, and Jill's mom had let her wear her grandmother's gold locket.)

"I thought you liked Arnie," I said. Arnie was Jill's mom's live-in boyfriend. He ran the big hardware store in town: Porter's: Everything for Your Projects. They had a good arts and crafts section, including lots of origami paper, even though the local origami crowd was mostly Takahiro and me, and Jill when she was trying to buy either of us a present.

"I did," she said. "But he's gone all—weird."

"Weird how?" Arnie has always been weird. He's the only person I've ever met who doesn't have a pocket phone. But he'd been a tireless piggyback-ride giver when he and Jill's mom first got together and Jill and I were eight, and he didn't stop because he got bored with his girlfriend's kid and her friend, but because we decided our third-grade dignity couldn't take it. And now he always looked at me like I was me and not a teenager, which is a rare gift in adults.

"Weird weird."

"That's clear and helpful."

She was silent a moment. "You know that selling-you-something face he has? Smiling and smiling and—like Mongo watching the hand with a dog biscuit in it? It's okay in the store. It's probably why he sells so much stuff. But he never used to wear it at home. He does now. It's like—I don't know what it's like. It's buggie."

Like Val noticing me noticing his shadows? "I'm sorry," I said uselessly.

"Well, I'm sorry you don't like Val," she said. "Doesn't do either of us much good, does it? Hey, there's a silverbug outbreak at Longiron. Dena phoned while you were primping. It's supposed to be pretty epic. Peak forecast is for tomorrow. Want to go take a look?"

"Silverbugs?" I said. "Again? That's the second flare this summer."

"Yeah," she said. "It probably doesn't mean anything."

There are always a few silverbugs around. If you see one you're supposed to report it. If you didn't mind stepping on them you were supposed to do that and then report it. If you did mind you were supposed to put a bowl or a bucket or your coat over it and then call your local Watchguard base and they'd send someone over to bash it for you. (There were silverbug buckets all over town, of course, like trash cans and mailboxes, but there was never one around when you saw a silverbug.) The auto-report buttons on pocket phones only came in a few years ago and that made it a lot easier, because you could snap the coordinates and run away. When I'd been a little kid you had to phone it in and wait. But if your Watchguard was having a bad day you could be there a while so mostly people like me who did mind stepping on them went and found someone who didn't mind and let them deal with it.

It's not that I'm totally squeamish about killing things. I kill things like slugs and aphids in Mom's garden (she pays me. She says it's the only way to get me to stay home from the shelter occasionally). But silverbugs aren't bugs, and they aren't really alive. Nobody knows exactly what they are, but they may be some kind of tiny cobey—cohesion break. I've stepped on a silverbug exactly twice. The first time on a dare when I was seven years old and the second time two years ago when it was suddenly *there* too late for me *not* to step on it, although I tried. I only clipped the edge of it but it still went pop and I fainted, like I did the first time, and then I threw up like six times and was sick for two days afterward, which was also pretty much like the first time. But the nightmares were a lot worse the second time, although that may be because I hit my head pretty hard on the sidewalk when I went down. Us bug woopies are in the minority but there are enough of us around it's not that big a deal, although I'm pretty sure Cobey Central keeps a list of us.

But a cloud of silverbugs is amazing to see and although if it's a really big cloud the army'll be along at peak forecast to zap it, they're usually happy to have some ordinary members of the public around to step on the ones that get away because some always do get away, and there doesn't seem to be a fancy army gizmo that works any better than people's feet. But the other thing about silverbugs is that if you step on a lot of them one right after another you get high. It varies from person to person, how many you have to step on. Jill says one is plenty for her, but Takahiro says he's never noticed any effect at all—and he stepped on eight or ten at the outbreak in June, which should have made him as off his head as a triple-fried. So while the army is happy to have company, they'll have a few spotters keeping an eye on how everybody's doing.

(Everyone was really curious about Taks' invulnerability, but when Steph tried to ask him about it he did the Patented Takahiro Silence so everyone rolled their eyes and gave up. It might have been something about being half Japanese, but none of us had ever heard that Farworlders are any more resistant than anybody else.)

One more thing about silverbugs. Big explosions of them might mean there was a cobey coming. One outbreak, okay, it happens. Two outbreaks . . . But it was like earthquakes. Sometimes you got tremors and sometimes you didn't. Sometimes the tremors didn't mean anything. Sometimes they did. But after a second big silverbug mob they'd probably be sending a few cobey troops to the local Watchguards. If there was a third they might even reopen the big old cobey unit camp, Goat Creek, out in the barrens. They'd put a cobey base there at all because a couple of generations ago this area had been kind of a hot spot for medium-sized cobeys—and Newworld mostly doesn't have cobeys, not like Oldworld, which has them everywhere all the time—but they closed it down after the cobeys stopped. At the moment the only thing that lived at Goat Creek was a lot of feral sheep. So Jill was right, it probably didn't mean anything. But . . .

"Let's go indoors," said Jill. "At least there's cake. And I think your mom would let us have a little champagne if we asked really politely."

Ran went home with one of his friends and I went home with Jill that night so Val and Mom could have one night alone with each other, although he'd been sleeping over for a while by then and I could (mostly) not think about it. But they couldn't afford a honeymoon: this was it. I tried to think of something nice to say to Mom before we left but I couldn't. The last thing I said was, "Don't forget to put Mongo out. I've walked him already. You can just put him out in the back yard. And bring him back in again."

She gave me a lopsided smile. Seven and a half years ago she'd been giving the A Dog Is a Big Responsibility lecture and here I was telling her what to do. "I won't forget," she said.

"And you have to close the kitchen door really tight or—"

"Or he gets out and sleeps on your bed," she said. "I know."

I hugged her. Val was standing behind her. I gave him a stiff little nod. If he tried to touch me I'd scream. He didn't. He just nodded back. It was so dark in the hall I couldn't see his shadows.

I watched Arnie that night. I actually looked for any weird shadows on the wall behind him and there weren't any. Arnie did look like he was carrying a little too much charge, but all of our teachers look worse by the end of the school year. Some of them look worse at the beginning.

Arnie was not a big thing in my life. When I went back to Jill's we usually went straight to her room. That night neither of us was very interested in supper after all the cake (and a little champagne) although we shared a bowl of broccoli and gravy to make Jill's mom happy about vitamins. Arnie and Jill's brothers all wanted to watch football so we had the perfect excuse to flee to her room as soon as possible. She closed the door like she was shutting something out (besides brothers) and sat down on her bed like she was falling. "I keep thinking—it's almost like he's under a spell," she whispered.

I gave a violent shiver. "There is no magic in Newworld, *baka*, stupid," I said, louder than I meant.

"Keep your *voice* down," said Jill. "I *know*. There's no magic in Newworld—which is why your lawyer aunt who defends magic users works seven and a half days a week."

Jill sounded maybe a little more stressed than just about Arnie. But Jill did something a little freaky herself. We called it the f-word. *F* for "foresight." She said I was the only person in the universe she'd ever told about it. And probably anyone could have seen that her mom and dad were going to break up, so that she knew it just meant she had been more plugged in than your average eight-year-old. But not anyone would have been home throwing up the day her best friend's dad was going to get killed in a stupid road accident. She didn't know that was why. She just knew it was her foresight, telling her something really bad.

She should probably have reported herself. But who needs trouble, you know? It's not like she ever tried to use it, like Gwenda's clients (mostly) had. After my dad died, Jill tried to figure out a way to deactivate it, but it was a little like deactivating breathing. You can hold your breath only so long and then your body makes you breathe. Nothing as horrible as Dad's death had happened to either of us since and she mostly managed to ignore it, like burying that really dreeping sweater you bought on sale during a brain malfunction in the bottom of the drawer. If you're careful you never have to see it, let alone get it out and put it on. There mostly wasn't so much of Jill's f-word that it was too creepo, but it was still more than waking up in the morning with a sense of doom because you knew you were going to flunk your algebra test (besides, Jill got As in algebra) and every now and then it did bug her. And she'd had the scan and the blood test like everyone else.

I didn't mention the f-word tonight. But I wondered.

"Keisha said Gazzy'll even get you spells if you have enough money." Gazzy sold what the local crazydumbs needed to get fried. Everyone knew about Gazzy. Even the cops knew about Gazzy. But he was still out there across the street from the high school nearly every day.

"*Spells?*" This was Newworld. Even if maybe the gene-chopping hadn't been quite as thorough as the big posters all over the walls in your local Watchguard office said, and even if Gwenda had more clients than she could handle. "But who would want to put a spell on a hardware store owner?" I objected, more to make Jill feel better than because that's what I thought. I didn't know what I thought. *Spells?* But since I'd seen Val's shadows, anything was possible.

"I guess," said Jill. She got off the bed and knelt on the tiny patch of clear space between it and the door. Since Jill was the only girl in her family she had her own bedroom but it was about the size of most people's bathrooms. We'd been sharing her single bed when I stayed over since we were little kids and fortunately neither of us had grown up to be a kicker. Jill pulled a box out from under the bed. "Hey, look what Mom brought us. She told me I had to wait till after the wedding though." Jill's mom was a beautician, and the shop she worked in was pretty amazing. Jill opened the box. There were about twenty little sample-sized bottles of nail polish, all of them in shades of blue and green and purple. "Oh, big bang," I said, feeling better than I had all day. Maybe they were just shadows, you know? Maybe Arnie had heartburn.

"Can I do yours?" said Jill. "You know I'll do it better."

"Yes please," I said. "Thanks."

CHAPTER 2

I PHONED MOM THE NEXT DAY AFTER WE WERE already most of the way to Longiron. (In a house with five guys who were all machineheads, there were always spare cars.) My excuse was that you didn't ring the honeymoon couple early in the morning but I should have gone home first and taken Mongo for a walk. But I was having trouble with the Mrs. Val concept and Mongo did occasionally miss his morning walk (now that he was a calm, mature adult dog) and all that meant was that I'd have to pick up the back yard as well as the sidewalk. And we'd work extra-hard on herding at the shelter this afternoon to make up. He probably wouldn't do any worse indoors than eat a curtain. He was still kind of a perpetual mouth machine. I didn't like the kitchen curtains much anyway.

The noise the car was making (some cars were past saving, even by Jill's brothers) was a good excuse to keep the conversation short. Mom sounded a little distracted, which was fine, and she agreed to give Mongo breakfast, and she and Val were going out in the afternoon, which was finer, because they wouldn't be there when I got back. The reprieve was only for a few hours, but I'd take what I could get.

The silverbugs were even more amazing than they'd been in June. A big outbreak takes a while to reach its peak and the army posts observers to calculate when that's going to be because that's when they want to take it out. The big zapper was just rolling off its flatbed transport when we arrived. The area had been cordoned off with the orange-striped rope that meant "cobey units" to the rest of us—that and the big orange cobey logo on trucks and uniforms. But there were quite a few people already in an advanced state of hilarity, which was probably the result of stamping too many silverbugs. I recognized several kids from our class . . . including Eddie. Which was probably why Jill parked on the far side of the green.

A mob of silverbugs tends to like an open space, which they'll fill up like a gigantic swarm of glittering silver bees. Longiron had a town green with a bandstand and a wishing well at one end and a softball field taking up most of the rest. The silverbugs were curled up, or maybe I mean spread out, over about three-quarters of the available area, hanging in the air like a kind of self-perpetuating firework only a lot more confusing. I couldn't look at a big silverbug display for long or I started getting sick and dizzy, but that first thirty seconds of staring was exhilarating in a way that was almost frightening—your mood *rushed* upward with the swirl of the silverbugs, and you felt like you were about to be told the ultimate secret of the universe, or at least how to fly by turning your feet into rocket blasters. "Come on," said Jill. "Don't sit here. I'll protect you," meaning she wouldn't let me step on any bugs. Reluctantly I climbed out of the car, but I was having a kind of f-word moment myself, which was that Jill's was bothering her.

We made our way slowly toward the orange rope. There were other cars and other people, but they were mostly (sober) grown-ups on this side. The bug center was toward the other end of the green from us—silverbugs like open areas, but they always collect off center. They were looking rather galactic today, with long, slowly spinning arms like your science textbook's artist's conception of the Milky Way. But the way the light reflected off them made me start to forget which way was up and which way was down. . . .

I looked away. There was a tree and I put my hand on it. I was seeing a kind of after-image, like a tiny checkerboard, where the black squares were pinholes into nowhere. "I think I'd better go back to the car," I said.

"I've seen enough too," said Jill.

"You okay?" I said. I'd've expected Jill to want to watch the light show a while longer. When they turned the zapper on, the air would tighten up like your skin when you get goose bumps and then there were great jagged anti-flashes—I don't know what else to call them, if you've never seen it, and lots of people in New-world have never seen a silverbug mob—as the bugs popped or squished or whatever it was they did in great sweeping swathes. (We'd been there when they turned it on at Hyderabad in June. But our moms didn't know that one of Jill's brothers had also taken us to the last big outbreak in Birdhill four years ago.) They were moving the zapper into position now. I wanted to be back in the car when they flipped the switch. The silverbugs that didn't get zapped would dart out through the crowd of onlookers, almost like they were deliberately fleeing annihilation. Almost like they were alive.

"I don't know," she said. "I feel more like the way you describe it. Up and down are all . . . peculiar. And I don't think I want to step on any bugs."

So after all I got back to our house sooner than I wanted. We were mostly silent on the drive, although not wanting to shout over the car helped. But I didn't like Jill looking all low amp and shut down like this. She's not the low amp and shut down type. It might just have been seeing Eddie acting loopy and even more of a *bakayarō* than usual, but I didn't think so. Finally I said, or shouted, "What's wrong?"

She hitched up a shoulder and let it drop, still staring at the road. "You know, or you wouldn't be asking," she said (unreasonably but accurately). "F-word."

"It's bad?" I felt slightly sick.

She looked at me quickly and away again. "Nothing like your dad. But . . . yeah. Something big and ugly and dramatic. And— public."

My stomach unclenched a little. Really not like my dad then. She might have just said that to make me feel better though. "A cobey, say."

"I don't know. But yeah. It might be." She was silent a moment and then added: "I don't mind knowing who Laura is going to fall for next. Or what Peta's Café is going to have on special next week. But big stuff—no. It feels wrong and bad. Maybe the wrong is making it feel bad."

"Yeah." But we both knew we didn't think so.

I heard Mom and Val laughing as I put my key in the lock and then as I opened the door it stopped like . . . like what happens when Mrs. Andover walks into a classroom. Doesn't matter how great you were feeling a second before. Mrs. Andover is the human version of dropping your ice cream on the ground, a big ugly tick on your dog that *you're* going to have to pull out, or getting a D on your algebra homework for the second time and seeing the *akuma* of summer school looming at you.

Bugsuck. *Iya. Iya na* creepo.

"I'm just taking Mongo out," I mumbled, keeping my eyes on the floor—they were in the living room, and I had the feeling Mom had been sitting in Val's lap—"And then we'll go on to the shelter." I put the lead on my overexcited dog and pretty much ran out the door. We didn't get back till it was dark, and even Mongo was (relatively) tired. But we'd been practicing herding both with and without sheep (or alpacas, which are majorly evil from a herding point of view) and he had been absolutely dropping in his tracks when I yelled *stop* or held my hand up. My brilliant dog. So I had something to be happy about.

It was a good thing I had Mongo and the shelter. Because it was pretty much keeping my eyes on the floor and running away for the next six weeks. It was too easy to hate Val once he and his horrible shadows were around all the time, even with how unhappy the way I was behaving made Mom. But it didn't make her as un-happy as being married to Val made her happy, so I hated him for that too. At the time I didn't think Val gave a bucket of battery acid whether his new wife's daughter hated him or not. Ran thought he was great, so he and Mom outnumbered me, right? I had to live in the house, but the garden had become a no-go area because of the way the shadows hung out around the shed. The slugs could just eat that end of the garden because I wasn't going near it. I got desperate enough I even once asked Ran if he'd ever seen anything like what I saw—what Jill had seen—Val's dreeping shadows. But it got obvious fast that Ran thought either my wiring was coming loose or I was playing some kind of joke on him, so I stopped.

One day when the shadows were particularly bad and I was to-tally absolutely sure one of them was following me around and trying to climb up chair legs to get at me so I couldn't even sit at the kitchen table to do my origami (Val was in the shed), I blurted out that Val had only married Mom so he could stay in Newworld instead of being deported back to Orzi-whatsit, and Mom went *rigid* with fury and sent me to my room. I was too old to be sent to my room, but I went anyway. I'd never seen her so angry. She didn't come around later and try to make it up either. So I hated Val for that too.

I tried to look up Val's shadows on the webnet, but what was I supposed to look them up under? I half-tried a couple of times to talk to Jill about them—she'd seen full-current weird about the shed, after all—but she wasn't having a good summer herself. It was like breaking up with Eddie had jerked her off her sprockets and she couldn't find her own rhythm again. She told me once, trying to laugh, that she had this sort of permanent half headache of approaching doom. "It's probably just knowing we've got Mrs. Andover for homeroom our senior year. How unfair is that?"

If it hadn't been for Clare and the shelter I don't know what I would have done. Run away from home for real and joined the army. (I'd be more likely to jump down one of the silverbug checkerboard pinholes.) Clare had lost a couple of workers over the summer (kids who looooove animals often find they don't looooove cleaning up after them so much) so she could even pay me for a few extra hours. I was there so much I was totally tight with the Family, which are the mostly reject animals that live at what used to be reception, but Clare's put a half wall across most of that room so you can sidle along this little aisle from the front door to Clare's office, although Bella (the wolfhound) can still reach you if she wants to. You can tell a lot about a potential critter adopter by how they react to ten or twelve dogs enthusiastically bouncing off a three-and-a-half-foot barrier in welcome. (There are usually also a few cats in the bay window ignoring the fuss, Suri the parrot screaming, and Sherry the chameleon silently turning blue.)

Mongo became an honorary member, since I usually brought him along, and he was good at enthusiasm. (He never learned to love the bus ride, but he learned to put up with it.) And by the end of the summer he could bring the ponies or the wethers to the top gate, or Clare's chickens back to the henhouse. (We were still working on the alpacas. Alpacas have minds of their own.)

The best times, that summer, were when Jill came to the shelter with me (mostly she was working too: she was a waitress at Peta's Café and put in a few hours a week at Porter's) and we took as many of the long-term residents for walks as possible. Clare tried to get all the dogs out of their kennels at least every other day, but her volunteer walkers didn't always show up. Mostly you could only walk one or two dogs at a time—no more than you had hands *and* the dogs had to get along—but Jill and I took the Family out in bulk. I'd have Mongo and Bella and Jonesie plus Athena and Eld and maybe Mugwump, and she'd have Camilla and Twinkle or Angela and Dov and Doodad, who usually wore herself out early on and came home in a pocket.

But the day we got home from a triumph about a missing chicken, Mom wanted to go to Pineapple and Pepperoni for dinner.

Once Mom was working for Tennel & Zeet and we weren't *utterly* broke all the time, she used to take Ran and me out for dinner at Pineapple and Pepperoni occasionally. P&P was the local pizza place that advertised *EVERYTHING for your pizza* and so every family in town with kids would go there and the kids would try to think up stuff they didn't have. They were pretty high wattage, and people didn't really want to waste their money on something they wouldn't eat just to give a pizza place a hard time. (Yes, they had chocolate sprinkles but Mom wouldn't let us order them.) Although Ran went through a period of *liking* peanut butter on his pizza. Tomato sauce, cheese, pepperoni and *peanut butter.* They only put it on his third but it was hard even to watch somebody eating peanut butter pizza.

The thing about P&P was that it had started up after Dad died, so when Mom and Ran and I started going there it was our new family ritual, a ritual that said we could still be a family and do silly stuff like order pizza with peanut butter or raisins or potato chips (Mom only let us order that once, unfortunately, it was pretty good), or zombie fingers (breakfast link sausages) or witches' eyes (green olives) or demon brains (red peppers. Green peppers were toxic sludge and yellow peppers were chicken toes). I think we may have started laughing again when we started going to P&P.

And then Mom married Val and she wanted to take him along when we went out for our pizza evenings. Which meant not only Val, but coming home after dark with Val, even though I wasn't alone with him. First time I said I had a headache and stayed home—and was tactful enough to be in bed when they got back, although I'd been reading by flashlight, and only turned it out when I heard the car in the driveway. Second time Mom phoned me at the shelter, and I said, more or less truthfully, that Clare had asked me to stay late. She had, but I could have made it home if I'd hustled.

Third time . . . I'd come through the door relatively cheerful and ready to tell everyone about how clever Mongo was. It would give me something to *say*, you know? It wasn't like I was having a good time being a sullen teenager not adjusting to her mom's second husband. It took me a minute to realize that all three of them were standing around like they were expecting to go somewhere. And then Mom said we were going to P&P. After a pause, while I could feel myself deflating like Mongo having been told to stop being a *bakayarō* and Go Lie Down, I said I wasn't hungry.

"Maggie," said my mother with an edge to her voice, "you have never not wanted to eat pizza in your entire life. Except when you have a headache," she added grimly, "or have decided to stay later at the shelter than Clare asked you to."

I flinched. I'd tried to keep Clare out of my problems. I stared at my hands, hoping that my stomach wouldn't choose that moment to growl. I *was* hungry. I was enormously, *takusan* hungry, and I hoped they'd leave soon so I could get to the refrigerator before I fainted or something. I'd had lunch but it seemed like several years ago. I would *love* a pizza. I even started to think about going and making my mother happy. Or less angry anyway. But I raised my eyes and involuntarily met Val's. He was looking at me with that cautious, wary expression he usually had when he looked at me. His shirt looked like something out of one of the dog beds at the shelter.

He was standing in front of the wall between the kitchen and the front hall, where usually Mom's grandmother's quilt hung on a long rail. But she'd taken it down for mending—it was so old it kept trying to disintegrate, but Mom would sew it up again and put it back on the rail. If the quilt had been there I wouldn't have seen much.

But tonight as I met Val's eyes this great *writhe* of shadows erupted up the empty white wall behind him. It was so startling I gasped and stepped back.

"*Maggie . . .*" began my mother, and she was really angry, because she thought I was faking it. But she must have seen how shocked I really was when I turned to her, and she stopped, and her face changed, and she almost looked like my old, pre-Val mom again. She put one hand on my arm and the other one on my forehead. "Sweetie, are you ill?" she said. "Do we need to get you to a doctor?"

"No," I said, or mumbled, because the fear spike on top of the too-long-ago lunch was making me feel kind of weird. "I'm fine. It's just—" And then I couldn't think of what to say instead of "your new husband is *hitodenashi*—some kind of monster." What is the polite alternative? "I'll be fine. I'll make myself some scrambled eggs."

Mom wavered. She'd moved the looking-for-a-fever hand to my other arm. "Maybe we should all stay home," she said.

"Oh *Mom*," said Ran. "She *said* she'll be fine."

My little brother, the soul of unselfishness. But in this case I was totally with him. "I make great scrambled eggs," I said. "I don't need help. Or looking after. You should go."

Mom smiled. "I know you make great scrambled eggs. Right after—before Tennel & Zeet, when I was working all hours, we lived on your scrambled eggs."

"Hey," I said. "I learned to cook."

"You did," said Mom. "But at first it was scrambled eggs. Are you sure you'll be all right?"

"I'm sure," I said firmly. Mom put her hand on my forehead one last time. It's a mom thing. You come home covered in blood from beating up (and being beaten up by) the playground bully, or wet, muddy and hysterical because you dropped your knapsack with all your schoolbooks in it in the river and it got dragged downstream a ways before you managed to get it out again, and the first thing your mom does is feel your forehead for fever. "Mongo will take care of me."

"I'll leave my phone on," said Mom. "Call me if you need to."

"Okay," I said, and she hugged me, and I almost cried. Before Val, we used to hug each other a lot. . . . I risked a look at Val. There was only one shadow left on the wall behind him and it was kind of saggy and . . . almost like it was sad. Margaret Alastrina, I said to myself, Hit the circuit breaker. Then Val moved . . . and the shadow on the wall was just the shadow of a short hairy guy in a really awful shirt.

I was in bed when they got back again, but this time I was reading by my ordinary table lamp. Mom came in to check on me. She sat on the end of my bed and we talked a little. But there wasn't really much to say. She was married to Val. And I couldn't bear to be around him.

Val spent most of the days in his shed. He'd already been tutoring before he met Mom, so now his students came here. Fortunately there was a back gate so we didn't have a constant stream of losers and dreeps through the house. Mostly he tutored math and science, not philosophy. I knew that Takahiro was going to be doing some kind of hot-wired super-science project with him starting in the fall semester. I was trying not to think about it because Taks was my friend.

It was something, I guess, that Mom hadn't found a way to cram an office for Val into the house. Our house was way too full already, even after Dad and Mom turned the garage into a dining room. Mom's cubby at the end of the dining room was pretty well impassable. It was known as the Lair, and Ran always roared or snarled when he mentioned it. There wasn't room in the living room even for a desk. If Ran and I wanted to do our homework downstairs (the better to torture each other) we did it on the kitchen table. So having Val in the shed was relatively great, as great as anything was about Val.

Except that every now and then Mom sent me out there with some kind of message. How lame is that? It would cost money to connect the groundline so that never happened and Val wouldn't have a pocket phone out there. When he went to the shed he left his phone in the house. Even Mom thought this was kind of weird, and kept asking him why. Eventually, one night at dinner the subject came up again, and Mom asked why again, and he got a funny little smile on his face and said, "I don't like the energy."

"You—what?" said Mom.

"I do not like the energy," repeated Val. "I would be without electricity and my 'top also, but that is too difficult, and I am lazy." He had an old-fashioned fold-up 'top that lived on a shelf in the kitchen with its power cord tucked behind the refrigerator where Mongo couldn't get at it. It was so old that when you unfolded it not only did you have to tell it to turn on, you had to tell it to plug into the webnet. And almost all the letters on the keyboard had worn off.

There was a creepo silence. Finally Mom said, "Oh, you philosophers," and changed the subject.

Philosophers. What Val had said sounded like the sort of thing the loopheads who studied the physics of the worlds might say, not that I knew any of them personally. How to Go Crazy in One Easy PhD: get it in physwiz and then get hired by one of the brain bureaus. There was one in Steelgate, called The Intellectual Trust, in a big grey building that was so ugly it looked like squashy purple methane-breathing aliens must have built it. *Trust.* Not likely. Mom's mysterious missing sister was supposed to have worked for a brain bureau before she disappeared—or maybe she disappeared because she worked for a brain bureau. There was a rumor that the one in Steelgate had a whole floor sealed off against stuff like electricity and groundlines and the webnet, and you had to work with paper and pencil by oil lamps. Doing *what*?

If Val had been a friend I'd've said *shut up.* Don't talk about *energy.* Maybe someone dropped a 'top on you when you were a baby and it bent a little piece of your brain. There's nothing wrong with groundlines and electricity. The rumor about those sealed-off brain-bureau areas was that they were trying to discover where science meets magic. Where the boundary is. And how they could cross it. But they got *rid* of magic because it made people crazy.

If Val was a magic *user,* instead of some kind of monster, he would make sure he *didn't* have shadows, wouldn't he?

And why didn't everybody see them? What was *my* problem?

I had kept my eyes on my plate. All my life Mom had been making us have dinner together at least two or three times a week. This had survived Ran's throwing-up phase when he was about two years old. It had survived Dad's job, although there were nights when Mom gave Ran and me most of our supper at the usual time and then we had dessert with Dad, who'd come home, yank his tie off, and sit down at the table immediately, his briefcase leaning against the wall below the quilt.

Dinner together had even—just—survived those months after he died, when Mom was working three jobs. When she was super late I used to put Ran and me to bed on the sofa (heads at either end and feet in the middle. He kicked, of course) and I'd get up and stagger into the kitchen and turn the skillet on for scrambled eggs when I heard the car. She didn't like this much and tried to tell me I should go to bed (Ran could sleep through the end of the world, and he was still little enough for Mom to carry him upstairs) but I said *we eat dinner together in this family* and I could see she didn't know what to do. I didn't dare tell her I was afraid of the dark when it was just Ran and me: I already knew she couldn't afford a babysitter and I was ten pretending to be thirty. I'd make scrambled eggs and heat up a roll and get the salad out of the refrigerator and sit at the table with her and drink a glass of milk and listen to Ran snore. It won't be for long, she'd say. I'll get a real job soon.

And she did. And we got Mongo. And P&P opened. And we all got older.

And then Val happened.

Dinner together two or three times a week was apparently also going to survive Val. I was careful to be out as many of the other nights as I thought I could get away with. This would be easier as soon as school started again. Val had only been around about half the time when it ended at the beginning of the summer. But the kind of thing you're out late for when it's school-related takes less explaining to your mom.

So anyway. If Mom wanted to say anything to Val when he was in his shed she had to go out there. Or send a messenger. Occasionally she managed to send me. Sometimes she just sent me out there with a mug of coffee because she was making coffee (all of us except Ran drank a lot of coffee). Because unfortunately I liked watching TV on the big screen in the living room instead of my weeny 'top up in my room and I'd decided this was something I wasn't going to let Val totally wreck. So there I was when Mom wanted someone to go. Although I guess this was part of her Make Maggie and Val Friends project.

I can't remember what message I was supposed to be delivering that day. I'd been out there a few times before and it was always creepo, but that's all, and I'd learned to say whatever I had to say, or hand him the note or the mug, and run away. That day I'd knocked on the shed door and he'd said "Come" so I had to go in.

When I went in that day it was like . . . I don't know what it was *like,* but whatever it was that made Val bigger in the dark was *living* in there, not just the shadows—suddenly the shadows seemed tame and harmless—this huge awful *unimaginable* thing—something like a combination of the silverbug checkerboard where all the little black void holes were gaping jaws with glinting silver teeth and a monster out of a fairy tale with too many eyes and too many claws as well as too many mouths with too many teeth. . . . I may have screamed.

Then Val had *his hands on my shoulders* like he was holding me up and he was saying, "Maggie, Maggie, it's all right," when it was anything *but* all right, and he led or dragged me out of the shed and kicked the door closed, which cut off some of the worst of it. But there was a breeze that day, and it was late in the afternoon and all the ordinary leaf shadows were running around madly anyway, as well as all the stuff following Val, because *yes it was still there* and dreeping *rioting* over the garden. I would probably have gone completely doolally in another minute, frothing at the mouth and biting his hands (*ewww*) but he let go of my shoulder with his right hand and made some weird twisty gesture where his hand seemed to *disappear* under a great dizzy-sparkling swirl of shadows, and at the same time breathing out some phrase I didn't understand, in Orzaskan or something I suppose.

It all fell away—whatever it was—like taking a coat off, and I was okay. Shaken—and *furious*—but okay.

He dropped his other hand and for a moment we stood looking at each other. I would have run away instantly except my knees were rubber. I noticed he looked weirdly shocked. That was my job in the circumstances. I was about an inch taller but I felt like unmown grass next to a bull: the grass may be taller, but . . . Val *loomed*, even if he was shorter than me.

"Maggie—" he began, but with the sound of his voice I stumbled away from him. I can't remember if I gave him the message or not, whatever it was. I turned and rubbery-kneed raced back to the house like there were devils (with mouths full of glinting silver teeth) after me. *Magic user*, I was thinking. *Magic user.*

How had he got across the border? They *never* let magic users across the border anywhere in Newworld, even if they'd been legal wherever they came from.

"Maggie?" Mom said as I blundered into the house, trying not to cry or gasp or be weird any way she'd notice. I failed. Mongo rushed up to me and whined.

"Maggie, what's wrong?" she said.

"Ask Val," I said in a squeaky voice nothing like what I usually sound like, and bolted upstairs, Mongo so close to my heels I nearly tripped over him. I ran into my bedroom and slammed the door. I don't know what Val told her, but Mom left me alone

43

that night. After everyone else had gone to bed I crept downstairs again and made Mongo and me a giant platter of scrambled eggs. Ran, who had the teenage boy's radar for food, followed the smell of coffee and toast downstairs, so then I had to make an even more gigantic platter of scrambled eggs. Ran and I had ours on toast and Mongo had his on dog kibble. Nobody else came down and asked us what we were doing.

"Mom said you were sick," Ran offered, around a mouthful of eggs. I'd dropped a handful of peas into the eggs so there was a green vegetable involved and Ran was separating them out and making a little pile on the edge of his plate. Mongo ate his.

"Yeah," I said. "More or less."

"She was worried about you," said Ran. "Val too."

I succeeded in not snorting my scrambled eggs out through my nose. I said, "You mean mad at me, don't you? Mom doesn't really think I'm sick." And I have no idea what Val thinks, I added silently.

"No," said Ran, distinctly, having swallowed his mouthful. "Worried. You know. . . ."

"Don't make me sorry I scrambled some eggs for you," I said.

Ran shoveled some more in and chewed. "Okay," he said. "But he's really not so bad. Val," he added, like I might not know who he was talking about.

"You can wash the dishes," I said. I took Mongo out, and then we both went back to my room again, and Mom never said a word about what happened with Val, or about Mongo spending the night in my room. Or about how she was married to an illegal magic user monster. Worried? Yeah. They could be worried. I

44

could go down to our local Watchguard and tell them I suspected my mom's new husband of being a magic user. They would check him out—especially after they found out he's a Commonwealth emigrant. And then . . .

This was so bad. Awful. *Hidoi.* The worst. *Saiaku no jitai.*

I didn't know what I should do.

Oh, and Ran did do the dishes that night. Not necessarily so that you didn't have to do them again, but he had definitely used soap.

CHAPTER 3

SCHOOL STARTED SIX WEEKS AND THREE DAYS after the wedding—and nine days after the last message I took out to the shed. I never thought I'd be glad about the start of a school year but nobody was going to argue with me that I *had* to go to school and any break was better than endlessly trying to figure out where the line was I had to walk at home. All lines were obscured by *shadows.*

At least I had Mongo. He liked everybody, including Val, but I was always his first choice. I might have had Bella and Jonesie too but I thought Mom would probably notice if I tried to smuggle a wolfhound and a Staffie cross the size of an ice-cream van upstairs to my room as well as Mongo. (Not to mention the dog food. Bella didn't actually eat all that much. Jonesie was an industrial-strength vacuum cleaner.)

The first day of school I stuffed my new paper notebooks and my old 'top in my knapsack and wished I was on my way to the shelter. I'd thought more than once this summer about trying to convince Clare to take me on full time and then I could not bother to finish high school, but I knew she'd tell me to come back when I had my first PhD and she'd be happy to hire me at minimum wage (she had about six PhDs in stuff like molecular biology, very useful for cleaning kennels), and that Mom would have kittens if I tried. No, pterodactyls. But if I lived at the shelter (there was a sort of staff apartment over Clare's office: it was pretty awful, but I wouldn't have to worry about keeping Mongo) it would solve brooding about living under the same roof as an illegal magic user *bakemono*—monster.

I knew that the stuff they teach you in school about magical hygiene and how all magicians are psychopaths is just grown-up nonsense like if you never kiss anyone you won't get pregnant (you have to wonder about adults sometimes; it's not the kissing that does it). But some of the deep Newworld distrust of magic must be for good reason or why did they go to so much trouble neutralizing the genes for magic in my grandmother's day? How was I supposed to know which was the little bit that was true? I worried a lot about Mom. She was married to the *bakemono*.

I hadn't been sleeping too well since that last message to the shed. I kept thinking that I should go to Watchguard and rat on Val. They'd probably throw him out of the country. But it's not like we'd go back to the way we were before—Mom would be totally miserable and I'd be the bad guy. And the idea of ratting out another human being—even Val—felt totally *kusatta*. Slime mold behavior. *Toxic* slime mold behavior. Especially ratting him out to Watchguard. Our local watch guys were mostly really nice, but they still sent their reports on to the big military Overwatch, and then if it was important Overwatch sent it to the niddles, NIDL, the National Invasion Defense League, and somewhere along the chain of command the sense of humor went out and the guns and zappers and the armored transport vehicles that looked ready to take on a galactic strike force came in.

I have a little trouble with authority anyway but when the army comes to town you get out of the way and that yanks my wiring. I don't like big ugly guys who think they're better than you are because they've got a cobey badge on their hats. (Cobey units are the elite of the up-themselves division. Yaaaaaawn. My uncle Darnel isn't so much up himself, but he's still a kind of a jerk.) Some state-level Watchguard gizmohead comes to every school once every year to give the standard lecture on reporting silverbugs and doing anything that a member of a cobey unit tells you to do and doing it fast. The major we'd had every year since I'd been in high school was so delighted to be himself that he could hardly stop smiling and throwing his chest out at us and *stroking* his medals and ribbons and the stuff on his uniform while he talked. (Jill said it was because the medals weren't his, he'd hired them for the day from Central Costume.) I couldn't hand anyone over to these bugsuckers, not even Val. I admit when I saw Val across the dinner table I wavered. But I didn't waver long enough to do him (and Mom) any harm.

But I was getting short of sleep. Takahiro had taught me to make *kami* guardians out of paper, and I'd folded so many the last nine days, or rather nights, when I couldn't sleep that every time I turned around or Mongo wagged his tail a few blew off wherever they were and fell on the floor. I had them along both windowsills and over the door to the hall and the closet door, and I'd run strings through more of them so I could tack them up near the ceiling and around the lampshade and anywhere else I could think of. I'd got pretty sharp at folding *kami.* There were different kinds of protective *kami*: earth, wind, sun, moon—and critters. I of course totally specialized in critters.

The first *kami* Takahiro had ever showed me how to fold was a fox—*kitsune*—and I'd adapted it so I could have a dog too, although it might have been a wolf. (Eventually I redesigned it further and created a border collie.) There were lots of others: badgers, otters, sika deer, cranes, doves, koi, hares, dragons. It was soothing, folding something familiar, over and over and over, and my stupid brain would settle down and everything would slow down and focus on the piece of paper in my hands, till I became Hands Folding Paper. I'm not sure I didn't fall asleep like that sometimes. I probably slept better sitting up folding than I did lying down in bed. And sometimes when it was like I'd woken up to find that I was still folding paper I'd find that I'd folded something I didn't recognize. I began to recognize it, though, because it always seemed to be the same thing: long, sinuous, with a big spiky crest on its head and neck and plates or feathers or something both down its back and along its belly. Unless the jags underneath were legs. I might have worried more about the legs except that I always felt better when I'd folded one of these things; they gave off a funny mix of both peace and strength. I could never do one when I was thinking about it though. I had to be in that Hands Folding Paper space, turn off, and let it take over.

When I picked up my knapsack for the first day of school, it weighed too much, of course, and as I dragged it across my desk about a dozen little paper critters headed for the floor. I don't like leaving *kami* on the floor—it's not polite—so I bundled them up and stuffed them in one of those useless little pockets knapsacks always have and ran (joltingly) downstairs, thinking that maybe I could stop at Porter's for more origami paper on my way to the shelter that afternoon. (Another of Arnie's virtues is that he doesn't mind kept-under-ruthless-control dogs in his store. He's even been known to have dog biscuits under the cash terminal.) I could hear Jill's (latest) car crunching on the gravel of our driveway as I chugged my coffee. Mongo had already guessed what his early walk and my unusual level of activity meant and was in tragic mode.

"Don't eat anything I wouldn't eat," I said to him. Mom was in the shower and Val and Ran were still asleep. At least I didn't have to say any complicated good-byes on the first morning of my senior year. I kind of felt that if Val had wished me a good year I'd have a bad one. No, wait, my knapsack was full of *kami*. They'd protect me. Maybe I should get a *kami* tattoo. Speaking of things that would give Mom pterodactyls.

If you're asking me, school pretty much sucks. It wasn't going to suck less because it was our last year, except that we could finally see the end of it. But a year was still a long time. And it wasn't the end because we were supposed to go to college after. I wasn't bright enough or didn't take tests well enough (you choose) so I hadn't been offered any scholarships that would have made it possible for me to go away to school. I'd been thinking I'd go to Runyon, which was near enough I could commute from home, and Dad had gone there, which didn't mean they had to take me but it helped. I could just about do it by bus, but I was—had been—trying to rewire the board for enough graduation money that with the money I earned at the shelter I could buy some kind of car. Jill's brothers would find me a cheap one that ran. But now . . . there was no way I was going to live another four years at home. With Val.

I also thought, what if someone else finds out he's a magic user? (Gods' holy engines. What if he's a *magician*. No. Too gruesome to consider. Also supposedly the anti-cobey boxes wired in all over the landscape would pick up magic use of that level. Since there wasn't supposed to be any serious magic or magicians in Newworld I'm not sure how they thought they knew this, or why it was supposed to be a good idea to waste the tech on something that didn't exist.) But even if she didn't have to hate her own daughter Mom would still be miserable if they took him away. And what if they decided Mom had been damaged or short-wired somehow? What about Ran and me? If we got put into care . . . I'd be eighteen next month. Maybe they'd let me be Ran's guardian. Maybe Mongo would find a hundred gazillion dollars under a tree and I could bribe someone to leave Mom alone. Maybe they just wouldn't find out.

Did Mom know? How could she not know? Was I supposed to tell her? *What* was I supposed to tell her? But she knew I hated Val—wouldn't she think I was making stuff up to be a creepazoid? She obviously didn't see the shadows and I didn't suppose Val kept a jar of powdered dragon's blood on his shelf (at least not with a label on it) or a spell book written on human skin or anything.

(Could you tell human from any other vellum? And what did spells look like? If it was in Orzaskani it might look like a cook-book. Boiled Rival Magician. Manticore Liver Pâté.)

What had Val told her about what happened nine days ago? I had thought things around home this last week were a bit lower watt than they had been with all the newlywed la-la-la stuff going on, but maybe that was everybody trying to avoid me. I'd been trying to make this as easy as possible for the last six weeks and three days with the result that I was beginning to feel as if I might as well go live with strangers, because I was already.

"*Chotto*, Mags, lighten up," said Jill. "This is our last year. All we have to do is not fail." Jill had accepted a place with enough of a scholarship that she could afford to go. I didn't want to get a job waiting tables—which paid better than the shelter: *everything* paid better than the shelter—and a horrible little studio apartment with cockroaches and two-hundred-year-old clanking radiators and a toilet that dripped all night and a No Pets rule so I'd be smuggling Mongo in under my coat, which would not be fun for either of us.

I had to let Runyon know what I was doing by the end of September. I didn't know what I was doing.

"Easy for you to say, *oni* face," I said. *Oni* are the bad spirits like *kami* are the good ones.

"*Oni* butt," said Jill. "Your problem is that you won't get off yours except for something with four legs and fur."

Jill parked and we strolled toward the main entrance. Most of the other students were smiling and talking animatedly about the summer (some of them more convincingly than others). I heard a lot of people saying stuff about Longiron and Hyderabad and the silverbug mobs. There were a few faces reflecting the range from resignation to dread. I figured I fit into that group. Jill got me by the arm and hustled me, shouting at the people we knew: "Hey, Becky-Ashley-Ryan-Keisha-Dena-Zach-Hadar-Hanif-Jamie-Laura"—she faltered—"Eddie-Jason-Steph. How was your summer? How many silverbugs did you step on? Are you ready to torture Mr. Grass-ass this year?" Mr. Garcia was head of the history department and deserved to be tortured. Jill took Mr. Garcia personally because history was her favorite subject.

We'd seen all of them some time over the summer except Ashley, who'd been with her dad in Spain. "Hey," she said to me. "I hear your mom's remarried."

I stiffened without meaning to—I was going to have to get used to this question—but before I thought of something to say, Ashley wrinkled her nose and said, "Sorry. That bad? I sympathize." She didn't like her stepdad either, but he was a super-plugged-in, rubber-soled type, a mechanical engineer who stopped people from building bridges that would fall down. And her dad was still alive, even if he was in Spain.

The first bell rang, and we moved toward the doors, the talkers doing the talking and the listeners doing the listening. I was a listener. Today Jill was talking as if she was going to get a prize if she said a million words before homeroom. Her chin was a little too far up and her hands were making gestures that were a little too large. I glanced at Eddie. He didn't look bothered. He was talking to Genevra, who was new this year; she'd moved in during the summer, near Jill. Maybe he'd met her there. Genevra was listening with her tongue not quite hanging out. Eddie could be very charming. Dreeping jerk.

I trailed behind a little, thinking about what I was going to say the next time someone asked me about Val. Ashley and Keisha were yakking away beside me. I glanced up when someone passed close by my other side.

I had to look up a long way. I'm not short, but Takahiro is majorly tall. He's also majorly quiet most of the time. He'd grown up in Japan but when his mom died he was shipped over here to live with his dad. The story was that he didn't know any English when he arrived but his dad enrolled him here anyway and told him to figure it out. Thanks, Dad. Nobody I knew had ever met his dad— he never came to any of the school stuff parents were invited to— and they lived in a gigantic house on the far side of town almost nobody ever saw either. I'd been home with Taks a few times so I could vouch for the fact that it existed and was enormous—and was full of Farworld art and *silence*. The only other person who lived there was Kay, the housekeeper. I'd met Kay. Kay was one of these people who thought food was always the answer. The way Taks ate, she was probably right. But I'd never met his dad, who traveled a lot, buying stuff for museums and then telling them how to install it and take care of it (according to Taks).

I didn't remember Takahiro's first couple of years here very well myself—he arrived the same year my dad died, and it took me a while to start noticing the rest of the world again. By the time I was noticing, Takahiro was famous for (a) not talking (b) doing origami all the time, which helped with (a) and (c) getting the highest grades in his class for almost everything. Since this included papers in English you have to assume his English was fine, at least at home alone and quiet with his books and 'top and not in the middle of the playground or the cafeteria with everyone screaming.

But he still didn't talk all that much, he still had a slight not-Newworld accent when he did, and he still tended to leave out words like *the* when he was upset about something because you don't have *the* in Japanese. Although I may be the only person who's figured this out, since Takahiro didn't get excited or upset in any of the usual ways. I noticed it because *the* tended to disappear when he talked about his dad.

So I looked up till my neck cracked and it was Takahiro. "Oh, *Taks*," I said, and, not knowing I was going to do this, threw my arms around him. He had spent the last couple of Augusts at this super-whizzy brainiac camp his dad had found to stow him away at so Kay could have a holiday. He was such a good student the school didn't make a fuss about him getting back a day or two late, as he had last year, for the beginning of term. Since I hadn't heard from him beyond the occasional text saying stuff like "meteor shower last night. Electric" or "Have scientifically proven oatmeal here made of bleached beetle carapaces" (I'd answered that one "Want my aunt to sue for you? She's good at it") I'd assumed he wasn't back yet.

He patted my back gently and I let go before I embarrassed him any more. He didn't hang out with Jill and me and our crowd of loose connections: he was a solid-state brainiac, and hung with other brainiacs. I nodded to Jeremy and Gianni, on Takahiro's other side, who nodded back cautiously: I was pretty sure the only things they ever hugged were their 'tops. They were either pretending they hadn't seen me do anything gruesome or were having a telepathic conversation about the atomic number of Venus. (Science: not my best feature.) Probably the second.

"Bad summer?" said Takahiro.

"Not the best," I said. "They got married."

"Ah," said Takahiro. "Yeah. They were going to."

"Yeah," I said. "You?"

"Not the best," he said, and smiled. "Some new origami though. I'll show you."

"Great," I said. "Can—" But the second bell went, and we had to hurry.

There was a mob at the back of Mrs. Andover's homeroom as we all fought to get into the last row. Jill and I lost and were in the middle row, but at least we were together. Takahiro sat in front of me in the second row, which instantly made my seat the best in the whole classroom. Even slouching (Taks was always slouching) he was taller than anyone else. Under the roar of conversation Jill said to me, "We're going to P&P tonight, okay? Laura says there's a seriously cute new guy making pizza."

When a gang of us went to P&P, we went later, after the family-supper rush. I took the bus home because Jill was going to the café after school, changed into my grubbies, hooked up Mongo (who had been very good and I only found the last shreds of a paper towel on the kitchen floor, although it might have started as a roll of them) and shot off for the bus that would take us to the shelter. By the time school started the days were already getting inconveniently short. I gave a few of my friends a quick walk (with Mongo accompanying) and settled down to cleaning kennels. I had to turn the lights on to see what I was doing.

Then Mongo and I went home on the bus and I spent some time looking gloomily at my course outlines. My main claim to scholastic fame is that I read a lot. I always liked stories but it got kind of out of control after Dad died. I read *The Count of Monte Cristo* in sixth grade (good choice, although Haydée is a dead battery) and *War and Peace* in seventh (bad choice, what a bunch of losers). But this will only get you so far. The class I was dreading most was something they were calling Enhanced Algebra. This was camouflage for college-track students who needed another math credit but had barely scraped through Algebra I and Geometry. But they'd found a unique way to punish us for being stupid: the textbook was *enormous.* It was not going to fit in my knapsack. So not only was it going to be a total pain to haul back and forth to school every day, carrying it was going to be this great badge of dishonor: Here's One of the Dumb Ones. Jill and Takahiro were taking calculus. At least I had friends who could drag me through Enhanced Algebra—as they'd already dragged me through Algebra I and Geometry. They weren't going to help me carry the book though.

Mom asked me how my first day went and I told her about the algebra book. Unfortunately that reminded her to ask if I'd accepted the place at Runyon yet—sent the paperwork back, she said, although most of it you can do slightly after the last minute on the webnet. No, I said.

"Why?" she asked, clearly surprised.

"I'm not sure I can afford it," I mumbled.

"Of course you can!" she said. "We've been through all this. Tennel & Zeet agreed last spring to underwrite a student loan for you. And you can live at home—" She stopped. I didn't say anything.

The silence turned loud and harsh, like a silverbug zapper. I went on brushing Mongo for about another minute while my ears rang and my skin blistered and then said, "I need a shower before Jill picks me up," and fled. I heard Val come in the kitchen door as I ran upstairs, and I could hear Mom's voice, really quiet so I couldn't hear what she was saying, as I locked myself in the bathroom.

Okay, this was *not* going to ruin the first night of my senior year. (Life with Val: saying "this is not going to ruin . . ." a lot.) Especially because by tomorrow we'd start having homework (and my life as a pack animal began) and I had to keep my grades up in case I was going to Runyon. If a good fairy zoomed in from Neverworld and gave me a fortune. A small fortune would do—I was okay to spend the rest of my life working off my college loan. But the end of September was only two weeks away and if I said "yes" I had to send them a (nonrefundable) check too.

So I *bounced* downstairs like the only thing on my mind was how much pizza I could eat (I burned a lot of calories working at the shelter) and there were Mom and Val holding hands at the kitchen table. Mom was staring at the table but Val looked up and our eyes met. I was even braced for the explosion of shadows up the wall behind him. This wall had photos and stuff so it wasn't like it was blank, but it turned *black* with them. If you believed in hell, which I'd never thought I did, it was like looking into hell—like one of those horrible old etchings of people getting eaten by demons—I was sure if I blinked a couple of times it would all come into focus. . . . I ran for the front door. Mongo was on my heels, half-hoping he could come with me and half-worried about whatever was worrying me. "You stay here," I said breathlessly, hoping that Val's demons wouldn't suddenly start eating dogs. "I'll see you later," and I closed the door as gently as I could. I hadn't said good-bye.

Jill wasn't here yet so I started walking down the road. I was shaking with adrenaline and—it might have been rage. How *dare* he destroy our family? How *dare* he turn my mother against her own daughter? How *dare* he . . . *be* whatever he was? Whatever *monster* he was?

Keisha and Lindsay were already in the back seat, or I might have blurted out the whole thing to Jill. I hadn't told her about that last day I took a message out to the shed. I didn't want to hear what she'd say. She would want to give me advice because she was my friend, and whatever she said would be the wrong thing. I also knew she still thought there was something wrong with Arnie, and it didn't feel at all electric that there was some kind of bad stepdad virus going around.

Jill's always been good at picking up mood, but she'd been almost creepily sensitive lately, so when she asked me what was going on I told her about the gigantic algebra book and how carrying the stupid thing was going to label me "loser."

Jill laughed. "I think it looks kind of cool. Math as art. Most textbooks are dead boring." Keisha and Lindsay—who were both taking trig, which had a normal, boring textbook—joined in with flipping Maggie's switches. I had trouble not hitting flashpoint. But I could go to P&P and act like a normal teenager beginning her senior year of high school or I could go home. No choice.

But I guess I did go into P&P with kind of an attitude. Just like Jill knew there was something up with me when I got in the car, she knew I hadn't been telling the truth that it was the algebra book. (Well, it *was* yanking my wiring: who wants to be wearing a big loser sign their senior year? But she was right it wasn't the most important thing.) Keisha and Lindsay had gone on ahead while Jill was still trying to get whatever it was out of me as we went through the door and I was being about as friendly as a bucket of battery acid till she said, "Oh, Magdag, don't be such a bugsucker," and she said it in one of those little quiet spaces that happen somewhere like a crowded restaurant, especially when you don't want them to. I know there's often a brief pause to stop and look when someone comes through the door, but it doesn't usually stretch past the first few tables, which may be having their breadsticks shot across the room by the draft, and it doesn't usually last more than two syllables unless whoever is coming in is a movie star or something, and we don't get movie stars in Station.

But—thanks a lot, fate—this time it was like everyone had shut up to hear someone call her best friend a bugsucker. The other weird thing was that the lights sort of flared and flickered for just a second, just enough to notice—which at least should have distracted everyone I might know from "Magdag." I used to punch Jill out for calling me that when we were six. I didn't think I'd get away with it at seventeen. I was still biting on "Val is *not* going to wreck my senior year of high school" like Jonesie on that burglar's leg (that's how he ended up back at the shelter, the family he'd protected decided they were scared of him, can you believe it?), and now Jill had called me Magdag in public. So I put my shoulders back and *glared* like the flickering lights were deference to my greatness. (Or that I was Jonesie and the restaurant was full of burglars.) I'm not usually the don't-mess-with-me type. In fact, I'm *never* the don't-mess-with-me type.

One of the people who looked up when the lights blinked was a boy delivering a pizza to one of the tables beside the aisle we were swaggering down. He straightened up at the commotion and I was sure I saw him flinch when Jill said "Magdag." So I was planning on giving him my very best death glare when he finished turning around, since he was clearly turning to get a look at us.

I always thought that "my heart turned over" was just a phrase. Also, Jill and Laura both find boys cute really easily. I don't. (Okay, I'm not *entirely* interested only in their minds.) But this one . . .

He was tall, but not a skinny phone pole like Takahiro. He had shoulders and arms—oh *wow*, those arms—his P&P T-shirt and apron were too baggy to guess what the rest of him looked like, but I guessed anyway. I saw the tight little butt before he turned around. I was pretty sure that my death glare had been neutralized by a nice curve of thigh through the apron as he finished turning toward us. And then he smiled. At me. At *me*.

My heart turned over.

He had long curly black hair tied back in a ponytail and gigantic chocolate-brown eyes—*dark* chocolate, not that feeble milk stuff.

Heavy black brows, but artistically arched, and long eyelashes—long like you figure there's probably a breeze if you're standing near him. I wished I was standing nearer. Dramatic cheekbones, straight nose, full lips, wide mouth (*smiling at me*), golden-brown skin somewhere between fourteen carat and caramel. If it weren't for the long square jaw and the *gorgeous* neck (the neck was obviously part of the package with the shoulders and arms) he might have been too pretty.

He wasn't too pretty. Trust me. He was *not* too pretty. Oh, did I mention the dimple? He had a dimple in one cheek. Oh. Gods. Oh. *Gods.*

"Oh, gods," breathed Jill next to me, like an echo of my thoughts. "Mags, he's staring straight at you. *Get his phone number.*"

I hoped I wasn't drooling. "Uh," I said. We were nearly on top of him. "Uh, hi," I said. It was pretty much the hardest thing I'd ever done in my life that I tried to keep going. But it was just too tacky to stop. He must be used to having nearly every female who's ever *seen* him asking for his phone number. And a lot of the guys too.

I was trying to remember how to smile. I'd managed to turn the death glare off but I'd kind of stalled at that point.

"Hi," he said back. To me. Still staring into my eyes. Still smiling. He'd smiled a little less while he said "hi" and then turned it back on again full blast, so the dimple showed.

"*Mags,*" hissed Jill, clutching at my elbow, dragging me to a stop. I probably didn't struggle all that hard.

"Uh," I said again. "I—er—I haven't seen you here before." And then felt myself turn purple. That was almost as bad as asking for his phone number.

"I have been here only a few days," he said. He had a slight accent, but I had no idea where it was from. Well, I had pretty much no idea about *anything* with him staring at me like that. "Now I am glad I came to this town," he said, still staring at me.

My jaw really did drop. I'm sorry, but it did. I'm not ugly or anything, or stupid (at least not usually, about things other than math and science and taking tests), but this guy . . . guys like this don't stare at girls like me.

"Her name's Maggie," said Jill. "*Usually* she talks," and gave my elbow a shake. "When's your break? Come join us. If you want."

"I would like that," he said. "Thank you." He flicked a little piece of his smile at Jill and then refocused on me. "I will see you later."

"Oh—great," I said (I think that's what I said), and then Jill was dragging me again, forward this time, toward our table.

Wolf whistles greeted us. Keisha and Lindsay had been sitting down while I was having my little encounter with Mr. To Die For, and one of the other waiters was putting down a pitcher of beer and some more glasses. "Hey, give her a beer," said Laura, only half-annoyed that Mr. TDF had noticed me, not her. She was pretty tight with Ryan, and Ryan was a good guy.

"Anybody get his name?" said Jill, who was apparently my agent for the evening.

"Casimir," said Zach. "Is that weird or what?"

"Not everyone is from No Town, Nowhere," said Jill. "I think it's a nice name. Casimir. Yeah." She grinned at me.

There was a lot about that evening I didn't take in very well. I was completely dazzled by Casimir, of course, but that wasn't all of it. It was like the lights that had flickered when we came through the door went on flickering in my brain somehow. As if something was turning itself on and off. As if my wireboard was being rerouted or something. I didn't like it.

But then again it might just have been Casimir. He was enough to make anyone short out a few circuits. He did join us during his break—Jill saw him coming and nearly shoved Hadar off his chair to make space for Casimir to sit down next to me. He'd taken the apron off but the P&P T-shirt underneath was still hopelessly long and baggy. He'd brought a cup of coffee with him, so I got to say something else totally lame: "Oh, I can't buy you a cup of coffee then."

He looked faintly puzzled—maybe he was having second thoughts about me: I wouldn't have blamed him—and then the smile (and the dimple) broke out again. "No, I have my coffee, thank you," and I *think* he was going to say something else—like maybe I could buy him a coffee some other night or even that he'd buy me something some other night? Maybe it was just my brain going *zot. ZZZZ. Zingo.* But Jason interrupted and said, "So, where are you from? You don't sound like you're from around here."

"No," said Casimir. "I learnt my English in England."

"That's not an English accent," said Jason, and I thought, what's he so pissed off about? Jason's really good-looking if you like them blond and stuck on themselves, but he's never thought I was worth more than "hi," and it's supposed to be girls who get rats'-assy about looks.

Casimir said that he'd been born in Ukovia and his parents were Ukovian and he had spent most of his childhood there, but then he had been sent to boarding school in England and only came home for holidays. He said some stuff about how different Ukovia and England were and then Jason interrupted again and said, "Are you here to go to school?"

I hadn't been paying much attention to what Casimir was saying, although the sound of his voice was making me feel all petted and velvety. He was sitting close enough—there were nine of us wedged around a table for six—that I could feel his body heat. When he moved his arm or his knee, it would brush mine (*that* made my brain turn on and off). I was trying to think of a way to say "Back off, Jason," without getting in his face about it. But I heard Casimir saying "Runyon" and I snapped back to attention.

"I accepted a place at Runyon," he said, "because it has perhaps the best physics of the worlds department of any school in Newworld."

"The physics of the *worlds*?" said Jason in a disbelieving voice, and a little silence fell.

My heart sank. Only loopheads wanted to know any more about physwiz than that silverbugs should be popped and where to find your local Watchguard. Senior year you have a bunch of required seminars in stuff the government says you have to know something about: history of magic, why they gene-chop you, what they think they know about cobeys, like that. They're all short—none of them lasts more than two weeks—and from everything I've heard they don't actually *teach* you anything, but it goes on your Watchguard record that you've been cranked through the informed-citizen education machine. Most of it's just stuff like all of school is stuff (although I was a little interested in what they were going to tell us about gene-chopping), but physwiz freaked a lot of people. Every year there was a petition from some of the parents that it's an inappropriate subject for high school kids and should be removed from the syllabus. Since these were usually the same parents who had meltdowns when a book their kid checked out of the school library had the word "vagina" or "dickhead" in it, the petitions were mostly ignored. But physwiz creeped out a lot of relatively sane people too.

I knew Runyon had an important physwiz department. But it was its own little territory and anybody who didn't have to go there didn't. When I had the campus tour last year our guide reluctantly waved a hand at a path through some trees and said vaguely, oh, physwiz is down there, and then flipped back into guide mode and started talking about advisers and food. I guess I knew, but it was the sort of thing you didn't want to know, that Runyon's physwiz department was a big deal, really more of a brain bureau with students.

The cutest boy in the known universe is a loophead. Well, that might help to explain why he seemed to like me.

"Oh, wow," said Jill, not willing to let my unexpected conquest go without a struggle. "Um. Are there, you know, jobs in physwiz—the physics of the worlds?"

Other than being disappeared by a brain bureau, I added silently.

"I want to study history," Jill went on, "but my mom keeps telling me I need to get a degree in something that'll let me pay back my student loan."

"I hope there are jobs," said Casimir, "because it is what I want to study. But there is a trust, the Nowak Trust, to bring students here, and to send some of your students to Oldworld, to study the physics of the worlds. I was offered a much better scholarship to come here than if I stayed home. And if there are no jobs, well"—and he made a short, graceful gesture that wasn't from around here either, but it meant that (momentarily) his shoulder pressed against mine—"this is a nice place to work. And the coffee is good."

Everybody but Jason laughed, and then Casimir's break was over and he left. I tried not to be too obvious about watching those shoulders and that butt walking away, but when I surreptitiously glanced around the table almost everyone else was watching too. Then our pizzas arrived, fortunately for me, because everybody got busy eating and forgot to give me a hard time.

When it was time to go—school-night curfews for another whole year, joy—Lindsay and Keisha were getting a ride home with someone else, so it was just Jill and me. We were all leaving when Jill suddenly said, "Oh, where is my—um?" and went back. She made a big show of looking around her chair and under the table, and then she glanced at the door, but Laura, Ryan, and Ashley were waiting for us. "No, you go on," she said, and flapped her hands at them. "I'm sure I'll find it in a minute."

Laura looked at me and grinned. "I'm sure you will," she said, and all three of them left. Jill was sitting down and digging through her purse with a scowl on her face, but as soon as the door swung shut behind them she was on her feet again. "I'm going to *go get the car,*" she said to me, slowly and carefully, like maybe I didn't speak her language. "You can *wait here.* I will pick you up in a few minutes. You have a *few minutes.*"

"Jill, I'll walk to the car with you," I said, exasperated. "I'm not going to ask for his phone number!"

"Tell him that," she said, and darted past. I turned around and there was Casimir walking toward us, looking slightly uncertain. "See you!" Jill sang out to Casimir, and kept going. He had a little piece of paper in his hand. "I—your friend—" he said.

"Jill thinks she's being tactful," I said, not sure whether to die of embarrassment or stare into his big brown eyes as a way not to stare at the piece of paper in his hand.

He held it out to me. "I was hoping if I gave you my phone number you would give me yours," he said, and turned the smile on again. "It is a large enough piece of paper that if you tear off the bottom, you could write yours on it."

Our hands met as he gave me the paper. So many connections exploded I could feel the smoke coming out of my ears. I could barely write, or remember my phone number—I had to sort of mutter it over to myself so the rhythm would remind me. I could have pulled out my pocket phone, put his number on it, and sent mine to his, but where's the romance in that? Besides, my hands were shaking so badly I'd probably have pressed the wrong buttons and sent my number to Joe's Live Bait House, which is a major local landmark on the edge of the barrens, but I didn't want Joe asking me out for a cup of coffee. It was my pocket number I gave Casimir, of course. I didn't want Mom or Ran or—worst—Val to answer the ground phone with Casimir on the other end. Supposing he did call, which still seemed to me about as likely as that I'd decide to go to Runyon after all to study physwiz. (It might even be worth living at home, if Casimir was my TA next year.) When I gave him my little piece of paper I could see that at least half the restaurant was watching. Some of the women were really old. He probably did this six times a night every night with different girls. I wasn't going to think about that.

"Talk to you soon," I said, and fled.

CHAPTER 4

JILL WAS STILL PUNCHING THE AIR WHEN SHE dropped me off. I went up to the front door smiling—and then noticed that the light was still on in the living room. *Shimatta.* And toxic pond slime. Margaret Alastrina, I said to myself, pull the circuit breaker. It's not even eleven yet (quite. It better not be, or I'm in big trouble). They're just watching television or something.

As Mongo hit me going at full escape-earth's-atmosphere velocity—*oof*—my mother appeared at the end of the front hall. Her eyes were red-rimmed. *Yabai.* Crap zone. I'd forgotten about our conversation earlier. Casimir was suddenly a figment of my imagination. This was reality.

"Hi sweetie," she said. "Good evening?"

"Yeah. Except for the school-tomorrow part," I said, petting the ecstatic Mongo (he *had* to have kangaroo blood, the way he could leap around on his hind legs), and hesitated. If it had just been Mom, I might have told her about Casimir. But I knew she wasn't alone. Val was in the living room.

I had a moment to think, oh, come on, I don't *know* that, I'm just guessing, they've been married less than two months, of course they've been smooching on the sofa after Ran went to bed. But I did know. I could feel him there as clearly as if I heard him cough. Or maybe it was his shadows I was picking up.

"I was about to make hot chocolate," said my mother. "Can I make you some?"

It was a peace offering. I knew it was a peace offering. I didn't want hot chocolate—well, no, I *always* want hot chocolate, but I didn't want to drink it with Val, and I *did* want to go to bed and think about Casimir. *Why couldn't they just leave me alone.* I could feel my head start to throb and I wanted to scream and throw things. But I hadn't had a tantrum in about fifteen years and this probably wasn't a good time to recharge that old skill.

I felt thirty years old. No, forty.

"Sure," I said. "That would be great."

Mom turned to go into the kitchen and I braced myself to join Val in the living room. I could do this. It was okay. Five minutes for Mom to make the hot chocolate. Two minutes to drink it—all right, five. Then I had to walk Mongo. It was a school night. I really did have to go to bed soon.

Where I was standing, about halfway down the front hall (next to the dining room that used to be a garage and the blank wall where the quilt should be), you can see the back of the sofa that faces the TV. You can't see anyone sitting on it unless they tip their head back or hang an arm over it or something. I couldn't see Val. He might be sitting in the big chair. Mom might have been sitting on his lap before I came in. It was a good chair for that. Jill used to sit in Eddie's lap in that chair while Takahiro and I folded little paper things, sitting on the floor next to the coffee table. Eddie used to say things like, Hey, that's amazing, what you guys can do with paper, that's a . . . potato chip! I can tell! And that's . . . Mr. Grass-ass' ass! Wow!

Eddie always was a broken tool. But he didn't have shadows.

As I was standing there in the hallway taking deep breaths and telling myself I only had to stay ten minutes, this *shadow* appeared over the back of the sofa—this long narrow *snaky* shadow—except it was too fat to be a snake, and it had this jagged outline like feathers or spiky plates or something—it drizzled along the top edge of the back a little ways, waggling back and forth, leaving a trail, or something, dark and shiny as a beetle's back except *as long as your arm.* It looked like maybe it was trying to catch my attention, but I was bent over and holding onto Mongo like a drowning person hanging onto a piece of broken boat. Disappointed, I guess, when it reached the end of the sofa, it slithered or unrolled or something down the front, and then *oozed* across the seat and fell or dripped to the floor. . . .

I'd had it. I'd *had it.*

I could have done one of two things. I could have screamed, run back out the front door and never come back. I could have become the Phantom of the Shelter, only coming out at night to clean kennels. Or I could get so furious I forgot to be frightened, thinking this *monster,* this *magic user,* living in *my* house, married to *my* mom—and run forward, straight *at* the snake-shadow thing, and screamed at *Val.*

I chose the second.

"What the gods' holy engines is it with you?" I shouted. "I'm *sick* of your stupid horrible shadows crawling around! What *are* they! What are *you*? What are you *doing* out there in the shed? *What are you? What are you doing here?*"

He had started to get up—he was sitting in the big chair—when I came in. It was one of those weird things he did, he stood up when Mom or me or Jill or any woman came into the room. But he kind of froze halfway when I started screaming at him.

There was a crash from the kitchen and Mom appeared in the archway looking like the end of the world, only madder. "*Margaret Alastrina, what do you*—"

Val finished standing up and said, "Elaine, it is all right."

Mom said furiously, "It is *not* all right that she should—"

But Val shook his head and held up his hand. Both hands. And then spread them out. I knew what he meant but it made him more alien. No one in Newworld did stuff like that, any more than Newworld guys stood up when women came in the room. "Maggie—Margaret—will you please tell me what you see?"

I turned my head to look at the sofa. The shadows were gone, of course. There weren't any on the wall behind Val either. They probably didn't like being yelled at. (Mongo had followed me and was pressed up against the backs of my legs. He knew I wasn't yelling at *him*.) "There's nothing there! And now you're going to say that teenage girls are sometimes *like this*, and it's okay, I'm just *crazy*, and then my mother won't hate me any more, she'll just have me locked up!" It had been kind of a stressful day. I burst into tears.

I'd've stopped if I could—I *hated* crying in front of Val—but I couldn't stop. I put my hands over my mouth and made hysterical gagging noises. I saw Val make a move toward me, and then stop before I ran away. Then Mom had her hands—not too gently—on my shoulders, and she pushed me sideways and down, till I sat on the sofa. Probably where the shadow snake had been crawling. I cried harder. My senior year had started, I'd met the most beautiful boy in the world, he *liked* me, then he turned out to be a physwiz loophead—and not quite two months ago my mother had married a hairy freak with a shadow zoo.

I bit down on my hand and poked my fingers in my eyes till I could finally stop crying. By then I also had most of a medium-large dog in my lap, licking my elbows and trying to get at my face and whining. Mongo wasn't allowed on the furniture.

When I opened my sticky eyes there was a box of tissues on the coffee table. Since I could hear banging and clattering noises from the kitchen—some of them sounded like something broken being swept up—I assumed it was Val who'd put the box there. Would one of his shadows bite me if I took a tissue? I'd been passing him the salt or the salad for the last seven months, but then I'd never admitted I could see his—friends either. They might not like being seen. Or maybe by admitting I could see them I'd *catch* them, like a monster virus. I was now shivering. I wrapped my arms around Mongo. Mongo liked this. His tail started thumping against my leg.

I leaned around Mongo and took a tissue. I didn't see any shadows. I took several more tissues, blew my nose so hard I nearly started crying again, and tried to dry my face off. This wasn't easy because Mongo was now trying to help. I petted him, putting off looking at Val, and watched Mongo's black and white hairs drifting away and attaching themselves to Mom's pale-gold-and-sage-green sofa cushions.

Little quiet clinks and then footsteps moving from the bare kitchen floor to the hall and living room carpet. The footsteps paused, and an indrawn breath as Mom saw Mongo on the sofa. Footsteps started again (the floor in the hall creaked just there), and then Mom silently set a tray on the table in front of me, pushing the box of tissues to one side. She poured, put one mug in front of me, handed one to Val (murmur of "thank you"), and sat down with a third. She was sitting in the other chair—neutral territory. Not close to me, not close to Val.

The hot chocolate smelled wonderful (my mom makes the *best* hot chocolate) but I wasn't sure if I wanted to let go of Mongo long enough to pick up my mug. Dogs are very comforting when your world has exploded.

"Margaret," said Val at last. "Can you talk?"

I nodded. And then I wanted to be *totally* sure I was being polite, so I added, "Yes." Except it came out a croak, so I had to say it again: "Yes." But totally polite probably meant looking at him, and I couldn't. I was still staring at the top of Mongo's head.

"Will you please tell me what you mean about—shadows?"

I thought I was going to tell him—him and Mom—about the snake thing, but what I heard myself saying was: "That first night you came to dinner, last winter. I opened the door and there were like *forty* of you. You and your shadows. They *loomed.* They made you look huge. It was like inviting an army in." They'll eat all your food and ruin your carpets and you don't even know whose side they're on. "And . . ." I trailed off. I couldn't think of a good adjective. Mom wasn't yelling at me but I thought she probably wouldn't like it if I said "scary" or "gruesome" or "some kind of monster."

"Do you see them often?" said Val in the same calm voice, like he was asking me to pass the salt or the salad.

"Pretty much any time I see *you*," I said, a little too quickly. "And there are more and more of them." I looked up at last, looked at him. There were like *hundreds* of shadows stuck around the room, mostly behind him, with lots of what looked like twisted legs and distorted heads—except how did I know where one stopped and another one started? Maybe there were only a few that happened to be the size of giant elephant-swallowing anacondas. They were curling around the windows and Mom's geraniums and Takahiro's and my paper things, perched on the picture frames, half-tucked behind the legs of furniture, lying raggedly along the gap between the tops of books and the shelf above them. I think I whimpered. I'd never seen them this bad before—never seen *this* many of them—although they weren't moving around much, and Val's shadows usually moved.

These weren't still though. They wiggled. There were so many of them it was like there was something wrong with my eyes. Have you ever thought about the darkness between a row of books and the top of the shelf? Of course not. You don't, until it goes all loopy, and little things like legs or tails or tongues hang down over the spines.

Oh gods. Oh *gods*.

I had my arms around Mongo, and he was leaning against me. I could feel something sharp digging into my breastbone—the broken cog that hung from his collar with the tag that had his pet-registry number on one side and our ground phone number on the other. The scientists cut magic out of us in Newworld two generations ago but they haven't quite eliminated superstition, and even Station has a charm shop where you can buy stuff like Mongo's cog. Some charm shops would sell you fetishy things with feathers and twigs and dried flowers, but if you sold too many of those the Overwatch goon squad would probably shut you down. If you stuck to broken chips and dead batteries they left you alone. Mom had bought Mongo's charm, to my amazement, when he stopped growing and got his first adult collar. She'd laughed a little—that funny non-laugh she had for years after Dad died—and said something weird and grown up about it being a good thing to be normal when you could. I thought of this comment a lot. Mom was not into charms. And her grandmother had been a magician. And one of her sisters had disappeared while she was working for a brain bureau.

I'd always thought most of the physwiz stuff was some kind of grown-up paranoia. The usual rumor around any high school was that the two weeks of physwiz we had to take was some brainwashing thing to make sure we weren't ever tempted to start making charms out of feathers and twigs and dried flowers or try to wake up the genes for magic we didn't have any more so what was there to wake up? Newworld was *all* about science. We were stronger than Oldworld and Midworld and Farworld and the Southworlds and everywhere because we'd got rid of magic, and science had all the important answers.

Everywhere had silverbugs—and everywhere had cobeys, Old, New, Mid, Far and South—but I'd never seen a live one and I didn't know anyone who had. I knew about the famous ones, of course, the ones even science couldn't make close up and go away, but since in Newworld the military always had them epically guarded I figured they could be anything. Uncle Darnel was in a cobey guard unit, and he said he had no idea what they were. You got special gear and you did what you were told, he said. It was just a job.

I knew the double R of course—Run and Report—because that was drummed into you from the beginning, with "please" and "thank you" and "don't throw your oatmeal on the floor if you want to go on living." But exactly *what* you were supposed to run and report was always left a little vague. It would look odd. It would be clearly out of place. Apparently you would know it if you saw it—it was maybe like a lot of silverbugs all stuck together. Which made me particularly sure I never wanted to see a real cobey. A mob of silverbugs *not* all stuck together was too much for me.

But I didn't know anyone who'd ever been worried enough by an oil spot on the road or a puddle of water where no water should be or a cobweb sparkling with too many prisms to run and report it, although I knew people did occasionally. Well, and there were people like old Mrs. Githers, who ran and reported about once a week. When the local Watch shift were having a slow day they gave her a cup of coffee before they walked her home again.

There was never anything to report around here. Before this summer the last silverbug outbreak had been four years ago in Birdhill, which was nearly thirty miles from here. Jill was right:

No Town, No Where, although some of the stories about the old Goat Creek base in the barrens were pretty extreme, and Station got its name from when it used to be mostly the train terminus and where the soldiers went when they were off duty. But they closed Goat Creek down because they didn't need a big army base here. Station didn't even have a regular scan any more. The mayor used to make a fuss about getting the sweepers here once a year. Fine. That was the sort of thing mayors were for, with kissing babies at the Fifth of July town gala. The sweepers never found anything and the last few scans had been canceled. We were a low-risk area: the anti-cobey boxes were enough for us.

I sneaked another look at Val, over the top of Mongo's head. He was wearing another of his ugliest-ever-seen-in-a-civilized-country shirts. He had a lot of them. He'd sat forward in his chair, his forearms on his thighs and his big hairy hands hanging between his knees. I thought magicians were supposed to have long slender fingers to write mystic runes in the air and twiddle wands and things. His hands looked like they'd be good at strangling people and hammering nails without a hammer. His head was bowed and his shoulders slumped. He looked really tired. Or overwhelmed. Or sad. He looked like someone who'd just heard some bad news he wasn't expecting. Or maybe he was expecting it, just a little, but it was worse now that he'd heard it.

I was trying to unglue my tongue from the roof of my mouth and for possibly the first time ever say something to Val voluntarily (that didn't involve shouting). But my mother beat me to it. "Val?" she said, hesitantly, in this little splintery voice.

I heard way too much in that one syllable. I heard how glad

she was to have him in her life. How lonely she had been before she met him. How much she loved him. I remembered how much more often she'd laughed in the last few months than she had in all the years since Dad died. In spite of me.

I put my face down on the top of Mongo's head.

I heard Val stir. "I didn't know," he said, so quietly it was almost a whisper. His voice always sounded kind of rough and hairy too, although maybe it was just his accent. "I didn't know. I did what they told me; I let them . . . Maggie, I have wondered, because . . . but . . ."

I didn't look up; I didn't want to see.

He went on: "They told me to go to Newworld. It would be easier here, they said. I already spoke the language. There were jobs for such as I . . . now was. They did not tell me they would let the government steal my money, or that I would not be able to teach, because the schools here would not accept my papers."

"Joanna"—Joanna was principal of the high school and a friend of my mother's, which was kind of a pain—"nearly broke a leg leaping over her desk to shake your hand when you said you could tutor science and math," said my mother, and I recognized this voice: this was the one she used when your best friend told you she didn't want to be your friend any more. (Jill and I had had our ups and downs when we were younger.) "You have more referrals now than you have time for."

It worked on Val too. I looked up to see him sit back and smile at my mother. Then he looked at me. We stared at each other till my eyes were drawn to the bookshelf behind his head. One of the legs or tails or tongues began to waggle harder when I looked at it. Maybe it was the thing that had been on the back of the sofa. I remembered that I'd occasionally thought one of the shadows was following me around. I stared at the waggling thing. It had moved to a relatively empty bit of shelf and was now bouncing up and down like it knew I was staring at it. If that was *all* of it bouncing, then it was not the size of a giant elephant-swallowing anaconda. I wasn't going to admit it, but it reminded me of a puppy hoping for action. In another minute it would bring me a ball to throw. "One of your shadows is waving at me," I said in a strangely calm voice.

There was a silence. "It might be Hix," Val said at last. "She would have come with me if any—could. Did. And she has always been friendly, and interested in—humans."

"*She?*" said my mother, taking the word out of my fallen-open mouth. "*Friendly?* All right, I'm glad she's friendly, but . . ."

Her voice trailed away, but it was a long minute before Val said anything. "I do not know where to begin or what to tell you," he said. "It was in the conditions of my visa that I tell no one anything . . . about my previous life. Indeed I thought they had laid a geas on me, so that I could not. But then I believed—I *knew*—that I had left everything behind. I had certainly left my—my—what Maggie calls my shadows behind me in Oldworld. They were very much a part of my old life. . . ."

I knew I didn't want to know, I thought.

"I admit I have wondered. I have wondered particularly—I know that it is not uncommon for a child to dislike a parent's new spouse but—I have told myself that it was my vanity that insisted that Maggie was reacting to something more than myself—"

The shirts, I didn't say aloud. The shoes.

After another pause Val went on. "Cohesion breaks—what you call cobeys—are much commoner in Oldworld than they are here—as you know. I will not repeat the tired old arguments about whether Oldworld would do better to embrace science as Newworld has; Oldworld has been plagued by cobeys for hundreds of years, long before Newworld turned away from magic. It is enough to say that at present Oldworld depends more on its magicians than its scientists. In Orzaskan a town this size would contain a dozen people trained to deal with cobeys. They would all be magicians.

"I was one of those trained. The training begins young; you learn your letters by puzzling out your first incantations."

He paused. I was thinking *you learn your letters by puzzling out your first incantations.* You didn't use the word "incantation" here unless you really wanted to get in someone's face. *What kind of a dreeping canty is that* was rude enough to get you sent to detention if a teacher heard you.

Val sighed. "My country is very old; its history runs deep into the earth; our word for cobeys means 'hole in the earth.' '*Gvaza-kimu.*' 'Earth hole.' 'Earth . . . bottomless.' 'Earth profound.' It is hard work, weaving the earth together again, across such a chasm."

He fell silent again. I had been listening to him and not watching the shadows. I glanced at them now and discovered that a lot of them had slid down off the walls and were pooling around his feet, and over the back and arms of his chair. Oh, *yuck.*

"I have wondered," he said. "I have wondered from the first. Since I stepped off the plane and joined the immigration queue. There were—shadows—in the airport arrival hall. There were

82

shadows on the hands of the young woman who stamped my new visa. There were many shadows in the small room where I was scanned and scanned again, and questioned, and questioned again. There were shadows on the face of the doctor who clearly did not like me, did not like my kind, and would have refused me entry if he could. This was so plain I knew that there was nothing there, that the shadows were only shadows, that what I was seeing was only the result of having had no sleep in thirty hours."

"And of leaving your home forever," said Mom, "and coming to a strange country. A strange world."

Val nodded. "Yes. I was very tired. . . . I had grown so tired that I had let them take my magic away. I was so tired I let them take everything away." He shrugged, his odd, dramatic, Oldworld shrug, and it was as though I saw him shrugging off a mountain or half a planet. "I thought it would be worth the loss, after . . . They took it all away, and sent me here."

"Not everything," I said. I tried to use my calm voice again, but the memory was making it hard. "They didn't take everything. That time I came out to the shed and—and—what was that?"

"That was such bad *livnyaa*," he said. "You knocking just then. *Livnyaa*, luck—a kind of magical luck—which is to say not luck, because there is no luck in magic. The—the *skha*, the web, or mesh of power, is very close—much too close for luck, for accidents. I wondered that that happened—that it happened with you, Maggie. I had brought a few old things with me to this new world—things that had been with me for a long time, but which had been denatured, when they took everything else, to be only what they appeared to be: a stone, a cup, a wooden wand beautiful only for the grain of the wood. I had been increasingly troubled—for a week or a fortnight before that day, Maggie—with a sense that some one or more of those things were . . . stirring. Were coming to life once more. They should not, and they should not have been able to. But I had to admit to myself that I kept them as if they were still tools of magic. Do you remember that you thought me mad that I will not have my 'top or pocket phone in the shed? You do not mix things of scientific power with things of magical power. I told myself it was habit, superstition. . . .

"That day, Maggie, I had been turning those old tools over, searching for any sign of returning power—wondering if I were capable of seeing such a sign, even if it were there. I had picked up the small wooden rod that had once been a very powerful tool when you knocked, Maggie, and it—I do not know how to describe it—*blazed*. That is what you saw. That is what you interrupted."

"Why on *earth* did you say 'come' to me?" I said angrily.

"I didn't," said Val. "I said 'nah! *Nah!*'—no. It sounds much like 'come,' heard through a door."

I goggled at him. But I couldn't not believe him. I couldn't. Involuntarily I thought about him tapping out Mom's fender after I'd dented it. I thought about all the times he hadn't ratted to Mom when I'd been horrible to him at the grocery store. He had even told me that he had never been to a supermarket till he came to Newworld. In the town he lived in it was all little shops: you bought meat from the butcher who wrapped it up in paper for you, and vegetables—sometimes with the farmyard dirt still on them—from the vegetable stall, and bread from the baker. If you lived in the village you could smell the fresh bread baking every day. I could feel something hard and cold in my chest cracking. It hurt.

"What did you tell Mom?" I said. "After I came screaming indoors? I was expecting to be grounded for a week at least for—for—" I looked at their drawn, anxious faces and didn't say what I'd been going to say. "For rudeness?"

"I told her as near to the truth as I could without admitting to my history," said Val. "I told Elaine I had an old charm. I admitted it was illegal. It was one of the few things I had from my old life. I believed it had been destroyed as a charm. That is true: my luggage was examined even more intensively than I was. I did not believe any live thing would have been passed by Newworld's border scans, which are notoriously thorough. Despite this it had held some grain of power within it somewhere—and this had regenerated. I told her it would not happen again. I was myself very shaken."

I remembered his face that day. Yes, he had been very shaken, even if I had misinterpreted why. "Has it?" I said, more sharply than I meant. "Has it happened again?"

There was a pause. "Yes," said Val. "I'm afraid so."

"Oh, Val," Mom murmured.

"Yes," repeated Val. "But if this had not happened, we would not be having this conversation. For what that is, perhaps, worth."

"Why not?" I said. "Why wouldn't we?"

"Maggie—" said my mother.

"It is reasonable that she asks these questions," said Val. "*Why* is that these things that have happened leave me open to what you are telling me today. I have not seen my shadows—my *gruuaa*—since I woke up in the hotel room the day after being successfully passed into this country. In hindsight now I think that I have spelled myself not to see them, with some fragment of that skill I should no longer have. But—Margaret—I would not have said that you were crazy, if you had told me this thing I could not believe. I would have thought there was something awakening in you—something I had been emphatically told did not exist in Newworld any more—but that might, perhaps, be roused by my history. I do not know how I would have answered you, however, because the compact was that they took *all* of my magic. But if I had no magic left, my wand should not have begun to accrue *skha* strength again. If it did . . . then perhaps the shadows, the *gruuaa*, were also as you saw them, and not only a reflection of what was happening to you."

"Anyone who reads fairy tales should know never to let a magician keep his wand," I said, firmly *not* thinking about what might be happening to me. I might almost choose being crazy. "Even if you've beaten him and taken his magic away."

"I have wondered about that too," said Val. "Wondered about that since before the beginning—since before they finished with me, and told me to come here. I am less surprised that your Watchguard and Overguard do not read fairy tales, but my countryfolk certainly do. It is also curious to me that two of my ex-colleagues from the Commonwealth are teaching the physics of the worlds at Runyon University."

"Runyon?" I said, or squeaked.

"There's no reason Maggie shouldn't go to Runyon next year,

is there?" Mom said. That wasn't what I was thinking about, but I didn't say anything.

He shook his head. "But it is odd. I do not like odd in these circumstances."

I didn't mean to say it. "I met someone tonight who—who is here to study with someone at Runyon. It's why he's here."

"What does he wish to study?" said Val.

"Physwiz," I said reluctantly, wishing I'd had the sense to keep my big mouth shut. "The physics of the worlds. Not magic. You can't study practical magic at any university here. Just history and stuff."

"I do not yet understand how it is here," said Val. "In Orzaskan you would not study what you call the physics of the worlds unless you were to be taught magic. The one balances the other, to the extent that balance is possible. Some of my students here have the most extraordinary lacunae in their education."

"You can get a degree in physwiz here," I said. "But only a loophead would, and everyone who does is swallowed up by the government. But there aren't that many of them—graduates with degrees. Most people stress out by their second year and switch majors." Or go crazy, I thought. "There are a bunch of required— short—seminars in your senior year of high school about it. But it's all history and safety and how Genecor was right." Mom, whose grandmother had taken her children to the Genecor guys, shifted in her chair. I'd noticed years ago that she did this little automatic pro-Genecor sales pitch any time they were mentioned. She didn't this time. I went on: "And there are still a lot of kids who bring notes from their doctors that they don't have to take

the physwiz one. I won't have to because silverbugs make me sick, but lots of people who could step on silverbugs forever and never notice anything still manage to get out of physwiz. Worst-attended class ever, year after year. That's how scared most people are of the whole subject."

Mongo stirred, and I let go of him. I'd probably been hanging onto him too hard. But he didn't get off the sofa to do his usual burglar patrol, checking all the windows he could reach, and all the doors (including cupboard doors. Okay, mouse patrol. Also cupboard-door-not-quite-shut-that-clever-dog-could-open-that-might-have-FOOD-in-it patrol). He just lay down and hung his head over the edge of the sofa. I looked down and went *"eeeee."*

One of Val's shadows had detached itself from the wriggly pool around his feet and slithered, or whatevered, over to the sofa. Mongo was—*ewwww*—doing something like touching noses—*noses?*—with it. If you can touch noses (or any other body parts) with a shadow. If it was a shadow *thing,* with a head—then it had too many legs. One of my big problems with Val's shadows all along: they all had too many things like legs. *Eeeee.* But Mongo's ears were half-back in the meeting-friend position, and his tail gave a flop, and then another flop.

"Maggie," said my mother, and I realized she'd said it a couple of times already. I must have said "eeeee" out loud.

I felt like if I moved or said anything (okay, any *words*) it would notice me . . . maybe it had only noticed Mongo? I stared at it. If this end was its head, the head was kind of spade-shaped—like a snake's head. Except it was all blurry and spiky around the edges. Your eyes couldn't actually handle what they were seeing. You

kept checking that the shadow was there at all by the fact that you couldn't see through it. At the same time that it was scaring you into a pile of rusty bolts.

My pulse was hammering in my ears and I felt like I might throw up. Mongo put his front paws on the floor and began to sniff along the thing's side—like he might do another dog—in spite of all the *legs*. In spite of it being a shadow thing. Against Mongo's black and white side I lost track of where all of the shadow was. I could still see too much tail (and too many legs) but the front end had kind of vanished. Maybe it was sniffing him back.

"Hix," said Val softly, and the part of the shadow I could see twitched—very much like a dog hearing the recall and deciding to ignore it.

I didn't mean to say its name—if I meant to say anything I meant to say "go away" or *"help"* (or possibly even *"Mommy"*). But what I said was, "Hix." And then its head reappeared from where it had been invisible against Mongo, and turned toward me. The head wavered a little, and then rose up higher—higher— two little spots of shadow like *feet* appeared on the sofa cushions barely an inch from my knees, where I was sitting with my legs bent under me. The head floated toward me . . . I *was* going to throw up. . . .

I think it was the smell. I want to say it was a sweet smell, or something dreeping like that, and maybe "sweet" is almost what it was. Nice. Friendly. Almost soothing. Definitely anti- throwing-up.

The smell reminded me, suddenly and hard, the way smells can, of the first time we went to visit Aunt Gwenda. The old family house where she and Mom and Rhonwyn and Blanchefleur grew up (Darnel was with his dad most of the time) had sat empty for several years after Grandmom died while the sisters argued about what to do with it. Gwenda lost. She moved her law practice to Highmoor and herself into the old house and started doing renovations. (I really didn't want to go there because Mom had said there was a *mangle* in the cellar. It was a long time before I found out it was about laundry.) Mom was obviously tense about the trip, which made me tense (I told you I was that kind of kid. Plus the mangle). It was going to be awful. We were staying for a couple of weeks and I didn't know anybody in Highmoor; my friends were all in Station.

We were in the car all day, going there. We finally got to the mountains about sunset. I'd never been in mountains before either; Station is flat. When we drove through Highmoor it was totally the sort of place where there'd be mangles in the cellars. It was after midnight when we arrived and Ran, who was still a baby, had been asleep for hours. Dad carried him indoors and Mom tried to rouse me enough to walk. All I wanted was to be at home in my own bed.

But as Mom levered me out of the car the smell woke me up. It was a nice smell. I wouldn't find out till the next day that it was pine trees. But it completely changed my attitude toward everything in one breath, standing there wobbling and clinging to Mom. (The house was still scary though, even when I found out what the mangle was.)

I hadn't noticed that Val's shadows had a smell, but then I don't think I'd ever been this close to one before. (Thinking about the one—this one?—who had maybe been following me around was still too creepo, so I didn't think about it.) This close she no longer really looked like a shadow, although I couldn't say that she looked like anything else either. Flat black only has two dimensions, you know? You can't see *around* flat black. You can't see if it *has* an around. And I still couldn't see *her.* And her edges were still blurry. I didn't want to throw up any more but whatever was happening was still pretty disturbing. If I didn't have a name (and a gender) for her I'd be wondering if she was some relative of a cobey. But Mongo liked her. That should mean something. Would he like something that could open a door that our world could fall through and shatter into infinite chaos?

Mongo? Yeah. Probably.

For a moment—just a moment—I thought I saw the flash and sparkle of what I guessed were eyes in the gentle weaving shadow in front of me. They looked a little like silverbugs. And there were three of them.

Val said, *"Hix."*

This time she listened. She dipped her head, patted *several* feet—there were at least four of them on the edge of the sofa by then, although there were also a lot of legs and tail left on the floor. But she was *snaky*—or at least long-bodied and short-legged. How was she getting those extra feet on the sofa? Maybe black cobey-like things handle all their dimensions differently and she could have put even more feet on the sofa and still been snaky to New-world eyes.

She dropped down to the floor and turned back toward Val. When, if she had been something like a dog jumping off the sofa, her feet should have hit the floor, there was a very odd little shudder in the air. It wasn't a hearing thing like a thud, and it wasn't a vibration through the floor like something heavy had just landed. It was something else, like the way she smelled was something else. Like the way she could put two pairs of feet on the sofa in spite of the way she looked was something else.

She walked or crept or *somethinged* and was swallowed up in the rest of the shadows around Val. But after a second or two there was a new bulge off to one side. I was pretty sure the bulge looked familiar—like I'd now recognize that shadow from any other shadows.

Suddenly I was shivering so hard I thought I might fall off the sofa myself. Mongo climbed back into my lap. And Mom got up from her chair and came and sat down beside me and put her arms around me (and some of Mongo). It was like the first real hug since Val happened. I put my arms around her (and some of Mongo) and burst into tears. *Again.* "Oh, sweetie," said Mom. "Oh, sweetie."

But I was seventeen years old and a senior in high school and this was the second time I'd burst into tears in an hour? Drog me. So I stopped pretty quickly. And then I wiped my face on the top of Mongo's head because the box of tissues was empty from my last crying fit. Dog hair up my nose. Unh. Never mind.

"Mom," I said. "What's the matter with me? There's no magic in our family. There's no magic in anyone's family any more—in Newworld—is there? They gene-spliced it out of existence two generations ago. Didn't they?"

There was a pause. Mom sat back, but she took my nearer hand and held it. A little too hard. "They tried," she said.

I didn't want to hear this. I knew I didn't want to hear this. Calories, I thought. Aren't calories good for shock? I leaned around Mongo so I could pick up my mug. I was amazed to discover it was still hot. This conversation felt like it had been going on for hours. Mongo didn't even try (very hard) to put his nose in my hot chocolate. He recognized some boundaries. In this case it was probably that he knew that if he did a "Mongo, *no*" thing he'd be put off the sofa.

I put the mug back on the coffee table empty. "Tell me," I said.

It still took Mom a couple of minutes to begin. Do you know how long a couple of minutes is when you're waiting for someone to tell you something you seriously don't want to hear? And I'd *already* heard too many things I didn't want to hear tonight.

"Your great-grandmother was a notable magician," said Mom at last. "When the government committee presented its report, she was involved in the campaign to change the recommendations from the then rather risky surgery to merely keeping a list of all who tested positive. You studied this in school, didn't you? It was nearly twenty years before the surgery was finally passed as reliable, but what doesn't get in the textbooks is that that had less to do with the progress of medical interventions and more to do with your great-grandmother and her colleagues—who were also working furiously on an intervention of their own.

"But by the time your grandmother received the letter telling her when to show up at the hospital for the procedure, she and her sister were ready. She said it made both of them quite ill while science and magic battled it out. The newspapers were full of reports on how the surgery was not as safe as the Science Party and its adherents wanted to make out—that surprising numbers of the young people who were having the "minor" operation to disable the dominant magical gene were very ill afterward, especially those belonging to families known to have a strong talent for magic." Mom smiled faintly. "If anyone guessed the truth—and I can't believe they didn't—there was remarkably little said or speculated about it.

"Your great-aunt liked to say that at one point your grandmother turned a pale rather streaky green and began to grow scales on her elbows and knees and down her spine. Your grandmother always denied it—but on the whole I think I believe Aunt Teresa. At any rate, afterward they tested negative for magic. As do I and my sisters, and your uncle Darnel, although for a week before we went in for the test we had to have these horrible green frothy drinks every day. By the time it was your and Ran's turn Rhonwyn had figured out how to distill what was needed into simple little pills. It probably wasn't necessary for Darnel or Ran—magic tends to run down the female line in our family, although your great-grandmother always said there was male magic in our family, but nobody had figured out what it was yet."

She turned her head to smile at me, but if I hadn't had Mongo in my lap I might have fallen off the sofa after all. "Mom," I managed. "You've never told me *any* of this. I remember those pills. You said they were just to stop us from getting sick when we had the tests."

"I know," she said. "I should have told you." She paused. "I'm sorry. But the fact that magic runs in the women of our family doesn't mean that every woman has it. Your great-aunt didn't although your grandmother had it very strongly. The four of us sisters . . ."

"*You?*" I said.

She took a deep breath. "When your father died—when—" She took another deep breath. I wriggled around, pulled my hand free, and put my arm firmly around her. "After your father died—when there had been nothing I could do—I turned my back on all of it. It had always been an uncomfortable secret to have. It was—is—still an uncomfortable secret to have. But it was easier, closing the door on all of it. Blanchefleur was very angry with me . . . but then I was the only one of the four of us who married and had children in the usual way. . . ."

I registered that "in the usual way" as well as mention of mysterious disappeared Aunt Blanchefleur but I was not going to ask. Darnel had a wife and three kids but Ran and I thought they were boring. It was one of the few occasions when Ran and I totally agreed on anything.

"Darling, I'm sorry. But there are signs you look for—the four of us all had them when we were children. You didn't. I've wondered, a few times, because of the way animals love you, but there didn't seem to be any magic to it. And you've trained your maniac dog, it seems to me, by nothing more than love and grim persistence—"

"And food," I murmured.

"And I felt that Clare trusts you because you are precociously responsible—"

Oh! I thought.

"—not because you have any kind of magical knack. I still gave you the pills—both times—before you had the test; they still don't really understand how the inheritance works—and it is perhaps not surprising that a gene for magic should not behave quite as science says it should. I thought in our family, better to be careful."

Magic. I stretched the arm that wasn't around Mom out in front of me and looked at it. I might have been expecting that if I turned it at just the right angle to the light it would be faintly greenish— and if I turned it farther, the elbow might be a little scaly. I wondered what creature the green scaly thing my great-grandmother hadn't turned into might have been. I wondered what Hix would look like, if she wasn't a shadow. And then Mongo, who didn't feel an outstretched arm was doing *him* any good, began to lick it vigorously, till it curled (scalelessly) back toward him and the hand began petting him again.

Mom said softly, "I wasn't at all happy when Val told me about his old charm coming to life again. My mother did not believe in coincidence either."

"You did not tell me any of this," said Val.

I stared across the room at Val again. He still felt like the cause of everything that had gone wrong. He was looking at Mom, so I didn't have to worry about trying to meet—or not meeting—his eyes. His shadows eddied and wrinkled, like a pond you've thrown a rock into.

"I know," said Mom. "Before, it didn't seem necessary. It was nothing to do with me any more, except for my sisters, and we will see any of them rarely. They behaved themselves around Ber. I would ask them to behave around you too. After . . . after you told me about your charm . . . I still wanted to keep that door closed, you see."

"Why didn't your sisters know—about Val?" I said. "Why didn't they, um, notice anything? Gwenda and Rhonwyn were at the wedding."

"Probably because they weren't looking," said Mom. "They know how I feel about magic—how I felt after Ber died, and how I still feel."

"*I* wasn't looking either," I said. "I haven't wanted to see anything that shouldn't be there!"

"I know," said Mom again. "I'm sorry. I wish you'd told me. . . . No, don't," as I opened my mouth. "I know why you didn't. I'm sorry about that too. You'll fall in love some day and—and I hope it doesn't make you stupid about something that matters."

"It is not a common skill to see the shadows," said Val. "Usually you must be trained to see them. And still not every magician can."

"I can't," said Mom. "Even watching Maggie and Mongo, I still can't see what they see." I wanted her to say "but I'm not a magician." She didn't.

She and Val looked at each other. It was like something in a cartoon. I swear I could see the hearts and flowers rushing back and forth between them like on a golden sunbeam. It was kind of cute. It was kind of icky. Mom said, "I knew I should have told you about my family after you told me about—what happened with Maggie. But I didn't want to think that the magic I'd renounced wouldn't leave me alone. That I had married someone with—with magic ability. Which my daughter, who I'd been relieved to believe had no magic in her, was apparently sensitive to—sensitive enough to be seriously disturbed by what she had seen. But I was still telling myself perhaps it was just one old charm . . ."

I tried not to sound accusatory when I said to Val, "But—if you're a magician, if you're *still* a magician, why are you here? Why did they let you in? What went *wrong*? I mean—"

Val laughed, more a kind of cough, with no humor in it. "I understand what you mean. I tested negative. It is a blood test, yes? It is the same test you had."

Mom nodded.

"Plus all the scans, the forms, the interviews. My tools were dead—I was dead, to magic. And there was no mention of magic in my background. It is not usually possible to—disable—someone's magic when they are an adult, when they have used it as much as I had done. I was a special case. My government gave me a new life when it took away my magic—a new life on paper, which I had to memorize. When I thought they had taken away my magic. All my magic. I did not want to tell even Elaine the truth. I too wanted— badly—to keep that door closed."

"Why?" I said. "Why did they take your magic away? Why did you let them? Why were you a special case?"

Mom didn't try to stop me from asking this time. She was waiting for an answer too.

The shadows around Val *exploded.* Even after seven months of watching them creeping and twitching and scuttling around, and flaring up huge and collapsing to almost nothing, I'd never seen anything like this. Even Mongo went very still, watching them: his ears were pricked, but he was stiff and tense against me.

Val said, "I killed my best friend. Upon the order of my government. I said that I would do this thing on the condition that afterward they took my magic away so that I could never do anything like it again. They agreed. I was too blind with despair at the time to realize that this was what they wanted: if I killed him then they would see me as potentially the threat he had become."

I killed my best friend. I heard Mom suck her breath in sharply. Val looked hundreds of years old as he raised his head, first to meet Mom's eyes and then mine. I had never seen anything so bleak as the look on his face. Not even Mom after Dad died.

I killed my best friend.

I couldn't say anything. I couldn't stop hating Val in a minute, or stop being afraid of the shadows, even if one of them had come and said hello, and smelled nice, and was a girl and not an it. Even if Val looked like most of him had died with his friend.

But shouldn't I be afraid of a man who had killed his best friend? Even if his government told him to do it. Even if doing it had made him hundreds of years old.

And he was married to my mom.

Had he grown up with his best friend, like I'd grown up with Jill? I thought of Jill and me getting piggyback rides from Arnie, borrowing each other's clothes, helping each other with her homework (Algebra I had almost destroyed me, but William Faulkner had almost destroyed her), *being* there, even when we were mad at each other. *I killed my best friend.* What . . . what if Jill's foresight got really powerful, and she could predict everything? What if our government decided she was really dangerous, and . . .

I couldn't imagine it.

I looked at the shadow lake again so I didn't have to look at Val. Hix had sidled farther off to one side so that she was detached from the rest. When she saw me looking at her—if *saw* is the right word, if what I'd seen was eyes—a little ripple went through half a dozen of the feet I could see. Pat-pat-pat-pat-pat-pat. It made me smile involuntarily. So what if she had too many legs, or feet, or hands, or paws, or whatever. Whatever it was she did a great wave.

The shadows had been scaring me crazy for seven months. Could I believe they'd come from Orzaskan with Val, despite whatever his government had supposedly done to him, because they wanted to stay with someone so powerfully evil he'd killed his best friend? What did I know about them? I looked at them, sprawled and splashed and dangling around him. If someone was asking me, I'd say they looked like a flock or a pack clustering around the wounded member of their company.

Pat-pat-pat-pat-pat-pat. And Hix, I thought, is trying to bridge the Grand Canyon between him and me.

Maybe I'm just too easily wheedled by anything I start identifying as a critter.

And then—speaking of too many feet—there was a noise on the stairs like a troupe of giants, and Ran appeared. "Hey," he said. "What's the big meeting? Maggie"—obviously disapproving— "what's wrong with you? And Mongo's on the *sofa*?"

I sat up straighter, and let my arm drop off Mom's shoulders. "I have a headache," I said, which was the first thing I could think of. The idea of telling Ran any of this was way too complicated. Also he told his buddies *everything,* as I had (horrible) cause to know.

"So?" said Ran. "I smell hot chocolate. I'm hungry."

"You're always hungry," said Mom, "and if you're hungry, hot chocolate isn't what you want."

"Yes it is," said Ran. "I want food *too.*"

Mom gave me a quick kiss on the cheek and stood up. "I think I'm hungry too. Who wants to start the sandwiches while I make some more hot chocolate?"

CHAPTER 5

IT WAS NEARLY ONE A.M. BEFORE WE ALL GOT TO bed. Ran kept falling asleep, but he still managed to eat three sandwiches. But I think both Mom and I were so glad that some of the wall that had grown up between us was (maybe) coming down that we kind of wanted to keep on hanging out, even if it was a school night. I tried not to flinch when Mom patted Val's hand or he put his arm briefly around her, when he said something quietly in her ear that made her giggle as she was peeling carrots at the sink, when she dropped a kiss on the top of his head after he sat down while she was setting the plate of sandwiches on the table (lettuce, cheese, and tomato or peanut butter, bean sprout and carrot—the second a house specialty, and *I* made them because I knew how to squish the sprouts and the grated carrots into the peanut butter so they didn't all fall out again). They've been married less than two months, I told myself. I also told myself: and this is the way they are when I'm not around. I tried not to startle when Val turned toward me a little too quickly (for me: I don't think he *was* turning quickly), as if he was one of his own shadows. As if he hadn't told us . . . what he had told us. And I tried to remember that the shadows were only his . . . I didn't know what they were, familiars? Did real magicians have familiars, like a witch in a fairy tale? I only knew that one of them was friendly. And that I was already starting to take her word (um, "word") for it that Val was a good guy. In spite of what he had told us. The baseboards were black with shadows as we sat down to eat in the kitchen, and more of them hung from the curtain railings like swags.

I wondered how long ago it was, since his best friend died. I wondered what the friend had done that was so awful and dangerous.

There were so many more shadows than there had been all those months ago, when I opened the door and saw Val for the first time. As if Station had suddenly become a popular shadow vacation spot. As if the first ones had written back to all their friends and relations and said, Come join us here! It's really nice, and we're having a great time freaking out this girl who can see us!

And Val has got *married*! they might have added. If shadows knew about married. Had Val had a wife before? Did magicians have wives? I tried to remember what he'd told me on all those trips to the grocery store, the couple of times we'd gone to the zoo. But I'd always tried to forget anything Val told me, or not to listen in the first place. I remembered some of what he'd said about Orzaskan indigenous wildlife. I didn't remember anything about family or friends.

Mom didn't say anything when I didn't shut Mongo in the kitchen after I took him out for his last pee. We went upstairs very quietly, as if we were shadows trying not to be noticed. I was exhausted but I found it hard to get to sleep. I had way, *way* too much to think about . . . and Casimir's face started drifting across my mind's eye and that made my heart beat even faster than thinking about Val's shadows did.

Funny, I thought vaguely, that Takahiro's face appeared a few times too. Takahiro was my friend, even if he was annoying a lot of the time, but he was too tall and too solemn to crush on.

I was almost asleep when the air in my bedroom did a tiny, funny, indescribable shift. I felt Mongo's tail lift once and slap down gently across my ankles as he lay along my legs. I smelled her as—I guess—she settled down on the bed. Do shadows sleep? I thought about freaking out but I was tired and finally beginning to relax into comfort . . . and Mongo liked her . . . and it was a nice smell, like pine trees at the beginning of your vacation.

She was gone in the morning. I woke up late and still tired—the way you do after you've really tapped yourself out, even if you've had enough sleep and should be ready for the next thing. Not only wasn't I ready, I didn't *want* any next things. There were too many things already and I hadn't been ready for them either. I also woke up stiff—stiff and sore, as if I'd been on a real battleground swinging a real sword or a real rocket launcher.

Pretty much my first thought was, She's gone. I wasn't even sure how I knew she was gone—how do you look for an *absence* of a shadow? It reminded me of those horrible proofs in math class—you couldn't ever say, this is right or this is wrong, you could only say, we've done this a hundred gazillion times and it's always worked out so far. But I knew she was gone, even though I thought fuzzily that there was still a faint trace of her smell . . .

Of course my second thought was, You made it all up, you pathetic broken tool. But Mongo was still here (watching me with eyes open just a slit, ready to turn into Two Ton Dog if I tried to move him) and Mom only let me take Mongo to bed with me if something really traumatic had happened. Well, but there were all kinds of traumas. It didn't have to be about shadows with too many feet. Or terrible things that had happened to other people. Maybe it was about having flu.

Maybe it was just the fading smell that meant it wasn't the first day of vacation. . . *drog me*. School. I looked at the clock. It wasn't un-catch-up-ably late—probably. I mean, I'd had worse mornings. Mongo's morning walk would be at full speed though.

I could hear people moving around in the kitchen. I wanted to go back to sleep, but that was more about not wanting to find out what had happened yesterday than how tired I still was. Why hadn't Mom banged on my door? Maybe she thought I was ill. Maybe I *was* ill. Maybe I really had flu.

Maybe I didn't. I sighed and swung my legs out of bed. I found my jeans and pulled out the little piece of paper with Casimir's phone number on it. Okay, that had happened. Maybe I could face the rest. Whatever it was. Once I was up and dressed Mongo agreed to accompany me downstairs. He was trying to decide whether to be unhappy about having to get off my bed or happy about the prospect of his walk. I wished I was a dog with this kind of choice to make.

The radio news was just finishing as I walked past the sofa and across the hall. I was looking at the sofa like there was going to be a big sign on it telling me what had happened there last night. I was thinking about last night hard enough that I wasn't paying attention to the radio. *Quack quack quack,* it said, the way it always does. I let Mongo out into the back yard and headed for the coffeepot. Ran, oblivious to everything, was eating cereal, with a book propped up against the box, which was going to fall over as soon as he turned a page. When the cereal box went over, the sugar bowl behind it was going to go over too. I picked up one of Mom's African violets in a stoneware pot and replaced the sugar bowl with it. Ran turned a page and the box quaked.

Having swallowed my first half a mug of coffee, I began to register that it was too quiet in the rest of the kitchen. Mom and Val were just standing there. Val must have students this morning; he wasn't a morning person if he could help it. I had an ingrained, seven months' habit of *not* looking directly at Val, but checking the immediate vicinity for shadows when I knew he was nearby. There was a clump of them under the radiator and the sideboard. I sighed, and reminded myself they—and Val—weren't the enemy any more. I hoped. There was a faint, something-like-whiskery touch against my bare foot and I looked down: Hix. Eeep. Wait, can you say "eeep" about something who's been sleeping on your bed with you? Un-eeep. If she'd been a dog, I'd've bent down to pat her. I knelt down, and she *unrolled* suddenly and was a shadowy, slightly weaving column in front of me again, except this time she was as tall as I was as I knelt on the floor next to her. I bit down on the gasp, or do I mean scream, and hastily put a hand down to the floor before I rocked too far backward and fell over.

The hand went down right in front of her, and she must have thought it was an invitation, because she dove forward—I bit down again, and this time tasted blood—but she was now swarming up my arm. . . . I shut my eyes and sucked (gently) at my wounded cheek. She slithered around the back of my neck—my hair blew aside and came down again, like when you pull your hair up from under your collar and let it drop—and stopped on my other shoulder. The rest of her finished shooting up my arm and stopped (I thought) on that shoulder. Accordion shadow? There was a little of her trailing down against my chest, but she was only about half the length she'd been when she stood up in front of me. Shawl shadow. Feather boa shadow. I could smell her again. It was still a nice smell. She weighed totally nothing, but you—I—were still kind of aware there was something there. Someone. I warily put a hand up. I could, I thought, *just* feel her—that whiskery feeling again, against the tips of my fingers, and that lovely, first-day-of-vacation smell fanned delicately against my face. I wiggled my fingers, trying to, well, pet her, and there was this faint hum or vibration—almost like she was purring.

Finally I looked up. Both Mom and Val were staring at the radio, even though all it was saying now was that it was going to rain tomorrow. Okay, I wouldn't invite Casimir for a romantic riverside walk then. I stood up slowly, as if I were balancing something heavy and fragile across my shoulders. "Mom?" I said. "Er . . ." Before last night I would have ignored Val unless he said something directly to me, but now, with one of his shadows draped around my neck, humming . . .

Val made it easier. He looked at me. "Val?" I said.

"There is a cobey in Copperhill," said Val.

"Copperhill?" I said. "*Copperhill?*" Copperhill was like two towns over—less than ten miles. Most of the kids in Copperhill came to our school—a few of them went to Motorford Tech on the other side of Longiron. "I mean—confirmed?"

"Yes," said Mom. "NIDL has just issued a statement."

The niddles were the practical branch of Overguard. If they were involved it was too big for the Watchguard, which was definitely bad news. I couldn't think of anything to say except, "But . . ." *But* probably everyone who ever had a cobey open up near them said that, so I didn't say anything.

"There was one in Greenwire when you were just a baby," said Mom, trying to be brisk. "It was pretty serious at the time, but they cleaned it up and I don't think there's even a scar. There wasn't any fuss about reclassifying land use. Most of our milk still comes from Greenwire."

And the niddles were nothing if not paranoid. I tried to breathe easier. I heard Ran pouring more cereal so I went to check on the African violet, and let Mongo back in, who was beginning to wail at the back door. He knew there was breakfast going on and he didn't want to miss anything.

I had to reach past Val to open the cupboard where Mongo's kibble lived (on the *highest* shelf and so relatively bad-breaking-training-moment-proof) and as he moved aside I got a better look at his face. He looked even older than he had last night, and haunted. "Val?" I said, and my reaching hand, almost without my awareness, fell on his arm instead of grabbing the cupboard handle. "Are you all right?"

He smiled at me. I didn't think I'd ever really looked at him—without looking away again immediately—when he smiled. The lines on his face looked like they went in a long way. Mom was thirty-nine (and said crisply when asked that forty was just a year like any other year and your point was?). I knew vaguely that he was older than Mom but this morning he looked as old as a magician in a fairy tale telling you how the world began, which he knew about because he'd been there. "A cobey in the area is never all right," he said. I was trying to decide if he was blowing me off when he added: "And last night—I spent the dark hours listening to the voices of things I thought were gone forever . . ." He paused.

Things, I thought. I wondered if he'd heard the voice of his best friend. Or of the beginning of the world.

"It will take me more than one night to adjust. I cannot even see the *gruuaa*—the shadows—as you can at present. And—if this were Orzaskan, I would be a—a niddle."

"I'm sorry," I said helplessly.

"No," he said. "Don't be sorry. The truth is usually to be preferred—especially in matters concerning magic, where untruth can be fatal."

Magic was fatal for your friend, I thought.

"And I never wished to distress you. That, at least, is better now, I hope?"

"Yes," I said, Hix still humming in my ear, although if I were one of his students I'd have trouble looking at that shirt for a whole tutorial hour. And—holy electricity—not just socks with sandals, but *plaid* socks with sandals.

There was a shadow rappelling down the wall behind Val. It

hooked my eye away from his feet, and as I looked up again I saw the clock. *Drog me.* I had to do time-warping things if I was going to make it to school, and Mongo was going to have the fastest sprint around the block of his life.

Jill hadn't been paying attention to any news reports. *"Well?"* she said when I climbed into her car.

I was only slightly breathless from racing Mongo. And I still had a shadow around my neck. I'd checked in the mirror and there wasn't anything to see—I didn't think—but then I didn't know if shadows—*gruuaa*—showed in mirrors or not. Maybe my hair looked a little thicker and darker at shoulder level. Maybe I was losing my charge fast.

"What's that smell?" said Jill. She sniffed. "I like it. New perfume?" Fortunately she didn't wait for an answer. "So—*well?*" she said again, louder.

"What?" I said. I'm not a morning person anyway, and a lot had happened since she'd dropped me off last night. I wasn't even thinking about the cobey—or Val. I was wondering if anyone at school would notice there was a *gruuaa* around my neck. Mongo had certainly noticed that she wasn't getting shut up in the kitchen with him when I left. "What's got into him?" Ran had said. I hoped Mongo wasn't going to take it out on the curtains. Or the furniture.

Jill smacked her forehead with a flourish that would have got her a lead in the autumn term play if Ms. Gratton saw her. *"Casimir,* you moron. Have you figured out a campaign?"

"Oh," I said. "No." It wasn't that I'd forgotten about him— I'd thought about him kind of a lot after I was in bed in the dark but still too wired up from everything. Including Casimir himself. And including wondering if you rolled over on a shadow if you'd squish it. I'd finished up sleeping with a pillow over my head so I couldn't see the shadows the streetlamp made out of the tree outside my window. It had been windy last night. But there wasn't really any way I was ever going to ask Casimir to go for a romantic river walk, even when it wasn't raining. I'd expect him to say, Who? if I phoned him up. I wasn't going to put it to the test.

"Well, you have to," Jill said decisively. "He's foreign. He's from—um—wherever he's from. It's up to you to help him feel welcome." She started telling me that Diane was having a party at her house next weekend, and she was sure Diane would be happy to invite him, but really I should see him a couple of times before I risked him in a group. Yeah right. I tuned out. There was a silverbug at the intersection between Zorca and Laburnum. I pointed my phone at it and clicked the coordinates on to Watchguard. Let them deal with it. If the niddles were taking over the big stuff Watchguard would have plenty of time for silverbugs. Jill was still talking. One of the banner boards was streaming about the cobey, but Jill wasn't paying attention.

We got to school just in time, before being mildly annoyed with each other for each other's dumb attitude escalated into a real fight. Eddie was standing with the rest of our crowd and flirting like mad with Becky. Ginevra was hesitating at the edge of the group looking confused and unhappy. I thought, Right, Jill, you're so clued in about romance.

Nobody seemed too stressed about the cobey, although I heard "Copperhill" a couple of times and Laura had also seen a silverbug on her way to school, not the one I'd seen. That made two on this side of town this morning. That was at least one too many.

I saw Takahiro coming through the school gates as the first bell rang. I waved and he waved back. He lived on the far side of town and wasn't a morning person either and usually caught the bus after the bus he should have caught. (I didn't know why he didn't have a car. Taks and his brainiac friends did computer stuff for money and Taks' dad could've just bought him a car. But Taks used the bus.) Maybe I could get him to invite me over for an origami evening so I could tell Diane I had other plans. You never knew with Takahiro: sometimes he was almost human. Sometimes you might as well try to be friends with a cobey box. That was how Jill and I had started using Japanese phrases—to try and get some kind of reaction out of him when he reverted to dead-battery mode. It didn't work, but Jill and I liked saying stuff our teachers couldn't understand so we kept doing it. Also, isn't *sumimasen* just *better* than boring old "excuse me"? It sounds more like "excuse me" than "excuse me." Also we were pretty sure it wired Takahiro. Probably because we got it wrong. But if he wouldn't help us, how were we going to know any better than what we got off the webnet?

I started to wait for him, but then I saw one of his gizmohead friends beetling toward him so I didn't bother. I'd catch him during morning break and check what kind of mood he was in, not that that would mean anything about how he'd be next weekend. To give the *warumono* credit, he kept his promises. If he had promised you something—like that he'd give you an origami lesson—he'd do it. It's just that if he was in one of his moods when you showed up you wouldn't want to stay.

There was an announcement over the PA system in home-room about the cobey in Copperhill. How it was no big whizzy deal but just in case it was a deal and the niddles weren't admitting it we were supposed to keep an extra-sharp eye out for anything *unusual.* They didn't say what unusual was, of course. Two silverbugs on the same side of town in the same morning? And, added the PA system, if we didn't have to go to Copperhill, don't. Huh. That almost certainly meant the niddles weren't telling us everything. A whole town shouldn't shut down because there was a new cobey. That's why we had cobey units and the Overguard.

If it hadn't been for the announcement we probably wouldn't all have looked around and started counting Copperhill kids. So I wasn't the only one who noticed that probably half of them weren't here today. Big cobey then. Like maybe the kind that ran along deep lines. There was a deep line that ran from Copperhill to Station. But we didn't even have regular scans any more because this area didn't have cobeys or any of the weird pre-cobey stuff that scans supposedly pick up. We didn't have silverbug swarms either—like we'd had two of this summer.

First class was geography and Mrs. Tarrant isn't nearly as anal retentive as Mrs. Andover, so we could sit where we liked. I was staring resentfully at my gigantic algebra book when Takahiro dropped down next to me. He dumped his shiny new geography textbook on the desk, but his hands were busy with a little piece of paper, folding and folding and folding. Taks was amazing. I'd been watching him fold for nearly eight years and he was still amazing. He got *more* amazing.

Even I remember that when he first moved here he was folding origami all the time, and I wasn't noticing anything right after Dad died. Taks was the shortest kid in the class that year, so there was this tiny boy crouched over these almost tissue-thin sheets of colored paper, his long-fingered hands going so fast you could hardly see them. I knew about origami, although I'd never tried it, but a lot of the kids had never heard of it, which made him even more exotic. Station has lots of Southworlders and almost as many Midworlders but not many Farworlders.

I guess the teachers had had a memo or something to be nice to him because they didn't stop him folding even during class. It might have been the uncoolest thing ever—and Taks dressed all wrong at first, of course, and he had too many pens and pencils, which he always lined up very carefully at the top of his desk, just before he went back to his origami—but his paper figures were so fabulous that everyone forgot about cool and wanted one. He must have made hundreds of cranes, and pretty much gave one to anyone who asked, including the teachers. Cranes are the first thing everybody finds out about when they finally learn that origami exists, which is maybe why he made them for us clueless Newworlders. The beaks and wings and tail tips of Takahiro's cranes are always knife sharp. If you've ever made an origami crane you know what I'm talking about.

Takahiro still made cranes, but he mostly made other things. He was making something else today although I couldn't figure out what it was. When the bell rang he put it down. He was a fully plugged-in member of the senior class and had to pretend to pay attention to the teachers like the rest of us. (He was also now too conspicuously tall to get away with much.) I don't know if he was paying attention to Mrs. Tarrant or not (it was an Oldworld unit, and Oldworld geography is much harder to study than Newworld, because Oldworld cobeys keep jerking it around), but my eyes were drawn to the little paper thing on Takahiro's side of the desk. Its body was long and curvy and its neck—supposing that was its neck—was arched like the general's horse in some memorial statue, and it had a spiky crest a little like a horse's mane blowing in the wind. I was sure if it was alive, whatever it was, it would prance. It had plenty of legs to prance with. Absentmindedly I put my hand to my neck. Yes. She was still there. I didn't hear a lot about whatever Mrs. Tarrant was talking about. (Maybe I didn't want to, with a new cobey in Copperhill.) When the bell rang again Takahiro picked up the little paper thing and kept folding while everyone else was picking up their books and moving toward the door. There were more little paper legs, and the mane got spikier. I found myself thinking of the Hands Folding Paper figures I'd made in my sleep recently. I put my 'top and my notebook in my knapsack really slowly so I could keep watching Takahiro. It was typical of him that he hadn't said a word to me.

He stood up finally, holding it in his hand. It almost did prance—if I blinked fast enough: it turned its head toward me, shaking its mane and dancing on too many feet. Okay, maybe I was blinking too fast. Or maybe I shouldn't have had that third mug of coffee for breakfast. There was a faint breath of sweet-smelling air against my cheek, like a little feathery or hairy foot had just brushed it.

Takahiro held the little paper thing out to me. "She's for you," he said. "I've been working on the pattern for her all summer and couldn't get it right. I was going to show you and ask you to help me—maybe you could see something I was missing. But it was like seeing you this morning, I suddenly knew what to do. So I knew she was for you. But it's been like she was trying to get through to me all summer. Nice perfume," he added. He moved his hands to hold either end of his figure, pulled gently, and it—she—flattened out. "You can keep her in your knapsack," he said.

It still took me about half a minute to raise my hand and touch her. I was pretty sure there was an almost-invisible something pattering down my arm—or *some* of an almost-invisible something de-accordioning down my arm—to meet her too. If Takahiro noticed anything funny about the shadows on my sleeve he didn't say anything.

"*Domo arigato,*" I said faintly.

He nodded once as if whatever was happening was perfectly normal, hung his own knapsack over his shoulder, and left while I was still staring at my new mascot. I'd have to get Taks to show me how to make her. Maybe with him helping me I could do it while I was awake. Slowly I tucked her into another one of those sixty-seven weirdly shaped pockets you (usually) don't need that every knapsack has, that I'd stuffed a lot of *kami* into earlier. Maybe I'd just discovered something. They're all for holding origami. I should have thought of that before.

When I looked up from zipping my knapsack closed, trying to

make myself think about algebra (ugh—and if I didn't hurry now I was going to be late) . . . maybe it was that third mug of coffee again, or my natural resistance to thinking about algebra. But for a second—half a second—the quadratic exponential thingy of a second—everything went dark. At the same time that I knew it all happened in a fraction of a fraction of a second, I was also hovering, *hanging,* in the darkness for as long as it took half the stars in the universe to pull themselves together, shine like crazy, and blow up into nothingness again. There were other flashes in the darkness—like meteors or comets or something maybe—I don't know. And. And something. Something shadowy in the darkness. While I hung, and there was nothing under my feet, and nothing holding me up.

I came back to myself with a little invisible hairy thing fanning my face like I'd had a touch of heatstroke. Not likely: it was cold enough this morning to see your breath outdoors. My first thought was that the lights must have flickered off and on again—which made me feel a little sick and scared because while there are lots of reasons for electrical outages, one of them is that a cobey is maybe opening somewhere near you. That was still preferable to anything else I could think of about what had just happened—including that Hix appeared to have noticed whatever it was.

It was ten o'clock in the morning and the sun was streaming in the big windows. Even if the lights had gone out you'd have barely noticed.

Mrs. Tarrant was standing beside me, frowning a little. "Are you all right?"

"Er—the lights didn't just flash off and on, did they?" I said.

The frown deepened. "No. Maggie, don't worry. NIDL are in Copperhill, the cobey has been contained, and they're working to shut it down. By tomorrow everything will be back to normal."

I could see her making her face stop frowning. She tried semi-successfully to smile. No, she hadn't liked the news reports this morning either.

"It must have been that third cup of coffee at breakfast then," I said. "Tomorrow I'll have orange juice."

"You do that," she said. "Er—do you want a pass for the nurse?"

I thought about it. Yes. No. Algebra would still be there tomorrow. I sighed. "No. Thanks. It's algebra next. I'd better get used to it." She smiled. It was a better smile this time.

I picked up my knapsack—sliding the strap carefully onto my shoulder so I didn't pinch anyone's toes—and my monster algebra book, and left. There were a bunch of strange grown-ups wandering through the halls. They could have been new teachers I didn't know but I didn't think so. They didn't walk or look around the right way for teachers—and they were too interested in the students. Most teachers get enough of students in class. They looked like plainclothes army goons to me. One of them stared right at me, like he was hoping I was carrying stolen goods so he could arrest me. Nope, just my algebra book.

And a shadow thing brought into the country by my mom's new husband who had had all his magic taken away from him, except that he hadn't.

There was another silverbug quivering a couple of feet from the ground under the tree outside the office. I could see it through the corridor windows. I aimed my phone at it and sent the coordinates in although half the school probably already had. Maybe the goons were watching to see how many of us were good citizens, and clicked it through. Did I get a point for responsibility, or minus a point for paranoia? Did the niddles have a scan for shadows?

I worried about my blackout the rest of the day. (Shadowy-darkness-out?) I pretty much missed algebra class without involving the nurse. I could see Ms. Dane's mouth going and hear words like "polynomial" and "vector" but nothing got as far as my brain. (Not that my brain would know what to do with them even if they did.) I didn't think the blackout had been the third mug of coffee. But then what was it? *Shadowy* had developed a whole new meaning in the last seven months—and a *whole* whole new meaning since last night. I put my hand up to my collarbone again, where something was tickling me. Had the big blackout thing been like one of Val's shadows? Only a lot bigger? I didn't think this one was friendly. He'd given them a name—*gruuaa*—but he'd avoided explaining what they really were, hadn't he? He just said that Hix was friendly. I put my hand to my collarbone again. I caught Ms. Dane looking at me, and moved my hand to fiddle with my necklace.

And, speaking of what things were, what was Val? Was he still a magician? (How could you *not* know you were a magician? Or still a magician? It wasn't like getting back on a bicycle and finding out you still could, was it?) I pulled my necklace a little too hard; if I wasn't careful I'd break the cord. The tickle on the back of my hand got longer and slower, more emphatic and more rhythmic.

Hix was (maybe) saying, *There, there, it's okay.* Mom said the only suspicion she'd had about me was the way I got along with animals. Possibly including invisible shadowy animals with too many feet.

By the end of the day I was the kind of exhausted that I just wanted to go home—except that's exactly what I didn't want to do, because Val was there, and I didn't know what I thought about him any more, except that everything was so complicated with him around. Him and his shadows, one of which had cleared off from the shadow mob and was now coiled around my neck. It had been easier hating him, and being sure the shadows were some kind of bad guy. As I pulled my jacket out of my locker Hix was humming again.

That Val had killed someone—that he'd killed his best friend—should have made him easier to hate. But it didn't. I remembered his face, when he told us. I didn't understand—I didn't understand anything—but I understood how he'd been willing to have his magic taken away after that. How he'd *wanted* it taken away.

And how he was having a bad time too. And how some of it was my fault.

Jill wanted to hang out and I didn't so I said I'd take the bus home. But I got to the bus stop and without realizing I'd made some other decision, kept walking. The park was not so far away that I would die carrying one million books and an old 'top (the new ones *weighed less*) in my knapsack plus my dreeping algebra book in my arms.

By the time I got to the park gate my feet and shoulders were both starting to hurt, but I knew I wanted grass and trees and the river, and that it was worth a few blisters (probably). I walked in as far as I had to to find an empty bench beside a tree and collapsed, letting my knapsack drop onto the bench beside me. My algebra book slid off my lap onto the ground. I looked at it. I wondered what the chances were that it had landed in dog pee. Benches are big favorites with dogs. I picked it up gingerly. It now had a slightly bent-in spine corner. Well, the flastic thing *weighed* too much.

There was a bunch of little kids playing on the grass in the meadow. There were a few moms on a bench near them. I could hear the kids shouting, but they sounded farther away than they really were. I was probably light-headed from my beast-of-burden thing. I hoped that's all it was. The river was over the little hill from where I was sitting; I'd get up in a minute. I'd come this far; I wanted running water. Running water was the classic protection against bad magic, right? Hix had wrapped herself way high up around my neck—since she didn't weigh anything, presumably gravity didn't bother her—maybe to get away from the knapsack straps. But she made me feel like I was wearing one of those Elizabethan ruff things, like in last year's history of northwestern Oldworld textbook.

I thought about leaving my algebra book in a tree for the squirrels. It had to be the biggest, dumbest textbook ever made, this huge square thing. It looked like it should have legs holding it up and a lamp sitting on top of it. It had pretty fractal pictures on the cover, but it also said *Enhanced Algebra* in huge letters which wouldn't go with most people's décor. I was sure I was sinking into the ground with every step. I would weigh about a third less if I weren't carrying it.

I worked my way back into my knapsack straps and then picked up *Enhanced* creepo *Algebra* and tried to figure out a way to make it ride comfortably against my chest. While I was wrestling with it I started to feel some kind of big solid silence pressing in on me from behind, almost as if attracted by my stupid textbook. Of course I was imagining it. No I was *not* imagining it . . . and *silence* was the wrong word anyway: I could hear the trees rustling in the breeze: *shhh. Shhh.* But the not-quite-silence was crowding up against me, spilling to either side of me, as real as a mugger or a silverbug mob. In a minute it would have reached out its arms far enough to wrap them—

I jumped forward and spun around—well, lurched around— holding my algebra book out like some kind of shield. There was a shadow as big as a forest bending over me—

I gasped and jerked back—and promptly overbalanced with the weight of my knapsack, almost as if it was trying to drag me out of harm's way. Maybe the shadow bounced off my algebra-book shield too: by the time I stopped staggering and looked up again it wasn't there any more. Maybe I imagined it? Like I couldn't be sure I hadn't imagined the blackout at school. My body thought there had been something: I was shivering with adrenaline. Hix seemed to have gathered herself together onto the top of my head as if on lookout.

And then my phone rang. I stood there with my phone going *roop roop* from my left hip: it's the theme song from *Sword-daughter.* My hands were shaking as I fished for it. I didn't recognize the number. I almost didn't answer. As it went *roop* for the last time I pressed the button. "Hello?"

"Hello?" Casimir's voice.

"Oh!" I said. I should have been thrilled to hear from him, but I wasn't sure if I was or not. Had he mixed my phone number up with some other, cuter girl's? Was he going to figure out his mistake in a minute and I'd have to try and pretend I didn't notice and let him hang up? "Oh, um, hi!"

"It is a beautiful day," said Casimir. "And the restaurant phoned me a few minutes ago and said I should come to work late. I thought I would walk along the river. I did not know if you are busy. Would you like to come for a walk? I could perhaps pick you up? I am sorry to give you no warning. I expect you have other things to do."

He sounded tentative, even a little sad, like he was waiting for me to say no. No, for the other, cuter girl to say no. "I'd love to!" I blurted out before I had any more chance to think about it. To think about how totally intimidated I was going to feel all alone with the most gorgeous boy I'd ever seen (who would by then be being gruesomely polite to the wrong girl) and how I wasn't going to be able to talk in complete sentences and he'd think I was a moron. And I had *all this STUFF with me,* which was so uncool as to be totally fatal. "I'm at the park now," I said hastily, drowning out these thoughts and the pictures that were starting to appear with them, about me falling in the river or breaking his foot when I dropped my knapsack (or my algebra book) on it, or . . . "but my knapsack is full of books and weighs forty tons."

"I will carry your knapsack," said Casimir, and his voice was now all bright and shiny (as if I was the right girl). "Where are you?"

"I'm near the Willow Street entrance," I said. "If you go straight up over the hill and down the other side, there's the river. I'll be there, by the red bridge."

"I will see you in ten minutes," said Casimir, and hung up.

CHAPTER 6

I FOUND I WAS SMILING, AND MY KNAPSACK DIDN'T weigh quite as much as it had a minute ago (maybe). I glared around as if daring any bad shadows to give me a hard time and then tottered up over the hill and down the other side and dumped my knapsack and algebra book on the riverbank. It was probably just the effort of climbing the hill with all this extra weight that was making the edges of my vision sparkle like everything was silverbugs. There *weren't* any silverbugs. I stopped a couple of times to look around carefully.

I sat down on the bridge and put my feet over the edge and swung my legs back and forth and got my breath back. And tried to think up a few things to say to Casimir when he got here and then *memorize* them for when my mind went blank. Although probably the stuff I memorized would blank out too. I was staring dreamily into the water when there was a shadow moving at the edge of my vision. . . . I jerked my head up and it was Casimir walking toward me.

He had an amazing walk, or maybe it was just that I was already hopelessly crushing on him. You know that sort of half roll, half stalk that long-distance runners and tigers have? He had it too. As he walked toward me it was like the trees were framing him not because he was on the ordinary normal park path that had been cut through the trees, but because the trees were leaning back to give him space, like a crowd parts for a king.

At the same time . . . weren't the trees framing him a little too well? They were just ordinary trees lining an ordinary path, right? Then why was it like he was walking down a tunnel of light through darkness—snaky, writhing, shadowy, bottom-of-the-abyss darkness. . . . *No.*

I yanked my eyes away from him and leaned down to haul up my knapsack. As I straightened again, Casimir was beside me, reaching out for the shoulder straps. I looked into his face and for a moment his eyes glinted like running water, like the surface of the river I'd just been looking at—like silverbugs—and his long curly hair seemed full of shadows.

He smiled, and his eyes were brown again, and his hair was just curly. Little springy bits of it had escaped the ponytail. "Hi," he said.

"Hi," I said, briefly riveted by his gorgeousness. He took the knapsack—swinging it up over his shoulder like it weighed *nothing*—and reached for my algebra book. I couldn't let him carry everything while I minced along beside him like a . . . girl. "Thanks," I said. "I'll stick to this one." He looked surprised.

"I have a new theory about algebra," I said. "I'm going to learn it by osmosis."

His face lit up in a fantastic grin and then we were more comfortable with each other. We turned and walked beside the river without saying any more. I knew my knapsack was a torture device but Casimir didn't seem to be aware of it. I kept surreptitiously trying to rearrange the algebra book so he wouldn't notice I was struggling with it, but it didn't want to rearrange, or anyway however I held it there was some corner that was digging into my ribs or my arm or my stomach. In another minute I *was* going to leave it for the squirrels.

What do you say to a gorgeous boy you're trying not to look like a moron in front of? One of the things I'd thought of while I was sitting on the bridge was that I could ask him if he'd heard about the cobey in Copperhill. An interest in current events is a sign of a mature mind, right? And he hardly could not have heard about it, by now it was everywhere, first header on your pocket phone local news and the live billboard ribbons too, but it was better than saying, Gods, I could *die* for your dimples. So I asked.

He nodded. "But it is only one so far, right?"

Only? So far? I thought, clutched my shield-like algebra book, and didn't think about deep lines like the one that ran between Copperhill and Station. I swallowed. "Only—one?"

"In Ukovia, we have them more often than you do here. You know this, yes? Oldworld has many more than you do." He looked at me, but my mind had gone blank just like I'd been afraid it would.

"*Nazoku*, we call them," he said. "Cobeys." He looked at me again, expecting me to behave like the other half of a conversation. When I didn't say anything he went on. "Eh, I was taught in school that they are something like bulges, like bulges into our world from another, like hands beating against a curtain, and we do not worry unless they appear as a series, eh, we say *toruna,* too many, too many strong hands against an old curtain which may tear if the hands beat too hard. Yes? This is the fear, that the boundaries between worlds may become weak in that *gron* of space. This is why you have your Overguard and your cobey regiments, and we have our *tesra torontona.* The new textbooks have decided that *flow* is a better word for the energy pattern of a *nazok*; not bulges but surges. What you see as the *nazok* is the crest of a wave; there are many waves because there are many worlds which interrupt the flow of the *bransti siir domnoor*; I am sorry, I do not know how to say this, the energies from which the worlds come. You hope that this *nazok* that troubles you in your world is the unusually tall one, and the others will pass without your noticing."

I had stopped to stare at him better.

"Do they not teach you this?" he said, stopping too. "I do not translate these concepts easily."

I made an effort to unblank my mind. "You translate fine. We're not taught—not that we're—what—a lot of little rafts on an ocean of—" *Chaos,* I was going to say, but I didn't want to say it aloud. A shield-sized algebra book and a humming shadow seemed like very poor protection. Plus a new paper mascot in the knapsack over Casimir's shoulder and a lot of probably by now pretty beat-up second-rate *kami.*

He shook his head. "It is only another part of life," he said. "We need certain qualities in the air we breathe and certain qualities in the food we eat—and certain qualities in the earth that bears us.

The wrong air, the wrong food can harm or kill us. It is no different." He looked at me again. "What *do* they teach you about—cobeys?"

"Not much," I admitted. "That we should leave it up to Watch-guard and if it's too big for them, then Overguard will send the niddles—NIDL. We're allowed—encouraged—to squash silver-bugs, but anything bigger or weirder, we Run and Report." I hesitated. "We have specially trained units to deal—"

He was nodding. "Yes, of course. We do too."

"But some of the training is about—er—resisting the effects of being close to a cobey."

He was still nodding. "Yes, of course."

"*Mental* effects," I said.

He stopped nodding. "It is very disorienting—"

"No, it makes you nuts," I said. "According to the big guys. Overguard. Which is why we have the niddles. That's why they ripped the gene for magic out of us a few generations ago. Using magic makes you more susceptible." They say. Until last night I'd never doubted it. Or wanted to doubt it. Now I did. Poor Casimir. A little more forcefully than I meant to I went on: "They decided that having magicians going loopy all over the landscape was bad for business, and all their wires and beams and boxes did it better anyway."

"Magicians are trained—trained for many years—to withstand the risks they take. There are other dangerous jobs. Members of the ordinary police force are sometimes injured performing their duty. Having no magic to use leaves you totally vulnerable," Casimir said. "You cannot be sure of a—niddle—being close enough to protect you. It is like you take a first-aid course so that you can stop the bleeding while you wait for the doctor."

"That is what Watchguard is for," I said. "There's always a Watchguard around the corner. And why we Run and Report. You have to know this—that it's all tech and gizmos here. They wouldn't have let you in if there was any magic in you." I wondered if he could hear the jittery edge to my voice. He was probably used to women getting a little manic when they talked to him. "So you're totally vulnerable while you're here. Like us."

He looked troubled. "I took many tests to be allowed to come here, yes. But the arrangements were made by the trust which is paying my scholarship. My country—all of Oldworld—wants to know more of your science, that it appears to keep your people safe without magic. That is why I am here—that is why my trust exists. There are other people like me here, and other organizations in Oldworld like my trust. And yes, I was told I could not use magic here, which did not disturb me, but also that I had to leave my talismans behind." He smiled a little wryly. "I was not happy about this. But I will take some risk to help my country, you see? But I have been surprised at the—at the vehemence against magic here. People recoil, as if someone were telling them to walk into fire."

Ask me about my mom's new husband, I thought. Or about humming shadows that smell nice. "That's supposed to be one of the side effects of the gene-chopping," I said. "At a cellular level we all have post-traumatic shock."

"But your system works."

I hesitated again. "Some people think that instead of having magicians going crazy right and left we have physwiz engineers and philosophers going crazy. That engineers are easier to organize, and the philosophers are all locked in the brain bureaus. Or that it's easier to see the signs that they're going doolally—magicians are halfway there all the time. Maybe engineers and philosophers go crazy more tactfully than magicians do."

"This is why everyone goes silent when I say that I am here to study the physics of the worlds," he said.

"Except Jill," I said. "Yes."

"I will not go mad," he said.

"That's what they all say," I said. "I have an aunt who may be crazy, but since we never see her I can't be sure. But it's why even the two weeks of physwiz in your senior year of high school is the worst-attended class, year after year. There are doctors who pretty much earn their living finding excuses to give kids passes to miss it, because their parents are freaking out. They say that all you have to know is to Run and Report, and who needs to take the chance?"

"And yet you go for a walk when a cobey large enough to call out two specialist units to ensure containment has opened less than ten miles away."

Two? I thought. That hadn't been on the radio this morning, or the billboard updates. "You're here too," I pointed out.

"I am trying to behave as you would," he said. "I am not—totally at ease. I miss my *chabeled*," and he touched the base of his neck, where perhaps a protective medallion used to hang. Gwenda had some of my great-grandmother's old medallions—carefully denatured of course. "When the restaurant rang," Casimir continued, "I said that perhaps I would go for a walk. They said, it is a beautiful day, that is a good idea."

I thought about the two cobey units and the deep line between Copperhill and Station and didn't say anything. Well, there had been no public announcements about anything—your pocket phone was supposed to ping at you if there was an emergency—and that's what authority is for, to know stuff, right?

"Also . . ." he said. And *smiled* at me again. How could anyone's smile be that perfect? How could anyone's eyes be that huge and deep? How could . . . *Margaret Alastrina, hit the circuit breaker.*

"I wanted to see you again," he said.

My heart or my stomach or my blood pressure or something did something not humanly possible and I almost had to sit down. There were sparkles everywhere I looked and I didn't think they were silverbugs. I blinked. They weren't silverbugs but I didn't think they were my brain exploding either. And there were more and more of them. I almost didn't notice when Casimir reached out and took my hand because by then the wind—when had the wind started?—was wailing around us with this awful squealing edge to it, that kind of noise when you think *I really can't stand this it has to stop*—I couldn't hear anything else and it felt like being stuck with hot wires. The silverbugs—or the things that weren't silverbugs—were joining up like pictures of fractals on the cover of an Enhanced Algebra book, only they seemed to *shake* themselves and every time one of these chains shook more chains splintered off and glittered away into an infinity that was stretching out in every dizzying direction—in more directions than there *were* directions—

Just before I totally lost my sense of up and down, my sense of *beingness*, of a human body with arms and legs and feet on the ground, on a ground that was *there,* and a brain unmelted by hot wires, I closed my eyes.

That was a little better. Up and down resolved themselves, and I was still standing on something although . . . it was quivering. More like a little raft on a sea of chaos than like the earth I thought I knew.

Cobey, I thought, distantly. The Copperhill cobey has moved along the deep line and opened up in a park in Station. The park where Casimir and I happen to be.

The wind howled. I tried to think about what I knew. But what do you still know when everything is wrong? I thought I could still feel Hix around my neck; she was doing her Elizabethan-ruff trick even more tightly, so there was a little hairy-ish band of almost-warmth against my skin. As I thought about her . . . there seemed to be more of her. One of her accordion ends was elongating, creeping—slowly, like a person feeling her way—down my sternum. Slowly it groped around my waist, sidled across my pelvis and slid down one leg. Eventually it—she—reached the ground. The moment she slipped over my foot and touched earth I was *real* again. I hadn't noticed that I'd become unreal. Only that everything else had.

The wind was still doing its unhinging howl but I cautiously opened my eyes. Mistake. I closed them again. I couldn't see anything but a kind of wild, broken craziness like the three-dimensional version of a two-year-old scribbling with a crayon. But I could feel two things that I'd forgotten when I became unreal: Casimir's hand holding one of my hands, and my other hand clutching my algebra book. Hix had outlined one edge of the algebra book on her way down my body and maybe that's what made the book feel so weirdly real. Live. Like it was alive and scared to death like the rest of us. Or maybe it was exhilarated. It was hard to tell.

Margaret Alastrina, you're talking about an *algebra book*.

I'm in a cobey. I think I'm supposed to die. This is better, okay?

Slowly I knelt down on the little patch of quaking earth that Hix was keeping real for me. I held onto Casimir's hand and pulled him down too. I didn't have any hands left. But Hix seemed to understand about Casimir and she unreeled herself even further—I felt her edging past my ankles, and I felt Casimir—I don't know how else to explain it—become *real* again when she touched him. So I could let go of his hand.

I was crouching at the edge of a cliff. When I laid the algebra book down I kept it as close to me as possible; I laid it so that it was touching my knees. I didn't know if I was going to be able to open it against the wind, but as I tried, a little place of quiet cleared itself as if by the act of opening it. . . . I was looking at an explanation of how logarithms are the opposite of exponentials. About balance.

I tore a page out and began folding. I didn't know what I was folding, but my fingers seemed to know. Back, forward, turn, turn over, keep folding. Open out, keep folding. Turn over, keep folding. Keep the edges sharp, no matter how shaky and sweaty your fingers are, however hard the darkness at the bottom of the cliff is pulling at you. Keep the edges sharp like your life depends on it. Keep folding. I was Hands Folding Paper.

I knew when she was done—when she began to move faintly against my fingers, like she was breathing—and without looking up (don't look over the edge of the cliff *don't* look over the edge of the cliff) I flicked her into the maelstrom around me. Since I didn't look up I couldn't possibly have seen her stretch long silver wings and soar like an albatross over this awful sea. I tore out a second page and began folding again. And then a third page, a fourth, fifth, sixth. Seventh. I looked up when I sent the seventh after her sisters, and I saw the long, long wings I couldn't possibly have made, and a shining silver crest erect from the top of her head down her long unexpectedly sinuous body, studded with tiny feet: very like a silverbug fractal, and nothing at all like.

I thought of Takahiro saying: It was like she was trying to get through to me. I thought of those nights when I slept better sitting up folding paper than lying down in bed.

I pulled out an eighth page and began folding. And then a ninth page.

I hadn't realized I had a headache till it began to ease. I hadn't realized that the hairy, whiskery, spider-footy, tickly band around my neck had extended its other end (but did *gruuaa* shadows only have two ends?) up around my face and wrapped itself, or herself, around my forehead like a pirate headband. Perhaps that was why when I looked up again the world I knew had begun to reshape itself around me.

The shrieking yowl of the wind dropped to the crackle of a thunderstorm that was still a little too close. The trees were rebecoming trees. The insane silverbug sparkle was no worse than when you stand up too quickly and briefly feel dizzy. The sun came out again; the only shadows belonged to things I could see, like trees and benches and the railing of another little footbridge. And Casimir. He was staring at me like he'd never seen a human girl before.

"Casimir—" I said, or croaked.

To my astonishment—and a cross between horror and maybe the biggest thrill of my life—he picked up the hand he had been holding earlier and *kissed it.* He said something in a language that wasn't English, and then flung himself down and over onto his back, flinging his arms out to either side. Which was a pretty good description of the way I was feeling too.

My knapsack had made it through—whatever had just happened—too. It sat a little behind where Casimir and I had been kneeling, all sort of hunched up, like someone sitting with her legs drawn up and her arms around them, her shoulders as high as they'd go and her face pressed down hard against her knees. I reached out and stroked it gently, over the pockets where the *kami* and Takahiro's new mascot were.

Casimir's pose reminded me a little of my algebra book. I looked at it, lying flopped open where I'd left it. I'd torn out twenty pages or so. It looked like more. I was so dead for mutilating a schoolbook.

On the other hand, we were in fact both alive, Casimir and I. One of the top still-attached pages of the book curled up briefly, which wouldn't have been surprising except that it was curling *against* the mild breeze, which was all that was left of the wind. Okay, maybe *all* of us were still alive. *Margaret Alastrina,* I started to say to myself . . . and stopped.

I patted delicately at my shoulders. I wasn't sure how far Hix had extended or retreated. Something moved. Something rubbed ever so gently down the side of my face. I didn't think it was a foot. It might have been another face. I thought, I want to say her scent shimmers, but how does a smell shimmer? "Hix?" I murmured, and the light almost-weight around my shoulders gave a faint acknowledging shiver. "Thank you," I said, and the patting thing against my face felt briefly like tiny kisses.

Casimir sat up. "I am sorry," he said. "There is no excuse for my carelessness. I must plead that I have only been in your country for a fortnight, and everything about it is still strange to me—including the air, the wind, the ground under my feet, the sound of a river in its bed. It is all a language I do not speak, and do not understand what I am hearing."

"Sorry?" I said. "Why are you sorry?" I thought, I should be apologizing to him that almost the first thing my country does to him is try and kill him. And if he hadn't had this dumb idea about seeing me again, he would be somewhere else. I looked up at the sky. It looked like the sky always looks on a clear autumn day.

"I should have recognized the approach of a *nazok*," said Casimir. "Nor did I sense your *gruuaa*. I am more dependent on my *chabeled* than I knew." Now he looked up at the sky. I wondered if clear autumn days in Ukovia looked the same. "I am as dislocated here as if—as if—" He made a gesture with one hand. "It is much stranger here than I was expecting, so much stranger I was becoming afraid that studying at Runyon might teach me nothing I can use." He looked down, and at me, again. "I thought, the other night, when I heard the word from the old prophecy, that it was a fault of my hearing—the foreigner who mistakenly believed he spoke your language. But I could not help being curious—and in Ukovia we are taught not to believe in coincidence. And you . . ."

He tailed off and I thought, You *what*. "Prophecy," I said slowly and carefully.

"Yes," he said. "When you came into the restaurant the other night, and your friend called you *mgdaga*. It is an ancient prophecy in Ukovia: the *mgdaga* is a young woman who can"—he murmured a few more words in what I assumed was Ukovian—"who can mend the breaks between universes. Who has a natural affinity for the physics of the worlds."

"No," I said.

"Most are legendary but a few have been identified as historical persons. There were never many, and there has not now been one in hundreds of years; our magicians say perhaps it always was only a tale, there were merely a few young women who seemed to fit the description. I was puzzled that I would hear of a *mgdaga* in Newworld, and more puzzled that the name should apparently be used so casually. I still do not understand—but—but it does not matter. The *guldagi*—spirits—of the between-worlds manifest and proclaim you."

What?

"It is the equations of this world that gives the strength, yes? This is an acceptable art in Newworld? Who taught you? They cannot have known it would be so harshly tested, but then if *mgdaga* is a casual epithet they will perhaps not have known whom they taught. I would very much like to learn—if perhaps some scrap of it can be taught. It is exactly to learn such practical tools that I am here." He touched my poor book gently. "Perhaps we—you—we if you will allow—should carry some pre-marked pages after this. If this is a true *toruna* I fear there will be more use for them."

I could feel my mouth pulling itself into that "I don't understand and I'm sure I don't want to" smile. Jill and I used to see it on the face of our first-grade teacher a lot. "Whatever you're talking about—it's nothing to do with me. Jill calls me Magdag when she wants to be especially annoying. I don't *know* what happened just now. I don't even know if that was . . ." I couldn't say "cobey," as if saying it out loud would bring it back. I didn't want to admit that that part of what he was talking about might be true. But none of the rest of it was. *None.*

He began to look unhappy and confused, which would make two of us. "I don't . . ." And then his face changed again: dismay, disappointment. "Is it that you may not speak to me of these things because I am not a citizen of your country? I did wonder, some of the questions they asked, before they would issue me a visa. I don't know—"

"What?" I said. "Citizen? Country? What are you talking about? *I have no idea what just happened*—I can't even squash a silverbug, it makes me sick! I don't *know* why I wrecked my algebra book! I mean—not to—*know,* not like I can tell you. I—I just—" I reached up and touched Hix, and felt that almost-but-not-quite imaginary flicker against my cheek in response. Meeting her last night for the first time had almost been too much for me—this morning I almost ran away when she climbed up my arm for the first time—and now here I was using her for reassurance.

Casimir's eyes had followed my hand and his expression softened a little. "Ah," he said.

"Can you *see* her?" I said. This entire conversation was so far off my radar I didn't know what galaxy I was in any more. And I was getting farther away from the one I knew with every word. Especially the words I didn't know.

"I can see the edge of a darkness," he said. "A shadow that is not quite your body or my body or the trees. I would not see—her?— if I were not thinking of the *mgdaga*, who I would expect to have attendant *guldagi*—and whose *gruuaa* indeed held me here while you addressed the *nazok*. But I believe the *gruuaa* cannot fully appear in this wo—here," he said. "They are one of the *guldagi*."

"In this world," I said slowly. "You started to say *in this world*."

"Yes," said Casimir. "But I did not know if . . ."

He trailed off again. I was so not enjoying this conversation with the most beautiful boy I had ever met. Aside from the fact that he had been interested in me for reasons other than, uh, *me*. Not that this was a surprise. I took a deep breath. "Let's go back a little. Let's, uh, pretend that I'm totally stupid and clueless, okay? Tell me what just happened. With the wind and the weirdness and everything."

Now he was wearing that "I don't understand" smile. Apparently it was the same smile in Ukovia. It looked a lot better on him than it had on my first-grade teacher. "It was a *nazok*. What you call a cobey. Since it is the second, we must consider the likelihood there will be a third."

I didn't want to consider anything. Except for the sitting-alone-with-Casimir-in-the-park-on-a-beautiful-day part, I wanted all of this to go away. The all of the rest of it that was ruining the alone-with-Casimir part. The rest of it would include that he only wanted to be here with me because I was this historical thing. "But—it's gone. It's gone, isn't it? They—cobeys—don't do that."

He made another odd gesture with his hands—a kind of folding over and winding together gesture. "They do if they are properly bound. And it is much likelier they will be properly bound if someone who can do this is present as the *nazok* opens. Which is why foreseers are so important to us. My mother is a foreseer. In Eruopa and the Slavic Commonwealth if everywhere that had been disrupted by a *nazok* was lost, there would be very little human land left."

I was silent a moment. I knew that about binding, of course; I was forgetting my basic history. Oldworld was pretty much a patchwork quilt of shut-down cobeys; most of Newworld was more like your favorite jeans with mends on the knees and the butt and one or two where you'd torn yourself up on your mom's rosebushes or a particularly badly placed nail. They were still mostly jeans.

But it had been kind of an overexciting few minutes, just now, and it was easy to forget stuff, like your name and what day of the week it was. And here in Newworld we were taught to Run and Report. There hadn't been time to run. And it didn't look like there was anything left to report.

He glanced at me. "Usually a team is sent when a foreseer predicts a *nazok*. But a *mgdaga* could perhaps bind a *nazok* alone."

I ignored this. "Is this the way they usually happen?" Was there a "usually" about cobeys? "Like—" Like what? Like a spider being washed down the kitchen sink? "Like a storm out of nowhere?"

He shook his head. "Not one big enough to swallow two people. That is why I don't understand why I did not sense its approach. My Oldworld instincts are of even less use here than I had begun to realize.

"Little ones may happen unexpectedly—ones like what you call silverbugs, only bigger. It is not wise to step on them, however; when they burst, they will throw you down, and the earth will not be where you expect it, when you fall down in the ordinary way." He smiled. "Every small boy discovers this. Myself included."

I wasn't crazy about big *ordinary* bugs—beetles and spiders and things, although the next spider I found in the sink I'd catch in a glass and put outdoors. The idea of big silverbugs made me totally queasy. "Big enough to swallow two people," I repeated, like it was a lesson I was trying to learn. I didn't want to learn it.

He looked at me again. Steadily, without glancing away. *I* had to look away. It was funny in a way because Run and Report, with the "don't think about it" that goes with it, always made me a little cranky, but I assumed it was either because I was a control freak or because I had a mad aunt (maybe) from her knowing too much about physwiz. "People disappear when big cobeys open," said Casimir. "No one knows where they go. But there has been work done on trying to find out. My trust thinks Professor Hlinka, at Runyon, is close to a discovery about this; it is why they placed me here."

Several things jostled for position in my poor bewildered brain. The first one was: his trust must think a lot of him. But, wearily, this thought also came: someone is always close to a breakthrough. The breakthrough never arrives. I knew people occasionally disappeared. Gwenda said it happened oftener than was reported. Not one of them has ever come back but they've never found any bodies either. I remembered this. With my name and what day of the week it was: Thursday. One more day till the first weekend of my senior year. The longest short week of my life.

I was still dazed from—whatever had happened—but I had a weird sense of uneasiness. A weird *increasing* sense of uneasiness. I looked around. Not that I knew what I was looking for. Another cobey? Please the holy electric gods not. Would I know what one looked like after this? I didn't want to find out. The afternoon was still clear and sunny and the breeze mild and smelling of leaves and that sharp clean smell of fast-running river water.

To me the breeze also smelled of Hix. She shifted a little and I thought, I'm picking it up from her. She's worried about something. Her anxiety was spilling over me like pizza sauce over your last clean shirt. "I—I think maybe we should get going," I said, and began to struggle to my feet. I was suddenly so tired that the weightless Hix felt like an iron chain. I picked up my algebra book and looked sadly at my gigantic knapsack . . . and if I wasn't already in desperate unrequited love with him (to him I was a historical figure like a statue or a chapter in a book) I'd have fallen in love with Casimir when he picked it up as if it was totally his problem (in Ukovia they teach you to be polite to little old ladies and historical figures).

"Yes," he said. He was frowning slightly. It made his eyebrows arch more and his eyes looked bigger and darker than ever. *Aaaugh.* As I stepped toward him, dropping each foot back to the ground again like I wasn't sure it belonged to me, he reached out and grabbed my hand again. Whoa. That wasn't why I was walking like a little old lady who had come out without her cane (how did historical figures walk?) but hey, whatever. And we did move a little faster that way. He wasn't exactly dragging me but I was walking a little harder to keep up. Some of the long sinuous Hix had moved to the top of my head again, to her lookout point. I could still feel her on my left shoulder, but not my right, and I thought I could feel feet on my forehead again. It was like wearing a fuzzy invisible crown.

Casimir and Hix were right. We were out of the trees and crossing the meadow when the army arrived. I was having to concentrate on walking and carrying my algebra book at the same time—I felt like *"I"* was a committee arguing among themselves: the keeping-head-upright part was arguing with the algebra-book-carrying part, which was also snarling at the one-foot-after-the-other part. (Nothing was arguing with the holding-Casimir's-hand part.) The *I* part was trying to keep them all doing what they were supposed to be doing instead of lying down and not doing anything. We'd've done lying down together really well.

I gaped at all these guys in uniform running toward us—bright orange cobey badges bobbing on their hats. I was retroactively aware that there'd been some kind of uproar at the gates as we started walking—and stopped. "No, don't stop," said Casimir, and tugged me on.

Most of the other people in the park were stopping and gaping too, although I had a faint sense that they'd been sort of standing there dazed already. I sympathized. But guys in uniforms were halting to talk to the other people—in an in-your-face, we're-the-*army* kind of way. Some of the people the army guys were talking to looked like they were then being escorted somewhere—with two or three or four guys in uniforms at their elbows. Oh, drog me. This didn't look good at all. Without meaning to I stopped again. "No," said Casimir, *"don't stop,"* and he didn't stop, so he nearly pulled me over when our linked hands came to the ends of our arms. I staggered forward and he let go of my hand to put his arm around me. I wished I was enjoying this more. Also, the algebra book . . . Okay, pay *attention.*

The army guys were streaming past us. Like they didn't see us. They were stopping everybody else. Not us. They broke and slid past us like water around a rock. The water doesn't care.

Casimir said, "Your *gruuaa* is hiding us. But there is only one of her, I think, and she is tired: she kept both of us here and—eh—steady, while you bound the cobey. She is tapping you now, which is why you feel disoriented. I thought she might be able to tap me too if I am touching you." Of course. He had his arm tightly around me because he wanted my *gruuaa* to be able to use him. I was almost too dizzy to notice what it was like, having his arm around me: the clean soap-and-skin smell of him, the way our hips brushed as we walked, the feel of his arm against my back. . . . I had a vague idea I would want to remember *all* the details later. Maybe I could manage to forget about my algebra book, when I was remembering everything else, which at the moment was digging a hole in my stomach. Carrying it was always a pain, but I couldn't blame it if it was mad at me for ripping a big hunk of *its* middle out.

There I go again, I thought distantly, thinking about my algebra book as if it was alive. Tell that to Ms. Dane, when you explain about the missing pages. It was getting heavier, I suppose as I was getting feebler. The feet on my forehead were going cold, like Hix was coming to the end of what she could do too.

We made it to the gate. I think Casimir was nearly carrying me. We made it *out* the gate and Casimir turned and marched us toward the bus stop. We lurched inside the bus shelter and collapsed on the bench—even Casimir. So maybe Hix had been using him after all. Fortunately there wasn't anyone else waiting, so we could sprawl. One boy, one girl, one knapsack, one algebra book, one long fluffy invisible thing. The army guys were still going into the park, but slower now, and fewer of them, although these last guys were carrying more equipment—big weird folded-up angular machinery with little red and white flashing lights.

The front end (I assumed it was the front end) of Hix slithered off my head and back onto my shoulder. I could feel how tired she was, not the way I'd been picking up her anxiety, but by how limp she was. If she'd been a feather boa a few minutes ago she was now a feather boa that had been dropped in the river, run over by a bus, and then used as a chew toy by a Saint Bernard. One or two of the army guys looked sharply into the bus shelter but no one said anything. I tried to look surprised and clueless. I should have been able to do that really well. Maybe I did.

I flopped my head over—I was leaning against the back wall of the shelter—to look at Casimir. He was slumped against the wall too, with his eyes closed. He looked exhausted. Perhaps he felt me looking at him, because he opened his eyes and smiled. Even with everything that had happened in the last half hour that smile made my heart grow two sizes and bang against my ribs. Then he reached out and took my hand again like it was the most normal thing to do. . . .

Hey, he started it. What would a *mgdaga* do if the cutest boy she'd ever met put his hand around hers? I closed my fingers and gave his hand a squeeze. "Thank you," I said. "I don't know what any of that was—I'm saying that a lot, sorry—but the *mgdaga* stuff is a nonstarter, okay? We *do* believe in coincidence in Newworld."

My eyes strayed to a big army van—big enough to carry a lot of soldiers to a park where someone had Run and Reported a cobey—or where a cobey had opened up that was big enough to set off all the cobey boxes in town. Or an army van big enough to carry a lot of ordinary people who had had the bad luck to be in a park when a cobey broke, to be taken away somewhere. Nothing to worry about, they taught you in school. If a cobey ever happened here, which it won't. The attending cobey unit would take your statement and maybe give you a decontamination pill and send you home.

Nothing to worry about.

There were three soldiers unfolding the legs on a box like the ones we'd seen other soldiers carrying into the park. It was long and thin and had too many legs, although these legs were long and spindly. It didn't look friendly. I bet it didn't smell good either.

"How do you come to have a *gruuaa* companioning you?" said Casimir. "They are not common anywhere, but I thought—well, I would have thought—there were none in Newworld."

"She—she has been—er—companioning—er—my mother's husband." That sounded awful, and I was probably only still here because of Hix. I was probably only here *twice* because of Hix. Which meant I was only here twice because of Val. "My stepfather," I amended reluctantly. "She—um—he introduced her to me." Electric gods, was it only last night? "And she seems—um—to like me."

"It is a great honor," he said. "You are very fortunate."

Yes. That was simply true. I put my hand up to where I knew Hix was, wrapped around my throat but also trailing in my lap. I felt that faint wispy not-fur-not-feathers-not-scales *something* against my fingers. It moved. Even in an invisible unknown creature I thought I recognized the "pet me" response. I stroked gently with the tips of my fingers. She was humming again. . . .

Except it wasn't a hum. Or it wasn't Hix. It was something big and bullying, trying to overwhelm both of us—something like the army tank rolling down the street toward us.

Army *tank*?

Now I could hear—feel—something—the crackles and frizzles and—something-going-wrong-with-the-air—as all the unbent unfolded steel-legged things made contact with whatever was in the tank. I knew about armydar. You got a few days of standard armydar with a standard scan. Our last scan hadn't been so long ago that I'd forgotten. This wasn't that. This was *big*. Something the army thought needed to be in a tank to keep safe. What were they protecting, the thing or us?

They were chugging it out, the something-wrong-with-the-air, in these big ugly disorienting throbs, the tank thing and the boxes on legs. I could see two of the boxes from where I was sitting. There were almost-visible ripples wandering, weaving down the road, past our bus shelter. I closed my eyes, but I could still feel them, like you feel a boat heaving up and down on a long slow queasy-making swell. I didn't like it. It made me feel heavy and slow. This wasn't anything I could lob little bits of folded-up paper at. I opened my eyes again.

There was a fancy kind of armydar that was supposed to have a squashing effect on an area around a cobey—or some kind of preemptive squashing over an area that might throw out a cobey. Like flinging a blanket or a bucket of sand over a kitchen fire. It may not put it out, but it slows it down. And if this was some big, super-whammy armydar . . .

There was an army guy—in fact, several army guys—and the one in front had more stuff on his cap and his shoulders than the other ones, and he was looking grim and maybe angry—and he was coming toward the bus shelter. He saw us all right. One of the guys with him was holding a sort of gun-wand thing out in front of him—oh, her—and she was pointing it at us. There were three little red flashing lights at the tip. The flashing was kind of hypnotic. It looked like it was saying, *Ha ha ha, got you.*

And suddenly the bus shelter was full of *gruuaa.* I was looking at the big angry army guy and as the *gruuaa* poured into the bus shelter I saw a medium-sized hairy black and white cannonball arc immediately in front of the army guy. Mongo. I wasted half a second thinking, no, it can't be Mongo, there's nobody home now, which is to say Ran, to forget and leave the door open. But you know your own dog. It was Mongo.

Mongo dived across the road immediately in front of the army guy staring at me, and broke his gaze. He looked at the dog, gestured to one of his aides, and looked back at me—

Except that he didn't look back at me. He looked toward the bus shelter and then he looked confused. His eyes skated right over the open front of the shelter where Casimir and I (and a very large knapsack and a very large algebra book) were sitting. He stopped and looked around like he was searching for something he had dropped. He looked up again, straight at the bus shelter like he was sure whatever it was was in that direction. Then the woman with the wand-gun said something to him, and I noticed the blinking lights had gone clear. *Ha ha ha yourself.* He scowled at the lights, he turned away . . . he was missing out the bus shelter, and heading toward the gate into the park.

By then my arms were full of Mongo. "Mongo, you *loophead*," I said, burying my face in his fur, "what are you doing here?" But my stomach was telling me something was seriously wrong. "What *are* you doing here?" I looked up, still clutching Mongo, who didn't anything like all fit in my lap. I could feel some kind of greeting going on between Mongo and Hix— Mongo was a licker, and since I could feel Hix, if faintly, maybe Mongo could lick her. I stared around. Even now, knowing the shadows were friendly—well, knowing that Hix was friendly, and since they'd just stopped the army guy I was ready to guess the way-too-many-shadows around us were okay too—it was pretty scary. I remembered that first evening, opening the door to

Val and seeing the shadows rearing up behind him like the end of the world as I knew it.

Which it had been, one way or another.

It was normal-shadowy in the bus shelter; it was late afternoon and both the park fence and the first line of trees were between us and what was left of the sunlight. But sun shadows and *gruuaa* shadows were as different as—oh, as two black dogs from each other—when one's a Pomeranian and one's a Labrador.

I looked at Casimir. He was looking a little green, although that might have been the normal bus-shelter shadows: the inside walls were painted seasick green. But Casimir was staring at the *gruuaa,* so I guessed it was more to do with them. He hadn't looked green when we first got here. "I have never seen so many," he said. He made it sound like a question.

I was trying to decide what to answer when I remembered Val saying that most people had to be trained to see them. "You *can* see them," I said. "And you knew that Hix was helping us."

Casimir went on staring at the *gruuaa.* Did he look a little shifty? I couldn't decide. But, I thought hopefully, if the border tech didn't stop him, maybe seeing *gruuaa* wasn't going to get me jailed for the rest of my life either. I glanced at my algebra book. I'd worry about cobey-folding later.

"Yes," he said. "My mother gave all of us some basic training. I had little aptitude for most of it." He glanced up at me and smiled, that mental-health-destroying smile. "If I were talking about cooking, I would say that I can boil water. I do not help in the kitchen at the restaurant." He looked down again and shook his head. "So many," he said. "So many."

"They all—er—belong—I guess—er—to my—stepfather," I said. Belong? Stepfather? I was still having trouble with *stepfather.*

"Your stepfather?"

"Val," I said, which was less creepo than going on calling him my stepfather. "He—er—he has a lot of them."

Casimir blinked.

"He's from Orzaskan," I said helpfully. "I think they have more of them there. Like you said. In Oldworld."

"Orzaskan," Casimir said thoughtfully. "Val . . ." He blinked again. "You don't mean . . . Val Crudon, do you?"

"Er," I said. I should have kept saying stepfather. "Yes."

"Your stepfather is Valadi Crudon?" repeated Casimir wonderingly.

"He *isn't,* any more," I said defensively. "A—whatever." I didn't want to say "magician" out loud. Even though that was maybe exactly what he was, then, now, any more, whenever.

I didn't want to ask if it had been a huge headline all over the Slav Commonwealth that Valadi Crudon had been his government's executioner. I didn't want to ask if Casimir had any idea how you took magic away from a magician. One of the things our mental hygiene class taught us about Genecor was that gene-chopping a young person was neat and clean and complete. On a middle-aged grown-up the magic gene had silted or fuzzed up and got tangled with its neighbors, and trying to chop it then was really dangerous.

Could a magician maybe rust out, like an old car? If he didn't use his magic any more? If his government had just kind of *contained* Val for a while? So whatever it was that happened that day out at the shed was maybe like the radio coming on when you twisted the ignition key of your old car, but the engine wasn't going to turn over?

"There is some great mystery about him," said Casimir. "He disappeared—years ago. I was still a boy. There were two of them—Valadi and one other. The other is known to have died. No one knows what happened to Valadi. My mother was very distressed. She said he was the greatest magician in the Commonwealth—even greater than his friend who died."

His friend who died. I rushed to say: "He's *here*, okay? Here in Newworld. He's been here over a year. He has a visa and everything. He tutors really bright kids and really dumb ones in math and science. They made him leave it all behind—like you."

"Yes," said Casimir. "But I had very little to leave behind. And his *gruuaa* came anyway."

My phone rang, and I was glad of the excuse not to go on with this conversation. Val was *famous*? Even if what had happened hadn't been a headline, there was a reason his government had chosen him to . . . I dragged my phone out from under Mongo with difficulty. Mom. I clicked on. "Hi," I said. "Mongo's with me."

"I—oh," said Mom. "Oh, thank the gods. He got out when—Where are you?"

"I'm at the park," I said cautiously. "I'll be home—er." I didn't know the drivers on this route, and it was all downtown. They might not let Mongo on the bus.

"I have a car," said Casimir. "I will take you home. It is not a good car, but it is a car. Your dog and your *gruuaa* are welcome." He smiled, and I lost track of my conversation with Mom.

"Maggie?" said Mom.

"Unh," I said. "Casimir's here too. He's got a car, and he'll bring me home."

"Casimir?" said Mom. "Is he another senior?"

You could be standing in a burning building and the firemen are all yelling, Jump! Jump! and your mom would still want to know about the person whose name you've just said for the first time in her hearing. "No," I said. "He's the person I told you about—last night. Going to Runyon. Jill has met him, okay?"

"I'm not sure that's entirely reassuring," said Mom. "He'll bring you straight home?"

"Yes," I said, wondering what was going on besides Mom being a mom. She shouldn't be home now, Mongo shouldn't be out roaming the streets—and I would be *totally* freaked about this on any other day that I hadn't almost been disappeared by a cobey— and this conversation should sound more like the standard mom-teenage-daughter face-off and it didn't. It sounded like we were both really worried and not telling each other about it. I had my mouth open to ask questions and realized I didn't want to know any sooner than I had to. I looked across the street at the long-legged army things. The human shapes standing stiffly beside them looked more like upright gizmos than like people, and everything looked worse and worse as the light faded toward sunset. In the leaf-shadowy twilight the tank was a monster out of a fairy tale. "See you," was all I said, and clicked off.

The big army guy who had almost busted us had long since disappeared into the park, but there were still a lot of other guys milling around. I hoped our reinforcement *gruuaa* could keep us hidden. If Hix had held onto both Casimir and me by herself,

154

surely this gang could disguise half of Station? But that was before these great icky, woozy, loopy weird-air waves had started.

I took my belt off so I had something to use as a leash—fortunately Mongo was still wearing his collar. The little broken cog rubbed at my hand as I fumbled my belt under the collar. You're working, right? I thought at it. You're making us safe and—normal. I thought my hands were maybe shaking a little. Casimir picked up my knapsack again. I had Mongo in one hand and my algebra book in the other, but Casimir stayed really close to me—because of the *gruuaa* of course. He even slid his free arm around my waist again. Because of the *gruuaa*. Of course. He wasn't stupidly tall like Takahiro. When he turned his head to look up the street, the end of his ponytail brushed across my cheek. *Odorokubeki.* Amazing.

CHAPTER 7

HE WAS RIGHT ABOUT HIS CAR NOT BEING A GOOD car, but I was used to the skanky cars Jill's brothers let her borrow. This one ran. Mongo insisted on staying in my lap (which is majorly illegal so I hoped the *gruuaa* would disguise this from any ordinary traffic cops) and when we got to my house he still wouldn't move and I couldn't open the door or get out. Casimir came around and opened the door for me. "Get *down*," I said, and heaved Mongo onto the drive.

I looked at the house. It looked totally normal. No—*shimatta*—there were *gruuaa*, trying to look like standard shadows, lined out under the rosebushes along the front of the house. They looked eerily like some kind of fortification. They also looked smushed and unhappy, if shadows that aren't really shadows can look smushed and unhappy. There was an odd little hum, almost a moan, from Hix. The rest of the *gruuaa* that had come with us washed across the lawn like a tide, and thickened—reinforced—the ones under the rosebushes.

It might have been the armydar. It was making me feel pretty moany. It was just as bad here as it was in the center of town.

"Do you want to come in?" I said. I didn't know what I was leading him into but I was feeling that I could use all the friends I could get, even ones who thought I was some weird mythic thing and not just a clueless seventeen-year-old girl. I looked over my shoulder like I was expecting a column of soldiers to be trotting along Ramage Avenue and across the mouth of our little street. Not yet. "I can probably give you that cup of coffee we didn't have downtown."

Casimir tried not to brighten, but he did. That'll be the thought of meeting Val, I thought drearily. Never mind. I got to look at him a little longer. The line of his throat when he turned his head . . . and that *dimple* when he smiled. "Thank you," he said.

It also meant he carried my knapsack up the walk to the door. Some of the *gruuaa* peeled off from under the rosebushes and joined us. Mom opened the door before I got my hand on the knob: she must have been looking out for us. Her face was all pinched up with worry. She shouldn't be worried and at home in the middle of the afternoon. Ran—no, if it had been something about my accident-prone little brother, she'd've told me. She was immediately distracted when I introduced her to Casimir, however. Her expression struggled between amusement and "wow." When she turned away to lead us into the kitchen and the coffee machine she shot me a look that said, "Yup. Gorgeous." Some other day this might have annoyed me. Not today. Besides, he *was* gorgeous. Even your mom could see it.

I noticed there were a couple of new little origami critters on the windowsill (not that there was room. One of them was arched over an African violet like a dragon protecting his princess) and a third on the kitchen table. I had known Takahiro was going to be taking some kind of gizmohead science tutorial with Val, and I hadn't liked the idea at all. When he'd told me I'd wanted to say, hey, whose friend are you? but I hadn't. Staring at the little creature on the table now I had this dumb spasm of feeling that Taks' origami made everything all right. I was sure it had been my new mascot that had taught me (somehow) to do whatever it was I had just done as Hands Folding Paper in the park. The throb of the armydar almost faltered.

This didn't last even as long as it took Mom to bring the mugs of coffee out of the kitchen. I looked into her face: she was really frightened. "Maggie," she said in this unnaturally calm voice, "would you take a mug out to Val? He's in his office." Which was what we called the shed when anyone else was around.

I couldn't very well ask her what was going on with Casimir sitting there, or why she was sending me instead of going herself and leaving me to entertain my guest. I flashed an "it's okay, Mom's harmless" smile at Casimir and picked up the mug, telling myself that whatever happened it was *not* going to freak me out like it had the last time something weird had happened out there.

I let myself out the back door, Mongo plunging through before I could decide whether I wanted him or not, and a lot of *gruuaa* with him. I didn't think they had to wait for someone to open a door, but maybe they were being polite. As I walked the few yards to the shed door it got harder and harder to put my feet down and *go* that way. It was so peculiar a sensation I couldn't decide if I was just feeling reluctant—which I was, although I wouldn't have said it was strong enough to glue my feet to the path—or whether there was something really trying to stop me getting to the shed. Hix patted my face. It felt like, *Go on, I'm here.*

If there was something trying to stop me, it failed. I knocked. "Val? Mom sent me out with some coffee for you."

There was movement that didn't sound like someone walking to the door—but it sounded like it had something to do with something *large.* Then the ordinary sound of footsteps, and the door opened. A crack. "Maggie," said Val.

I held the mug out. Whatever was going on, I was happy to stay out of it. The day had been dreepy enough already.

"I would like you—I would ask you to come in," said Val carefully. "But—please prepare yourself."

Prepare myself for *what?* Hix was silent and motionless. I looked down. Mongo was wagging his tail. It was a happy, hopeful wag. Well, so it couldn't be too bad—could it? Huh. Mongo was an optimist.

Val opened the door the rest of the way. Behind him on the floor was a huge shaggy grey and silver dog with yellow eyes lying on a heap of rags. It looked tense and miserable. Val looked pretty tense too, and worried. Like Mom. Mongo's tail beat harder. The huge dog was panting heavily, although it was cool in the shed, and its tail was clamped between its legs. I looked down. Mongo had his head lowered and his ears not-quite flat, his eyes wide open but soft, and his tail was going like four hundred and twelve. Friendly but submissive. I looked at the other dog again.

It looked awfully like a wolf.

"Please come in," said Val. "Mongo too, if he wishes."

The shed wasn't that big. To get the door shut behind me I had to go closer to the huge dog (or wolf) than I wanted to. As soon as the door was shut I backed up against it till I couldn't go any farther. I could still feel that keep-away sensation I'd felt outside, but inside the shed it was weirder. Much weirder. It was both go-away and please-please-please-stay. The shed had *gruuaa* everywhere—there was even one wrapped around the cord that the little ceiling light hung from.

Mongo got down on his belly and crept toward the other dog. One of the other dog's forefeet gave a funny twitch and then it whined—a pathetic, heartbreaking sound. I knew that sound; I heard it at the shelter all the time. I also knew that the last thing you do is rush up to a strange animal and touch it just because you know it's miserable.

Well, okay, I didn't *rush*. I took two deliberate steps—past Val, who made no move to stop me—and knelt down by Mongo, who was by this time licking the big dog's chin. Petting this monster seemed rude somehow . . . not that what I did was *sensible*. I sat down next to it and reached out for it like it was Mongo. Like we were on the sofa, and he was sitting next to me. I reached out as if I was going to drag the front half of it into my lap.

Never, *ever* do this.

It gave a moan, and shoved its gigantic head under my arm and . . . there was a totally doolally blur, I don't know, all teeming and boiling and wildness . . . not wholly unlike a smaller denser version of what had wrapped around Casimir and me in the park . . .

. . . and I suddenly had my arms around Takahiro. A *naked*

Takahiro. Val produced a blanket out of somewhere and dropped it over him, and then knelt down beside him and hung on: Takahiro was shivering like he was having some kind of fit. He still had his head under my arm, and his arms were across my lap. One of them reached around behind me and grabbed the pocket of my jeans like it was saving him from drowning. I didn't know what else to do, so I wrapped my arms around his naked chest and back and held on too.

It was over in maybe a minute. Then he went limp, and his hand fell away from my jeans pocket. Val and I let go, but Val was tucking the blanket around him, as tenderly as if Takahiro was his baby son. A six-and-a-half-foot baby son. I realized the rags that the "dog" had been lying on used to be clothes. I thought I recognized what used to be a sweatshirt with our high school logo on it. He rolled away from me and tried to sit up. Val had begun chafing his blanket-covered back and shoulders like you might do someone you've just saved from drowning. "You're all right," said Val, pausing to retuck a bit of the blanket. "It's over. You're all right."

"I'm not all right," said Takahiro in a voice I barely recognized. "I have never been all right. I have always been *this*."

I wanted to scream or throw up or run away or all three, but I couldn't. Takahiro, as many times as I'd wanted to kill him in the last more than seven years, was my friend. And werewolves were a myth. Like *mgdagas*. I got up, a little unsteadily, and picked up the mug of coffee on Val's table. "Coffee?" I said inanely, and held it out toward Takahiro.

He glanced up and away again as if he couldn't meet my eyes.

The blanket slipped down over one shoulder. He had the most beautiful creamy skin, like a golden pearl. He pulled the blanket up over his shoulder again—Val was still kneeling beside him, rubbing his back. I kept on holding out the coffee (Taks was as much of a coffee hound as Jill and me) and eventually, without looking at me, he took it.

I sat back down on the floor too, immediately in front of him, where he would have to look at me (I hoped). I was fighting wanting to scream or throw up, and if I still wanted to run away—and with the army out there cranking its zappers and wave machines, I *did* want to run away—I wanted to take Takahiro with me. Far away from this world where everything was going so rats' assy. Mongo, however, was thrilled by the situation. He crammed himself between Taks and me. Taks got the soulful brown eyes. I got the being beaten to death with a tail.

"Can you tell me what happened?" I said in my calmest voice.

Takahiro didn't say anything, and after about a minute Val said, "They were doing a sweep in this area. I was surprised; Copperhill is over ten miles away, yes? And you have not the assumption of a cobey series in Newworld, I believe. Takahiro and I were out here, but I could feel something going on—as, I believe, could Takahiro." He stopped and looked at Taks. And waited.

Eventually Takahiro muttered, "Yes. It was the best thing that had happened since I came here, when they stopped doing regular sweeps. And this one's fiercer than I remember."

"The *gruuaa* did not like it either," said Val.

"Then you're seeing them again—er—you know they're there," I interrupted.

"Yes," said Val. "I do not see them as well as I once did—"

How well is well? I wondered. Do you know how many legs and how many eyes, and are there teeth? For that matter, are there mouths? Is it vocal cords in a throat that Hix uses to hum with?

"—but the skill is returning—now that I am employing it. I guessed Hix had gone with Maggie this morning, which was both good and bad; good that she would protect you, bad that she thought you needed protecting. In Oldworld, when a big cobey opens, usually at least one more opens near it, and *gruuaa* are very sensitive to the energy shifts this causes. Sometimes they can damp these effects for their human colleagues. Sometimes they cannot." He glanced at Takahiro again. "As I say, we were out here when this powerful sweep began. . . ."

The throb of the armydar was less awful in the shed, maybe because of all the *gruuaa*. "Why would a cobey sweep upset all of us?" I said. "It's just supposed to make the cobey easier to manage, isn't it? But it feels like it's trying to turn me inside out." Armydar didn't use to make me feel like that. But the regular sweeps stopped right around the time I hit puberty. Which is supposedly when your magic gene tended to flick into active status. Back in the days when anyone had a magic gene.

"Yeah," said Takahiro very quietly.

"It interests me very much that they do such a sweep," said Val, "here in Newworld, including a bandwidth that apparently disturbs magical effects. In Oldworld the sweep after a new cobey is for any sign of another one in the area, but it is also for any local use of magic. The dimension shift of a cobey will distort any magic done within its range of influence."

"Foreseers," I said. "Um." Not wanting to say Casimir's name. "Aren't there—foreseers?"

Val looked at me in surprise. "Yes. But foreseers are human, like the rest of us, and even a very good foreseer can miss a little cobey, which may nonetheless cause local disarray. It is perhaps Newworld's lack of foreseers that explains the strength and extent of this sweep, if it is still the result of the cobey in Copperhill. Although perhaps there has been some further activity nearer at hand."

I sighed. "I think—I think there was—well, I don't absolutely know it was a cobey, but it was something. At the park. This afternoon. It was pretty electric. And the army *hammered* down."

Val looked at me. I looked at Takahiro's long-fingered hands holding onto his blanket. The silence got kind of thick. "I hope you will tell us about it some time," said Val at last.

Maybe. Just not right now. I could hear Val really wanting to know, and I should tell him, but I was thinking about how beautiful Taks' hands were. When he'd been a bony little boy his big hands had been part of his strangeness. But they were elegant and graceful now, even holding a ragged old blanket closed with one of them, and petting my hyper dog with the other.

"About half an hour ago many of the *gruuaa* left abruptly," Val said. "I did wonder if that was to do with you, Maggie. Shortly after that the quality of the sweep changed, and I could see it was causing Takahiro increased distress." Val stopped and waited again.

Takahiro said reluctantly, "Yeah. The first whatever—sweep— was like olly-olly-oxen-free on the playground. The second was like they'd got the bloodhounds out and were coming in after you."

164

"At this awkward juncture Elaine knocked on the door and said there was a man in a military uniform who wanted to talk to 'everyone in the house,' which meant Takahiro as well as me. I could not risk that he might know that Takahiro was here. This man—Major Donnelly—asked me many questions, most of which I did not know the answers to, but I did not like that he was asking. I have suspected for some time that I may be on a list of potential malefactors—that if anything unusual happened in this area they would wish to re-examine me. Until last night I found this ironic. Today . . . I was as stupid as possible without, I hope, being deliberately rude."

Takahiro said softly, "Val's English got very bad." He was almost smiling. Mongo was in one of his rubber-skeleton poses, licking the hand that was petting him. Dog therapy. It's good.

"Yes," said Val. "Very bad. I might not have gone to pieces quite so quickly except that I knew what was happening to Takahiro by then, and I wanted the good major out of the house before it did."

Takahiro's head snapped up. "How did you know?" he said. *"How did you know?"*

Val patted his shoulder. "I have met your kind before, of course. They are not widespread anywhere on this world, I believe, but we have a few in Orzaskan and the rest of the Commonwealth. They frequently have a talent for magic."

I remembered the sense of something trying to stop me from going to the shed—and the go-away-stay-stay-stay once I was inside.

"As the change approaches, there is an unmistakable smell."

"Hormones," said Takahiro bitterly.

"They peak just before the change becomes visible," Val went on, cool as spring rain. "It was rather close by the time we finally saw the good major through the door again. I'm afraid that's when Mongo escaped, although he did us a favor—the major had the decency to be embarrassed, and wished to help Elaine catch him. I escorted Takahiro back out here where—er—there is less to break. But you were remarkably self-restrained."

"I might have *killed* you," said Takahiro. "You don't know. You go nuts when the change comes."

"You were not nuts at all," said Val. "I have seen much worse. And it is in the highest degree unlikely that you could have killed me."

There was something about the unshowy way Val said this that made me for the first time feel that I was seeing a little bit into Val's old life. Perhaps including why his government had ordered him and not someone else to do . . . what they'd told him to do. Why Casimir's mom thought what she thought. How it wasn't an accident—or a coincidence—that eight hundred zillion *gruuaa* had followed him into his new life, even though he hadn't known they were there. Or that Newworld, even though they let him in, maybe had him on a list.

"It would—I would—" Takahiro sighed, a long, long, weary sigh. "Thank you. It's—more awful when you're alone."

"Yes," said Val. "I have been told that by other young weres. But—have you not finished your training? If Maggie hadn't come home soon I was considering going through your wallet for the name and phone number of your mentor. I hadn't done it immediately only because I hadn't decided how to manage the conversation with someone who might not be your mentor. I assume it is not your dad?"

Takahiro gave a creepily bark-like laugh. "No, not Dad. Dad's not—like me." There was a pause, but Val was clearly waiting for more. "I don't have a mentor," muttered Takahiro to Mongo. "I just . . . cope. Mostly."

Val stood up. He looked like he wanted to pace but there wasn't room. He sat down again, this time on the chair. "That's . . . inhuman, if you will forgive the term. I am sure weres are uncommon in this country, but . . . in Orzaskan it is illegal for a young were not to have a mentor—an authorized, trained, experienced mentor."

"I had my mom. Till she died. Then they forced my dad to take me."

I didn't mean to but it burst out: *"Forced?"*

"Yeah. I'm why he left, you know? When he found out."

Val rubbed a hand over his face, as if wiping the look of pity away before Takahiro saw it. "It's genetic. Both partners must have the gene to produce a shape-changer. He may not be able to change himself, but he has to have known he carried the gene."

"If he knew he had gene, he is not saying," Taks said jerkily. "But my mom is—was—*kitsune*. She say—says—he knew before he married her. I don't know if he'd've liked me any better if I changed into fox. But I changed into good old unmistakable New-world timber wolf and he freaked out."

"But he's your *father*," I said—and kind of realized, as I said it, some of the echoes of what I was saying, with Val standing there.

Takahiro shrugged. "Yeah. And he pays housekeeper me—to feed me. But I was ten when Mom died and they sent me here. I was a little old for leaving in basket at police station door. My mom's family didn't want anything to do with me. They hadn't been happy about her marrying *gaijin.* When I turned wolf, they cut her off. Me too of course."

"But—don't you—I mean, when—"

"Don't ask me about the full moon," said Takahiro even more wearily. "Full moon is no big deal. I mean, you do feel it, but it's about as dangerous as having a bath. It's worry and stuff makes you turn. You want to know why I'm such a grind? Why I get straight As in everything all the dreeping time? It's not because I'm so incredibly brilliant, or because I *like* studying my brains out. It's because I can't afford to be worried about tests. Just in case."

Val said gently, "Your mother must have taught you how to turn voluntarily?"

"She tried. But I'd figured out my dad left after he found out I was 'shifter, you know? I think it kind of shorted out system. I think also it was different for her—woman and fox—although she never said so. She used to say, it's okay, we try again later. . . ."

I couldn't think of anything to say. There was a faint tap on the door, and my mother's voice said, "Are you all right in there?"

Val opened the door and my mother looked in. "Oh, Takahiro, I'm so glad you're safe," she said. "You were right about Maggie," she added to Val.

Val shook his head. "My experience with shape-shifters is limited. But we didn't have many options. Takahiro, how do you usually shift back?"

Takahiro grinned. Fiercely. "Oatmeal," he said.

"Oatmeal," my mother said blankly. She slid inside the shed and shut the door behind her. Val put an arm around her, but he almost had to, there was so little floor space left.

"Yeah. That's something my mother taught me. Human food you have strong reaction to will probably give you way to shift. Not if you've just 'shifted. You have to wait till you've kind of—settled into that body. Then if you eat something you think of as really, really human it'll probably bring you back. When I still lived with my mom, *umeboshi* used. It was what she'd used when she was first learning to do, when she was little girl. After she died . . . *umeboshi* hard to find here is, and it so much part old life was. It *was* so much a part of my old life. I wanted something Newworld. I loved *umeboshi* . . . I hate oatmeal. But Kay—my dad's housekeeper—kept trying to make me eat it because she thought I was too small and thin."

I remembered Takahiro when he'd first come here. He had been too small and thin.

"I was too stunned, right after my mom died. I felt nothing—not even grief at first. That got me through—everything. And it got me here. But after I began to get it that I was going to have to stay here . . . I 'shifted once after—it was one of those placement English exams. I think they wanted to put me in special school, and my dad say, 'No way, he can speak English.'" Takahiro closed his eyes briefly. "Kay was supposed to bring me home. It was after normal school hours. I run to boys' restroom, there when change hit. I had to get out—went through window. But I was only cub then, you know? Anyone who saw me, think it was student joke. They might report it, but they'd report big puppy.

"I got home all right—your sense of direction amazing as wolf, and you can run what feels like forever—but I had to shift back before Kay got home in car. . . . I was clawing my way through kitchen, looking for anything that might shift me back. I didn't really have any idea what I was looking for. I was also sure I'd failed test, and my father would be furious. I knocked over trash bin and there was morning's oatmeal. It rolled out, big congealed lump, and went splat. It was so gross, like somebody's brains. I thought about how much I hated it—then thought *yeah* and ate it—and 'shifted.

"I just got to my room and into pajamas before Kay arrived—bringing knapsack I'd left behind in test room. I don't know what anyone thought about the wrecked clothes on boys' room floor, but I guess there wasn't anything that made them mine—jeans, T-shirt, cheap sneakers. Nothing in pockets but lint. I didn't have much trouble being so out of it I couldn't answer any of Kay's questions—and then I think my dad got to her because next day she left me alone. Oh, and I passed the test. I didn't pass it very well, but I passed it."

Takahiro stopped but we were all totally listening. I kept thinking, he's been my friend for nearly eight years and I don't know *anything* about him. As the silence went on and got kind of heavy Takahiro glanced around at all of us: my mom, Val, and me last. Last and longest. He really looked at me. I smiled. It was probably kind of a shaky smile, but that was because I was trying not to cry for the little boy who got sent to the other side of the world to live with a dad who didn't want him. The only sounds in the shed were the vines outside the window rustling in the breeze and Mongo's tail still thudding (slower now) against my leg.

Takahiro said, "For a while I kept a box of instant oatmeal on the top shelf of my closet and I used to keep some made up in a jar on the floor. If Kay ever found it I don't know what she thought, but she had no business in my closet, you know? And then I 'shifted again . . . after another bugsucking English test . . . and I found out the instant stuff *doesn't work*. That was very bad.

"I could have figured out how to make real oatmeal, but I couldn't have done it regularly without getting caught, you know? Kay rules the kitchen. So I told her I wanted a bowl of oatmeal as a bedtime snack—oh, twice a week or so. It gets moldy after three or four days. She was kind of surprised . . . but Kay's not bad really. She makes me oatmeal. And we have a lot of fat wildlife in the woods behind our house. Raccoons are like *waiting* for me when I take the old stuff out."

Takahiro had never been much of a talker—even after his English caught up with living in Newworld. I wanted to tell him, it's okay, he didn't have to tell us all this. But I realized he wanted to—oh, not *wanted* wanted to, who would *like* telling someone else that his dad didn't love him? but to have someone to talk to. I sometimes thought my dad's death might have killed me if I hadn't had Jill to talk to—and I'd had Mom and Ran too. Takahiro didn't have anyone.

Casimir, I thought suddenly. Oh, drog me, I'd forgotten about Casimir! I'd *forgotten* about Casimir! I looked up at my mother. She was looking down at me—maybe just a little ironically. "Your friend," she said in a neutral voice, "had to go to work. So I came out here to find out if — well, if things had gone all right and if so, if you might need clothing or anything."

"He's not going to wear anything of mine well, that is certain," said Val, who was easily a foot shorter and twice as wide as Takahiro, although "well" was a nonstarter concerning any of Val's clothes.

"Nor Ran's," said my mother. Gods, I'd forgotten about Ran too. "Ran's at Alec's this afternoon," she added as if she was reading my mind again, "so I can go to the mall and pick him up on the way home. Most of it's open till late. Tell me what you need. No, wait. First tell me what *happened*."

Val said, "As I said, my experience with shape-shifters is limited. But one of the things anyone — anyone with my background — will learn is that physical contact — preferably unexpected or sudden contact — with someone they have a strong incorporeal connection with — for example a long friendship — will bring them back. Especially if they want to be brought back. I thought of Maggie."

I remembered my insane urge to drag the front half of something I now knew was a timber wolf onto my lap. It was funny in a sort of death-wish way.

I didn't remember Takahiro and me getting to be friends — mainly I remember that by the time we were both coming out from under — my dad's death and his mom's, and his being shipped here like some kind of package, and having to learn to live in English and in Newworld — we were already friends. Friends who seemed sometimes to exist to zap the electric crap out of each other, but still — friends.

I remembered him showing me how to make my first origami fish. That was before he was talking—pretty much at all. He sat down beside me in some class or other—I don't remember which—and started folding, because that's what he did all the time. He used to sit beside me because I'd leave him alone. A lot of kids would try and take his paper away from him, or flick what he was working on out of his hands. I'd sneak looks at him. It was hard to remember now that he'd been little for his age. But his hands were already big even then and his fingers really long. I used to half-imagine they had extra joints in them. I didn't understand how he could make paper do all that. But I remember the first time I picked up a piece of notebook paper and folded it over into a triangle and then folded and tore off the end so what was left was a square. He'd stopped what he was doing when I folded my paper over. I opened it up again and held it toward him. He stared at me—it felt like a really long time. He hardly ever looked at anyone and he never stared, and that's when I found out his eyes were the darkest darkest *darkest* brown, the barest bit not black—like he was wondering if I was just going to start teasing him too.

He pulled out a fresh piece of already-square origami paper, folded it over, and opened it again like I had. I nodded. Then he started showing me what to do. After I made a horrible mess of my piece of squared-off notebook paper he gave me a piece of origami paper to mangle. Then he gave me a second one. The second one actually turned into a fish.

There's a really big gap between being able to make origami fish and hats and boats and those fortune-telling boxes where you write silly things under paper folds and make people choose one, and your first crane. I wasted *a lot* of time (and paper) trying to fold a crane. I could follow the directions—by this time I had my own *How to Do Origami* book at home—but the results were always smudgy and lopsided and bent-looking. And then one day I got it. The folds were all crisp and sharp and right first time and the little hole in the bottom was centered and square and when I set it down it stood up straight. I couldn't remember the last time I'd been so happy—probably not since Dad had died—maybe the day we brought Mongo home. I went racing into the dining room and the Lair to show Mom—Ran had been totally unimpressed but he was still pretty little. Mom got it although I think she mostly got it about something making me happy.

"What are you going to do with it?" she said. "We could make space on a shelf somewhere." Mom has a collection of family china and stuff that takes up most of the corner cupboards in the dining room. The gaps and corners had silted up over the years with stuff like report cards with gold stars on them (not a lot of these) and family photos and candles too pretty to burn and tiny vases that weren't at that moment holding deadheading accidents from Mom's garden and a few of my china dog statues although by unanimous vote Mom and I made Ran keep his car models in his room. The crane would have looked right at home.

I thought about it. "No," I said. "I'm going to give it to Takahiro."

Mom didn't say anything about how Takahiro must have made millions of cranes and the last thing he'd be interested in is another one. She nodded. "He'll like that."

I took it to school the next day in a box, I was so afraid of crushing it. I found Takahiro on the playground—off in a corner by himself, folding paper. I knelt beside him. He looked up, startled. I opened the box and took my beautiful crane out. It suddenly looked a lot less beautiful than it had the day before on the kitchen table where I'd made it. It was the cheapest origami paper and the red on the colored side was streaky, and there were flecks of white on the borders where the ink hadn't quite gone to the edges. And it was just a crane. Takahiro had made millions of them. Just like Mom hadn't said.

My hand shook a little as I took it out of the box, but it was too late now not to do it. I held it out to him. I know my voice shook. "It's for you," I said. "It's the first crane I've ever made that isn't awful." I'd looked up how to say something like "Please take this, it is a gift for you" in Japanese on the webnet, but all of it but the "please" had gone out of my head: "*Dōzo,*" I said.

He took my crane gently, as if it *was* beautiful. He looked at it and then he looked at me again. I think it was the first time I'd ever really seen him smile. I was staring straight at him—terrified he'd laugh or be bored or something—and I saw his mouth say "thank you" but I don't think he said it out loud.

"You're welcome," I said, hugely relieved. (I'd looked the Japanese for "you're welcome" up on the webnet too but I couldn't remember it.) "Um—do you want the box?" He nodded, and was putting the crane carefully back inside it when the class bell rang. We stood up together and just before we turned to the school door he *bowed* and said clearly: "*Dōmo arigato gozaimasu.*" Which means "thank you very much."

Of course it took me about fifty more cranes before I made another one that was anywhere near as good. But a crane did finally get put on the dining room shelves: Mom gave me some patterned origami paper after I'd been doing it about a year, and I made her a crane out of the prettiest pattern, and a peony out of the pinkest. I also made Ran a *Tyrannosaurus rex* and a racing car, although he went on and on about what kind of car it might be (the book I got the pattern out of didn't say) till I was sorry (I told him) I hadn't made him a guillotine instead. (There was a pattern for a guillotine on some extreme-origami site I'd looked at—you can make *anything* out of paper if you're good enough. A guillotine is probably beyond me, but Taks could make one.)

I looked at Takahiro now. He was looking at me with an expression I thought I remembered from that day I'd given him the crane: surprise. Wariness. Hope. Although there'd been an awful lot of chain-yanking between him and me since that day. The weeks he suddenly wouldn't talk to me—which were pretty dreeping aggravating anyway, and worse when he'd been helping me study algebra and it was like he made *me* look like the bad guy when I wouldn't let him help me any more just because he wasn't *talking* to me. Or I'd see him at Peta's after school with his geek crowd and when I waved he'd look straight through me like I was, I don't know, a nongeek. Which I was of course.

That's how Jill and I started using Japanese phrases—when he wasn't talking to me he wasn't talking to Jill either, and it was Jill's idea to speak Japanese to annoy him, since he never did—speak Japanese, I mean. That thank-you when I gave him the crane was probably the only Japanese I'd ever heard him say. And that was before I started needing to annoy him. Then it kind of caught on. It was all Newworld girls and their 'tops—Steph joined the Annoy Taks group when she had a crush on him and he looked through her too, and then Laura and Dena did because they were tight with Steph, and he ignored all of us. But I like to think we were irritating. Also, some of us—Jill and me anyway—just liked the way the words felt in our mouths. Like *sumimasen*. *Shimatta* was a lot more satisfying than *damn*. And *sugoi* is a whole different kind of amazing than amazing.

I guess I was maybe feeling a little guilty now. "I was thinking about you teaching me origami. And that crane I gave you."

He nodded. "I still have it."

"You do?" I said, astonished.

He glanced at me and away again. "It was the first time anyone I'd ever showed how had actually gone on with it and done stuff. It was the first day I . . ." He didn't finish what he was saying, but I thought I could guess: I'd probably been his first friend. He didn't start hanging out with his geeks and gizmoheads till his English was up to arguments about servebots and why physwiz did or did not rule (there's a gizmohead tough-guy thing about physwiz). At the beginning though it was just me and origami. And the origami was really visible. It could have gone either way: the rest of the kids could have exiled me the way they'd exiled Takahiro. That they didn't was mostly Jill. If I liked Takahiro then she did too. And everyone liked Jill. It was Jill who first got him talking (in English) at all. She just started talking to him and I don't know how she did it, but she made it seem like they were having conversations, till they were, till he started talking back. He showed her how to fold paper too, and she was pretty good but I was better. It was a pity I couldn't take Enhanced Origami instead of Enhanced Algebra.

But then Taks grew about two-and-a-half feet, discovered geekery, and periodically forgot how to talk again. I think he'd always been like this, it's just we only started noticing after he was talking *sometimes*. And you never knew what was going to set him off. You'd think you were having a conversation and then you'd ask him something like what he thought about the movie the other night and he'd go silent and then just *walk away*. If this happened to you (as it happened to me) in the middle of the corridor at school with a lot of other people seeing it happen you felt like a *total* dead battery. But you know that thing about how a friend is someone you could call at three o'clock in the morning if you needed to? I could call Taks at three a.m. if I was in trouble. It was the day-to-day "hi, how are you" stuff that wasn't so good.

Mom was writing down the sizes Takahiro gave her and then said, "Wait a minute," went away, and came back with Val's dressing gown. "Come along, Maggie," she said. "Leave the boys to cope." Mongo, after what was evidently a terrible struggle, came with me, after wildly licking Takahiro's wrist one last time.

"Are you okay?" Mom said softly to me. "Er—it's been a rather harrowing day. Again. And I don't even know what happened to you at the park."

"I think I could sleep for a week," I said. "But I'm okay."

"How do you—you and Jill—know Casimir?" she said, trying not to sound like a mother and failing. I knew she didn't approve of college kids hanging out with kids still in high school: imbalance of power, she called it. And Casimir was *terrifyingly* good-looking. What did a nineteen- or twenty-year-old who looked like Casimir want with a seventeen-year-old who looked like me? I didn't think I could tell her about the *mgdaga* stuff; even to mention it was dinglebrained and woopy. And he had come in with me and talked to my mother. That would rate with her.

"He works at P&P," I said, trying not to sound like a teenager being asked personal questions by her mother, and also failing. "We met, um, today at the park."

There was a little silence as we went through the kitchen door. Casimir hadn't remotely hinted anything to her about the new cobey or she'd have been all over me with panicky-mom questions. I owed him for that. She thought we were having a standard mother-daughter conversation. It was still better than Hey, who would have guessed Takahiro was a werewolf?

"Casimir told me he's from Ukovia," Mom said finally. "His English is very good. He sounds a lot like Val."

"He's *heard* of Val," I blurted out. "He said 'Valadi Crudon?' like it was some big deal."

Mom turned and looked at me. The day before yesterday I'd've said it like an accusation. Today I was just frightened. Her husband was an ex-magician who had killed his best friend because his government had told him to. Except that he wasn't ex-. One of my best friends was a werewolf. I had an invisible humming creature with too many legs and eyes wrapped around my throat. There had been a cobey in the park—the park less than two miles from where we lived. A cobey that Casimir, who had heard of Val, recognized as a cobey. A cobey that I . . . *I* . . . I looked at my poor algebra book, lying on the kitchen table. You could see the gap the missing pages made, a little black hole against the spine, and the closed cover lay at a slight angle. Mom hadn't noticed, or she'd've gone ballistic—textbooks are *expensive*. But she wouldn't expect me to be a book mutilator. And how was I going to explain?

Two days ago Mom would have heard the accusation in my voice and shut me out. Two days ago we hadn't met Hix or seen a werewolf in Val's shed. Or heard why Val had been exiled. Today she said, "I knew there were things Val hadn't told me. But there were things I hadn't told him too; why should he tell me everything? I had even guessed—before last night—that Val was more important in his old life than he wanted to talk about. And I can't imagine anyone who has moved so far away, and to a new country, wouldn't have some mixed feelings about what they've left behind. Until last night it hadn't occurred to me that anything he hadn't told me might be dangerous."

Mongo, not getting the response he wanted merely leaning against me, was licking my hand. I sat down abruptly on the floor and started petting him fiercely with both hands. He lay down and stretched out to make this easier. His feathering—the long stuff on his neck and belly and legs and tail—needed brushing. His feathering always needed brushing. His eyes said, Don't stop. Hix flowed down one arm and across Mongo's ribs. His eyes moved—I guess he could see her better than I could. She curled up under his chin, and he raised his head not only as if he knew exactly where she was, but as if she took up space, which I still wasn't clear about.

Mom said carefully, "Casimir seemed to think you were a bit

special too." I didn't know what to say so I didn't say anything. Mom waited and then added, "Something a little unusual. About a prophecy."

I exhaled. I reminded myself that us Newworlders *did* believe in coincidence. And that he hadn't mentioned the cobey so I still owed him. But maybe a little less. "That's just some dumb folk tale. It's a *joke.*"

"I don't think . . ." Mom began, and stopped. I was thinking about my grandmother turning green and scaly. I was thinking about magic winning over science. I was thinking about Takahiro. I had a headache.

"Oh—a *thousand* dead batteries," I said. "Clare was expecting me—"

"No, she's not," said Mom. "I phoned her while I was waiting for you to come home. Whatever happened with Takahiro, I didn't think you'd make it to the shelter this afternoon."

"Oh, poor Clare," I said. "I wonder who—"

"She told me to tell you that she wasn't surprised, that everything was a hot wire this afternoon, and that she'd already called her brother."

Clare's brother was still pretending to be a farmer with a few acres at the other end of what had used to be their family farm, but he earned his living as a legal aide for a family law practice specializing in abused children. They both had the rescue-things gene, speaking of genes. He and Clare shouted at each other a lot but he always came when she needed him. I relaxed as much as I could relax. Which wasn't very much. I'd much rather have spent the afternoon cleaning kennels because nothing else was happening.

The default position in this household was that you boiled water and made a hot drink. Mom filled the kettle and put it on the stove. She took four mugs out of the cupboard and lined them up on the counter. The kettle began to make that faint far-off hissing noise that means it will produce hot water before you die of thirst (probably). Mom stood staring at the cupboard. There is a long time for thinking thoughts you don't want to think while you're waiting for a kettle to boil. She got the milk out of the refrigerator and put a lot of it into a pan. It was going to be hot chocolate then. That meant it was serious.

Well, it *was* serious.

CHAPTER 8

WE HEARD THE SHED DOOR OPEN, FOOTSTEPS—
one pair with shoes, one pair without—and then a hand turn the
kitchen door handle. Val's dressing gown went nearly twice around
Takahiro but didn't quite reach his knees. He'd wrapped the belt
round and round and tied it in front, like a samurai's obi. He looked
almost as unhappy as he had as a wolf: all curled in on himself like
he used to be eight years ago, and it made my heart ache. I wanted
to believe that it didn't make any difference that he might turn into
a wolf any time he was stressed out—but it did, you know? It meant
he was in danger *all the time*. Which meant that his friends were
also in danger all the time. There was no way the niddles *wouldn't*
believe we all knew. I said I didn't know Takahiro at all. But I did
in some ways. I knew that was one of the things he was thinking
about right now. Because now some of us did know. No wonder
he'd never really finished becoming one of us. We just thought it
was because he was half Japanese, and lived in a huge house on the
other side of town with a dad who was never home and who none

of our parents had ever met. And possibly because he was an arrogant moody stuck-on-himself creepazoid. And here he wasn't even a real gizmohead. He was just a grind. And a werewolf.

The kitchen was starting to smell of chocolate. It was probably my favorite smell in the whole world, and all I could think of was that we'd just had it last night, and I'd thought last night had been serious-enough-for-an-emergency-hot-chocolate-ration enough. I looked down along the floor. There were *gruuaa* everywhere. I could see them more and more easily even when they were hidden by normal furniture-and-people's-legs shadows. I didn't know if that was Hix's influence, or that I'd stopped trying to ignore them—or stopped hating Val—or what. There was a heap of them in the shadows under the table and a coil of them wrapped around and through the bottles in the tall skinny bottle rack between the edge of the cupboard and the refrigerator. There were several more of them winding around Mom's flour-sugar-coffee-tea canisters at the back of the counter by the sink. (Which contained, of course, two kinds of pasta, rice and dried beans.) I wasn't going to mention this. Mom was kind of a hygiene freak and I didn't know if shadow feet could carry germs or not. Hix had moved slightly to between Mongo's front legs and he was dementedly trying to lick the top of her head. If that was her head.

It was. Her three eyes blinked open to look at me. "Hey, sweetie," I murmured, which tended to be what I called all friendly critters. All the long-term residents at the shelter knew their name was "sweetie." Hix's eyes still glittered but they didn't look like silver-bugs to me any more.

Mom brought the tray with four steaming mugs and a plate of cookies to the table. She picked up her mug and chugged it. "I'd better get going," she said. "Takahiro, can you stay for supper? I'm stopping by the deli."

"Buy twice as much as you think you need," said Val mildly. "Changing is hard work." Takahiro gave another wild shiver, almost a spasm, looked at Val and away again, but he didn't say anything.

"I'll do that," said Mom. "Er—do you need—er—meat? Our usual from the deli is their tomato and chickpea stew."

"It's just calories," Takahiro muttered to the table. "It doesn't matter what kind."

Mom patted Takahiro's arm and my shoulder, dropped a kiss on the top of Val's head, and left.

The cookies disappeared in about forty seconds. Val got up and started making sandwiches. "A question, Takahiro," he said. "May I ask?"

Takahiro, to my surprise, took a moment to answer. "I don't really know how to say this," he said. "I'll tell you anything I *can* tell you." He flicked another sideways glance at me and fiddled with his mug. "So, yeah."

Val bowed his head briefly in one of his funny not-from-around-here gestures. "Do you know how your father got you into this country?" said Val.

Takahiro looked up at that. "Yeah," he said. "I mean, no. *I've* wondered about that. At the time I didn't think anything. Eh . . . My cousins told me, once, when my mom was still alive and the rest of the family hadn't completely cut us off yet, that I wouldn't be able to visit my dad in Newworld even if he wanted me to, which he didn't, because the border police would know I was a 'shifter, and kill me. That was about eleven years ago. I had to have about a million tests before they let me in, including blood work and scans and stuff, and I was kind of waiting for them to kill me."

"Oh, Taks," I said.

He looked sort of in my direction but not quite at me, and away again. "It was a long time ago. And then they didn't kill me after all. So I had to figure out how to stay alive. At the time I just thought they'd missed it somehow, which was almost comforting, you know? It meant I might manage to—pass. It wasn't till later, when I was older and more suspicious, that I began to wonder. There's not a lot out there about 'shifters that the ordinary public can access, and I didn't want anyone tagging me because I was too interested in this weird subject. But I don't see how *all* the border tech can have missed what I am. There's a lot about my dad I don't know," he added.

"What is your father's employment?" said Val.

"He buys stuff for museums. He's an expert on all kinds of stuff. Especially Farworld stuff. So he keeps being called in to make decisions."

"He travels a great deal," said Val.

"Yeah. All over the world. Over lots of national borders. Newworld, Oldworld, Farworld, Midworld, the Southworlds. He ought to be so suspect—with a 'shifter son. Who did he pay off—or something—to get me through? Why doesn't whoever it is have him totally at the end of a hot wire?"

Val finished cutting the sandwiches in halves and put the plate on the table. "We don't know," he said. "But the world does not work in some ways we are taught to believe that it works."

Takahiro grunted. "Dreeping," he said. "Crap zone." This was seriously bad language for Taks.

Val sat down, smiling a humorless smile. "It is inevitable at your age—yours and Maggie's—that you should still be learning how the world works. It is a little embarrassing that I should be learning the same things now. I should not be here with my shadows—"

"*Gruuaa,*" I said. "Casimir also called them *gruuaa,* although he's from Ukovia."

"Most terms concerning the use of magic are the same throughout the Commonwealth," said Val. "I fear then that Casimir may be yet another person who is not as the world says he should be. Yes. *Gruuaa.* If there is a Newworld word, I don't know it. My masters said they were stripping me of my magic and that, naked, the best place for me was Newworld. And so I came here, obedient little *dokdok* that I am."

"You probably mean clueless drone or dead battery," I said.

"Dead battery. Yes. Very apt. Except that I am not. But I have no idea how the *gruuaa* managed to protect me both through the lengthy dispossession process in Orzaskan and the intensive examination at the Newworld boundary."

Val and I each ate half a sandwich so it didn't look like it was all for Takahiro—and Takahiro ate the rest. You might almost say *wolfed.* Like he couldn't help himself. There were now a lot of *gruuaa* around Takahiro—looping over his chair, hanging from the picture frames on the wall behind him—and I figured the mob under the table were probably clustering around his feet. The armydar was still going *unh unh unh* so he probably needed them worse than Val or I did.

"Val," I said. "The *gruuaa*. They, uh—"

"They ground, protect, stabilize. And hide. I did not know their gift for concealment was so great."

"Yeah," I said. "They hid Casimir and me this afternoon. . . ." I tailed off. I'd nearly *died* this afternoon—or anyway been disappeared to nobody-knew-where. It had been awful and horrible and terrifying and also amazing and thrilling in a sort of sick way. Also there was Casimir. And yet it seemed almost a no-story after what had happened to Takahiro. After finding out what Taks lived with every day.

"Tell us," said Val.

"Oh. Well, after—um." I still wasn't going to talk about the cobey if I didn't have to. I'd shoved my wounded algebra book down to the end of the table where it was a little less obvious. "At first it was just Hix, but then there were too many of them—army guys—*and* they had brought all this *gear*—and Hix was tired. This big army guy had this wand thing and was about to nail us. Then the *gruuaa* arrived—I don't know, did Hix call them somehow?— Loophead, I mean Mongo, broke the army guy's concentration just long enough and the invisibility curtain dropped over us, I guess. It was pretty electric though, seeing the army guy suddenly *not* seeing us." I hoped no one was going to ask me why Hix was tired. It was probably okay about wanting to hide from the army. It was like you felt guilty when you saw a cop car. Even if you didn't have any reason, you just did.

Mongo, hearing his name, came out from under the table and presented himself hopefully. Mostly I was careful only to use his name when I wanted him to do something—which he would then get a treat for. I made him give me both front paws (one at a time) and roll over (in both directions) and then he got a piece of sandwich. "That's *all*," I said firmly—or he'd run through all his other tricks, including a few, like jumping over the sofa, that I didn't really want any grown-ups to know about. When dogs jump over things, they tend to push off with their hind legs at the top. I was always careful to check Mongo's feet when he came indoors. Still. Also it's a small living room. "But what are they—the *gruuaa*?"

"We don't know."

I stared at Val. "What aren't you telling me?"

Val laughed, a real laugh. It was a nice sound. "You are too quick. We don't know what they are, or where they come from, or why they seek us out—perhaps I should say we don't know who or what else they seek out. But they are parasites—energy parasites. They are attracted—they seem to be attracted—particularly to magical energy.

"Mostly they take what we do not or cannot use—like the pilot fish around the shark—but they will sometimes tap you in a way you will sense."

I put my hand up to Hix, who was wrapped around my neck again. Not just magical energy. *Not.* Hix began to hum, as if responding, either to my hand or to my sudden emotional spike of dismay. Could she pick up emotional spikes? Could she sense if they were happy spikes or unhappy spikes? She'd tapped into me today—but that was also when she was hiding Casimir and me all by herself. "Pilot fish and their sharks are sometimes pretty good companions," I said. If it was about animals, I'd probably have read up on it.

"Yes," said Val. "*Symbiote* is perhaps a better word than *parasite*, and a *gruuaa* or group of *gruuaa* and their human or humans are stronger and more flexible and resilient in—er—many situations than those humans alone. Those whom the *gruuaa* befriend are generally considered lucky. But I have seen old, experienced, commonsensical magicians disturbed when they learn that we are, in effect, the *gruuaa's* food."

I looked down. Mongo hadn't quite given up on the possibility of more sandwich. He was sitting beside my chair with his head pressing down rather heavily on my thigh. When he saw me looking at him his tail, of course, began to swish back and forth. "Trombone," I said, and he leaped up and shot away to look for his rubber trombone. It wasn't a fair command: I should know where it was before I sent him after it. You want to reinforce your training with success. But I wanted my parasitic dog to show off how clever he was. I heard him scurrying around the living room. Not there. He made a quick pass down the hall to the front door, but the dining room door was closed. It wouldn't be in the dining room. He scampered upstairs. I heard him nudging the door to my bedroom open. It might be under the desk or the bed. No. Not in the bathroom either. (Dog toys occasionally got in the bathroom as a result of the drama of baths.) Bugsuck. It was probably in the back yard then. *Leaking* dead battery. Use your *brain*, Margaret Alastrina, not your stupid emotions. He's not going to find it and he's going to be unhappy and feel that he's failed. Which will be *your* fault.

Mongo flung himself downstairs again. I might be giving up hope but he wasn't. I was just about to get up and open the back door, which was better than not doing anything, but dogs have a strong sense of fairness and Mongo would know I hadn't played fair with him, even if he forgave me, which he would. But he went to the back door himself without looking at me. And reared up on his hind legs, took the handle in his mouth and *pulled down.* The door snicked open.

I had never taught him to do this.

He ran outside and found the trombone under a rosebush. He came *dancing* back in with it again (I admit he didn't close the door behind him) and laid it proudly at my feet. "You are wonderful and amazing," I said. "*Sugoi.* Double *sugoi.* Good dog. *Good dog.*" I got up and fed him the last slice of chicken from Val's sandwich-making. I also closed the back door. Then I put the plate that had had the sandwiches on it on the floor so he could lick up the crumbs.

"I can live with 'parasite,'" I said. "It doesn't bother me."

I sat down again and Mongo fell over on his side, sighed deeply, and went to sleep. With his head what should have been really uncomfortably on his trombone. Usually a sleeping Mongo is soothing—it means he isn't running around looking for something to eat/destroy—and he'd also so totally showed off how clever he really is I should have been happy for a week on the memory. But I wasn't going to be. I wasn't. And it wasn't just Takahiro—or the cobey—

I snapped my head around. There was something behind me. No there wasn't. I looked at the *gruuaa* on Taks' chair, on the wall behind him. They were restless, but then in my experience so far they usually were a little twitchy. But there were sudden little bursts of sparkles in the corners of my vision—there was another one. With that icky silverbug resemblance. *Ugh.* So far as I knew silverbugs only ever appeared outdoors any more, since they figured out how to wire buildings against them, fifty years or so ago. The company my maybe-crazy aunt (maybe) worked for had done that, long before she was hired, if she was. Our house was only about twenty years old.

"That's the armydar," said Takahiro. "That's making you see stuff that isn't there."

"What?" I said intelligently.

"It's well known that if you have one cobey in an area, you'll probably have another. It's one of the reasons the army guys mobilize so fast."

"It—is?" I said, expanding on my theme of *intelligence*. Why did people keep telling me this? Was I the only person who didn't know? "I thought that was just Oldworld."

"Well, you have to look for the info, if you live in Newworld," said Takahiro. "Because they don't want you to know. They want you to think they're just being thorough. But the information is out there. And the latest is—this. It's got a fancy name. It's still armydar. I've been hoping I wasn't going to find out about it first-hand."

"I thought the quality of the disturbance was rather extreme for any standard scanning device," said Val. "Takahiro, are you—?"

Takahiro shivered. "The—the pressure is off now, for a while. I won't change again. I don't think. But I don't know. In Japan— my mom took me out of school, the one time a cobey opened really near us. Nothing happened, but I think that's because she was there. . . ." He shivered again. "But I guess if this goes on for very long I probably won't be able to stay—me."

"You are still you as a wolf," said Val. "It is the stupidity of the people who make rules that is your problem, not what you are."

I felt like saying, *you* haven't been in school with a mean stupid teacher in a long time. But I didn't say it. It was a horrible grown-up version of mean stupid teachers that was the reason Val was here in Newworld at all.

Val went on: "I would expect that this—er—special armydar will not last long. Your Newworld cobey units are very efficient."

"I don't know," said Takahiro. "According to the geek webnet meetspaces they think they're onto a way to stop the series thing— stop more cobeys from opening. And if they're bothered about what happened in the park today—they may keep it running for a while."

There was a little silence. Takahiro reached out a very long arm and swept my algebra book back toward the center of the table. Then he picked it up, gently, like it was an injured animal. "This is what you used," he said. "This afternoon, in the park."

"Yes," I said, startled. "How did you know?"

"Deductive reasoning," said Takahiro. He laid it down again. "I can't think of anything but an emergency that would make you tear pages out of a book." He ran his fingers lightly down the slightly collapsed spine, like stroking a sleeping puppy. "Then it *was* another cobey. This afternoon. In the park."

There was another thick silence. Val was looking fixedly at his hands. Never stare into the eyes of a dog who doesn't trust you; she will find that threatening. I tried not to growl. "Yes," I said. Val exhaled: a long, long, long breath. He kept looking at his hands.

After a shorter thinner silence Taks said, "I've been—well, I've been working on an origami figure for a cobey." He raised his eyes from my algebra book and looked straight at me. He smiled. Faintly, but it was a smile, and it didn't fall off his face immediately either. It was the first smile I'd seen since I'd met what I'd thought was a big dog, out in Val's shed. "I wasn't trying to find a way to stop one from opening or anything, uh, useful. I was just trying to get my head—and my fingers—around a shape in paper that would reflect the reality of a cobey. . . ." He tailed off. Maybe he knew how loopy he sounded.

"You gizmoheads," I said. "You've got too much charge." But I understood better than I wanted to. There was something a little freaky about origami, about what it could do. About the way folded paper could *explode* into something else.

"My mother believed . . ." he said and stopped. "My mother almost . . ." and he stopped again. "It—origami for a cobey—was my project this summer at camp. I almost didn't get it accepted—neither the physics teacher nor any of the math teachers liked the idea. They thought it meant I was nutso. But the headmaster likes my dad's money. So he passed it on to the art department and they said fine. You're allowed to be crazy if it's art.

"Since you know the rest . . . I've been trying to figure it out since my mom died. It was like if I could crack it I could crack *me.* Never mind that almost everybody who ever wrote an equation—or folded a piece of paper in half—has been looking for the same thing. And this summer it felt *close.* But what was coming was a lot more like an animal than like physwiz—but if it was an animal, it must be for you, Maggie. The art department gave me an A because I spent so much time on it. But you felt it too, didn't you? That it wasn't just—paper?"

"Yes," I said. "And Hix liked it. Hix thought it was a—a colleague or something." I got up, stepped over Mongo, and knelt beside my knapsack, feeling for the right little pocket. I pulled out several of my ordinary *kami* before I found her. The *kami* looked strangely dull and crooked—my folding isn't *that* mediocre—and Takahiro's new figure was . . . *limp.* You need paper that will hold a crease properly to do origami with. You'd never use anything soft. I carried her carefully to the table and laid her down. She's just tired, I thought. Like Hix. I looked at my algebra book again. Looked away.

"I wouldn't have thought of it if it hadn't been square," I said. "I know you can—well, Taks can—make origami out of any shape of paper, but I'm pretty stuck on classical square. And I've done so much of it that if you show me square paper I think origami. I know about as much algebra as Loophead here," I said, looking down at the sleeping Mongo, "but this afternoon I had to do something and—and—oh, I can't explain! It sounds so *girlie* to say it felt right. But I was carrying this like *warehouse* of square paper, and Taks, you'd just showed me your new figure. It—she—was in my knapsack with a lot of paper *kami*. I've been making *kami* all summer, like—" I stopped. I'd been making *kami* against Val and his shadows. "And the pages were big enough—I'm nowhere near as good at microscopic folds as you are—and strong enough. I think the wind would have ripped ordinary paper to pieces before I finished folding. It was—it was something to *do* besides sit there and wait to disappear forever."

Val had drawn the book toward him and put his hands—gently, as Takahiro had—on the cover. "I'd bandage it, if I were you," he said.

"*Bandage* it?" I said. I looked at it again and felt another pang—of conscience. It was a *book*. It wasn't a wounded soldier.

"Yes," said Val. He looked up at me and smiled. "Go on, humor a mad old man."

He wouldn't have dared to say that to me two days ago. I smiled back, hesitantly. "Okay." I picked the book up and—yes, I cradled it, like I would a half-grown puppy at the shelter who doesn't understand that its ghastly ex-owners dumped it on the street for the crime of being a puppy.

We heard Mom coming in the door then, making crackling noises as her shopping bags bumped each other and the walls—and then there was the unmistakable sound of Ran talking about cars. The smell of the deli's fabulous chickpea and tomato stew reached us first. I took my knapsack and my algebra book upstairs and then pelted downstairs again before the rest of them ate everything.

Ran's obliviousness was comforting. I don't think he even

noticed that Takahiro was wearing a dressing gown, let alone Val's dressing gown. Mom handed Takahiro most of the shopping bags and he went off to the bathroom to change. The *gruuaa* seemed to stay in the kitchen. Maybe they were interested in the stew too. I ran after him a minute later, with scissors for the tags: "Thanks," he said, reaching a long bare arm around the door. "The nail clippers weren't working so well."

The way he was standing I could see his reflection in the mirror over the sink: that golden-pearl skin gleaming on a long naked back and butt. Oh. Wow. *Great butt.* Not that I'd seen a lot of other teenage boys' naked butts to compare it with . . . but I was pretty sure this one would still rate. I don't think he knew, but I still turned away really fast, giggly with embarrassment.

Mom had turned the radio on and clicked it to the local station. Every time an announcement-type voice came on the conversation faltered as everyone but Ran stopped to listen. But it was only ever about weather and traffic reports and big bargain sales at the mall. With the armydar still thumping away this began to seem kind of surreal. Or maybe . . .

"Hey, Ran," I said. "You can feel the armydar, can't you?"

Ran gave me one of his little-brother looks. The one that says, You are so clueless a creepazoid, but Mom'll get mad if I say so. "You think it's some kind of critter, and you want to take it to the shelter?" And then he laughed like only a thirteen-year-old boy can laugh.

I was very good. I didn't say anything that would make Mom mad either. I said, "So you *can't* feel it."

"What do you mean, *feel*," said Ran. "It's airwaves. It'd be like feeling the radio signal." He reached his hands out and made clutching gestures like a zombie in a horror movie.

Takahiro rejoined us and ate and ate and ate and ate and kept eating. Finally even Ran noticed this, probably because Ran believed himself to be in a permanent state of semi-starvation due to grown-up stinginess. "Holy electricity," he said to Takahiro, half-admiringly and half-resentfully. "You're *really* hungry."

"Hard day," Takahiro said offhandedly, and poured more stew into his bowl. Mom had bought the feeds-twelve size and it was almost gone. Val got up and began slicing more bread. I fetched the peanut butter. Val hadn't adjusted to the Newworld addiction to peanut butter, and Mongo had had the last slice of chicken. I wondered what Casimir thought of peanut butter. I thought of Casimir with both a thrill and a flinch. Already what had happened in the park seemed to have happened to someone else in another century. And I'd only met Casimir yesterday.

Takahiro had been my friend for nearly eight years. I looked up and Taks' eyes were on me. He looked back at his bowl immediately.

The radio eventually reported blandly that a cobey unit was making a sweep through our town as part of the standard backup procedure after a cobey has been successfully contained. "General Kleinzweig has declared the all clear for the Copperhill event, but further states that a military presence will remain in the area for a few more days."

Takahiro waited till Ran was "helping" Mom do some mid-meal cleaning up to say quietly, "I bet General Kleinzweig isn't happy about whatever happened in the park today. Which may be why the fancy armydar is still on."

"Which might mean another round of knocking on doors and asking innocent civilians difficult questions," said Val. "Yes."

Takahiro's eating was finally beginning to slow down (perhaps because there wasn't anything left to eat) as Mom put a big platter of deli brownies on the table. "Mom, you're the best," I said, and she grinned at me. I felt like I hadn't seen her grin in years. It made even the armydar less gruesome for a couple of minutes.

She said to Takahiro, "You're welcome to stay here as long as you like, but shouldn't you call your dad or someone and tell him where you are?"

Takahiro said in that blank, flat voice he'd used when he told us about being a werewolf, "Dad's not home. I don't know where he is. He hasn't been around in a few weeks." He glanced up and I guess we were all staring at him. "It's all right," he said. "Kay says he's phoned a few times. And I call her if I'm going to be really late, and she leaves the porch light on."

Okay, we were really retro, we'd had these sit-down-and-*talk*-to-each-other dinners at least twice a week my entire life—which had been fine till Val happened—but I was aware that not everybody did this. Steph used to say she didn't recognize her mom after she had a haircut, she saw her so rarely, even though they lived in the same house. Becky said that it was really a good thing she had to watch her weight because there was never any food in her house. So my family was weird. But I could see the shock on Mom's face and Ran even stopped talking.

Mom hastily passed the brownies around again (like any of us needed reminding) and the moment passed. And then we played Scrabble. On a board you take out of a box and unfold, and little plastic tiles with letters on them. Val really liked Scrabble. He said it helped with his English. He'd been totally language-school and academic-seminar fluent when he came here, but living in it is different. It was Val, Takahiro, Ran and me. Mom had brought work home but rather than locking herself away in the Lair she propped her 'top and her cardboard folders at one end of the kitchen table. We had to fish under papers for lost tiles.

I was almost embarrassed. But I didn't want Takahiro sitting around by himself right now, and if we took him home that was what he'd be doing. I'm who got the Scrabble board out. I knew Val would play, and Taks would be polite, and Taks was Ran's new hero because of how much he could eat. There'd been a couple of years after Taks started teaching me origami that I'd brought him home pretty often, but that had mostly stopped when we got older and started hanging with different people—and Takahiro had turned into a moody jerk. But now I knew he had reason.

About halfway through the game—while Ran was agonizing over his turn, which involved a *j* and a *z*—I got up to make coffee. I'd been pulling Takahiro's chain for so long I didn't think about it: I sang out, *"Taks-san, kohi ka?"* Do you want coffee? He'd say yes or no or he'd ignore me, and then I'd pretend I'd scored another point against all those times he'd looked through me at Peta's. There's another joke about this—the English adjective *much* in Japanese is *takusan,* which is pronounced "Taks" plus the standard honorific *san*. Jill started calling poor Taks that when he cracked six feet in ninth grade.

There was a pause, and I remembered what I was doing, and then I was *really* embarrassed, and promptly made it worse, the way you do, by saying *sumimasen,* and then I was so embarrassed I wanted to die, and couldn't remember any words in any language.

"*Hai, arigato,*" Takahiro said. "*Kohi kudasai.*" Yes thanks. Coffee please.

I gaped at him. I couldn't remember the last time I'd heard him say even one word of the language he'd grown up in. My few words of Japanese instantly deserted me, of course. I wasn't up to *conversation*. Jill and I just used a bunch of words and phrases we'd looked up on the webnet. I also had a paper copy Japanese dictionary in my bedroom, but I didn't admit to it. "Oh—um," I said. "*Daijōbu.*" All right. I probably made more noise with the coffee machine than was strictly necessary.

"*Dōzo,*" I added—the one word I'd managed to remember eight years ago when I gave him my first good crane—and put the mug down in front of him.

"*Arigato,*" he said. His voice sounded rusty, as if Japanese was a door that hadn't been opened in a while. "*Ii nioi ga shimasu,*" he said thoughtfully, as if listening to himself. He looked up at me and smiled. "Smells good."

Mom only had a vague idea of the Japanese thing. You don't really discuss winding your semi-friends up with your mom. But she'd raised her eyes from her 'top screen and was looking at us. And Val, who didn't, or anyway shouldn't, know anything about it at all, was watching us carefully. Maybe it was just the Japanese words. I didn't think so. Grown-ups, so clueless most of the time, occasionally catch on at really the wrong moment. (Ran was still going "*Zaj. Jaz. Zja.*") I said, "Sorry. Jill and I learned a little—really a little—Japanese a long time ago. Because—er—"

"I'm Japanese," said Takahiro. "Half." He was *enjoying* this. For about a third of a second I was furious. And then I thought, Okay, I guess he's earned it.

"*Wā*'," I said tentatively, which maybe meant "wow," and he laughed.

"*Ee, sugoi,*" he said. "Yeah, amazing." And picked up his coffee mug.

By the end of the game (he won and Val was second by three points) Taks was beginning to look and move more like himself again. His shoulders had dropped by at least two inches and he no longer looked like he was sitting on the edge of his seat because he was expecting to have to run away somewhere. As I put the game away Ran was telling him unbelievably lame thirteen-year-old-boy jokes and Taks wasn't offering him even minor violence, which is pretty *sugoi*.

And the *gruuaa* weren't juddering around so much. Hix had dangled over my shoulder for most of the game like she was watching. Mongo had been asleep and was now cruising. He was cruising in that I've-slept-long-enough-I-want-something-to-*happen* way. After I put the game away I went to fetch a few more dog biscuits. I had three choices: I could take him for a walk, I could give him something to do, or I could watch while he started running through his repertoire, hoping for the trick that *this* time would make praise, petting and dog biscuits appear. If none of his tricks worked, then in his despair at discovering he was no longer loved and appreciated he'd look for something someone—probably Ran—had carelessly left at dog level and destroy it tragically. (I have been known to accuse Ran of leaving something at dog level *for* Mongo to destroy. Like those fabulously expensive sneakers he then decided he didn't like. Very old history. But it made *my* job as dog trainer harder. As I pointed out to Mom when she stopped me from gnawing off all of Ran's top surfaces.) I usually managed not to let it get this far. And Mongo was a lot saner than he'd been as a puppy but he was still the same dog. It was hard to believe he was almost eight years old. He was already doing pirouettes as I closed the cupboard door.

The radio had been burbling away for the last hour with gardening tips and the health benefits of bicycling to work, and I heard a plug for Clare's shelter. We had a bunch more kittens to find homes for and usually managed to move a few grown-up cats as well during a kitten rush. And then there was the kind of pause that isn't supposed to happen on the radio and totally gets your attention, and then a new crisp official voice was saying, "I have an announcement. While General Kleinzweig wishes to emphasize that there is no cause for anxiety, he has decided it would be prudent to leave additional patrols in the area overnight, and to reassess the security of the situation in the morning. Please do not be alarmed if you should see soldiers on your street; they are there in your best interests."

The radio went back to burbling but we sat in silence. Some of the *gruuaa* climbed up the wall and started doing their spiky dance—the dance that had so freaked me out that first night Val had come to dinner. I looked at Val: the heavy lines down the sides of his mouth seemed even deeper and heavier than usual. The *gruuaa* had climbed higher and higher on the wall behind him and were making a kind of pointed filled-in-arch shape. All of it kept moving and *seething* and little bits of wall flickered through as—I don't know—legs and bodies and heads moved and left gaps, but the overall shape remained weirdly steady. Usually when the *gruuaa* threw themselves around they just threw themselves around. Val's grim face and the dark pointed arch behind him made him look like Evil Cobra Man or something. I didn't like it. It was only two days ago that Val was still my worst enemy.

Val moved, like someone jerking himself out of a bad dream, and the *gruuaa* fell back down the wall and made thornbushes over the baseboards. I knew that jerk: Jill did it when her foresight was hurting her. I stopped not-liking and started worrying.

Takahiro stood up and said, "Thanks for"—and his eyes fell on Ran and he finished—"everything. Dinner was great. Sorry I ate the last brownie."

"You aren't sorry," said Ran.

"I'm not sorry," agreed Takahiro. "Maggie, the bus stops at the end of your street, doesn't it?"

"I'll take you home," said Val, standing up like there was a cobey regiment on his shoulders. There wasn't, but there were a few *gruuaa*.

"I can catch a—"

"Yes, you can, but I'm going to drive you home." Val snagged the car keys off the hook on the wall.

Takahiro hesitated.

"I'll come too," I said. "If I stay here, Mom'll make me clean up the kitchen."

"Or do your homework," said Mom, but she didn't mean it. She was worried about Takahiro too.

I waved to Mongo, and he shot out the door in front of us, trailing *gruuaa*. I didn't know what happens if you shut a car door on *gruuaa* and I couldn't see them in the dark, so I left my door open while I clipped Mongo into his car harness next to me and put my seat belt on. Then I closed the door so cautiously I had to do it twice. Nothing squealed. I really had to learn about doors and *gruuaa*. Both Taks and Val had just got in the front and closed their doors.

We were on a corner lot of a street near one edge of town, and we had to go clear across town and out the other side to where Takahiro lived. We saw a car turn and come down our street, and several passed by on the main road as we drove toward it. Val stopped at the intersection.

"Look," whispered Takahiro.

There were three soldiers standing on the sidewalk, watching the cars pass. They had the big orange cobey unit badges on their hats, and one of them was holding something like a video tablet or 'tronic desk up and looking at it.

All three of them turned their heads and looked at us.

Suddenly the car was full of a *smell*. I can't describe it, but anyone who has spent as much time at an animal shelter as I have knows smells like it. It's a clean smell—it's not about dirty bedding or food bowls or anything—but it's a *critter* smell. I reached forward and put my hands on Takahiro's shoulders. And squeezed. Hard. "You're okay," I said. "You're here, you're with us, you're okay."

His hands came up and grabbed mine. Really hard. "I shouldn't have eaten so much," he said in a muffled voice. "This has never happened before. But if I were still weak and hungry I bet I couldn't . . ."

"You're not going to," I said, trying to remember how Ms. Dunstable—who was also Mom's friend Joanna— made her voice go all solid-state when she was talking to the full school assembly. "You're going to stay the way you are right now because while Val and I are okay with you no matter what, these soldiers aren't." Takahiro was panting—way too much like a dog. Or a wolf. Mongo whined. The soldiers were sauntering toward us, like daring Val to step on the gas and make a run for it. Val was looking out the window, his hands motionless on the steering wheel. I thought, *Oh, gods, he's performing for them.* Mongo whined again. Just before the first soldier leaned down to tap on Val's window Takahiro let go of my hands. I sat back but twisted around and slid my right hand between the car door and Takahiro's seat, and his hand dropped and grabbed it. Mongo whined a third time and with him straining toward the front seat I could just reach the snap, and flicked it loose. He was through the gap between the seats in a flash, sitting in Takahiro's lap. Takahiro's lap was nearly big enough. I saw Taks' other hand rise, as if involuntarily, and run down Mongo's silky head and back.

Val opened the window. "Good evening," he said.

"Good evening, sir," said the soldier with a kind of ugly politeness that reminded me of a teacher who is about to destroy you and is enjoying making you wait for it. "Our orders are to stop cars at random and our random-number generator chose you." He showed his teeth and held up his box.

If that's a random-number generator, I thought, I'm a werewolf. That crawly, itchy, something-behind-you feeling was so strong with him standing next to the car shoving his box almost through the window at Val that I thought I might very well morph into something myself—a gopher or a chipmunk maybe. Takahiro was still breathing in little sharp jerks like he wanted to pant—I could feel it through his hand—but he had his mouth closed. Possibly because Mongo was licking his face.

"And you are, sir?" said the soldier with the box. One of the other two soldiers aimed a flashlight in through the window. The blaze gave me the excuse to keep my eyes down.

"I am Valadi Crudon," said Val. "This is my stepdaughter, Margaret, and her friend Takahiro."

Val sounded perfectly calm, as if being stopped and cross-examined by soldiers was all a part of daily life, while I was thinking, *What the bugsuck is it to do with you, assface!* maybe almost loud enough for their hot machine to pick up. The *gruuaa* were all crammed against the floor of the car—a lot of them had come with us. Hix was between me and the back of the seat. I was at such a peculiar angle, hanging on to Taks' hand, that if she was trying to stay hidden, there wasn't that much shadow for her to disappear into. I was sure the soldiers couldn't see her, but maybe the box could. The rest of the *gruuaa*, I realized, were eeling forward, to cluster around Takahiro.

"And you live, sir?" said the soldier with the box.

"Margaret"—*nobody* called me Margaret; it was like he was talking about someone else, which was maybe just as well—"and I live at the end of this street, 87 Jebali Lane. Takahiro lives on Sunrise Court. We are taking him home."

"Out late on a school night, sir?" said the soldier with the box, smiling a smile as ugly as his politeness.

"Takahiro is an old friend of the family," said Val, still calm. "And the school year has only just begun. There is little homework yet."

The third soldier had been doing something I couldn't see, behind the glare of the second soldier's flashlight. I had only a sudden writhe from Hix, and heave from the *gruuaa* on the floor, as warning. I let go of Taks' hand and flung myself back in my seat just before this searchlight big enough to light up the Marianas Trench blazed in at us. I could see *gruuaa* plastered around the window frame next to Taks, over the dashboard, along the strip of seat left empty by Taks' narrow butt (although there was some hairy black and white Mongo tail in the way too). I thought maybe it was a good thing that the inside of Mom's old car was a weird swirly pattern of black and grey, even if it meant it always needed vacuuming. Mongo yelped, Takahiro jerked, and Val sat like a stone, his head still a little turned toward the soldier with the box.

The light went out. I slithered around again and felt for Taks' hand. Although even if they'd caught us holding hands, so? But I was glad they hadn't.

"That dog shouldn't be loose in the front seat," said the soldier with the box, but now he sounded angry.

"No, he shouldn't," said Val. "Margaret?"

"Mongo," I said, and my voice sounded funny, but the soldiers didn't know what I usually sounded like. "Mongo, come on."

Taks gave Mongo a last pat and a little push—and let go of my hand again. I reached between the seats and grabbed Mongo's collar. He let me drag him into the back seat again, and clip on the harness strap.

"You'll pardon us if we keep an eye out for you when you come back, I'm sure, sir," said the first soldier, still angry. "For your own good, of course."

For our own good? I thought, chewing on the insides of my lips.

"Of course," said Val. "Good evening, sir." His "sir" sounded like "zir." He pressed the button and the window glass slid up again. Then he waited patiently for a break in the traffic—there were a lot of people out late on a school night—and drove calmly across the intersection. The critter smell was fading, so I assumed Takahiro was all right. I reached forward again and patted his shoulder.

"What *was* that?" said Takahiro. He still sounded a little muffled.

I could see, under the flash of passing streetlights, that Val was frowning. "I'm not sure," he said. "They certainly pulled us over because they were getting readings off their—whatever it was—that made them want to look at us more closely. I didn't recognize it, but Orzaskan technology is different and I'm several years out of date. I doubt it was generating random numbers. That dazzle at the end was full of assessment radiation: the light was just a, er, blind. They didn't find what they were hoping for, however, or they would not have let us go so quickly."

"You told the *gruuaa* to protect Takahiro," I said. "Didn't you?"

Val shrugged. "He's the most vulnerable of us. If they care to look me up, or if my name is already on their list, they will know who I—was. You, Maggie, have Hix, and through her the other *gruuaa* will also serve you."

Takahiro said, "I can't see them—the *gruuaa*—but I can feel them, or . . . the wolf can. It's—it's a little like someone putting a wet washcloth on your face when you have a fever. It's better and you relax a little even though you know you're still sick."

Val nodded. "Good," he said.

We were silent till Takahiro had to give Val directions. Sunrise Court was this huge non-development development—all the houses had like twenty bedrooms and eight-car garages and cottages for the staff, and the lots they were on were the size of football fields. You wouldn't know they had anything to do with each other except that there was this gigantic gate that said *Sunrise Court* and then once you were through it you had to choose the private drive you wanted. There were only five of them but I still couldn't imagine five families in Station wanting houses like that. The gate to Takahiro's drive had to read his palm print before it would let us in.

Taks' house was dark when we got there except for a porch light. "S'okay," said Taks. "I told you. Kay's left the porch light on. That means she got my text."

"Taks—" I began.

"I'm fine," he said quickly. "Really. You guys are great. Including Mongo. Thanks. See you tomorrow, Mags," and he got out. I did too, so I could sit in front. To my surprise he gave me a quick hug—and then sprinted to the house. Well, I don't think it was a sprint, it's just his legs are so long. He didn't look back. *"Jā, mata,"* I said softly. See you later. But I saw . . . I thought saw . . .

I got back in the car and closed the door. "A lot of the *gruuaa* are going with Takahiro," I said.

"Yes," said Val. "As I said, he's the most vulnerable of us."

"What . . ." I said. And then didn't know how to go on.

Val said, "They respond to fear and anxiety—not perhaps unlike how Mongo does. He may be hoping to sleep on your bed instead of in the kitchen, but he also wishes to comfort you—to stay near his person in her distress. Hix is important in the hierarchy of the company of *gruuaa* who befriended me many years ago—the rest will have accepted you because she so clearly does."

I thought, Some day, some other day when there isn't anything else going on, I want to hear about *gruuaa* society.

"We have demonstrated Takahiro is important to both of us. They will have drawn their own conclusions. I have some authority by long association, and I can say 'yes' or 'no.' I said 'yes' to their staying near Takahiro. Which is not to suggest that they always do what I ask them—rather like a dog again, perhaps, although *gruuaa* plan and conjecture more than dogs. They are neither domestic nor domesticated. But right now they are so pleased to have me recognize them again they are eager to do what I ask."

"That's really nice of you," I said after a pause. Here I was doing something alone after dark with Val. And with his shadows. And saying "nice" to him. He'd called me his stepdaughter to the army creep. I suppose it made us sound more united or something.

Val glanced at me. "Takahiro will be all right once the military leave the area again, taking their equipment with them. Then the *gruuaa* will come back to us. Unless one of them develops an individual bond with Takahiro and decides to stay."

"Do they all have names?" I said.

"Oh yes," said Val. "But I do not know all of their names. I had—have wondered if the names they give us to use are the same as the ones they use to each other. Indeed I am not sure they use names among themselves."

"But . . ." I said, and then couldn't think how to go on. "But . . ."

"I was trying to be what I had promised to be," said Val. "What I believed myself now to be."

"How long?" I said. I didn't know how to ask what I was really asking: How long ago was it that you killed your best friend? How do you—what do you do after that? Did your government just— knock you out somehow, like a zoo vet with a trank gun knocks out a tiger? Did they tie you up for two months, two years?

But he heard me anyway. "Seven years," he said. "It took my government five years to . . . some of it was for their safety, but some of it was for mine."

He was silent a minute, and then went on: "It has been a somewhat full two years, at last, when they let me go . . . since I came to Newworld. My old habits and instincts have no place here; and I had been out of the ordinary world entirely for five years. That there was a great swathe of my old skills and—facilities simply gone did not seem any more surprising or difficult than much else I found here. That I dreamed of much I had lost—including the *gruuaa*—that I imagined even that I saw them sometimes—did not seem surprising either. I still see my friend's face. . . ." He was silent for another moment. "And then there was Elaine." He shrugged again, that very un-Newworld shrug. "I suppose I will sound old and foolish to you when I say that Elaine has made my new life worthwhile, whatever I have lost."

No, I thought, I think it's about the most romantic thing I've ever heard anyone say who wasn't in a book or a movie. For just a flash I was seeing Casimir's grin in my memory. But then it faded, and it was Takahiro, looking at me levelly over a bowl of chickpea and tomato stew, and then looking away. Saying *ee, sugoi,* and smiling into his coffee. I barely knew what Takahiro's smile looked like. I was pretty sure I'd like it if I got the chance to develop a relationship with it.

We stopped at a red light. When the light turned green Val added, "And now I am discovering—I must discover—what I have not lost."

"And not get screwed up by Kleinzweig's goons while you're at it."

"Yes."

"Loophead," I said.

"Yes," said Val, who had (fortunately) caught on to my Mongo-nickname routine. You want your dog to react to the sound of his name, so you need to call him something else when you don't want him to react. "I think it is a very good thing you brought him to-night," Val continued. "We have proven that the army do not have a reading for werewolf, but Takahiro will have been emitting some-thing that their meters might have read, if it weren't for the *gruuaa* and—er—Loophead."

"But they didn't."

"They did not, or we would be in three little rooms being asked questions," said Val grimly. He glanced at me again. "I apologize. Perhaps it is not that way here."

"I don't know what way it is, any more," I said. "But—you said you did have weres in Oldworld."

"We do," said Val. "But any not known to the government will be in a great deal of trouble if discovered." He glanced at me a third time. "It is, as Takahiro said, stress that causes involuntary change. A properly trained and mentored were will not change, even under extreme stress. But the myth lingers that weres are untrustworthy and unpredictable. Therefore the government can do what it likes with you, or your boss or your neighbors will come to learn what you are."

"That's—blackmail," I said, appalled.

"It is," agreed Val.

When we got to Jebali Lane the soldiers were still there. Still waving their box. The same one strutted over to the corner as Val made the turn. Val stopped and slid the window down again.

"All well, sir?" said the soldier.

"I believe so, zir," said Val.

The soldier glanced across Val to me. "Glad you've got that dog in the back seat," he said, and patted the roof of the car like giving us permission to live.

"Bugsucker," I said under my breath as Val slid his window closed and drove on. Val laughed.

Mom was opening the front door before we were out of the car. I thought: Elaine has made my new life worthwhile, whatever I have lost, and looked the other way when he put his arm around her. I slowly clipped Mongo's lead on and then (quite a lot faster) took him for a walk.

CHAPTER 9

I PICKED MY ALGEBRA BOOK OFF THE KITCHEN table and took it and Mongo upstairs with me again. He threw himself on the floor and then bounced on and off the bed several times. *"Hey,"* I said in my best dog-trainer voice. "Stop that." Usually he jumped onto the bed immediately and lay flat, trying to look invisible, in case I changed my mind and made him sleep in the kitchen after all. (Note that I wouldn't *dream* of bringing him upstairs at bedtime and then taking him back to the kitchen. In the first place it's *totally* unfair and in the second place he has a heart-rending poor-sad-dog routine that would make a stone weep. Or possibly General Kleinzweig.)

Mongo looked confused for a moment, standing stiffly, tail up . . . and then I realized *Hix* was caroming around the room, very much like a dog inviting another dog to play chase-me. She was making a tiny half-imaginary sweet-smelling breeze. I had no idea what a *gruuaa*-trainer voice sounded like—or to what extent *gruuaa* would accept "training" from a mere human. "*Stop that,*" I said.

Hix collapsed. I could only see her because I had been looking straight at her when she went from lightning strike to stain on the carpet. "Bedroom rules," I said to the stain on the carpet. "You lie down and be quiet. Or you sleep in the kitchen." Like she had a collar and I could drag her downstairs. And she could probably slide under closed doors. The stain on the carpet roused itself and twinkled. "You're allowed on the bed," I said, and patted it, "as long as there's still room for me."

I didn't see her move, but I knew she was now behind me—and the (new) stain on the carpet was gone. Mongo fell on the bed with a happy sigh. No one does a happy sigh better than a dog.

Quiet.

I looked at the algebra book. I was supposed to bandage it. Right. Um. I had some really pretty origami paper Jill had given me last Christmas that I was still waiting for the right moment to use. I got it out and started folding a chain. It took a while, but I finally had a long enough chain to wrap once completely around the book and enough left over to tuck in the space where the pages had been torn out, like a bookmark. I made those links extra-thick so when I closed the book the covers were almost parallel again. I laid it gently on the desk.

I got into bed gingerly. It's one thing to wake up with a semi-visible, mostly intangible *gruuaa* having joined you some time in the night. It's something else to worry that you're lying down on top of her. Mongo gave another happy-dog sigh and I thought there was almost an echo to it, like the noise a semi-visible, mostly intangible critter might make. Her smell and the smell of clean dog went rather well together, like chocolate and vanilla. As I drifted to sleep I heard her start to hum.

When I woke up groggily the next morning to my alarm going NOW NOW NOW NOW my algebra book was on the bed. Mongo had his chin on it. I was *sure* I'd left it on the desk. I was pretty out of it last night but I wasn't out of it enough to take the textbook from my least favorite subject to bed with me, even if it had saved my life yesterday. Was I? Maybe I was. I stared at it. The paper chain was gone. I blinked, trying to convince myself my eyes would focus before my first cup of coffee. Mongo had been a terrible paper shredder as a puppy (he'd been pretty much a terrible everything shredder as a puppy) but I was pretty sure he wouldn't stoop now to eating an origami paper chain. Besides, if he'd tried, it should have woken me up.

Could a barely visible, semi-intangible critter have a taste for three-dimensional paper? I wasn't sure if Hix was still here or not . . . and then a shadow on the wall moved in a way that nothing else in my room could have made a shadow of. Barely visible semi-intangible critters might very well be able to eat a paper chain silently and without making the bed shake. I wondered vaguely if there were any house-training issues with *gruuaa*. I didn't think there'd been any weird stuff in the corners since Val moved in—well, any more weird stuff. Neither Mom nor I was big on housecleaning, Ran was hopeless and Val fit in with the family pattern very well. If *gruuaa*, uh, excreted, what *was* it? No-body would notice more dust.

I climbed out of bed awkwardly, carrying my algebra book, and set it on the desk, feeling a bit like a dog trainer taking her dog back to the place she'd put him the last time she'd said "stay." "Stay," I murmured, thinking there was something funny about how it looked. Or rather there was something funny about the fact that it didn't look funny . . . The covers were parallel. The top one didn't slant down over the empty space in the middle. Okay, maybe that's where the chain was. It must have got folded up inside somehow.

I opened the book. No chain slid into view. I couldn't remem-ber exactly where the ripped-out place was, so I fanned the pages, looking. It was toward the back—I thought. It should have been obvious. It had been very obvious last night. I yawned. Maybe I should get the coffee first. No, this was dumb. There was a dreep-ing great *hole* where I'd torn all those pages out.

No hole. There was, however, about two-thirds of the way through the book, a big clump of some rather odd pages. There was algebra stuff written on them—awful-looking equations with lots of letters and squiggles, but I wasn't going to think about that now—but the paper was strangely shiny and there were faint pat-terns printed on it, as well as the textbook stuff. Colored patterns in a range of mostly pastels and some deep violet. Very like the pretty paper Jill had given me for Christmas, which I'd folded into a chain to make a bandage for a wounded algebra book. I flipped the strange pages back and forth. They were (apparently) bound into the spine with the rest of the ordinary pages, although if I ran my fingers over them they were slightly textured, like Jill's paper had been, but the patterns were much fainter than they'd been on Jill's paper. I thought, since the entire situation is totally screw-loose and doolally, what's a little more? Who cares?

The new pages were also more flexible than paper—either than algebra-book paper or fancy origami paper. I riffled them again. And while I was having my it's-all-screwloose-so-who-cares attack, I looked at them waving back and forth and thought that it wasn't me that was providing all the waving, and the way one of those pages felt between your fingers was almost *muscular*. Well, the book had to have got to my bed somehow. . . .

What was I *saying*?

I had to sit down kind of abruptly. Fortunately my desk chair was right there. I slapped the book shut and stared at it. It lay as still as a dog who knows you mean it this time. I kept staring at it. Of course it lay still. It was a *book*. And the shadows on the wall were just shadows. I kept my eyes averted from where Hix was playing with the pull cord of the curtain. I didn't want to think about any of it—which included Takahiro's secret—I wanted everything to be like it had been two weeks ago—two months ago—before Val—before Dad died. Especially before Dad died. I grabbed the edge of the desk and held on hard for a moment.

One of the great things about dogs is they don't do regrets and what-ifs and all that useless human-thinking stuff. Mongo got off the bed and put his nose under my forearm and gave it a heave. It meant, Hi, I'm here, and, by the way, it's morning, and I want a pee and breakfast. If Dad hadn't died it might have taken me a few years longer to convince Mom to let me have a dog. And I'd rather not hate Val. And Hix was a friend. And Casimir. And Takahiro . . .

I got up—maybe a little unsteadily—put my dressing gown on and took Mongo downstairs. There was a faint breeze around my ankles that might have been Hix. I let Mongo out (with or without Hix) and groped my way into the kitchen to make coffee. Mom or I was nearly always the first one up. It was me today. It had seemed to me unfair for years now that it was like this. Ran got up cheerful but you needed a blowtorch or a jackhammer to wake him. Val was the same. Maybe it's something to do with the Y chromosome.

I poured my first mug and chugged about half of it. I put the rest of the coffee in our big insulated pot, put it on a tray with three more mugs (although Ran was still drinking milk out of his) and brought it to the table.

Where my algebra book was lying.

I may have whimpered. I stared at it. Maybe it stared at me, I don't know.

Mongo, who was watching through the glass for when I plunked the tray on the table, whined at the kitchen door to be let back in. So I did. Several *gruuaa* came with him; it wasn't just Hix. They arranged themselves along the baseboards very like long thin shadowy dogs and . . . fell asleep? I don't know that either. I sat down in my chair. The algebra book had sidled a little closer to where I'd left my mug on the table while I was letting Mongo in. I finished my first mug of coffee and poured my second. My hands were shaking.

Mom came into the kitchen yawning and rubbing her hair. She fell—well, sat—in her chair and started on her first mug of coffee. Halfway through it you could see the possibility of articulate speech returning. "Cramming already?" she said, nodding at the algebra book. "Is your teacher this year that bad? Poor you."

"I—er—the book's so huge and such a weird shape it won't fit in my knapsack, and I'm afraid of leaving it behind," I said, thinking fast. I was pretty sure I was supposed to have read the introduction, or else why had I hauled it home in the first place? Maybe I could do it at lunch. The introduction should be mostly *words*. I knew what it would say: that algebra was fun and easy and we were going to have a really good time together this year blah blah blah. Dreeping dreeping *dreeping*.

"It *is* a weird shape," said Mom, pulling it toward her. "What on earth were they thinking when they made a textbook half the size of a coffee table?" She lifted the front cover. It opened, it seemed to me, lazily, like a cat stretching; the cover, when she let go of it, didn't drop inertly to the tabletop the way it should, but subsided gently, and the pages started fanning *themselves*. They fell open, of course, about two-thirds of the way through, where the paper was silky and printed with something besides algebra. I could see $x^2 + 6x - 8 = 3x + 7$ all wound around a flowering vine: the x's were tiny four-petaled flowerets. I didn't know if the right answer was "*ugh*" or "*awww.*"

"How extraordinary," said Mom, stroking one of the pages (which was stiffly standing straight up, like a cat being petted). "Whatever is the paper made of?"

I had no idea how I was going to answer that one, but fortunately she looked at the clock and said, "Oh, flastic, Ran has got to get up," finished her coffee and went back upstairs to throw shoes at my brother (I wish. I've been known to do that, but it got me in trouble).

I took my algebra book (and more coffee) back upstairs with me, got dressed in record time, and brought my knapsack downstairs again *with* the zootronic book, as camouflage. As I snapped Mongo's lead on I was aware of Hix climbing up my arm from Mongo's back and arranging herself around my neck in what I guess was becoming her standard position. I straightened up and glared at my algebra book. "You stay *right there*," I said. "I'll be back."

I hadn't noticed it in the house—maybe our remaining *gru-uaa* had figured out how to block it?—maybe I just wasn't awake enough. But outdoors I could still feel that creepy it's-behind-you-and-it-isn't-friendly new armydar. Were they still at it? Ugh. It was like finding out the playground bully was waiting for you when you'd been hoping he'd given up and gone home. Green pond scum. *Smelly* green *dreeping* pond scum.

And there were still soldiers at the end of our road. Bugsuck. *Shimatta.* We turned around. At this end Station butted up against what was kind of the edge of the barrens. There was a jagged hedge of little trees between the last of the houses and the scrub that gave way pretty soon to the barrens. You could make your way along the far side of the trees (it was pretty rough going but all the local dog walkers did it), and then duck back in again when you got to the next street. We went up Singh Lane. There were no soldiers at the end of it. We stopped on the corner and looked around. From there you could see five streets dead-ending into Ramage, this side of town's main avenue through Station: Jaboli, Singh, Jenkins, Korngold, and Drisk. Only Jaboli had soldiers on it.

When we got back, Ran was eating cereal and my algebra book was still lying next to my knapsack. Mongo, who knew perfectly well what my school knapsack and rushing around in the morning meant, was doing his, You-don't-mean-you're-leaving-me-*again*-you-call-that-a-*walk*? and getting in the way. It seemed to me a little more intense than usual, but if he and Hix were now great friends, he probably knew she was coming with me, and I don't suppose a dog gets it about semi-visible and mostly intangible being easier to sneak past the teachers.

I was stuffing a piece of toast in my mouth when I heard Jill's wheels crunch on the driveway. "I will see you this afternoon," I said, getting down on my knees to give Mongo a hug. When I stood up, Val was standing in the hallway. I hesitated. I didn't really know what terms we were on with each other. Even remembering Takahiro—and the conversation coming home in the car—it was still really hard to stop thinking of Val as a villain and start thinking of him as a hero, like turning a page in a book. In books that kind of thing really annoys me. Even when the person who was wrong about the other person who is really a hero has been being a creepazoid, which I guess was me.

He gave me a little nod, as foreign as his shrug.

"Morning," I said. "Sorry. Jill's waiting."

He stood aside immediately, but said, "How are you?" His voice was furry with sleep, and it seemed to me his accent was stronger than usual, like it took him a while to fit back into his Newworld life in the morning. I could relate to the fitting-back-into-reality problem. But I'd spoken to him yesterday morning too. I guessed I'd better get used to it.

"I'm okay," I said. "Still kind of freaked out. Worried about Takahiro." I paused. "You?"

"I am well, thank you," he said, alien as a Martian. "You will see Takahiro today?"

"I'd better," I said, picked up my knapsack and algebra book, and headed for the front door.

"You've got soldiers at the end of your road," said Jill. "What's up? This whole area is making my hair stand on end. It feels like invisible things with legs crawling on you. Ugh. It's much worse near you than over where we are." She'd got the short straw in the family vehicle lottery that day: she was driving the Mammothmobile. It had probably started life as a muscle car fifteen years ago for you and your eighteen closest friends to intimidate the locals in. You could get several kegs of beer in the back seat and maybe a small buffalo or the basketball team.

I glanced guiltily at Hix, who was a slightly odd pool of shadow in my lap. "Um—Val says it's some kind of hyped-up armydar. Because of the cobey." I'd put the algebra book on the floor, leaning against the wall of the footwell. When Jill turned out of our driveway it tipped over so it was leaning against my leg. It might just have been centrifugal force. (Yes. I know about centrifugal force. Yaay me.)

"Val says, eh?" said Jill. "So, you didn't punch him out for talking to you, did you?" I didn't say anything and she went on: "Where were you last night? I tried to call you but your phone was turned off. We all went to P&P again. Casimir was there and he asked after you. He said he'd *seen* you yesterday afternoon."

"Yeah," I said, trying to sound casual. "We ran into each other at the park. He gave me a ride home."

"At the park?" said Jill, slightly distracted from the fascinating topic of Casimir. "There was a really big whizztizz at the park yesterday. Army all over the landscape. Steph lives in the street opposite the main gate, you know? She saw like forty units all rushing through the gate at once. She was afraid it was another cobey but there haven't been any announcements or anything, and school's not canceled—dreep it. I don't know, I suppose it wouldn't really be worth a cobey in the park to have school canceled."

I tried to smile. "Yeah, we saw them arriving as we were leaving. I don't know what they thought was happening." Which was true enough. Although I knew it wasn't what they were expecting. I wanted to tell Jill about yesterday but I didn't know where to start. Or what I could say. I couldn't tell her about Takahiro. Not even Jill.

Jill finished backing out of the driveway and turning around, and stopped so she could look at me. I tried to look at her steadily but it was hard. Sometimes it's a big flastic pain to have a friend who sees more than most people. "Maggie—" she began, and stopped. She looked away from me, down at the steering wheel, as if only just noticing that she was driving the Mammothmobile. She sighed. "Okay, whatever," she said, and put her foot back on the gas.

"There they are," she said. "The soldiers." I looked warily out the window. I didn't know if they had my scan profile from last night on their 'tronic or anything—or what my algebra book might be giving off. Two of the soldiers were looking toward us but nobody tried to stop us. I didn't mean to be holding my breath, but I let it out as Jill crossed the intersection. "No, I don't like them either," said Jill. "Although some of them are probably cute and nice and everything and joined the army because they needed a job."

There was something about the atmosphere in the car I didn't like, and I didn't think it was the armydar. I glanced at Jill's profile. Tentatively I said, "Casimir says that his mom is—um—a foreseer. That in Ukovia the magicians use foreseers so they'll know where to be, ready and waiting, to shut down a cobey as fast as possible."

Jill was silent for a moment. "I live in Newworld, and I want to be a historian. And if you're asking me, I'd've said that it *was* a cobey in the park yesterday, and if something that *isn't* a cobey could make me feel that crazy and off the planet then if I ever am near a real cobey opening I'll probably start running around on four legs and howling at the moon or something."

I shivered. I wondered if there was any particular reason why that metaphor had occurred to her. I wished there was a way to tell her about the park yesterday—and Takahiro—without *telling* her. Abracadabra or something. Ha.

"I think I've just decided I want to study the history of science," she added grimly.

We weren't any later than usual, and the bell hadn't rung, so we stood around with our usual group. Steph was full of what she'd seen yesterday and everyone else was listening. Eddie was trying to catch Jill's eye and I could see by the way she had her lips pressed together that it was taking some effort not to let him. Although it might have been the armydar—or the cobey. It wasn't quite as bad here as it was outside at home but it was pretty bad. It was making me feel a little pressed-lips too. I put my arm through Jill's and she gave me a sidelong smile.

Then the bell did ring, and I realized I hadn't seen Takahiro. My stress level instantly soared. Jill was glad enough to drop to the back of our gang because Eddie was at the front—his homeroom was on the other side of the building. I looked around. My heart was thumping unpleasantly hard. There were three silverbugs in the trees beyond the edge of the parking lot. *Three.* Not a good sign. The arm that wasn't through Jill's was full of algebra book; someone else had probably reported them by now anyway.

It was Hix who told me. I felt that whisper of air against my cheek, the darkness at the edge of my vision that was Hix, and I looked in her direction, the way you turn toward someone putting their hand on your shoulder. I almost didn't see him, the *gruuaa* were wrapped around him so tightly, but once you had seen him you had to notice how *off* he looked, like he was walking in a forest in bright daylight: lots and lots of leaf shadows with little twinklings of light, almost like miniature silverbugs. Suckfest. There were no shadows on the big paved courtyard outside the high school, or beyond the first row of cars in the lot. But it shouldn't matter—I hoped. Almost nobody could see the *gruuaa*; I hoped the armydar didn't mess with that.

"Oh, there's Taks," said Jill, sounding relieved. "I've been having one of my feelings that he might be in trouble. I'm *tired* of having—feelings. Gods. Does the armydar mess with your eyes? He looks all, I don't know, patchy."

I remembered that she'd seen the *gruuaa* on the shed, the day of

Mom and Val's wedding. "Oh, Jill," I said, or rather wailed, "I have so much to tell you."

"And none of it is good, is it?" said Jill. "I've been hoping that it's just the armydar screwing up whatever it is that I do, but I've been having . . . Maggie, I don't think Takahiro is very well."

I was thinking the same thing, and was already moving toward him. I was beginning to feel that the *gruuaa* were holding him together somehow—like a mummy's bandages.

"Taks, you should have stayed home," I said. "You look awful."

He almost smiled. "Thanks."

"You know what I mean."

He stopped trying to smile. "Yeah. But it's worse at home. I think it'll be better here—lots of other people. Distraction. I'm not . . . you know." I'd been sniffing cautiously, and there was no wolf smell. "It's just the armydar makes me feel like I'm being pulled apart. We haven't even had a scan in this town in years."

"And they weren't this bad and they didn't go on this long," I said. "I know."

"If it isn't better here, I'll go home," said Takahiro, but he looked as grey as the cement-block front wall of the school entry as he said it. There were shadows draped around his chest and shoulders. Black was not a good color for him today.

"No," I said. "If it isn't better, I'll take you to Val."

Jill was looking at each of us in turn, frowning. "Tell you later," I said, but I looked at Takahiro. He gave a tiny nod, and then went limping on toward the front door.

We were the last ones inside. It was suddenly a lot darker after the glare of the courtyard and we paused, and didn't notice immediately the last of the kids ahead of us going through a big arch thing set up in front of the double doors into the school from the entry hall.

There were soldiers standing on either side of it. They waved us forward.

"Oh, gizmos and dead batteries," murmured Takahiro.

"The *gruuaa*," I murmured back. "They've got you." I hoped. I could feel Hix tightening around my neck. It tickled, but it wasn't funny.

Jill said under her breath, "The *what*?"

"Later," I said. "We don't want to look like we have anything to hide." I was rearranging my algebra book like that was the only reason we'd stopped. I marched forward, thinking, What are they looking for? I reached up and found what I hoped was a trailing end of Hix and draped it/her over my algebra book. What would happen if the archway didn't like me? Portcullis? Boiling oil? Or would they just arrest me? I thought I might prefer to take my chances with boiling oil.

"Morning, miss," said the soldier on the left. "Just walk on through. This is only a formality, don't worry."

"Good morning," I said, trying to sound as if I believed him.

There was a funny swipe against my skin as I walked through, like walking through a spiderweb. It should have been kind of like walking through trailing *gruuaa* but it wasn't. *Gruuaa* aren't *sticky* and don't leave a nasty feeling behind them that you can't wipe off. I disliked even more the sensation of Hix bushing out like an angry cat, and the algebra book cringing back against me. Also, *oof*. It was a big book and it was pressing my stomach into my backbone, which wasn't leaving much space for the three mugs of coffee and a piece of toast that were there first.

The machine beeped. I stopped. My heart was beating way too hard and my mouth was suddenly so dry I couldn't swallow.

The soldier on the left sighed. "That machine is a total waste of electricity and palladium."

"Shut up," said the soldier on the right. "If you'd come back through again, miss."

"May I put my algebra book down?" I said, laying it on the hall monitor's desk. "It weighs a ton."

"Sure," said the soldier on the left.

"No," said the soldier on the right.

"Get a grip, Sherston," said the soldier on the left. "It's a textbook."

"Keep your knapsack," snapped the soldier on the right. "And come back through."

Hix seemed to have unwound or unrolled or something, like she'd done yesterday in the park. I could feel her against my face and hands, but I was pretty sure she had taken a loop around my waist and was brushing against my legs too. Unless that was one or more of Takahiro's *gruuaa*. *No,* I thought at them. *If any of you are his, don't. Go protect Taks.* I walked back through the archway, turned, and came through it a third time. The machine remained silent. My heart was still hammering away and I felt a little ill. One down and two to go. I put my hand on my algebra book.

Takahiro was next. I swear the archway turned black with shadows as he went under it. But the machine didn't say anything.

Jill was last. The machine beeped again. I put my hands up to

231

where Hix was leaning against my cheek. *"Go,"* I whispered. Hix disappeared—I may have seen a little scamper of shadow from me to Jill. She looked at me, frightened, and put her own hand to her face. "If you'd walk back through, please, miss," said the soldier on the right. Jill turned and stumbled through the archway and then turned around again and walked slowly through, joining Takahiro and me. The machine was silent. The soldier on the left sighed again. I saw Jill twitch and then there was Hix around my neck again, tickling my chin.

"Thank you for your cooperation," said the soldier on the right.

"Sure," said Takahiro. I noticed he was standing up straighter—as straight as Takahiro ever stood, and his voice sounded normal. The *gruuaa* had turned themselves into a kind of jacket. Taks wore a lot of black anyway. Usually he looked really good in it. We moved down the corridor toward our homeroom. My heart was slowing down to normal. "What?" I said to him.

"The school's shielded," he said softly. "You can feel it, can't you? It's better in here. I'd forgotten. This morning I was just thinking, more people around to soak up all that buggie crap in the air. But the school's shielded because it's a designated relief shelter, you know? If there ever was a cobey around here they couldn't immediately contain, this is one of the places they'd tell us to go. That means it's shielded from armydar too. Which is why they were running us through that thing. I wonder if the machine beeped for anyone else?"

"It better have," I said, "or somebody is going to notice it was two out of the three of us."

"What were they looking for?" said Jill, still upset.

Takahiro shrugged—a nice normal Newworld shrug. "Dunno. Contamination, probably. They probably graph it out on a map."

Senior homerooms were all over the place. It was supposed to help traffic flow in the corridors. Used to be senior homerooms were all near the front so seniors could stroll in after the rush. But we had to hurry. Jill dropped back to walk beside me, lumbering along with my algebra book. *"What was that,"* she said flatly. "At the archway."

"Gruuaa," I said.

She looked at me, and then we went through our door, and there was Mrs. Andover glaring at us.

I spent the rest of the day worrying about what to do about Takahiro after school. We nodded to each other at lunch like everything was normal, although I noticed him folding paper instead of eating or talking—okay, that was still pretty normal for Taks. Jeremy and Gianni were waving their arms around and pushing a 'top back and forth at each other and not eating much either. But that was normal for them too. When they weren't redefining the universe they were inventing 'tronic games about redefining the universe.

There were a lot of shadows under Takahiro's table but I couldn't tell if any of them were *gruuaa*. You'd better be there, I thought. We have to leave the school again this afternoon. Although you could go home long enough to check on Val. I frowned. Val didn't need checking on, did he? Besides, there were still *gruuaa* at home, just not as many.

I had left my algebra book in my locker. I had told it to stay, but the long down had never become Mongo's best trick either. I had no idea what I was going to do or say if it suddenly materialized on the lunch table—or I saw it waddling across the floor on its edges. I decided I wasn't hungry either. I pulled some paper out and started folding too, but I couldn't settle to anything. Everybody else at the table was full of whatever had happened at the park yesterday. There were some pretty wild theories. None of them wilder than the truth though. I saw Jill glancing at me occasionally, but she didn't mention that I'd told her I'd been at the park while it was going on. She was the kind of friend who knew when to keep her mouth shut.

What was it I'd folded yesterday, with that awful wind trying to gouge bits out of me, and the universe falling to nothing around me? My fingers had seemed to know what they were doing. Well, but it was some cousin or close personal friend of the figure Taks had given me—I hadn't done it consciously, but I often tried to figure out one of Taks' new figures without asking him how he'd done it. Although I almost always did have to ask.

I had put the new one back in my knapsack this morning. I took it out and looked at it for a long time. Her. She'd gone stiff and sharp again, like she'd been re-energized by a good night's sleep. If an algebra book could regenerate pages and follow me around, why couldn't an origami figure feel better after a good night's sleep? I wasn't thinking about it. If I was thinking about it, which I wasn't, I could think that I'd imagined her being limp last night. (I wasn't thinking about the algebra book *at all*.)

Taks made a lot of critters, and then usually gave them to me. Everyone knew I worked at the shelter and that if you said the wrong thing to me I'd start spouting about proper care and feeding and the right environment to let the critter be itself and natural behavior blah blah blah. It was like flicking a switch. I couldn't help it, any more than a light bulb could. Takahiro had started officially making me critters in seventh grade, when someone, probably Eddie, he's always been *warugaki*, wanted to know what to feed an octopus and said I didn't know anything. Because I'm like that I looked it up (on my 'top in my lap in math class) and made sure to tell Eddie in front of as many people as possible: mollusks, mostly. Takahiro made me an octopus that day.

I looked at the new critter. I started to fold . . . and then had a kind of vision of a kind of movement inside my locker . . . and hastily turned the little paper thing into a dragon. I was good at dragons, and usually someone wanted it afterward. Laura picked this one up, got out her green pen (green was Laura's thing), and gave it eyes with long eyelashes. Oh well.

I put Taks' away and started on another one. This one was *not* going to end up with long eyelashes. But it kept refusing to fold into a dragon. I would position the paper for a perfect crease and my hand would slip and the crease would go somewhere else. My hands *don't* slip when I'm folding paper. I knock over full mugs of coffee on a regular basis, but I'm good at folding paper. I'm just not as good as Takahiro. I turned whatever it was over to make the same (wrong) fold on the other side.

There was an odd little change of air—no, of air pressure, like

I was a tire being pumped up—and again I felt Hix stir against my neck. When I noticed that there was a new gentle weight leaning against my ankle I knew what it was. I kept folding.

The bell rang and I picked up my new critter. "*Nani*, what's that?" said Laura, waving her dragon like a fan.

"It's a *baku*," I said at random. I had no idea what it was.

"A what?" said Laura.

"A dream eater. If you have nightmares, you put a *baku* under your pillow."

"Remind me to ask you to make me one the night before our first algebra test," said Laura, who was in my class. She stared at it a moment and then shook her head, got to her feet, and picked up her knapsack. I bent down and picked up my algebra book, which was now under my chair. I tucked my new paper critter inside the front cover.

"You brought your algebra book to *lunch*?" said Laura. "Magsie, you are a sick woman."

"It doesn't fit in my locker," I said, almost truthfully.

"Isn't it the worst?" said Laura. "Whoever designed the dreeping thing really wanted to punish us. You know calculus doesn't even have textbooks? It's all on their 'tops."

"If you'd let me help you last year," said Jill, "you too could be in textbook-free calc."

"Thanks, I'd rather carry around a book almost as heavy as my car," said Laura. "See you."

Jill said quietly, "I saw you put—well, wedge—your algebra book in your locker before lunch. And I walked here with you."

I didn't say anything.

"Is your algebra book a—um—*gruuaa*?"

"No," I said. "I don't think so." I remembered Hix trying to protect the algebra book too when we went through the soldiers' scanner.

The cafeteria was emptying out. "You said you had a lot to tell me," said Jill.

"Yes, and a lot of it isn't mine *to* tell," I said. Without meaning to I reached up and touched Hix. It should have looked like I was patting myself on the collarbones for some reason but Jill said, "That's your *gruuaa*. Isn't it." It wasn't a question.

"Yes," I said.

"And it's what got me through the soldiers' thing this morning."

"She," I said. "Yes."

The second bell rang. "We're going to be late," I said. "Can you take Takahiro and me to the shelter after school?"

"Only if we don't get detention," said Jill, and we sprinted for the door. The late bell was just going when we burst into Mr. Jonadab's classroom. Mrs. Andover would have marked us down, but he just smiled.

CHAPTER 10

THE SOLDIERS AND THEIR ARCHWAY WERE STILL
there when we left, but we didn't have to walk through it again. I
didn't like the way they were looking at us, but that was probably
my guilty conscience. I was standing close enough to Takahiro that
I felt him quiver when we opened the front door and spilled out
onto the concrete. "Taks," I said.

"I'm okay," he said quickly. "It's not as bad as it was this
morning."

"Yes it is," I said, fighting the urge to brush myself off, as if it
was something you could brush off. It was nothing like the soft
tickliness of Hix. And despite Hix and Taks' shadow coat we
were still feeling it. I glanced around, wondering if I'd catch any
of the other students uncomfortably or absentmindedly trying to
sweep invisible crawling things off themselves. I saw Jeremy with
his shoulders up around his ears, scowling so hard his eyes had
disappeared under his eyebrows and his hands clawing at the op-

posite shoulders, but that was just Jeremy in the throes of game invention.

Takahiro sighed. "Okay. Yes, it's just as bad. But your—things—are really helping. Thanks."

"*Gruuaa,*" I said. "But don't thank me. Thank Val."

Jill pulled up in the Mammothmobile and I opened the front door and shoved Taks in in front of me and climbed in after him. "Where are you taking me?" he said. "Should I be worried?"

"Yes," said Jill, staring at the road. "You're—he's—*covered* in—in *gruuaa*. I can see them better when I'm not looking at them. They look kind of like feather boas. Only they sparkle. Sort of. And they have too many eyes. And I think those are legs. Too many legs. Maggie, what is going on?"

She saw them better than I did. "A cobey opened in the park yesterday and we're being taken over by niddles," I said. "Isn't that enough?"

"No. Then it *was* a cobey," said Jill.

"Yeah," I said. "Um."

Jill said carefully, "How do you know it was a cobey? And why wasn't there an announcement?"

I tried to think of some other way to say it. Maybe I shouldn't have told her. But I always told her everything. And it was bad enough I couldn't tell her about Takahiro. "I closed it down," I said.

Jill exhaled rather hard. "You. A *cobey*," she said. "You *closed* a cobey?"

"Yeah," I said. "I wouldn't have known that's what it was, except Casimir told me."

"*Casimir?*" said Jill. "You didn't know what it was and you *closed* it? It takes a *regiment* to close a cobey. According to the board banners we've got two cobey units in this town now!"

I looked down at the floor of the car where the algebra book was leaning lovingly against my leg again. "Yeah. Well," I said. "Maybe Casimir was wrong."

"Talk to me, damn it!" said Jill.

"*I don't know, okay?*" I said. "I don't dreeping know! I pulled some pages out of my algebra book and folded them up and threw them into this big—*big*—wind and it went away!"

"And now your algebra book won't stay in your locker and is following you around," said Jill.

"Yeah," I said. "At least you saw that."

There was a pause. "At least I saw that," said Jill. Another pause. "Why am I taking you to the shelter like it's some safe place? None of us is a homeless lost animal, are we?"

The silence that followed this remark was so deadly that Jill took her eyes off the road for a second and looked at us. "*What?* Now what? What else? What *else?*"

"I'm a werewolf," said Takahiro matter-of-factly.

The car did a tiny zigzag, but only a tiny one. "A werewolf," Jill said cautiously. "This isn't a joke, right?"

"No," said Taks. "It's not a joke. And stress makes me turn. This armydar stresses me hard."

"Yeah," said Jill. "The scans were never like this. It makes me feel like a silverbug with the zapper turned on. The *animal* shelter?"

I had a headache. Maybe it was the armydar. Maybe I was going to turn into a turkey or a mutant chipmunk. "I don't understand how any of this works, okay? But the *gruuaa* suck up random energy or they block the fact that stuff the niddles aren't going to like is present or something like that. Oh, Val's a magician," I added, and the car did another zigzag.

"He can't be," Jill said, sounding increasingly stressed herself. "They'd've never let him into the country."

"*Gruuaa*," I said. "He came with a lot of *gruuaa*."

"Those shadows on the shed," said Jill, remembering.

"Yeah," I said. "He didn't know. He didn't know they were there till—till night before last." Jill shot me a look but didn't interrupt. I went on: "He's been teaching dead batteries that the square root of ninety-six is double fudge cake with buttercream frosting—"

Jill snorted.

"—and people like Taks that—that science can *make* the square root of ninety-six be double fudge cake with buttercream frosting—"

"For the record," said Takahiro, "my project is about how we define the integrity of one world as differentiated from another."

"Holy electricity," said Jill. "You don't want much, do you?"

"—and back wherever Val is from he was . . . I guess he was a pretty big machine."

"Not machine," said Jill. "Magician."

"Whatever," I said. "But the *gruuaa* are working really hard and Taks is still not happy, you know? Neither am I. And I didn't like that scanner thing at all, and the way it almost . . . And Mongo really liked Taks . . . um . . ."

"As a wolf," said Takahiro. "Yeah. I noticed that. Kay's cat avoids me like—well, avoids me for weeks after, but she would, wouldn't she? She's a cat."

"As a *wolf?*" squeaked Jill. I could see her clutching the steering wheel but the car didn't zigzag this time.

"Yeah," said Takahiro. "Yesterday. Val saved my life. And after . . . these are his *gruuaa.*" He did that vague touching thing you do when you're groping in the dark for something that is probably fragile, if you can find it. "He sent them home with me."

"And when we took him home, the soldiers at the corner stopped us, but Mongo sat in Taks' lap and I think that helped too," I said. "Val has tutorials till about six tonight. So we go to the shelter first. Where I'm hoping whatever—er—the armydar either puts out or picks up may be a little more confused. If it works we might even adopt someone."

"Do you have a wolfhound?" said Takahiro.

"Yes, actually," I said. "Her name's Bella. She's one of the Family. They have to turn the armydar off eventually, don't they?"

"Mom says it can be weeks if it's a big cobey," said Jill unhappily. "First there was Copperhill and now—well, whatever they think happened, they're slapping us down hard with this new amped-up armydar."

"What's it supposed to *do?*" I said. I think I may have howled.

"It's supposed to stop it—them—from spreading. Cobeys. They run in series," said Jill. "I guess they think yesterday was trying to be a second cobey."

"Does everyone but me know that cobeys run in series?" I said. Takahiro's hands had found something and were cradling it. It was liking this: it twinkled. But I was pretty sure he'd heard "weeks." Maybe he already knew.

"Everybody who doesn't zone out and end up in Enhanced Algebra with the biggest textbook on the planet, yes," said Jill.

Jill turned in through the shelter gate. Rob Roy and Gertrude were barking, but Rob Roy and Gertrude were always barking. Clare came out of the office but her face cleared when she recognized us. "I could really use some help," she said. "I don't suppose you're all here to work? The army have been here half the day—it's an animal shelter, are they expecting me to be hiding a cobey generator in an empty kennel?—and nothing's done."

"Sure," said Jill. "I can spare a couple of hours."

"Cats don't like me much," said Takahiro. "I'm okay with dogs."

"Can you face cleaning kennels?" said Clare, looking up at him and smiling.

He smiled back. Good. Maybe the shelter had been one of my better ideas. "Can't be worse than Mrs. Andover," he said.

Clare laughed. "Joan Andover? She was a dead battery when she was your age and still Joan Ricco. I'd rather clean kennels too."

It *was* better at the shelter. Clare was completely obsessed, and spent all her spare time getting grants from various animal charities and papering downtown with posters for volunteer dog walkers and special critter-education events—that's human education about critters, you know, not the other way around—and open days, and as a result the animals at the Orchard Shelter were a lot happier and better socialized than in most shelters. (Or a lot of people's homes, but we won't go there.) The turnover for all the standard adoptable critters was high but Clare managed to sort of *solder* the ones that were too old or too ugly or too large or too cranky or too something into a kind of on-site family—the Family—which sometimes made them so charming to susceptible visitors a few of them got adopted after all. (Some of these also got brought back. Clare never refused a returnee.) But the *soldering* thing—I think it made a kind of critter-energy net. You felt it— okay, *I* felt it—as you turned up the driveway and through the gate that had *Orchard Shelter* on the left-hand post. I was hoping that even the armydar would have trouble punching through it.

Takahiro and I were sent out to the kennels. I showed him how it worked and let him get on with it. I hoped the dogs wouldn't mind Taks' *gruuaa* escort, if Mongo's reaction to them was any guide. I kept the slightly dubious-tempered ones for myself. It seemed to go okay. I could hear him making the occasional comment about the weather and tonight's homework. I grinned. Critter therapy is the big bang. I was even relaxing a little myself.

It was just after five-thirty when the *gruuaa* suddenly went crazy. The room filled up with small bursting stars, so many and so bright they made me dizzy, or maybe it was the odd scattered wind, or winds, which were sort of semi-something, like the *gruuaa* themselves were semi-something, which was so disorienting. It was like wherever they were really from was suddenly much closer than usual.

I'd been at the grooming table brushing Florrie, who was probably a Shetland sheepdog and was definitely more hair than dog. I dropped the dog brush and it went *thud* on the floor and skittered a little way, like any ordinary thing, wooden back and plastic bristles and a strap for your hand . . . like any ordinary thing . . . like . . .

The brush stopped when it ran into my algebra book. Which I'd left in Clare's office with my knapsack.

The tiny exploding stars thinned out and disappeared, but I felt almost as sick as if I'd stepped on a silverbug. I couldn't see or feel any of the *gruuaa,* not even Hix. Florrie twisted around so she could lick my hands in a "pardon me but don't just stand there" way. I let go of her and bent slowly down to pick up the grooming brush. I had to hold onto the table. I had to bend over a second time to pick up my algebra book.

I put the book carefully on the counter. It didn't seem right leaving it on the floor, even if the floor had been its choice. Maybe it couldn't leap, but only slither or waddle. I moved around the table so I could keep an eye on it while I went on brushing Florrie but I was worried about Hix. No, here she was, shinnying up me like a kid up a tree. If she weighed more I'd've said she flopped across my shoulders, but it was hard to say "flop" about something that landed as hard as dandelion fluff. "You okay, sweetie?" I said, and Florrie wagged her tail—*keep brushing*—but I was talking to Hix. "What was that about? Where are the rest of you? Is Taks all right?" Nobody was barking, so I wanted to assume nothing too awful had happened, although I didn't know what domestic dogs might do if suddenly confronted with a wolf: flatten themselves into doormats and hope for the best, maybe.

I hadn't realized how accustomed I'd become to the presence of *gruuaa*—or how sharply I'd notice their absence. How much heavier and more ominous the air was without them. I didn't like the sensation that Hix had buried her face under my hair at the back of my neck, the way an unhappy dog will put his head under your arm.

I was feeling the armydar more strongly again, like the return of a fever you'd hoped had gone away for good. I could guess that Takahiro was feeling it too. It was nearly six o'clock, so time we went home and looked for Val. (And Mongo, who was used to coming with me to the shelter, and would reach the destructive stage of tragic mode soon.) I was carefully not thinking beyond that point.

What was I expecting Val to do? He couldn't stop Takahiro from being a werewolf, or being stressed out by the armydar, and he couldn't shut the armydar down. And two nights ago he hadn't even known he was still a magician. Whatever that meant. For the first time since all this began—since meeting Casimir, since really talking to Val for the first time, since Hix, since the Copperhill cobey—I remembered that Aunt Gwenda's house was called Haven. She'd told me when I was still really little that its name had originally been Witchhaven. They'd changed it to just Haven after they cut the magic gene out of everybody in Newworld—and *witch* became a word you didn't use in polite company. (If you had to say anything, you said *magician*.) At the time my interest level in this information was a degree or two below "do you want a peanut butter or roast beef sandwich for lunch?" But I'd remembered it. I also remembered my mother saying, irritated but also uncomfortable, to my dad, as we bumped down the long narrow driveway after a visit to Haven, that one of the reasons she loved him was because he was so normal. I wondered if I counted as normal any more. Val didn't.

I finished Florrie and put her back in her run. She sighed, shook herself all over, and collapsed on her bed. I envied her. I picked up my algebra book and went to look for Takahiro and Jill. Maybe it had just been time for the *gruuaa* to all go do—something. The stars and the weird wind and everything were their version of the late bell at school.

The three of us met up and headed back to the office to sign off with Clare. I was clutching the algebra book like it was my last friend, and while Hix had looped herself around my neck again I still felt that most of her was curled up under my hair. "You didn't take your algebra book up to the kennels, did you?" said Jill.

"No," I said.

"I didn't think so," said Jill.

Takahiro was walking more and more slowly down the little hill to the office and the front gate. Jill was giving him the same worried looks that I was. "What happened with the *gruuaa*?" she said. "They all just kind of cleared off about a quarter hour ago."

"I don't know," I said. "Um—what did you see?"

We were walking so slowly she had time to think about it. "It was like being caught in an electric storm," she said finally. "I think my hair sizzled. I didn't like it."

When we got to the office building the Family were lying over all available surfaces. It was after public hours so the barrier gate was open. Most of the dogs rolled immediately to their feet and came over to say hello. Bella was tall enough that Takahiro could pet her without bending over—although Jonesie had the answer to that one by rearing up and putting his front feet on Takahiro's stomach. Jonesie is a Staffie cross—Staffordshire crossed with Sasquatch—and he wants you to know he is a dog of power and influence. The cats withdrew to the far side of the room and hissed.

"*Off*," said Clare, making a grab at Jonesie. She glanced at the cats, clustered at the far end of the bay window and making a sound like a nest of snakes. "I guess you're not kidding about cats not liking you," she said. "But the dogs are making up for it, aren't they?" Jonesie was back on all fours, but his place had been taken by Athena the greyhound, who, with her feet on Takahiro's chest, was licking his face. Clare sighed, but Takahiro was (gently) pulling Athena's ears and Athena, not a big tail wagger, was wagging her tail. I could see him unstiffening, but as Clare went off to raid the cash box to pay us, Takahiro looked at me and said softly, "I don't think I can do this."

"Do what?" I said, but I knew. Where were the *gruuaa*? What else had happened?

"I don't suppose there's any chance—no," said Takahiro. "I could just sleep on the couch."

"No," I said. "But we can take some of them with us. Clare's got lots of spares."

"What?" said Jill. "You mean in my car?"

"We'll take the ones who don't throw up," I said.

"Oh, thanks," said Jill. "I'm so relieved. *Why* are we taking them with us?"

"The *gruuaa* are all gone. All but Hix." Jill's eyes rested on my collarbones. She nodded.

"And the armydar—makes Taks, um, sick," I said, conscious of

Clare maybe being in earshot. *Gruuaa* could just be a weird teenage word. *Werewolf* she'd hear. "The *gruuaa* were kind of holding it off."

"Sick," said Jill. "Okay. And it can't be good news that they're gone either, right?"

Clare came back and shoved some money at us. "I need a favor," I said. "I need to borrow some of the Family."

"Borrow?" said Clare. "You know I'd let you adopt any of them in a second. Half a second. Adopt two and I'll throw in a free set of steak knives. Adopt all of them and I'll help you build the fence."

"Ha," I said. "I'll take it up with Mom. But right now I need to borrow—several of them. Er. The big ones."

She looked at me. "You know I trust you," she said. "But . . ."

"The armydar," I said. "It's making Takahiro sick. Having critters around kind of—damps it, you know?"

She gave Takahiro a sharp look. In the office light he again looked grey, and it was like he'd lost weight just in the last few hours. He didn't have any weight to lose. His face was all sharp angles like a connect-the-dots in a kids' coloring book. She looked away again, at the Family. Several of them were picking up that there might be something going on. Jonesie, Bella, and Athena were looking from me to Clare and back again.

"Actually I do know," said Clare. "I was thinking about sleeping on the sofa here tonight because the buzz in my head isn't nearly as bad here as at home, even though it's only the far side of the pony field." The shelter stood on what had once been the orchard of Clare's family's farm. She lived in the old farmhouse.

She looked at Takahiro again and he smiled faintly. "Okay,

249

since it's you, hon," she said to me. "But . . ." She stopped. "Who do you want? We'd better do the paperwork. We'll just have a lot of 'rehoming was not successful' later. I'll give you some dog food. And a blanket to put on the back seat. The big ones? I hope it's a big back seat."

"It's pretty big," I said.

Jill sighed, and went off to fetch the Mammothmobile.

One of Takahiro's hands seemed to be welded to the top of Bella's head, which was a good beginning. I also chose Athena and Jonesie and Dov, a Newfie cross who looked like a medium-sized bear, and Eld, which was short for Elder Statesman because that's what he looked like, if elder statesmen were ever mastiffs. But the jowls and the look in the eyes were dead-on.

I was signing everything and Clare was dragging out a large bag of dog food when Majid came strolling in from whatever havoc he'd been creating outdoors. He looked around interestedly, twitching his tail. He took in the windowsill full of hissing, fluffed-out, bottle-brush-tailed cats and spurned them, as he usually did. Whatever was going on, he wanted his (un)fair share. He went straight up to Takahiro, lay down at Bella's feet, and began purring.

Majid is the biggest Maine coon cat you've ever seen, and he doesn't take any crap from *anybody.* This would be okay if he had a less all-inclusive definition of "crap." I know Maine coons are mostly sweethearts, but Majid is a mutant. Clare had given up trying to rehome him. Most of the Family end up that way because nobody wants them—Bella's too big, Athena has a torn lip from her racing days that healed so she looks like she's snarling all the time, Jonesie is one big battle scar from before Clare rescued him from his previous so-called shelter and reformed him, and so on. Angela (spreading herself out ecstatically on the empty sofa) has only one eye; Mugwump growls at everybody. Majid, aside from being huge, is gorgeous—whorls of brown and mahogany with a little white on his chest and front paws—and people keep trying to adopt him because he's so spectacular to look at, and can be very charming when he's in the mood.

The mood never lasts long. He always comes back in a week or two having eaten the mailman or given the neighbors' Rottweiler a nervous breakdown. He and Bella have reached an immovable object/irresistible force compromise, and he (mostly) accepts his role as a member of the Family, but Clare now locks him up (when she can catch him) when the shelter is open in case he takes a dislike to someone who, barring traumas involving a pissed-off saber-toothed tiger, might take one of our other tenants home with them.

"Oh, hi," said Takahiro, surprised, and bent down to pet him with his other hand. Majid's motor went into overdrive. When a thirty-pound cat purrs, the walls shake.

"No," Clare and I said simultaneously. Taks looked up. Majid had rolled over and presented several acres of hairy belly for rubbing. Bella stood looking dignified (and disgusted). Athena and Jonesie turned their backs (which is a bit risky with Majid, although he was pretty good with the Family). Most of the cats on the windowsill were now staring in the opposite direction and trying to make their fur lie down, with mixed success. "We are *not* taking Mr. Destructo with us," I said.

"I don't think I've ever petted a cat before," said Takahiro. "The undercoat is so soft."

"That's not a cat," I said. "That's Majid. He's a force of nature. Any resemblance to a real cat is bogus."

"I'll get the gloves," said Clare. Pretty much only Clare or I could remove Majid from somewhere he wanted to be, but it was still a good idea to be wearing gloves when you tried it. The Majid gloves were heavy leather gauntlets with the cuffs extending most of the way to your elbows. He *could* just bite your head off, but he (probably) wouldn't to Clare or me.

The Mammothmobile pulled up and stopped. I heard the bang of Jill's door. So did Majid. Furthermore he was smart. As soon as I started clipping leads on our new escort he would know exactly what was up. Clare had better hurry with those gloves. I went out to spread the blanket in the car. With the back seats down there was a lot of room, although we humans were going to be squashed in front with the bag of dog food. Plus three knapsacks and an algebra book.

"It's kind of interesting you're driving a car big enough for a wolfhound and a mastiff to get in the back of today," I said.

"And a greyhound, a dark brown bear, and a brindle utility vehicle," said Jill.

"Greyhounds don't take up much room," I said. "They're like dog silhouettes. But why today? Usually the Mammothmobile is stuck to the side of your house by several months' worth of cobwebs because nobody wants to pay for the gas."

"Nah," said Jill. "Greg takes it out at least once a month and runs over any small annoying children that have piled up in our neighborhood since the last time he took it out. But I had an f-word moment this morning—although I didn't know it was going to be animals. I almost funked out at the gas station. Mammoth gets the mileage of like the space shuttle." She was tucking a corner of blanket under the seat, where it might conceivably stay put for twenty seconds after twenty paws started clawing at it. "What's Mongo going to think?" she said.

"Mongo will be thrilled," I said. "It's bringing them back again that's going to be hard."

Clare had reappeared with the gloves at last and gingerly picked Majid up. He went ominously limp—you have the idea that cooperation is not Majid's central reason for living—while Jill and Takahiro and I took the dogs out to the car and persuaded them to jump in the back. We started with Bella because what she did the others would all do, but she was too tall. We had to straighten her forelegs out and then lift her back end up and shove. I got the front end and Taks got the back. She put up with all this with her usual supernatural courtesy. "What a good girl," I said, and gave her a dog biscuit, which made all the other ones want a dog biscuit too, so the rest of the loading was pretty easy, if ridiculous. It was *very* crowded back there, although everyone was looking bright-eyed and interested. It should be okay: they slept in heaps most of the time anyway.

I slung a bag of kibble almost as big as I was on the front seat. There were going to be four of us: Jill, Takahiro, me and a bag of dog food. Even the Mammoth wasn't *that* large a car. I stuffed a few cans of wet food in the footwell under the folded-down back seat.

"I'll get in the middle," I said. When I wasn't dealing with immediate stuff, like funneling five large dogs into a three-and-a-half large dogs' space, my brain kept reverting to *where are the gruuaa where have they gone and why?* Hix was still wrapped around my neck, but she was too still, and if a feather boa could be stiff she was stiff. I couldn't tell if my increasing sense of doom was just the *gruuaa's* absence or something else: the armydar was making me stupid in spite of Hix, and we were about to leave the relative safety of the shelter and go back out on the street. Both Jill and Takahiro looked a little drawn, and Clare looked positively wasted, but that might have been because she was carrying a deadly weapon with a history of sudden unpredictable detonations.

Takahiro jammed himself in beside me while Jill started the car. There was a little panting going on in the back seat but I hoped nothing too severe. Jonesie was trying to get at the cans of dog food but I was pretty sure he wouldn't succeed. And even with a Staffie's jaws he probably wouldn't be able to open them. Probably. "*Ow,*" I said.

"Sorry," said Taks, and scooped my legs up and draped them over his knees. "Oh," I said, startled.

I could hear Jill trying not to laugh as she said, "More."

"Okay," said Taks agreeably, rearranging my legs so they were over only one of his knees. Then he put his arm around me. I felt myself nestling up to his side as if I wanted to be there—I also felt myself blushing so hotly my head might explode and never mind the armydar. Jill put the Mammoth in gear and we started rolling downhill toward the gate. The pressure increased immediately: it was so bad you could almost hear it, although maybe that was just the bones of your skull grinding together. "Drive slowly," said Takahiro.

"Of course," said Jill. "There are a lot of loose animals in the back seat."

As if on cue Bella put her head through the gap in the headrest. "Oh, sweetie," I said. "I hope you're all all right back there." Bella, who was usually pretty reserved, lowered her massive head and gave me a brief lick with a tongue the size of a bath towel. I instantly felt better, and Hix stirred like someone waking out of a deep, drugged sleep. My head cleared—although whether it was more the armydar or Taks' nearness that was messing me up I don't know. I could feel Taks' breath against my hair. If I snuggled—I mean turned—just a little bit, I could rest my cheek against his shoulder. This would be a good thing, because then maybe Hix would curl around him too. That was all I was thinking about. I wasn't thinking about the warm weight of his arm around me, the way it tucked under my elbow so the long-fingered hand could lie palm up in my lap. I hadn't thought about how long Taks' fingers were since he had been that silent little boy folding paper. It was only because I was worried about how my old friend was doing that I picked up his hand and held it with both of mine. But I felt him relax a degree or two—like I had when Bella had licked me.

"Oh, big hulking suckfest," said Jill. There was an army truck turning in at the gate, with the cobey unit logo splashed on its side.

"Pretend to ignore them," I said. "Keep going."

"They won't be for us," said Jill. "Not specifically."

"I don't want to find out," I said. "Remember we've lost our *gruuaa*."

"Yes," said Jill. "I'm missing the sparkly shadows."

The army vehicle had clearly seen us . . . and they wanted us to stop.

"Don't stop unless they aim a zapper at us," I said.

"Drog me," said Jill. We kept rolling down the hill. The army guys didn't quite want to turn in front of us, maybe because there wasn't room, maybe because the Mammoth made even an army van nervous. But they went up the hill like someone who was planning on turning around and coming down again in a hurry. We got to the gate and Jill was bumping onto the main road and I was just saying, "You might turn up Rodriguez, they might not see us by the time they—" when there was a terrified scream from Clare, a shriek of overstressed brakes and . . . the sound of a large heavy metal object slamming into a cement post, like the ones that line the shelter driveway.

"Wow," said Jill, looking in her rear view mirror.

"Did they miss him?" I said.

"What?" said Jill. She looked back at the road in front of her and finished turning. Then she turned again, down Rodriguez. Even the Mammoth knew it was carrying a load: you could feel it settle on the corners. There was the sound of scrambling in the back, but the panting wasn't any worse. "I don't think they'll be following us any time soon," Jill added.

"Go to the end of the road and stop," I said.

"What?" said Jill again. "What do you mean, did they miss him?"

Even if some overeager army drone raced down to the gate and looked for us, they wouldn't be able to see us sitting at the end of Rodriguez. "Just stop," I said. "Please."

She stopped. "You can kiss her if you want," she said. "I won't mind. And you've got a major bag of dog food for chaperone."

"I—*what*?" I squeaked. I turned, but somehow I turned the wrong way. I put a hand out—just to steady myself. The dog food was trying to shove me farther into Taks' arms. I wasn't entirely sure Jill hadn't given it a push from her side. My hand was on Taks' shoulder. His arm tightened. His other hand reached across, smoothed down the back of my head, cupped my chin briefly. And then he kissed me.

Jill opened her door and got out. "I'm going to move those cans," she said. "The clink, clink, clink is really annoying."

This was so totally the wrong moment. Not to mention the tactical difficulties. I wound my arms around Taks' neck (Bella gave the nearer one another lick as it slid past) and kissed him back. I unwrapped one arm so I could pull my fingers slowly through his incredibly thick hair. He moved a little, and slid one hand under me so he could lift me the rest of the way onto his lap. Fortunately the Mammoth had amazing headroom, even if not quite enough for a wolfhound. Taks' other hand patted leisurely, delicately down my back—I shivered. He pulled me closer to him. I couldn't get any closer.

Jonesie put his head through the gap between Taks' headrest and the door. I could see him checking the situation for dog biscuit probability. And then I kind of lost track. I'd kissed a few boys before, but nothing like this. I had a sudden, *extremely* flustering memory flash of Taks's long naked back in the bathroom mirror. . . .

There was a soft thud, and purring. Jill was just closing the rear door. I sighed, and let myself sag back a little. Taks let me go. Sitting on his lap made me seem as tall as he was: I never looked straight into his face like this. He smiled. Cheekbones to die for. How could I never have noticed?

"I'm sorry to break it up," said Jill, "since this is obviously quality time, but if one of those army goons did get as far as to cross the street and look down Rodriguez, they would see us. Is this the him you wanted them to miss?"

I turned away from Taks, but this time I leaned against him quite comfortably. Majid, of course, was sitting in the driver's seat and the bag of dog food was canted at an angle like an army truck had run into it from the other side. "Yes," I said. Majid gave me a brief dazzling golden stare and then half-lidded his eyes again. I know when my life is being threatened.

"Well, he's our hero," said Jill, "So I guess it's okay he's coming with us, right? Will he eat me if I try and move him?"

"I don't know," I said. "Wiping out a cobey truck may have put him in a good mood." I reluctantly climbed off Taks' lap, gently pushed Bella's head out of the way, knelt up on what there was of the seat to lean past the dog food, heaved Majid by a kind of levering process, and spread him over Taks' and my laps, which he nobly consented to. He purred harder. He was making my teeth rattle. "We'll go to your place the back way," said Jill, and started the Mammoth again. It sounded a lot like Majid.

It was at that moment there was a tiny, whispery touch against my forearm. It might have been floating cat hair—Majid was a mighty fur factory, and there was the gang behind us as well—but it wasn't. It was a *gruuaa*. A—tiny? Miserable?—*gruuaa*. It crept up my chest and lay just below my collarbones—and, trust me, it's not like there's an enormous shelf there for lying on. But the *gruuaa* aren't into gravity much. There was some communication going on with Hix, I thought, and I was pretty sure whatever it was was making me feel tiny and miserable too. Maybe it was just that it was too easy to be expecting bad news. Even Hix's sweet smell seemed faded and sad.

I laced the fingers of one hand through one of Takahiro's—the one that wasn't petting Majid—and he kissed the top of my head. I wanted to be happy, and instead I was more frightened than ever. My old friend and brand-new boyfriend was a werewolf and the army was after him. Us. Probably. And Val . . .

I wished I could talk to the *gruuaa*. Well, we'd be home soon enough. Too soon. Even draped with unhappy *gruuaa* (and a bone-shaking megacat) I could still concentrate on Takahiro sitting next to me—sitting next to me so close I could feel him breathing. (The bag of dog food was kind of a romance wrecker, but I could live with it. I could even live with Jonesie trying to catch my eye so he could express outrage at the presence of Majid in the front seat, when he, The Jones, was in the back.) Takahiro . . . *sugoi.* Super-quadruple *sugoi.*

A brief vision of Casimir's grin lit up my mind's eye. The grin and the *dimple.* I felt a brief rush of what-might-have-been. But Taks would never mistake me for a magdag whatsit mythic super-gizmo. He was there when Mrs. Fournier hadn't believed me that

I was feeling sick and I threw up all over the floor in seventh-grade science class. He'd been first on the scene in ninth grade when I stumbled and fell spectacularly over the broken paving stone outside the high school office—where I'd been summoned to *discuss* my failing grade in pre-algebra. I had not only skinned both knees but cracked my forehead on the step, so there was blood *everywhere*—and Takahiro had been the one to pick up the test paper that had flown out of my book with the big red *F* on it, across which Mr. Denham had scrawled *Even you are not this stupid*—and had never once said a thing about it afterward. Takahiro wasn't ever going to think I was some kind of legendary hero.

Although right at the moment I wished one of us was.

CHAPTER II

THERE WAS NO REASON FOR OUR HOUSE NOT TO be quiet on a weekday evening but I didn't like it. I was sure it was the wrong kind of quiet. Val's last student should have just left. Mom should have just got home—and her car was in the driveway. Ran was maybe home or maybe not yet. But it was always quiet when I came home after school. I only felt so funny because the armydar was scrambling my brains. Or Takahiro was scrambling my . . . whatever.

The *gruuaa* mobbed me the moment I slid out of the car. Me and Takahiro, but especially me. Something wrong. Something awfully, horribly wrong. Val. Of course. It had to be Val: Val who had brought them here, or who had brought him here. And there still weren't as many *gruuaa* as there had been last night, when Val sent most of them with Takahiro—they'd left us at the shelter, and they weren't here either.

"Maybe you'd better stay with the car," I said.

"No can do, white girl," said Jill. I knew that voice. It meant her f-word was telling her stuff, and she wasn't going to tell me what. "I'll just roll the windows down a little for our friends." It was pretty chilly; the Family would be fine. And I was shivering just because of the weather. Just because of the weather. Takahiro held my hand. I had a cape and a hood of *gruuaa,* and more of them were winding around my feet like cats: they were so urgent and insistent I was almost tripping over them, although there was nothing there to trip over. I waded down the path and opened the front door—and was promptly knocked into Taks, behind me, by a frantic Mongo. He didn't behave like this: he did enthusiasm, not panic. Nor was he the least bit interested in the car, and he adored other dogs. Majid, I realized, was with us too, and Mongo was even ignoring a cat the size of a wolverine coming into his house.

Mom was sitting curled up at the far end of the sofa, in the dark. The streetlights were coming on outdoors, the curtains were drawn, but she hadn't turned any lights on. "Mom?" I said. I turned the overhead light on, and she turned her head toward me. Her face was wet with tears. *"Mom?"*

"They've taken him," she said. "Val. They came and took him away." Jill slipped past me and went into the kitchen. I heard the kettle banged down on the stove and the little *whoosh* of the gas lighting. I went and sat by my mother, and took her hands. Several *gruuaa* climbed up the front of the sofa and pooled in her lap. Mongo pressed up against my leg from the other side and put his nose against her knee.

"Who?" I said. "Where? Where were they taking him?"

She shook her head, but her voice sounded a little stronger when she answered. "The major who was here yesterday—when you were here," and she nodded at Takahiro, who was sitting beside her on the floor, also wrapped in *gruuaa*. "Donnelly. He came back with a warrant. He said that Val is . . ." Her voice broke, and the tears began again.

"Mom," I said. I hated seeing my mother cry. I'd seen her cry after Dad died—but not like this. She'd been shattered by Dad's death—but she'd also been angry, and full of a blazing energy, determined to protect Ran and me, and keep our crippled family a family. But now she was crying helplessly, exhaustedly, despairingly. It made me feel five years old, and more scared than I'd ever been in my life.

"The warrant says he's a magician and a spy," she said softly. "That they know who he really is, and that he only got into this country by some—some trick. They said they were *sorry* for me, for having been—" She stopped talking, pulled her hands away from mine and put them over her face. I put my arms around her and she laid her head on my shoulder and wept like a little girl.

Jill arrived with a tray. "Coffee with extra sugar," she said. "And a ham sandwich. Shocky people should eat." Mom sat up and was beginning to shake her head. "*My* mom says," added Jill, although it was exactly what my own mom would say if it had been happening to someone else. Jill picked up the plate and offered it. It was three against one (four, counting Mongo. Five, counting Majid. Even if they were staring at the sandwich rather than Mom). Mom reluctantly took a half, looked at it, and bit into it doubtfully.

Jill's mom was right (of course). You could see my mom settling down a little. She got through nearly half of her half sandwich before she laid it down. "We're going to my sister upstate," she said in what was almost her normal voice. "They've taken my husband, why shouldn't I want to go to my sister for a while?" Even if she is notorious for pro bono work for people accused of magic, I added silently. "There are a lot of people leaving town till they get this cobey rift shut down thoroughly—and turn the armydar off. They're starting to call it a rift—there's a rumor that another cobey opened at the north end of town." The park—and us—were near the southwest end. So it was a series, and it was getting longer. A lot had happened while we were lying low at the shelter. "Tennel & Zeet is closing, and they've canceled school for the rest of the week—Val's last tutorial didn't bother to show up—the army has decided they want the sheltered buildings for military use.

"I've already called Gwenda—her groundline crashed after about a minute, but she's expecting us. I was just thinking about what we need to take with us when . . . when it all kind of caught up with me." She took a deep breath. "Takahiro, you should come with us. We can go past your place on our way out of town for whatever you want to bring with you. I'll talk to Kay. . . . Electric angels, what is *that*," she added, having just caught sight of Majid.

"That's Majid," I said. "We—er—there are a few more in Jill's car."

"Cats?" said Mom, baffled.

"Well, dogs, actually," I said. "But the *gruuaa* all left while we were at the shelter—when they took Val, I guess. And Taks said the animals—our ordinary animals help. There are a few *gruuaa* here, although most of them must have gone with Val. . . . How are you?" I said to Takahiro.

"I'm okay," he said. He smiled at me. "Don't worry."

Mom, who has Mom Instinct and knows me way too well, was distracted from everything—even Val—by Takahiro's smile. Taks wasn't a big smiler, ordinarily, and the situation wasn't exactly a big-smiley one. She turned to look at me pretty hard. "Hmm," she said. "Jill, your mom called and wanted to know if I knew where you were—the armydar was interfering with the signal for your pocket phone and she couldn't get hold of you. I'm sorry, I should have told you at once. She called before . . . before . . ." Mom's voice wavered briefly. "She sounded pretty upset. We've got a groundphone in the kitchen."

Jill jumped up to phone.

"I've been trying to phone Ran, tell him to come home, but I can't raise him either. I guessed you'd be at the shelter—but even Clare's groundphone is out. I'd've started worrying about you too if you hadn't come home soon." She tried to smile. Usually she was a really good smiler. Not tonight.

"Drink your coffee," I said. "It'll get cold."

"Eat your sandwich," said Takahiro from the floor. "Or the invasion force will get it." Majid was (mostly) in Taks' lap but his eyes were clearly trained on the sandwich on the coffee table.

There was a muffled yell from the kitchen. "*What?*"

We all turned toward her, but werewolf reflexes are faster even than Majid's and Takahiro had the plate over his own head before

Majid finished his pounce. Majid disappeared. I hoped this wasn't the end of a beautiful friendship. Majid, foiled, tended to be cranky.

Jill reappeared at the kitchen door. "They took Arnie. They took *Arnie.*"

"They—?" I said.

"Major Blow-it-out-your-ass-and-set-fire-to-it," she said violently. "Donnelly. The same bugsucker who took Val."

"I don't understand," said Mom. Neither did I. Arnie sold drain cleaner and soldering irons and barbecues and birdseed. I could see why they took Val—they were wrong, and I wanted to solder their asses to a barbecue, but I could see how their ugly minds were working. But Arnie?

"They say his mother and grandmother were magicians, and he didn't have his genes chopped off or whatever it is they do because his grandmom figured how to fake it and then his mom did it for him too."

Mom and I carefully didn't look at each other, but Jill was staring at the wall. "And they can't arrest her because she *died.* But he's still got the genes."

"They can't mean to do it now?" said Mom, and I could hear her being appalled. "They'll—they could kill him."

"Or turn him into a vegetable," said Jill even more violently. "Magdag, what do we *do*? Mom's saying to come home, we're leaving town too, that if I don't get back there fast she'll pack my suitcase for me. I—I don't even like Arnie all that much. I mean, he's okay, and he keeps my brothers from killing each other, but—" And she burst into tears.

I bounced off the sofa and put my arms around the second

wildly crying woman in half an hour. I loved Jill as much as I loved my own mom. And my hatred for Major Blow-it-out-your-ass was getting kind of out of control. "What do we do?" Jill wept into my shoulder. "What do we *do*?"

"We go after them," I said suddenly. "I'm sure the *gruuaa* will show us where."

"Good," said Takahiro, and got to his feet. "I'm coming too."

I looked at him over Jill's bent head. I wanted him to come—I wanted really, really badly for him to come. I wanted it even more badly as I began to realize that I meant it, about going after them—going after Val and Arnie. We had no idea where they were, or if they were anywhere near each other. Or who else might be with them.

"Don't be absurd," said Mom, but she didn't sound grown-up commonsensical angry, just bewildered.

"I think absurd is what we've got," said Takahiro. "Being a werewolf is pretty absurd. I'm used to it."

"I really want you to come," I said. "But—"

"You might be able to use a hundred-and-sixty-pound wolf," said Takahiro. "Think about it."

"Okay," I said. We smiled at each other. Absurdly.

Jill was still crying, but she raised her head and looked at me. "Are you serious?"

"Yes," I said, but I was thinking: All very well, the *gruuaa* might be able to get us—as far as we can get, but then what? Major Blow-it would hardly be holding them somewhere that two teenage girls and a hundred-and-sixty-pound timber wolf could break them out of easily.

There was a knock on the door. Jill and I startled so hard our heads banged together. We stood there clutching each other—nobody's idea of a courageous rescue party. Mom got up, wiped her face hastily with one hand, and answered the door.

It was Casimir.

"I am sorry," he said, and looked over Mom's shoulder at Jill and me standing like incompetently reanimated zombies at the end of the front hall, in the little space between the kitchen table and the back of the sofa. His eyes met mine and he smiled, but it was a worried smile, and it didn't dazzle me the way it had yesterday. Jill and I moved apart, and Takahiro walked around the end of the sofa to stand beside us. Takahiro and Casimir hadn't met before; Taks didn't eat a lot of pizza. They looked at each other. I couldn't see Takahiro's face but I could see Casimir's, and I couldn't read his expression: it might have been shock. Even if he could read somehow that Taks and I had been kissing, I didn't think that would qualify for shock. I didn't like the other possibility.

"I can see I am here at a bad time," he said, and I waited for him to finish, I'll come back some other day. *And next time, call first*, I thought. He'd phoned first yesterday. Maybe the armydar was getting to him too.

But instead what he said was, "May I come in?"

Gods' engines. We didn't need any more complications. Even beautiful ones with heart-stopping dimples.

Mom, probably still a little confused by recent events, stood aside, and he walked in with that same wild-animal grace I'd noticed yesterday. He didn't need trees and daylight; he had it walking down a short narrow hall in a boring little house at the dull end of town. Takahiro, who really was a wild animal, walked like a human boy who thought he was too tall.

Casimir stopped in front of me. "My mother is a magician. She did not like it that I wished to study science. I almost did not accept the scholarship to Runyon, even though I had applied for it, because she disliked it so much. And then they almost did not let me come, because my mother is a magician. But at last they did let me come. I have been in this country only a fortnight. I began the job that my mentor found for me at the beginning of the week. On the third day of my new job, a large cobey opened in a town less than ten miles away from the town I now lived and worked in. I had been told during the two days of induction seminars the trust gives to all its students on arrival that we would not see a cobey here, that big ones were so rare it was not worth wasting time telling us what to do if we did, that if there was one anywhere the army cobey units would have contained it before we knew it existed.

"That night, before the cobey was announced, two young women walked into my new workplace, and one of them called the other one *mgdaga*. The *mgdaga* is our great heroine; there have been several *mgdaga* in the history of my country, although the last one was over two hundred years ago.

"On the fourth day," Casimir continued, his eyes never wavering from my face, "I met the *mgdaga* again, and saw her perform a magic I have never heard was within the skill of any magician, and my mother knows a great deal about magicians and what they are capable of, and I have learnt much of what she knows merely by being her son. I discovered that the *mgdaga* was a friend to *gruuaa*—and that she was stepdaughter to Valadi Crudon, himself a great magician, who had disappeared from his homeland in some mystery seven years ago. My mother taught me that there is no coincidence, only shortsightedness."

Most of this had washed over Mom, fortunately, but she reacted to Val's name. She said sharply, "He did not disappear. He uses his own name. He has always used his own name."

Casimir nodded, although the way he did it was almost a bow. "It is only other magicians who—who revere him. And I imagine the *olzcar*—bureaucrats put a—a blind on his name, so that it did not stand out. So that if you looked for it, it would look like—like—"

"John Smith," I said. "And the *gruuaa* followed him. He believed they—his old masters, his old government—had taken all his magic, but the *gruuaa* followed him anyway. And hid the fact that not all of his magic was gone. He came here, to Newworld. And the *gruuaa*—hid him."

I raised my hand in what had become a habitual gesture, to run my fingers gently across the slightly-disturbed-air that was Hix where she was looped around my neck.

"I believe no human has ever really understood *gruuaa*," said Casimir. "But they are very loyal to those they choose."

There was a little silence. There was no way I was going along with this magdag thing, but we still needed to get on the road after Val—before the non-magdag's nerve broke.

"He did no magic," said Mom. "He didn't even know about the *gruuaa*—till Maggie told him. But he did no magic."

Thanks, Mom, I thought, but Casimir was already staring at me.

"But—Takahiro—" Jill said cautiously.

Taks shook his head. "What Val did for me was just from knowing about . . . There wasn't any magic."

Casimir looked thoughtfully at Takahiro. "You're a were," he said. We all stiffened and I moved involuntarily closer to Taks as if I could protect him. The hamster protecting the mountain lion. But hamsters are more acceptable in small social groups.

"How do you know?" said Takahiro levelly, not trying to deny it.

Casimir ducked his head again. "I'm sorry. But I would like to convince you that I am on your side."

"On the—the what?" murmured Jill. "The magdag's side?"

"The *mgdaga*," said Casimir. "Yes."

"Why?" said Mom. "Why do you want to convince us? Why do you think it's about sides?"

"A *mgdaga* only appears when there is need of her," said Casimir calmly, like we were discussing pizza-topping choices. "I know Takahiro is a were because my mother has friends who are weres, and after they have worn their animal selves recently there are traces left on their human selves. You have been your animal self recently, I think."

So that's how you managed to move the plate before Majid got it, I thought, as Takahiro said, "Yes."

Casimir nodded, and then looked around at us again. "Is Valadi not here?" he said. "He will know of the tradition of the Ukovian *mgdaga.*"

"They've taken him away," said Mom, and she was beginning to sound angry. That was better than desperate and fragile. "The army came—and took him away."

Casimir looked at me again. "Don't *look* at me like that," I said resentfully.

"Magdag," breathed Jill.

"Oh *stop,*" I said. "Okay, Casimir, listen. We're going after him—Val. And Arnie too. Jill's mom's partner. They've taken him too, which makes even less sense. He's born and bred Newworld, he was never a magician in the first place. Do you want to help us?"

"That is why I came here," he said. "I do not like this—army-dar. And I hoped the *mgdaga* would have something I could do."

"Stop it," I said. "That's my first—er—whatever. No *mgdaga gomi*—garbage. I know about the *gruaa,* but that's all."

"You are joking," said Casimir. "I was in the park with you yesterday. When you folded up a large cobey and tucked it in on itself so tightly it could not come loose while we escaped—and then called the *gruaa* to hide us from the army."

"They never have announced a cobey in the park," Jill said. "Mags *is* a good folder."

My eyes went to my algebra book, lying innocently on the coffee table next to the empty tray. Innocent except for the fact that I'd left it in the car. "I didn't call the *gruaa,*" I said. "They came. Fortunately for us."

Casimir shrugged, his elaborate, not-Newworld shrug, very like Val's. "They knew to come," said Casimir. "They have chosen you. And they knew you needed them. It is very nearly the same thing."

Mom said, "Maggie?" It was half her Mom voice and half something else. It reminded me a little of Gwenda's voice.

"I don't *know* what happened," I said, a little too loudly, not wanting to remember the wind that felt like it could rip the earth to shreds—the feeling that the earth was crumbling away underneath me. Or the feeling of folding the torn-out pages of an algebra book, and that awful, falling-into-the-void feeling that every fold I made was creating another endless invisible line that was trying to drag me down into that nothingness. That I was trapped in a web that I was weaving—folding—myself. "Takahiro's a better folder than I am," I said. "Enormously better. And it was that critter you gave me, Taks, that I chose to fold—to try to fold." The fox-wolf-dragon. Like my Hands Folding Paper critter. I was talking to Taks now, as much as anything to make everyone stop staring at me. "I didn't know what to do, and I remembered you'd said to keep her close."

Takahiro nodded. "I—I don't get this, but my mother was"—he glanced at Casimir—"also a magician, sort of. She taught me origami, and she taught me about the *kami*, and she taught me how—stuff crosses borders sometimes."

Like being a were, I thought. That's a great big border crossing.

"There's been some buggie thing crossing borders anyway," Jill said. I already knew she'd been picking up more lately—foresight stuff—more than just seeing *gruaa* and having premonitions

273

of doom while the armydar crushed us like a boot on a silverbug. And choosing to drive the Mammoth today. She went on: "I don't know if that's because of the cobey—the cobeys—with the number of silverbugs we've had around for like the past six months— or the armydar, the last couple of days. But—it's like the borders are getting all messed up. I can almost see—it's a little like the way the *gruuaa* twinkle in the corners of your eyes. And"—she was using her you're-going-to-pay-attention-to-what-I'm-telling-you-and-then-you're-going-to-pass-your-math-exam voice—"I think the armydar is making it worse."

"Yes," said Mom wearily. "It was *my* mom who taught us that, us four girls, when they were first inventing the armydar. That this is what would happen, sooner or later—that the army's technology is itself unbalanced and could, and probably would, further unbalance the dangerous situation a big cobey creates."

There was an ugly little silence.

"Then we'd better go," I said, still too loudly—or maybe it was the armydar making my voice echo. "Do what we're going to do." Whatever that was.

"Maggie—" began Mom.

"Look, I have to," I said. My cape had scattered, but there was now a single *gruuaa* trying to wind itself up my unoccupied-by-Mongo leg. I absentmindedly put my hand down to help her. Him. Whatever. It curled around my arm and up onto my shoulder. There were faint furry greetings or—what do I know— gossip-exchanging waggles. I was pretty sure—for no reason— that I had been clambered on by this one before. It wasn't the one who'd come back to tell Hix what was going on after they'd all left us at the shelter, but it still felt half-familiar. I was going to have to learn more of their names. There was the faintest— the *faintest* drift of something across my mind—something that wasn't me. *Whilp*, it said.

I shivered. "I have to," I said again. I sounded like I was telling the truth.

Mom stared past Casimir to the wall. She'd rehung Great-grandmom's quilt. The only light was from the lamp I'd turned on in the living room, and the quilt gleamed in the twilight, green and gold and palest pink and cream and deepest red and purple. I thought suddenly that I was wrong about this being a boring little house: no house could be boring with that quilt hanging on the wall. Many of the squares had plants on them, mostly flowers, a few with just leaves; you could see where Mom's gardening instincts had come from. But quite a few had animals on them, and the animals were often watching you through some plant or other. I hadn't thought of it in years, because this particular square hung near the floor, but it had fascinated me when I was shorter: it had a little round, furry or feathery face, peering out through leaves so dark they were almost black. You couldn't see much of the face— except that it seemed to have three eyes.

I was pretty sure Mom knew I'd go whatever she said, but I'd rather she accepted it. But she was my mom, and I was seventeen years old, and it was kind of a jump from being a reliable dog owner to being a magdag.

We were all silent. We should be making plans, I thought. What plans are there we can make? We didn't even know where Val or Arnie was. Maybe if I took Great-grandmom's quilt off the wall again and laid it on the floor it could do the enchanted-flying-carpet trick. I couldn't remember if flying carpets in fairy tales could go through walls or not. And the armydar might mess up its homing instinct. *Dōshiyō*, I thought. *Dōshiyō, dōshiyō.* What do I do?

At last Mom nodded, a stiff little jerk. "Gods' holy engines," she said grimly. "I don't think I can stop you, much as I think I should. And it'll be easier afterward for both of us if I say okay now. But I also think the usual systems have broken down. That's the cobey, perhaps—or the armydar. And I find Casimir's version of events rather compelling." She smiled at me; it was not a happy smile. "You are so much like your grandmother," she said. "It doesn't really express it to call her stubborn. When she made up her mind about something . . . she made granite look soft and pliable." She paused. "Your grandmother—like your great-grandmother—was also a powerful magician."

"And you, Mom?" I whispered.

"I'm the sister who gave it up," she said. "I'm the one of the four of us girls who wanted to be normal. I'm the one who fell in love with someone whose family had never been gene-chopped because there was no gene to chop, who went to secretarial school so I could get a job sooner, because Ber was going to graduate from Runyon in a year and we could get married. And then I went to accounting classes in the evenings before you were born, because I liked arithmetic. You know where you are with addition and subtraction." She leaned forward, over Mongo, still attached to my leg, and put her arms around me. Hix (and perhaps Whilp) did her bodiless-shadow thing: I felt her patting my face and I think

Mom's too, not at all dismayed by there being no space between us for her to *be*. I thought I felt Whilp making a nest in my hair. I have bad hair most days; a *gruuaa* couldn't make it much worse.

"Go with love and luck," said Mom. "And with magic. I send you with all that I can offer you." She kissed me on the cheek—and there was a funny little tingly feeling, almost *gruuaa*-like.

"Giving up magic didn't work so well for Val," I said.

"No, it didn't," she agreed. "Which is probably why I'm not shutting you up in a closet right now. But you'd better leave before I break down entirely—before I remember that I'm your mom and you're seventeen years old. Ran and I will go to Gwenda as soon as he gets home, which had better be soon. Come . . . come after us . . . as soon as you can. That house is not called Haven idly. There is still magic there—Gwenda will help us. I wish I were taking you and Val there now."

I turned and nearly ran out the door. I also nearly tripped over Majid. "Come on," said Jill, grabbing my arm. "No falling down. I'm sure we need you in one piece."

We went down the sidewalk together while I said to myself, I am *not* going to cry, I am *not* going to cry. It will be fine, Val will like Haven, and he'll figure out how to get along with Gwenda (my dad used to call her *formidable*). Takahiro appeared on my other side carrying Majid, who was (astonishingly) purring again. Mongo had come out with us and then shot ahead and had his forepaws up on the rear door of the Mammoth (this was not allowed, of course: dog claws scratch paint) and was wagging his tail so hard it was in danger of coming off, while Bella strained to get her muzzle through the quarter-open window to touch noses with him. "That's a yes then," said Jill. "If I open the door, will he get in, or will everyone else come out?"

"He'll go in," I said, "if we make it obvious enough that that's the plan." By the time this had been achieved, not without a certain amount of swearing and being hit in the face by wagging tails, Casimir had joined us. "If we put this end of the rear seat up, I can get in the back," I said, pulling dog hair out of my mouth. "It's either me or the dog food—that's an easy one. And it's dumb to take two cars. Then Casimir can get in front." It was nearly dark; the streetlights had all come on and there were shadows everywhere. Some of them were *gruuaa*.

"I'll come in the back with you," said Takahiro. "You can sit on my lap." I didn't quite laugh, remembering how crowded the three of us had been on the drive over—and Casimir was a lot wider than either Taks or me. *Shoulders.* Yes, I know, I'd been *kissing* Taks and liked it a lot. And I wasn't minding the idea of sitting in Taks' lap at all either. But Casimir totally won on the shoulders and a girl can look. And if Taks was in back with me we could stuff everybody's knapsacks under Casimir's feet. He'd brought one that looked like he was going camping for a week. I didn't want to think about what he imagined the magdag was going to need.

Supposing we found Val and Arnie and wanted to take them away from wherever they were, where were we going to put them? On the roof?

"And Mongo, Majid, and Bella will sit on us," I said loudly, to drown out my thoughts.

"*Odoroku beki,*" said Takahiro. "We'll cope somehow."

We were pretty cozy in the back. It had been crowded back

here *before* Takahiro, me, Mongo, and Majid. I settled down—trying to be less heavy is not really very constructive—and Takahiro put his arms around me. Hix and a few of her friends redraped themselves around both of us. I was way more comfortable than I should have been. Briefly. Till Mongo ricocheted off one of the front headrests and ended up in my lap. Bella put her head over his back, and I could feel Jonesie whuffling in one of my ears. Oh well. At least Majid didn't seem to be killing anyone. Yet. Casimir got in the front, and Jill last. I could see the bag of dog food through the gap in the headrests. Bags of dog food can't laugh, can they?

Jill put her hand on the key and then sat back. "Er—where are we going?"

Good question. Suddenly I wasn't comfortable at all.

Casimir turned around so he was looking out past us through the rear of the car—or would have been, if there hadn't been a lot of hairy bodies in the way. "There," said Casimir, pointing.

I looked at him. "What?"

He smiled at me. It was a better smile than it had been earlier, and I felt Taks' arms tighten—just a little. "There are a few small things that my mother gave me," Casimir said.

"That got through the border guards," I said.

"Like sewing your money into the lining of your coat," said Jill. "So maybe the robbers won't notice."

"Good attitude, *manuke*," I said. "I wonder if it's generally known that the Newworld border is as full of holes as this car is full of dog hair." But Jill wasn't listening to me; she was trying to pick up what Casimir knew. Our eyes met. I could see that she was succeeding. And then . . . I began to pull it too, or it to pull me. It was a bit like a loop of *gruuaa* tugging in their insubstantial way. Maybe that's what it was. Jill nodded, turned to face the front again, and started the car. It roared to life as befitted a giant hairy thing with tusks.

"Oh!" I said as Jill backed the Mammoth around in a deliberate, star-pupil-driver-ed way that said she was every bit as frightened as I was. "My algebra book! It had better come with us—"

"I'm sitting on it," said Takahiro.

I relaxed again (sort of). I supposed it really wasn't going to let itself be left behind now. I reached down past Takahiro's skinny butt and gave its spine a pat.

"How close are we going to be able to come?" said Jill conversationally a minute later, negotiating the main street, which was unusually empty—and there had been no soldiers on the corner of Jebali. We were the only car at the midtown stoplight, which never happens except in the middle of the night. Two cars passed in front of us—both of them loaded to the roof with suitcases and boxes. Leaving town. Heading north and west, which was where Mom and Ran would be going soon too. With a car full of suitcases and boxes.

The newsboard banners were empty. There were silverbugs everywhere I looked—clustered in dizzying little clumps on the overhead power lines, glinting on storefront windowsills, and scattered apparently at random on the sidewalks. And ironically every one of the big metal anti-cobey boxes had a crown or swirl of silverbugs. So much for *you*, I thought at them. They didn't reply. Two days ago I wouldn't have expected them to. Today . . . today it was probably just the throb of the armydar making me spacey. I was almost getting *used* to the armydar. This couldn't be good.

My stomach felt funny. I hoped we didn't drive over any silver-bugs.

We went our solitary way across the intersection. "To wherever," said Jill.

"I am not sure," said Casimir at the same time I said, "Probably not very."

Takahiro said, "Even if we could drive up to the front door, we don't want to, do we? It's not like we're coming to the local lockup for official visiting hours."

I was beginning to feel that hazy tug more strongly. The *gruuaa*, I thought, had stabilized their line on Val.

"There's that falling-down army base a few miles out of town in more or less this direction," said Jill. "Out at the edge of the barrens. Goat Creek. Maybe it's not as falling down as it looks."

"There have been rumors for years that it isn't," said Takahiro. "Even that it's completely in use. They're just not saying for what. I've always wondered why—and who—runs the sheep out there, you know? The perimeter fence is from when it was a firing range and special-ops training and stuff, but the fence is still there. And so are a lot of sheep. So like now I'm wondering if they're using them—like we're using our guys here." Mongo was doing one of his I-am-a-spineless-rubber-dog things and had twisted his own head around so he could lick Bella's face as her head rested on his back. Of course there was a lot of face to Bella.

"Dad used to say that it was a conservation thing, the sheep," I said. "Managing wild grassland or something."

Takahiro snorted. "The only stuff that grows on the barrens is what *can* grow on the barrens. They don't need sheep for that. And they had to import some kind of tough little feral sheep that could survive on what does grow there."

Jill glanced in the rear view mirror at Takahiro. "The things you know."

"I have the secret gizmohead insignia tattooed over my heart," said Takahiro.

"Whatever," I said. "This feels like the right direction."

"Good," said Casimir. "You feel it too."

"It's the *gruuaa*," I said. There were a lot of them in the car with us. They seemed to be twisting themselves into a big, irregular, ever-so-slightly glowing net. I could both (kind of) see them draped all over everything in their usual raggedy globs and clusters of shadow, and also (kind of) see them as this big glowing network thing. It seemed to throb in time with the armydar, and with the flash of the streetlights over Mongo's back. Light sometimes did strange dimensional things when it hit the dramatically black and white markings of a border collie. Such as the border collie in my lap at the moment. Flash. Flash.

"Perhaps, when this is over, you will teach me to speak to the *gruuaa*," said Casimir.

I shook my head, but that made the flashing-network thing worse. "I can't teach you anything," I said. "I don't know. It's not really speaking." Flash. Flash.

"But I like the idea there's going to be an after," said Jill.

The landscape changed as we got closer to the Old Barrens. The big lush trees put in by the town council disappeared and the tougher, scrubbier trees of the barrens took their place. The sourleaf grass that the sheep around the old army station had to live on began to show in clumps, especially in breaks in the paving. The farmland was all on the other side of town, toward Copperhill; this side there was only a polite strip of cultivated public land before it began disintegrating into the barrens. At first there were warehouses and big ugly slabs of grey industrial something or other and then they disappeared too. Now we were in the barrens for real. There were occasional sandpits and increasing stretches of scraggy, grey-green sourleaf grass, turning yellow for autumn, and looking kind of ominous in the twilight. We went *click clack* over the abandoned stretch of auxiliary railroad that had served the army base when Station had been a big town and the base had been open. Officially open.

Jill turned the local radio on. Even the usual burbling sounded subdued. There was still nothing to worry about, said the presenter, trying to sound chirpy and failing, but since the schools and many businesses had decided to close temporarily while the army finished securing the situation—

"Situation?" said Jill.

"Securing?" said Takahiro.

—much of the town had decided to take an unscheduled vacation.

"*Vacation?*" Jill, Takahiro, and I all said together.

But if any citizens had any concerns, there was an army presence at the high school, the local Watchguard offices, and city hall, and would be glad to answer any questions.

"Presence?" said Takahiro. "Concerns?"

"Well, at least they all seem to be busy elsewhere," I said. The road was amazingly empty, except for silverbugs. There were way too many silverbugs. We saw one pickup truck with something like a lawn mower in the back and one closed van, which could have had anything at all in it. A small traveling plastic cobey model for educational purposes. Major Blow-it. Val. Probably not Val, since the *gruuaa* didn't react.

Jill turned the radio off.

CHAPTER 12

WE'D BEEN ON THE ROAD ABOUT HALF AN HOUR
when Jill pulled over onto a sandy, gravelly spot that looked like
other cars had stopped there too, but why? I doubted there were
enough people who tried to break into Goat Creek to need a parking space. She turned the car off and we sat there listening to the
ting of cooling metal and the noises of dogs hoping this meant they
were getting out of this jiggle factory soon. She said, "We need a
plan."

Nobody said anything, but both Jill and Casimir turned around
and looked at me. Taks' arms tightened around my waist again,
Hix many-footed up my chest and wrapped herself back around
my neck—and Mongo started wagging his tail, till I grabbed it and
held on. He looked at me reproachfully.

"It's not a very good plan," I said.

"Good would be too much to ask," said Jill. "Although if I
wreck this car I'd better have Arnie to show for it, or I'll be in so
much trouble I probably won't see you again till I'm eighty."

"I don't think wrecking the Ma—the car is part of the plan," I said. "Do you know how much farther to the gate?"

"Nearly two miles," said Casimir at the same moment that Jill said, "Two miles, give or take," and Takahiro said, "About two miles."

"What?" I said. "Have you all been here or something?"

They were looking at each other. "No," said Jill. "It's the picking-up thing I do. More of it lately."

"The wolf knows," said Takahiro. "The rest of me just translates."

"It is one of the little skills my mother sewed into the hem of my coat," said Casimir.

"It's a pity we couldn't have spread all this talent around a little more," I said. "Like one of you could rip chain-link fence apart with your bare hands and somebody else could hypnotize army guys into opening the doors and letting everyone go."

"We'd still have a transportation problem," said Jill, giving Dov's butt a shove back through the gap between the seats. Dov's entire butt didn't anything like fit through that gap, but you could almost see the edges of the seat bowing under the strain. He shifted forward again, had nowhere to go, and collapsed on Bella. Bella sighed.

"And a winged chariot drawn by flying horses in your pocket," I said.

"I'll work on it," said Jill.

"Okay," I said. "Does anyone's radar tell them when the army guys are going to start noticing our car?"

"No," said Casimir. "But not yet. There is little to make an unremarkable car—"

"Unremarkable!" said Jill.

"Their scans will not care that it is large and full of animals," amended Casimir. "They will not think it remarkable till it comes too close."

"Okay," said Jill. "Less far to walk." She started the car again. "Keep talking," she said over her shoulder.

"Don't hit any sheep," I said.

"That this road is being left to go to pieces is bogus," said Takahiro. "There've been a lot of vehicles over it recently."

"Wolf?" I said.

"Wolf," he agreed.

"Do you always know this stuff?"

Takahiro hesitated. "I'm not sure. It's not usually very relevant. Mostly I try to ignore it. It's harder to ignore when I've been wolf lately."

I was starting to feel seasick as the car jolted over the increasingly bumpy road past the perimeter fence—despite the fact that the armydar pressure dropped off abruptly and there were fewer silverbugs. Which told you something, although I wasn't sure what. I should have felt better, not worse. But it wasn't the road, it was the plan. It was bad enough that I was putting my human friends in danger. I was putting the critters in danger too, whose only crime had been a willingness to trust me and get in the car. But we were going to need the distraction—just as Taks had needed them for a different kind of distraction.

"It depends on if I *have* figured out how to talk to the *gruuaa*," I said. "Or . . ." I pulled a little on the glowing network in my mind, and there was a kind of chirrup, as inaudible as the *gruuaa* were insubstantial, in reply.

"Okay," said Jill. "Then what?"

I was watching the network. There was a shimmer, like Hix's wiggle only more so—and it was getting stronger, or I was getting more able to pick it out. Something, like the way Whilp's name had, drifted across my mind. The shimmer was Val, I guessed. Val surrounded by a lot of *gruuaa*. Now if only I knew what was left and right out here in the real world. "Hey, can you stop again? A minute," I said, staring at the *gruuaa* web.

The Mammoth stopped. "What—" began Jill.

"Wait," I said.

There was silence, except for a lot of breathing. The eleven of us weren't breathing anything like together or to any kind of pattern, but as I stared at the invisible glowing web the breathing began to make sort of *chords* with the subtle pulse of the network. It was something like what the passing wash of streetlights did to a black and white border collie's fur, which was creepily a little like the checkerboard of a mass of silverbugs.

. . . Um . . . Hix?

Then there was the worst rubbing-your-tummy-and-patting-the-top-of-your-head-at-the-same-time exercise that you can imagine—with your other arm (what other arm) you're slaying a dragon with a rubber sword, and I think you're probably juggling a hoop around one ankle. Or maybe there's a pogo stick involved. I felt like a piece of origami paper being folded by clumsy hands. . . .

But for a moment something—something distracting and confusing—flickered into *this* world.

"*Sugoi,*" murmured Jill.

"Holy hot electricity," said Takahiro.

"Yeah," I said, and it all snapped off again . . . or slid back where it belonged. I was panting worse than any of the dogs. "Val is being held—somewhere—I *think* off to our right. I hope I'll know better as we get closer. . . ." and I plucked at the web like a guitarist who's lost her A string. Or her magic-loophead-other-world string. "But that disappearing thing the *gruuaa* do . . . it's variable."

"That was *gruuaa*, just now?" said Jill.

"Yes," I said. "So the idea is that while the army guys are all falling out the front door to see what the giant glowing weirdness on their doorstep is, we're, or some of us, are going to be having a look around the side where they're holding Val. And maybe one of you will suddenly discover an ability to melt holes in the sides of buildings by pointing your finger."

"That's your plan," said Jill.

"Yes."

There was a pause. I listened to all the breathing.

"This is probably a good place to leave the car," said Jill eventually. "It might even be here when we get back."

I could have gone upstate with Mom and Ran. . . . But I knew I couldn't. And the *gruuaa* would have prevented me if I'd tried. I held onto that thought, and tried not to think of the ten other people (two- and four-legged) that I'd dragged into my dangerous insanity. The feeling in my stomach was familiar. This was how I felt when I had been the last kid chosen for the volleyball team in seventh grade. Or when I'd seen that *F* on that pre-algebra exam.

We were so squashed up in the back that when Casimir opened our door Mongo and I *spilled* out. Takahiro unfolded himself behind me and stood up straight, like he never did at school, and sniffed the air. *Sniffed the air.* I turned back to the car. Bella was holding them in check, but looking at me hopefully. I groped for leads, and snapped them all on. I didn't want to lose anybody, and things were only going to get more confusing from here. "Okay, you guys. Out."

There was a brief furry river of brown and black and white, and then the dogs were weaving around me (while I tried to avoid being tied in a granny knot by leads) and Majid was standing a little distance away looking around in what was probably lone-conquering-hero mode. I didn't think even the *gruuaa* would have much luck persuading him to be a member of a team.

"We can start off together," I said. The other three humans took four dogs, leaving me with Bella and an off-lead Mongo. I retrieved my algebra book and my knapsack, as if Jill and I had just driven into the school parking lot for a long day of extreme boredom with occasional brief shocks of learning something. I had a flashlight in my knapsack because I was that kind of girl. Tonight it was going to be useful.

Everyone else had shouldered their own knapsacks. Jill and Casimir were getting something out of the trunk, and then I heard Jill locking the car. "Don't want the dog food stolen," she said.

They didn't seem to be running the armydar at all out here, which gave me less excuse to be this confused and blurry-brained. If we did, by some miracle, get Val and Arnie away, they'd probably turn on something even worse. And then we'd need a regiment of grizzly bears to damp it out. Maybe we could just ask the bears to eat anyone who got too close.

The *gruuaa* network was showing me what I guessed was the layout of the army base. Jill had the car flashlight; the boys were following us, although I doubt Takahiro was paying much attention to my feeble little beam. I glanced up at him once, and he was looking up at the sky, and his eyes gleamed golden. Taks' eyes are so dark brown they're almost black. And while you could hear us humans and the dogs crunching through the undergrowth I swear Takahiro made no more noise than the *gruuaa*. I had no idea where Majid was.

I had been thinking that the *gruuaa* network left a lot to be desired as a way of guiding solid people over solid ground as I stumbled in the dark, trying to keep the flashlight beam nearly straight down in case anyone from the base happened to be looking out an ordinary window in this direction. And then simultaneously Takahiro said, "Maggie—" and Bella, walking in front of me, stopped. She had her hackles raised, which made her look almost as big as the huge ugly block of building that had appeared just ahead of us. On the far side of a complicated, clearly unclimbable fence, chain link and barbed wire. The high-voltage-with-extra-lethal-kick sensation beat out at us like wind from a wind tunnel.

I stopped. Takahiro and Jill and Casimir stopped. The rest of the dogs stopped too, most of them with one foot raised and ears stiffly pricked, as if they were expecting interesting and dangerous prey to burst out at them. There seemed to be no windows and no lights on this side. Just the fence. And the punch of extra-muscular voltage.

"Whew," said Takahiro, except it was more like a growl.

We stood there. I waited to feel my pathetic plan disintegrating. But the *gruuaa* web was brighter than ever. "Can you see that?" I said in this insanely calm voice.

"Yes," said Jill, just as insanely calm.

"Good," I said. "You're in charge. Um." Someone—some *gruuaa*—ran down my leg, disappeared in the dark, and then reappeared in Jill's flashlight beam, swarming up her leg. "Oh," she said, slightly less calmly.

"That's Whilp," I said. "Um—"

...She... drifted to me from somewhere.

"She'll help you."

Jill nodded, put her flashlight in her pocket and made the collarbone-patting gesture I knew so well with her free hand. Hix was still around my neck, and there were two or three more *gruuaa* wrapped around various bits of me too, separate from the network, focused uncomfortably on me: anxious, insistent, determined. The real-world wind was cold but I was feeling, if anything, increasingly warm, like bread in a toaster someone has just turned on. Even if Jill and the rest managed to create a diversion, what was I supposed to be doing for them to be diverting *from*? I clutched my algebra book, and I swear it wriggled, like a critter you're holding too tight.

My algebra book.

"Okay," I said, back to the insane calm. "I've just decided this is where we split up. Which way is the front door, do you suppose?"

There was a pause, like they thought this was a rhetorical question, and then Casimir said hesitantly, "That way, I think," and pointed.

"Fine," I said. "You take the dogs, and Jill's got one—at least one—*gruuaa*, as—as translator, because the network is going with you, and you're going to try and create a—a disturbance that they'll want to check out but that turns out just to be some loose dogs, okay? Mongo," I said to my dog, who knew something was up and had reattached himself to my leg, because whatever it was it was up to him to protect me and maybe there would be sandwiches at the end of it, "you go with Jill."

Mongo didn't move. "*Mongo,*" I said, and repeated the go-to-that-person gesture. He knew Jill; he even sometimes obeyed her. He wasn't moving. Jill walked over to me and took Mongo's collar. "Come on, loophead," she said. "The magdag wants us to go save a different part of the universe."

Mongo had never bitten anyone in his life, but he gave a wild despairing whine as she dragged him away. It made my heart rip loose and turn over; I felt like I'd betrayed my best friend. I hoped that wasn't what I'd just done. I took a deep breath and held my algebra book hard enough to hurt. Taks kissed the top of my head and murmured, "*Ganbatte.*" "Do your best." I wanted to cry. I wanted to run home, where Mom's hot chocolate would make it all better. I listened to my friends moving away from me. I took another deep breath, and it hurt worse.

I knelt down and put my algebra book on the ground, propping my flashlight to give me a little light. The *gruuaa* who had stayed with me swarmed down and poured over the book, patting it in their faint, fuzzy-hazy, too-many-footed way. Even all together they wouldn't have been able to heave the cover open. And I didn't want them with me. *Go,* I said, I hoped I said, and did a sort of wave at the network, which did seem to be moving away in a this-world direction similar to Jill's. *Go with them, help them,* I said, I may have said, or I may have said, *Urgly flump duzzy blah,* in *gruuaa* language—or I may have said nothing at all.

There was a brief, even peremptory hum from Hix and a faint sharp explosion against my neck like a butterfly losing its temper. Several of the remaining *gruuaa* scampered away. Something like a *hmmph* from Hix then, which I translated as, *Okay. Your turn.*

I refocused on my algebra book. The cover opened and the pages fanned themselves out. The oddness of the regrown pages seemed to have spread; most of the pages now were that too-flexible, almost-muscular substance with the faint pattern that resembled the decorative paper Jill had given me for Christmas last year. "I'm sorry," I said, and ripped a page out—a page standing straight up from the spine, like a kid in a classroom waving her hand and saying, Me, teacher! Choose me! The page came out easily, like untucking a bookmark, not like tearing a bound page. I held it up in front of me and briefly I saw the shape I needed in a kind of shimmer, like a tiny private aurora borealis.

I laid the algebra-book page on the ground, thinking about Casimir's comment that I'd folded a piece of the cobey. Of course the cobey had come to us; the ground here, so far as I knew, was just ground—unless the inaudible thump of the barrier was doing more than guard. Carefully I took a page corner between my fingers and put the tips of the fingers of my other hand in the center of the page. As the pressure of my fingers made it settle farther into the dead leaves and grass and dirt it seemed to quiver like the skin of an animal. I tugged ever so gently on the corner and of course nothing happened, because paper is paper even when it's weird paper . . .

. . . and at the same time it lengthened, as if it was made of something like an Ace bandage or crepe paper, and my pulling hand . . . disappeared.

I froze. My ordinary hand, clutching the tip of the torn-out paper page, was still there, in front of my kneeling knees, against a background of dirt and slightly crushed autumn grass. But I could feel the *other* hand, the one that had disappeared, also holding the tip of a torn-out page, which, by my feel of it, was almost a hand's breadth farther out in that direction. What do I do? I thought in a panic. Are there now two of me? If I keep folding is all of me going to disappear—or double? Will there be some other me wandering around some other where? Where will *I* be?

I felt Hix unwind from my neck, slip lightly down the arm(s) that was (or were) holding the tip (or tips) of the page and . . . when she got to the place where there were two choices, chose the invisible hand holding the stretched-out corner. Against that hand she was suddenly *solid,* and, having been licked by more animals than I could remember over the years, I immediately recognized the sensation of a tongue on the back of my hand—scratchier than a dog's, less scratchy than a cat's—and kind of *frilly,* like it had extra edges. Is this the *gruuaa* home space? I thought confusedly. I could feel the pads of her tiny feet. They were warm and soft and, I thought, very slightly sticky, like a gecko's feet. They pattered down the length of my forearm and stopped and clung. I was pretty sure there were at least ten of them.

But I still didn't want to go there, or *unravel* brand-new bits of me there, even if some of the natives were friendly. What if I couldn't breathe or something? If the other me can't breathe, will *I* die?

I folded the corner over, and as I creased the edge, my other hand came back from wherever, and there was only one hand and one piece of paper again. I felt a little sick, but that could just be . . . everything. When I took hold of the opposite corner of the page with my other hand, I hesitated and then tugged it gently too. That hand too developed an identical twin, and an invisible corner of that page stretched into *gruuaa* space. I felt Hix move (in the dark, unreliably sort-of lit by my flashlight on my ordinary hands, I couldn't see her, whatever space she was or was not occupying) and then I felt her ruffly tongue on the back of that hand too.

I kept folding. As I did, the other remaining *gruuaa* scrambled up higher, hooking themselves over my shoulders, and reached around with—what? Small slightly sticky feet?—to pat my face and forehead. One of them was humming: a much deeper note than Hix's. There was a faint sweet smell like strawberry jam.

I turned the almost-paper figure over and kept folding. And folding. The figure was beginning to throw off little crinkly gleams along its creased edges—or maybe that was something to do with the narrow beam of the flashlight, and the shadows my fingers made. I turned it off and stuffed it into a knapsack pocket. I took a deep breath. This was better, even if I couldn't see very well. *Because* I couldn't see very well. Last fold went in with an almost-audible tap like the last bang of a hammer against a nail already flush with the wall. I picked the little thing up, pulled its two extended ends, and . . . it *bloomed.*

Both my hands disappeared as they pulled, and the figure boiled over where my hands and wrists ought to be—my heart was thundering like a stampede—let me tell you it is *terrifying* when a piece of you disappears—although I could feel the figure against my invisible skin the way I could feel Hix, and the invisibleness was solid enough to be a darker darkness.

Hix streamed back up one arm and around my neck; the other few *gruuaa* were holding onto my hair and tucking themselves down the back of my collar as if preparing for the worst. This was not helping my state of mind. At least yesterday in the park Casimir had been there too. I wondered, wildly and frantically, as if I was never going to see them again, what the others were doing. I was rapidly losing track of up and down and there and here and sound and silence—and me and not-me or extra-me or super-me. I saw my algebra book flopping, no, clapping its covers open and shut almost like it was applauding; briefly I saw my *baku*, still tucked in against the front cover. I'd only used one page, but there was a huge rent out of the middle.

I shifted my (invisible) grip on my new figure, which seemed to be still unrolling and unrolling and unrolling like an infinitely long reel of some thistledown fabric—a swell of it touched my face and blew back over my head—I clutched at it as if it was real fabric, yanked a billow of it forward, till it caught around my algebra book too—

—And then as the invisible, inaudible, intangible *other thing* began to lift me up out of the world there was a frantic flurry of feet, a *thump*, and a tiny anxious yelp as something only too my-world real slammed into me. "*Mongo!* I told you to—" But the other thing was pulling me away. *No. No. I can't—* I heard the even-more-frantic scrabbling of those feet and a don't-leave-me-behind whine, and I writhed, half in and half out of the world I knew and the world I didn't, grabbed for his collar, wrapped an arm around as much of his body as I could reach—

—And dissolved into not-me. Mongo was gone with everything else. *Mongo,* I thought. *If you've killed yourself because you're too stupid to obey orders—*

I was pretty sure I was crying, if not-me had tear ducts.

Maggie? said a shocked, familiar voice with a thicker-than-usual Orzaskan accent. *Is that you? Don't do it! Go back! It's much too dangerous!*

Shut up, I said. *We're rescuing you.*

Mongo, I thought. *Where are you?* But there was no answer: no not-Mongo not-yelp or not-whine. No not-tail whumping against my not-legs.

I banged into something hard and found myself sprawling—on a rough cold cement floor. My knapsack slammed painfully into my back. Even through my jeans I lost some skin as I skidded across that floor. But at least they were my legs, my jeans, and a cement floor I could understand. There was a shout—a way-too-audible shout—and then confusion, and something big and silvery-grey seemed to bound over me and toward the shouting—and then there was a thud, like a heavy body hitting the floor, and silence.

But as I pushed myself painfully up to a sitting position there was a sense again of something *blooming* against my hands—no, in my arms—pressing against my bruised chest—something furry—

"*Mongo!*" I wrapped my arms around him so tightly I managed to get nearly all of him on my lap as I sat with my legs bent under me on the cement floor of . . .

A tattered little paper thing that had somehow inserted itself under Mongo's collar came loose, and floated to the floor.

Mongo was shivering and panting and making tiny frightened noises—even while he was licking my face he was whining, unhappy little *anh anh anh* noises, and I didn't know what to do: I'd had a hard enough time being not-me, and I could guess that a dog, with no semi-comforting intellectual concept of a division between body and mind, would have found the experience of not-me even worse than I had. But here was Hix, pattering down my shoulder, onto Mongo, winding herself around his neck. She began to hum. Mongo put his head under my arm and I got an arm around his butt. This was about the most uncomfortable position I had ever been in in my life, and I was going to be able to stand it for about a second and a half. But I could feel him beginning to relax. In a weird way he seemed to get *heavier,* as if he was finishing the journey, bringing the rest of himself through to this place.

The billows of non-fabric thinned like cloud wisps and disappeared, and my eyes cleared, and I was looking at half a dog and a very-stretched-out T-shirt that would never fit me again. I began to notice the dusty, shut-in, windowless feel of the air that went with the cement floor. The other *gruuaa* who had tied themselves up in my hair untied themselves and scampered down to the floor . . . to throw themselves ecstatically into whatever the equivalent of "arms" is for *gruuaa*: there were a lot of them already here. I registered their presence, raised my eyes slowly up, and . . . met Val's eyes.

Val. A small mean frightened part of me said, *None of this would have happened without Val.* A slightly larger but just as frightened part of me said, *Yeah, that's right. Especially the part about* not *dying in the park yesterday when the cobey swallowed you.*

Val looked really bad in the fluorescent light. Bad and *stressed.* Well, duh. But there was something about the look on his face. The pro-Val part of me said, *He's worried about you. About* you.

He was trying—again, I guess, helplessly, the way you can't not try, sometimes, even when you know you can't do something—to stand up out of the chair he was chained to. *Chained.* I felt like I was seeing him being tortured. *Chained.* We don't chain people—that was something they did in the Middle Ages, when Charlemagne was caroming around Oldworld knocking the creepy human heads off manticores, and in Newworld the witch doctors ruled. These were big thick heavy chains—like the meanest, toughest bicycle lock you ever saw. Like too big and heavy to carry on a bicycle: your wheel rims would sag like rubber bands.

He couldn't do it and dropped back to his seat. *Clank.* He must have read the expression on my face, because he said, "It's not as bad as it looks." He held up his hands. "It's just to stop the mighty Oldworld magician from turning this place into a garden shed full of rusty tools, with a broken lock on the door."

Still holding onto my dog, who had now pulled one of the knapsack strap ends under my shirt and was chewing on it, still sitting on the very uncomfortable floor of the cell where they were keeping Val *chained,* I said, "Which otherwise you would have done at once, of course."

He started to smile. I don't think he meant to. I smiled back as a way not to start crying again. I had my dog, wasn't that enough? I tried to concentrate on Val's shirt. Most horrors would pale in comparison, but the chains came top here.

"If we get out of this," Val said, "which I very much fear we won't, I am going to find someone to apprentice you to, if I have to smuggle you into Orzaskan."

"I don't think I'd like the big guys in Orzaskan," I said. "Why don't you just apprentice me yourself here?"

He was smiling now as if his face hurt. "Very well. That is what we will do. Unless we discover that Gladonya the Great has emigrated recently too."

Gladonya the Great? No, I didn't want to know. Maybe it was an Orzaskan joke.

"Maggie, no one should be able to do what you just did." Another Commonwealth accent saying that. This could get boring. I wished it would get boring. Anything was better than being this frightened. "But you should not have done it." The smile disappeared and he was completely a stern, responsible grown-up. Who happened to be chained to his chair. "There is nothing you can do here, and it is unlikely you can leave as you came."

However it was, exactly, that we came. I looked to my left, which I thought was more or less the direction we'd arrived from, and there was a big ugly grey cement wall. I could still see some kind of maybe-cobey-like swirling running under the rough cement skin but I could also see that it was getting weaker and fainter. It would be gone completely in another minute. Leaving me here.

I looked back at Val, but he glanced over my shoulder and

so finally did I. There was a gigantic silver-grey wolf—*wolf*—standing over what seemed to be a rather small unconscious man. As I looked, the wolf stepped delicately over the body and sat down beside him, wrapping his tail neatly around his front feet.

Wolf.

I made a little squeaking noise, rather like the noise Mongo had been making when we first arrived here. *Anh. Anh.* I took a deep breath and held it, like you do against hiccups, till I stopped making that noise. "Takahiro?" I said. "Takahiro?"

"I doubt he could have come through your gate in his human form," said Val.

The wolf bowed his head, but continued watching the man. The man looked familiar. . . . I crawled a little way toward him and Takahiro. This was a complicated maneuver, involving, as it did, the knapsack I was still wearing and a large traumatized dog chewing one of its straps while in my lap with his head under my shirt. I did it on two knees, one hand, and Mongo's butt. "Oh, gods' engines," I said, horribly conscious of the huge wolf who was also Takahiro, "that's Paolo. His wife works at Jill's mom's hairdresser's shop. He's the nicest of our local Watchguard."

And now he was unconscious on the floor of some stupid horrible military warehouse thing and Val was in the same room wearing *chains*. And, oh by the way, my dog was having a nervous breakdown and my new boyfriend was in his wolf shape. I could feel a bubble of either tears or hysteria rising in my throat. I scooched Mongo a little farther so I could touch Paolo's face. I could see he was breathing.

"He fainted," said Val behind me. "He stood up from his desk when the—doorway you made opened, and fainted. You cannot blame him," he added as if apologetically.

I didn't blame him. I just wished none of this had happened. Well, duh. When Paolo's wife had brought their two little kids to the shelter to pick out a dog a couple of years ago, I'd helped them choose. I saw them out walking Goldie sometimes.

I couldn't deal. I was a senior in high school. I'd only just passed my driver's test this summer. I'd be eighteen next month. There was no magic in Newworld, and the army were the good guys, keeping us safe.

I had to deal.

I looked at the desk. Maybe the key to the chains was in one of the drawers?

"The key will not be in the desk," said Val.

I turned my head to glare at him. "Don't *do* that," I said. "This is—weird—enough."

"I'm not doing anything," said Val mildly. "It is an obvious thing to be thinking. But I am in chains because they are afraid of my magic, and because they don't understand it they have some poor fellow in here with me, with a panic button to press if he is able to do so before my secret miasma of evil overcomes him. They will not have left the key with him."

"Secret miasma of evil," I said admiringly, but I knew I was stalling. I had no idea what to do next. But whatever it was . . . "Sweetie," I said to Mongo's butt, "do you suppose you might be ready to come out from there?"

I felt a familiar light pressure against the sole of one foot as I sat with my legs now folded under me. I felt behind me for my algebra book, and dragged it as gently as I could around to one side.

It flopped open at once, and presented one rigidly upstanding page, which again pulled free as easily as tearing a page off a memo pad. I looked at the little shred of paper lying on the floor that had fallen away from Mongo's collar. Folding this new page on and around Mongo's back was awkward but it so wanted to be folded I was barely keeping up with it. It was clearly a border collie, head down, tail straight out behind, intent as anything. Border collie *kami*.

I felt around under my T-shirt for Mongo's collar, and tucked it underneath. Then I wrapped both arms around him, put my face in his fur, and waited.

He came out looking embarrassed—gnawing on narrow chewy things like belts, long woolly scarves, shoes, coat sleeves, chair legs and knapsack straps had been one of the things I'd had the hardest time convincing him to *stop* doing, back in the days when he was learning to be a dog rather than a weapon of domestic demolition. He plastered himself belly-down on the floor and looked at me up through his eyelashes, judging how much trouble he was in. I reached out and curled the little paper collie another turn around his collar to make it more secure, and he immediately leaped up, licked my hand, licked my face, and then raced around the room twice while I tried to unfold my legs and find out if I could stand up. Ow. Sort of. When I bent over my algebra book again it flew open and another page presented itself, which I drew out softly.

I stood staring at it a minute. I held it stretched lightly between my two hands. I could vaguely see equations scrawled on it, tangled up in the leaf-vine flower-stem pattern of the ornamental paper. It was like one of those Can You Find? games in kids' magazines. Here was a numeral two, which was also the little nobbly green thing that the petals of a flower unfurl from, and one of the petals of that flower was bent over in a square-root sign. I hadn't noticed the bees before, which were also number eights, or maybe they were infinity signs.

"Maggie—" said Val, who was way too bright for his own good. My own good anyway.

"Shut up," I said. "I mean, please don't talk."

I knelt (stiffly) down on the floor again. The algebra book immediately clunked over to lean against my hip and Mongo stopped cavorting like a loony and threw himself down on my other side. He had at least two *gruuaa* along for the ride: one of them climbed up my leg to tickle my forearm. Carefully I made the first fold. I wasn't sure how many legs this one was going to need. . . . By the time my fingers couldn't find anything left that wanted to be folded I had a thundering headache, and the many-legged, spiky-backed thing in my hands glittered like an oncoming migraine.

I stood up again, not realizing till then that I had developed a billowing, quivering *gruuaa* cape—I could see it, dark and dazzling, skittering out on either side of me. I wondered if Val might be seeing me now as I had seen him, that first night he came to dinner—in my old life, where things (mostly) made sense. I walked over to him and, wordlessly, he held his hands out toward me. There was a lock, unnervingly rather like a bicycle lock except for the little flashing lights that looked creepily like a tiny scowling red-eyed troll face, between his wrists. Now what? Don't think about it. I grabbed one of Val's hands and slapped my paper figure down on the troll face.

There was a brief, queasy, up-is-down-and-down-is-nowhere-and-I-really-hate-nowhere-here-we-are-again moment. There was a kind of whistling gasp, and then Val's hands were holding onto my wrists, and he said, "Maggie!" I blinked, and I was standing in the awful little grey cement room at the back of the Goat Creek Military Base.

"Well done," said Val, smiling faintly.

CHAPTER 13

I LOOKED DOWN (NOW THAT I KNEW WHERE DOWN was again). There, of course, was my algebra book, although it was half-buried in . . . "What?" I said. Whatever it was, it looked a little like the compost heap in Mom's garden and a little like the remains of a fire in a 'tronic factory. "Ex-chains," I said, kneeling to pick up my algebra book. "*Really* ex."

"Really ex," agreed Val, standing up cautiously.

I looked at my book. I had only used three pages, but better than two-thirds of it was gone. The covers were still there, still saying *Enhanced Algebra* in big stupid letters, and there were some pages left inside, but not many. Val was right: we weren't leaving the way I had come in.

Val knelt beside Paolo, who hadn't stirred. "Do you have a torch?"

I set my algebra book down on a clean part of the floor and wiggled out of my knapsack, fending Mongo away from helpless-person-lying-on-floor-*meant*-to-be-licked while I fished for my flashlight. Val finished taking Paolo's pulse and then gently peeled his eyelids back one after the other and shone the light in them, gave the flashlight back to me, and ran his hands lightly over Paolo's skull. Then he rolled him over tenderly in what I recognized as the recovery position from the yearly-once-you-reach-high-school required first-aid class. I'd only ever done any of this stuff on my classmates and even with them cooperating wrestling someone else's body into any position was difficult. I wondered if there had been a lot of unconscious people in Val's life in Orzaskan since it didn't seem to faze him at all. "I guess he hit his head when he fell," said Val. "But what I can easily check is all normal." I went around to the chair behind the desk. There was a cushion on the seat, and a jacket over the back of it.

Val slid the cushion under Paolo's head and I knelt to put the jacket over him. One of the things they taught us in first aid is that unconscious people can sometimes hear you. I awkwardly patted Paolo's shoulder and said, "It's me, Maggie. I'm sorry you hurt your head. I hope you're okay." I looked up at the wall opposite the desk. There was no trace of the gateway my little origami figure had opened.

Then Val and Takahiro and I turned toward the door. "We can't just leave," I said, and Val laughed. "Indeed, I doubt it," he said.

"No," I said, glaring at him. "Not like that. Well, worse," I added reluctantly. "We also have to rescue Arnie."

"Arnie?"

"Jill's mom's partner. He owns Porter's—the hardware store."

"Ironmongery," said Val thoughtfully. "He is here too?"

"Well," I said uncomfortably. "I hope so. You were."

"Ah," said Val. He put his hand on the doorknob. I held my breath. He turned it.

The door opened. I let my breath out.

Hix was around my neck again, but the rest of the *gruuaa* skittered out in front of us, turned right, and raced down the corridor like some bizarre tide. The corridor was only dimly lit and the *gruuaa* might almost have been black water, their leading edge ragged like it was pouring over pebbles, and occasionally splashing up the walls like they were piers. Val, Takahiro the wolf and I followed, me holding Mongo's collar with one hand and my much thinner algebra book (it still wouldn't fit in my knapsack) in the other arm. We passed two doors on one side and one on the other, but the *gruuaa* were still on the trail, so we followed. At last they piled up in front of a fourth door.

We stopped too. "I will go first," said Val quietly.

"You will not," I said, annoyed. "The minute anyone sees you, they'll know something has gone wrong."

"I feel that a seventeen-year-old girl in torn and bloody jeans will be just as easily recognized as not a standard member of staff," said Val.

The army probably wasn't into denim blood chic, no. I let go of Mongo and put my hand on the door and threw it open, planning to do some kind of heroic first thing, but Takahiro beat me to it: he was through the door in a flash. There was a kind of grunt like the noise you make when the breath is knocked out of you and a sort of strangled scream, and someone, probably the screamer, said, "Gods' holy engines. Gods' *exploding* holy engines."

I was through the door too before they'd finished saying it—a hundred-and-sixty-pound wolf is pretty worrying close up, and I didn't want anyone doing anything radical. But Val nearly dislocated my shoulder when he grabbed me and jerked me back behind him—and Mongo got between most of our legs and we both almost fell down. Someone laughed.

"Arnie," I said.

"Babe," he said. "What are you doing here?"

It hadn't been Arnie who screamed. He was the one who'd laughed. There was another man at another desk against another grey cement wall. This one was conscious, however. Conscious and standing up with his hands above his head like we were holding a gun on him. Sometimes I'm too dumb to live. I blurted out, "*You're* the one with the gun." I could see it on his belt, with a weeny little strap holding it in its holster.

"Oh, man," he said. "I am *so* not going to shoot anyone." But to my horror—and Val's hands tightened, and Takahiro growled—the man lowered one hand and started fumbling with the strap. I hadn't seen Taks crouch for the spring but I grabbed him anyway—Val's hands on my shoulders meant I couldn't reach very far, but I let go Mongo's collar again and grabbed Taks' tail and then I did see him *stop* crouching . . . at about the same moment as the man behind the desk got his gun free and laid it clumsily on the desk. It skidded a little way and stopped, barrel pointing back toward the man, who had both hands over his head again.

"All I wanted was a *job*," said the man despairingly. He didn't look much older than me. "And there aren't many jobs around here, you know? And Paolo told me to try out for Watchguard, silverbugs are no big deal, and you spend most of your time walking little old ladies home anyway. Then there were all those silverbugs last summer, and suddenly we had the military crawling over us. . . . They're reopening this place, Goat Creek, you know? They aren't talking about it, but everyone knows they're doing it."

Not everyone, I thought. Bugsuck.

"I had *two hours'* training about use of a sidearm, okay? It was between how to step on a silverbug and how to fill out a form that you've stepped on a silverbug. I didn't join Watchguard to shoot people. I joined to walk little old ladies home."

"Aren't your arms getting tired?" I said.

He lowered them. "You'll tell your wolf not to eat me, okay?" he said. "That is a wolf, isn't it?"

"Er," I said. "Yes."

He nodded. "You ever been to that wolf rescue place, far side of West Turbine?"

Of course I had. It's got critters. After Clare ended up with a bobcat I wanted her to diversify into wolves too.

"I tried to get a job there but they didn't need anybody. Your wolf is really huge. I've never seen such a huge one. Hey," he said. Mongo was doing his big-friendly-eyes-wagging-tail thing. Mongo wagged his tail harder, went down on his belly, and began to creep in the man's direction. I could have called him back, but I didn't. When Mongo got close enough the man sat down suddenly on the floor and Mongo, immediately ecstatic, sat up, and the man put his arms around him and buried his face in his fur. You *so* don't do that with a strange dog, but Mongo's tail had gone into blur mode and he had found a piece of the man to lick.

Val walked the few steps to the desk slowly but the man didn't move. Val picked up the gun, clicked something, and a lot of bullets fell out into his hand. I wondered some more about what Val's life had been like in Orzaskan.

This time I didn't even have to open my algebra book: there was a page sticking out between the covers. I slid it the rest of the way out, set the book down, and started folding. The *gruuaa* came to help, pitter-patting over my hands, brushing against my face, and, I guess, billowing out into a quivering—I don't know, maybe like the curtain at the back of the stage, only wigglier.

"Whoa," said Arnie. "What *is* that? The shadows?"

"*Gruuaa,*" I said briefly.

"Of course," said Arnie. "I knew that."

Val gave a little snort of laughter. "They're Oldworld creatures," he said.

There was a tiny pause and Arnie said, "You'll be Val."

"*Be quiet,*" I said. "Please."

This one went much faster, and the headache wasn't nearly as bad. It was kind of funny in a not-ha-ha way that lock-picking gave me a worse headache than interdimensional travel. I held up another long spiky thing with a lot of legs and—this time—really almost managed not to think, What if it doesn't work?, slapped it on the lock between Arnie's wrists and—I hadn't heard Val come up behind me, but he grabbed me again when I sagged. The sag wasn't as bad this time either. And then Arnie was free, and there was more weird crumbly stuff on the ground that had been chains.

"Oh, wow," said the man with his arms still around Mongo, but he had lifted his face and was watching us. "Oh, *wow.*"

"We must leave," said Val, as if we'd dropped by for a cup of coffee. "What do you want to do?"

"Run away," said the man immediately. "I suppose they'll sue me or court-martial me or something. You couldn't tie me up, could you? So it doesn't look so much like . . . at least take the dreeping gun, will you?"

Arnie stood up and stretched. "Thanks, babe," he said. "I didn't know you were one of us."

"*Us?*" I said.

"Honey, there are so many of us," he said. "But I've never seen anyone do what you just did."

"*Us?*" I said again.

"Why do you think I run a hardware store?" Arnie said. "It's a good way to confuse the sweeps. You don't think it's all about cobeys, do you?"

"I—" I said. "Well, I *did*. But—hardware? I—er—I mean, the last few days, um, animals—"

"Yeah," said Arnie. "Animals are good too. It kind of depends on what kind you are. Clare's one of us. I should have guessed you were, since you're there all the time."

"I *wasn't* one," I said a little wildly. "Till about three days ago." Years. Centuries. Eons.

"Poor babe," he said. "It's rough when you find out like that. Happened to me about your age too. My mom had tried to tell me it was going to, but I didn't want to hear. But I'm the cold-iron end. Handling a lot of it every day also means I don't blow up fancy technology so much, which is kind of a dead giveaway. You still don't want me using your 'tronics."

"Maybe I could come with you," said the man sitting on the floor with his arms around my dog. Mongo had finished with one side of his face and was now working hard on the other side.

"If you're a friend of Paolo's," I said, "you could see how he's doing. He—er—fainted."

"Oh, man, Paolo," said the man. "Paolo's like my best friend. Even if Watchguard was his idea. I walk his dog sometimes. I babysit his kids."

"What's your name?" I said.

"Jamal," said the man. "Where's Paolo?"

"We'll show you," I said. "We—er—we have to go out that way. I guess."

"Good luck," said Jamal. "If you can blow stuff up, the 'tronics for all the barrier stuff to get out of here are in the front office, on your way out." He stood up, to Mongo's sorrow. Mongo settled for nibbling delicately on his fingers. I was ready to intervene but apparently Jamal knew (crazy herding) dogs well enough to realize this was a sign of affection.

"Thanks," I said.

"The office may be empty," said Jamal. "There's some kind of whiztizz out front. Bill just told me him and Benny were going to go take a look. You guys weren't supposed to be here at all"— he nodded at Arnie and Val—"but there've been like three more cobeys open up on the deep line and they haven't got the human-power to cover everything. So they were blasting on with opening Goat Creek up because this was going to be the big central what- ever, and they were sending in some kind of shielded truck to take you away but it got sent to one of the cobeys instead." He shrugged.

I looked at him. He looked nervously back at me. "I know you had your hands over your head and everything," I said. "I don't think you were exactly bluffing. But why aren't you more afraid of us? And why are you telling us how to get out?"

Jamal's eyes slid away from mine. "Oh . . . well," he said. "My mom . . ."

Arnie laughed. "I told you, babe. There are so many of us."

I heard myself saying, "If there are so *many* of—if there are so many, why are only you and Val here?"

"Huh," he said, and opened the door. Takahiro tactfully retreated behind me and Jamal went out first. "I'm worried about Clare," Arnie said. "But most of us are pretty half-volt. Little 'uns. Not me, although I'm stiff as a seized brake. Not your stepdad. Not you. Not you either, whoever you are," he added, looking at Takahiro.

We all followed Jamal out the door, including Mongo and the *gruuaa* flood, I for one feeling bewildered and rather silly. The corridor was still grey and empty. "There," I said as we went past the room where Paolo was, and Jamal opened the door and went softly in. "Oh, man," he said.

"I'll lock you in, shall I?" said Val.

"Oh yeah, thanks," said Jamal's voice from behind the door.

Val's hand lingered on the knob before he closed it. "If you need to get out," he said, "the charm will break from your side."

"Thanks," said Jamal's voice.

We went on. The *gruuaa* were still rolling on in front of us but as we went farther down the corridor it was like they were hitting some kind of shoal, and getting humped back toward us.

The corridor suddenly widened, and the ceiling got a lot farther away. From feeling like we were walking into an ambush I felt like we'd just walked out onto the open battlefield and the guys with the cannon and the air-to-rescue-party missiles would blow us away in a minute.

We were maybe all breathing a little hard as we approached a big open door on the left. The corridor was badly lit all along its length, but there was a lot of bright flickering light shining out through that door. It didn't look friendly. Well, it wasn't likely to *be* friendly, was it?

"Wait here," said Arnie. "Let me scope it out. And I'll leave Jamal's gun under someone's desk."

I began to notice that there was some kind of confused noise going on—I thought outside the building. Some kind of whizztizz, Jamal had said. Maybe Jill and Casimir and the *gruuaa* had found a way to make my non-plan work after all. We were about twenty feet from the end of the corridor, which was barricaded by a gigantic pair of double doors, like they sometimes used this end of the corridor as a garage for their cobey-unit trucks. But I was mostly thinking about Jill and Casimir and Bella and Jonesie and the others. The sick feeling in my stomach, which had mostly gone away while we were talking to Jamal, was coming back, and had brought friends. Uggh.

The light flickered in a different pattern. There were some pinging and popping noises and the double doors cracked open. Not enough to let me squeeze out, let alone Val or Arnie, who was Val-width and a good head taller.

But the crack let the noise rush in. There was crashing like an army getting lost in a lot of undergrowth, and there was shouting like an army getting mad about getting lost in a lot of undergrowth, and there were revving engine noises like army trucks having trouble bashing their way through a lot of undergrowth—and there was one voice shouting all by itself like whoever it was was really mad at someone else for doing something stupid—like maybe getting locked out of their own compound?

And there was barking.

There was Bella's deep bay, and Bella was not a barker. I'd heard her bark maybe once before—but the noise a wolfhound makes is pretty memorable. There was Jonesie's no-nonsense not-completely-ex-fighting-dog bark and then Dov's mess-with-me-at-your-peril warning bark. *No,* I thought. Don't do it. Those guys have guns. The *gruuaa* can't protect you from bullets. My sick feeling was getting a lot worse.

Val said, "Wait here," and followed Arnie through the office door.

Mongo and Taks and I went to the front door and peered out cautiously. It was strangely hard to breathe; it was like there was a giant hand pressing against my chest. I had my own hand on Mongo's collar. I wasn't sure what the *gruuaa* who had been with us were doing; in the weak shifting light I couldn't tell them from the real shadows. Maybe they were swirling out to join their friends in the field. I tried to look for the *gruuaa*-network thing that I'd hoped Jill and Casimir could use—but that had been when we'd been assuming the army guys we had to deal with were inside the buildings, not outside. It was just supposed to look weird. It wasn't supposed to have to stop anybody.

Yes. There it was. It was all mixed up in the undergrowth that the army guys were having trouble with. And I was pretty sure there were more *gruuaa* weaving themselves into it now—the ones that had been with us, presumably. Somehow my stomach didn't feel any better.

I jumped back as the doors jerked open a little farther, dragging Mongo with me. I was just thinking, It's dark out there, and the corridor lights are really showing up that the door is opening—when the corridor lights went out. Then there was the mother and father of all BANGS and the office lights went out too—but at the same time an alarm went off, *WOOP WOOP WOOP WOOP WOOP,* the loudest thing you ever heard, and a bunch of emergency lights burst on outside as the front doors ground slowly about three-quarters open.

We could get out. But so could the bad guys get in. Or see us trying to get out. And there were a lot of bad guys out there. There was certainly something going on besides picking up two prisoners. I could see three trucks branded with the cobey logo from where I had flattened myself against the corridor wall.

I couldn't hear anything through the alarm, but I could see the two guys with rifles running toward us.

Then three things happened simultaneously. The guys with rifles stopped like they'd run into a wall of something like extra-strength plastic wrap—invisible in the murky twilight and slightly springy—and I found that I was breathing and blinking and moving more easily.

Not quite invisible. As I stared at it I could see spiky, too-many-leggy, wiggly, faintly sparkling shadows. But there were new . . . strands, like skinny wires, that the leggy-wiggly things seemed to be winding themselves into. Were these what Arnie and Val were doing in the office? I didn't think the *gruuaa* alone would have that rubbery strength.

I took a deep breath . . .

. . . As a familiar furry shadow that turned mahogany-brown under the emergency lights leaped out from somewhere, raced toward us, and . . . sat down in the middle of the doorway between the three-quarters-open doors.

Majid stuck out a hind leg, examined it carefully, and began to wash.

The lights and siren began doing complicated dropping-out things. The alarm would miss a WOOP and then a light would go out. Then that light would come back on and another light would go out. The alarm would WOOP twice and miss again. Under other circumstances it might have been kind of interesting. Or it might just have made you crazy.

WOOP. Flash. Dazzle. WOOP.

It was hard to see through the plastic wrap. Everything looked kind of swimmy, like looking into a scummy pond. It was pretty manic back there though. In the silences I began to hear voices:
"That's—"

"—*and* all the dogs—"

"—*monsters*—"

"—damn cat—"

"—shelter—"

"Of course I'm gods'-engines sure!"

Jonesie gave one last sharp bark and subsided—I hoped that meant some human had told him to shut up. And that that meant that the critters and the humans—*our* critters and *our* humans— were okay and *together.* Except, of course, for the one enjoying the spotlight while he went on with his left hind leg.

Majid glanced back at me, as if he knew I was thinking about him. He did that a lot at the shelter. You'd think, Now what we particularly *don't* need right now is Majid—and there he'd be. The shadows around him in the doorway moved. Some of them were *gruuaa.* Majid turned his attention to his right hind leg.

Val and Arnie were using him for some kind of focus. Now I could feel sharp little splinters of whatever-it-was glancing off him, sliding toward me.

If you didn't know Majid, you might think he was only a cat.

Only a cat would have run away.

I hoped Casimir and Jill and the dogs were running away as hard as they could.

WOOP. BANG. WOOP. I thought they sounded like they were getting tired—the woops and bangs. Like when we got out of here—*when*—maybe the army guys wouldn't be able to turn them back on again.

I'd've almost said that Majid was having trouble holding his leg up at that angle. A perfectly normal cat-washing-leg angle.

There were at least three different voices. Maybe four or five. I could hear them through the plastic wrap.

"—evil spirit!"

"Get real, it's a cat. An unholy big cat."

"—*twice?*"

"We don't have evil spirits. This is Newworld, you moron."

"Then what about those shadowy things? The ones that aren't dogs."

"They *are* dogs. They're just—"

"—cobey. The rules change with a big one. You know there's a fourth one over at—"

"—a fifth at Nofield—"

"Yeah, it's why we're so short-handed. Why they're sending everyone who's left here. But it's still only—"

"—not. Where are Paolo and Jamal?"

"Five—when's the last time we had five?"

"—this unit twenty years, never—"

"My dad said that Genecor didn't get everyone—"

The plastic wrap caved so suddenly the guys with rifles all staggered forward. I could see the quality of the light change as whatever it was fell apart. The road seemed to have disappeared; there were saplings down all over the place, and brush—and three big army trucks parked at funny angles. But there were seven or eight guys with rifles now, facing us. No, ten. And one of them was shivering, and his eyes were so wide and crazy I could see them from where I was, hiding in the shadow behind the door.

The siren stopped.

About half the lights went out. Not the ones on the open doors. Not the ones shining on Majid.

I thought I saw a lot of shadows, spilled on the ground, racing outward. Some flung themselves into the suddenly flimsy-looking heaps of brush and scrub. Some of them shot off to the right, as if following someone. Some of them joggled and slithered back toward Majid and the door.

"—evil spirit if you like." This was the shouting, authoritative voice I'd heard first. "I don't dreeping care. We need to get back in there since Paolo and Jamal are too dumb to live. So go ahead and shoot it if it makes you happy. Or anything else you see. It's just a couple of illegal magicians. We'd be doing ourselves a favor. If they've got out, then they're dangerous, you know?"

What?

Several more riflemen came trotting forward. They were lined up now like a firing squad.

No way out.

The crazy guy's rifle came down and pointed at Majid and the doors the fastest. . . .

But werewolf reflexes are a lot faster than human ones. Takahiro had already bounded forward and was in midair over Majid's head, his silver-white fur shining like the moon in the lights, when several rifles fired. I should have dropped to the floor, but I'm not used to being shot at. I watched in horror as several bullets missed and caromed with tiny evil screaming noises against the corridor walls behind me—and then our Hounds of the Baskervilles unit burst out of somewhere and knocked several of the riflemen over. I'd never seen Bella snarl before. Jonesie bit someone and threw him down like a dog toy. It took me a minute to realize that they were draped with *gruuaa*—and that the soldiers couldn't see them properly. Monsters. Shadowy things that weren't dogs. I could barely see dark brown Dov, but I saw where he'd been when more soldiers behind the riflemen fell down, yelling and kicking. More confusion.

More bullets *wheeeeeeeed* gruesomely past me, and a few thudded into the walls—but at least two of them struck.

Not Majid. Not me. Takahiro. Majid bushed out his fur till he was as big as Dov and *ran*—and Val and Arnie picked me up, one under each armpit, and ran like fury. The Baskerville unit turned and flung themselves back into the fray—Mongo was beside me—no—he turned *back—Mongo!* But I saw—I thought I saw Mongo *ram* Takahiro as the next volley came past. That volley missed.

But there were too many of them, and some of them were looking at us. More riflemen were lining up. I just saw Takahiro stop and rear up on his hind legs, the blood *pouring* down his neck and chest, his eyes more dazzling-bright than the emergency lights, more beautiful than a dragon or a unicorn out of a fairy tale. I swear he got bigger and bigger till he was as tall as a tree, and his shining curved fangs were as long as swords, and then Val and Arnie were dragging me through grass and little saplings, and I realized I was hoarse with screaming Takahiro's name.

We stumbled into Jill and Casimir—and the rest of the dogs. Jonesie was the last of the dogs to rejoin us: in the light there was something dark on his teeth—it might have been blood. Blood. *So much blood. His white fur red-black with blood.* When Arnie dropped my other arm, I felt Mongo's head thrust itself under that hand, but I was still screaming. Val wrapped his arms around me and shoved my head down on his shoulder. "Listen to me," he said into my ear. "Takahiro is a *werewolf.* He is not dead. *He is not dead.* He has covered for us long enough to let us run away. You must run, Maggie. Don't waste what he's done for us."

Another shot rang out. I heard it slice through one of the little trees near us.

I screamed again because I couldn't help it, but I also nodded, and Val let me go, and we ran, or anyway we stumbled. Val had taken my knapsack. Val and Arnie seemed to know which way we were going. There were still shots shrieking past us, but I almost didn't notice. I followed Val blindly—he looked back for me every step or two, and sometimes I felt his hand under my arm again, but all I could see or think about was the blood on Takahiro's chest. So much blood. So much blood . . . Vaguely I knew the story that ordinary bullets couldn't kill a werewolf—Val should know, he knew real werewolves. Or would he have said that just to make me keep going? If Taks wasn't dead, why wasn't he catching up with us? We weren't going that fast—there was a little part of my brain that wasn't thinking about Takahiro, but about the bullets, the bullets that were still chasing us, faster than a werewolf, much faster than I could run, half-paralyzed with shock. . . . Even if the bullets didn't kill him, they must hurt. So much blood . . .

Sssssss whump. Whump.

I don't know how long we kept going till we stopped for a rest. I didn't think I'd heard any bullets in a while. Jill was now the one hanging back with me, putting her hand under my arm when I staggered. I was exhausted, but Taks . . . where was Takahiro?

I'd dropped my algebra book when they shot Takahiro. It had saved my life and rescued Val and Arnie and I'd left it behind.

It hadn't rescued Takahiro.

I think we didn't exactly stop. I think I fell to my knees and couldn't go any farther, and everyone else stopped too. I heard Val and Arnie talking in low voices: ". . . puzzled them for a while; I can make nav 'tronic go wrong easy as breathing, and your *gruuaa* are still on the job."

"We're still leaving a trail of magic the *gruuaa* can't begin to abolish, nor the six dogs either and one large cat, and when Takahiro rejoins us it will be much, much worse."

When Takahiro rejoins us. I took a deep breath.

"Takes an awful lot of critters to damp me, even when I haven't just been taking out army headquarters," said Arnie. "Not much we can do about it. Keep going. I can carry Mags a while. She's not all that much bigger than when I used to give her and Jill piggyback rides."

I wanted to protest this but I was too tired. Jill was crouched beside me with her arm around me. I think she was pretending we weren't listening. I hadn't noticed my face was wet with tears. I thought it had been that way for a while. Mongo was lying next to me with his head in my lap, worrying, wanting something to do to make me feel better. I took his head in my hands. "Mongo, my love," I said. "If you ever, ever felt like taking the initiative in your life, now is the time. We need all the critters we can get."

I stood up and took the Dog Commanding Posture. Mongo sat up eagerly. "*Away,*" I said, and threw my arm out in the go-get-those-balky-alpacas-at-the-bottom-of-their-field-*now* gesture. The one that said, and don't let them give you any nonsense either. Alpacas are notorious for giving herding dogs nonsense.

Mongo disappeared. I looked at Jill. Jill looked at me and gave me a tiny worried smile.

We joined the others. "I can walk a while longer," I said. "I'm sorry, I'm just a little tired."

"You have every right to be extremely tired," said Val. "But we must keep moving."

"You start folding up, babe, you let me know," said Arnie. "I bet I remember how to give a good piggyback ride."

It was only a minute or two later when the first rabbit dashed across our path. Bella turned into a blur and snatched it out of the *air*, and brought it to me, unhurt, kicking like sixteen pistons, and obviously terrified out of its mind. I looked around for Val. "Say *yalarinda orfuy la* and then put your hand on its head," he said.

"Uh—*yar*," I said.

"*Yalarinda orfuy la.*"

I got it the second time. Bella was the most patient of dogs, but I didn't want to try her too far. Reluctantly I reached out to touch the frantic bunny. It went limp. I took it from Bella. Its little heart was going five hundred beats a minute, but its ears were relaxed and it snuggled up against me like I was its favorite littermate. Fleas, I thought. "Good *girrrrrl*," I said. Bella was too dignified for mad tail-wagging, but she flattened her ears briefly. She caught the second rabbit too, and the third. We were up to five rabbits— Athena caught one of them, and we put the other three Basker-villes back on lead (Casimir having *amazingly* tucked the leads in his knapsack) rather to their disgust, but nothing was going to escape Jonesie's jaws still breathing, and I didn't know about the other two.

There was a pause after the fifth rabbit, and then the first sheep came hurtling through. Val shouted something—it was *yalarinda* again with something else—and then there was a second sheep, and a third.

And a fourth, fifth, sixth, seventh and eighth. At about that point I lost count.

"I can't hold them long," said Val, sounding pretty strained. "It's not much more than a conjurer's trick, what I'm doing. And I haven't time to teach Maggie to contain something so large."

"Where are they coming from?" said Arnie, sounding kind of amazed. "Are you calling them?"

"No," said Val. "It's Mongo, isn't it?"

"Yes," I said, with a lump in my throat for my very fabulous dog. "I told him to—to herd what he could find toward me."

Casimir said, "A *mgdaga* is resourceful, and has good friends."

About six more sheep went streaming past us in a mob, but this time there was a black and white shadow racing parallel on their flank. He managed to turn them, but rather than dodging past us as you'd expect they plunged into the middle of us, possibly because there were a dozen or so sheep there already. Uproar. Between Val and Mongo nobody got knocked over, although I thought Jonesie was going to have a heart attack. You could see him thinking, *I'd have order in ten seconds. Try me.*

If I'd been a real shepherd, I would have been telling my heroic dog what to do now, but I didn't have the faintest idea. He dropped in behind us, creeping along in classic style, as if he'd been watching the Teach Your Dog Herding videos with me—which he had, of course, but I hadn't realized he'd been paying attention. Also, sheep-herding usually happens in a field in daylight, with sheep that know the drill, and this was patchy scrubland in the dark, with sheep that probably hadn't seen a dog or a shepherd in a couple of generations.

When a sheep began to drift off to one side or another Mongo was on the job instantly. There was one especially large, especially raggedy one that didn't like its present circumstances at all, despite Val's conjurer's trick, and kept trying to make a bolt for it. Mongo wasn't having any of that, and I was afraid if I tried to tell him to let that one go we'd lose the rest of them—Mongo and I hadn't practiced much but the basic *bring them over there to here and stop.*

Val managed to comb a handful of the rebel sheep's wool loose with his fingers, trotting along beside it as it tried to get away from him. It stopped and stamped at Mongo, but Mongo eeled around behind it and it shot forward and bumped into another sheep. *Baaaa,* said the bumped-into sheep. Jill and Bella and Athena were now walking along one side of our weird herd, and Casimir with Jonesie, Dov and Eld on leads were on the other side. Arnie was leading, with four sleeping bunnies down his shirt: two in front and two behind. I doubted the shirt would recover. I was carrying the fifth, wrapped up in the hem of my Mongo-stretched T-shirt.

Val and I were bringing up the rear, Val so he could keep an eye on the sheep. I kept looking over my shoulder. I might have been looking for Mongo, but Mongo was more often to one side than behind us. I was looking for Takahiro.

Val was spinning the wool out roughly between his fingers in a long sort of whorl, longer, longer, longer, and then looping it around in a big circle. I could hear him muttering, but I couldn't

hear what he was saying. I thought there were some extra *gruuaa*
draped over him—to the extent that I could see them in this light I
thought most of them were clustered around Arnie. Val seemed to
get what he wanted, and trotted after the devil sheep again—which
was now trying to barge its way through the middle of the herd,
like someone trying to jump the line. Val worked his way up beside it, pulled his loop over its head and let it fall around its neck.

It stopped barging. It dropped slowly to the back of the herd—
Val was now walking with me at the rear again—and looked
around, rather like someone who's gone into a room and can't
remember why. It gave a forlorn little *baaa*, turned around, saw
Val . . . and trotted happily toward him, clearly *baaa*ing, *Where
have you been? I've been looking for you!*

It sidled up beside him and bumped him lovingly with its
head. Val looked at it sadly. "I am sorry, you ugly creature," he
said. "I have not used my magic in a long time, and I am very out
of practice."

If it hadn't been for Takahiro, I would have laughed.

There were no more bullets, no wicked little singing hums, and
no sense of being followed.

And no Takahiro.

We walked on and on and on and on. I don't know when Jill and
Bella and Athena dropped back again to walk with me, and Val
(and the devil sheep) went up ahead to walk with Arnie. The sheep
(and Jonesie) had settled down, and Mongo was still on watch, and
Casimir still had the other three dogs on leads. I don't remember
when or who told me that Val or Arnie or all the rest of them had

decided that we couldn't stop till we got past the fence around the Goat Creek camp, that while, thanks to Mongo, we weren't leaving a blazing neon trail that said THIS WAY any more—and that thanks to Majid and the *gruuaa* Arnie thought they'd shut down most of the Goat Creek base's 'tronics—Val and Arnie thought they could probably hide us long enough to get some sleep outside the compound, but not inside. I staggered on, thinking about Takahiro. I wanted to lie down and never move again. How many more times had they shot him as we *ran away?* Maybe bullets couldn't kill a werewolf the way they could a human, but *enough* bullets would slow him down enough for them to . . .

Old stuff I hadn't thought about in ages—stuff I hadn't known I remembered—about Taks kept prodding me, sharply, like being stuck with pins. I remembered offering him a bite of my peanut butter sandwich—I'm not sure when, but it was pretty soon after I gave him the crane. He'd never had peanut butter before, and at first he thought I was playing a practical joke on him. (His mom had been pretty traditional. Lots of rice and tofu and adzuki beans.) But then I'd thought my first taste of wasabi was a really mean practical joke, although Taks had warned me to take only the littlest bit of little and a really big mouthful of rice. . . .

I remembered him and Jeremy and Gianni deciding when they were fourteen that *Sworddaughter,* everyone's favorite TV series when we were all eleven and twelve, was only for babies who couldn't see how old and pathetic it was. I'd been mad at him for months after that. I remembered him telling me that hating Mr. Denham was dumb—I had just failed another pre-algebra quiz. *That's because* I'm *dumb!* I screamed at him, and ran away before he saw me burst into tears, because then I'd have to hate him too. I remembered winning first place in the summer reading challenge, the summer between ninth and tenth grades, and he was the only one of the people I thought were my friends who didn't congratulate me, because he was in one of his moods. I'd been really *proud* of that award. I'd read twenty-three books over that summer, including some really long ones, like *David Copperfield* (good) and *Anna Karenina* (what a bunch of dead batteries).

I remembered him sitting at the table in our kitchen, wearing Val's bathrobe and following me with his eyes.

I remembered kissing him. . . .

I was crying again. I seemed to be crying all the time. We'd been walking forever. I'd been crying forever. My head and my bones had ached forever.

Taks, where are you? You'd have caught up with us if you could.

A couple of times we paused for a handful each of chocolate and peanuts and a swallow of water. I didn't know where any of it came from: maybe Val had made them out of mushrooms and dead leaves, like Cinderella's godmother raids the vegetable patch for transportation. I love chocolate, but this chocolate tasted of nothing. I didn't think anything would ever taste of anything again if Takahiro didn't come back.

The fence, finally. It looked like any old stupid mean fence: plain chain link with a roll of barbed wire at the top. Not like the fence I'd stood staring at, clutching my algebra book, when Takahiro had kissed the top of my head, said, *"Ganbatte,"* and pretended to go with Jill and Casimir. A million years ago.

"I don't suppose any of you thought to bring wire cutters?" said Arnie. Jill, Casimir, and I all shook our heads. Casimir was carrying my knapsack now: he'd managed to tie mine down over his somehow. It was the sort of plain practical thing I could never do, like I couldn't do algebra. Casimir still moved like a panther too, even in the middle of the night on bad ground with army riflemen behind us, and a big lumpy heavy awkward bundle of knapsacks on his back.

I felt as if I was still carrying my knapsack, and it was full of bricks. I missed my algebra book.

I missed Takahiro worse.

"Hey," said Arnie. "You still got those bullets?"

Val pulled them out of his pocket and held them out.

Arnie picked one up and looked at it. "You think *you're* rusty, son," he said to Val. "This may be gonna rain on the Fifth of July." He closed his hands over it and blew, like you do before you roll dice, to make them lucky for you. Then he threw it at the fence, picked up the next bullet, blew, threw, picked up the next. . . . The bullets shone like bumblebees with the sun on them, black-and-gold-striped, even though it was full dark, and there were stars overhead and only a quarter moon. They buzzed rather like bumblebees too, and when they struck the fence, the wire they struck turned all gold. Arnie threw bullets till Val's hand was empty, and when he was done there was a big almost-rectangle, about the size of a bedroom window, gleaming gold. He rubbed his hands on his pants and then stepped forward, hooked his fingers through some of the gold-edged holes, and pulled.

The whole golden panel fell out. "Ouch," he said, and dropped it. "Hot." It *sizzled* as it landed, and then turned black, like chain link that has been in a fire. He put his foot on the bottom edge of the hole in the fence and shoved it down a bit more so we could climb through easily. Val was moving among the sheep, touching them one after another, murmuring words . . . and they were trotting away. Mongo pressed up against me, watching. I curled my fingers through his collar, to make sure he understood that this was okay. The little broken cog that still hung there rubbed against my skin. It was good to be normal when you could. But sometimes you couldn't afford normal. "You're wonderful," I said to him. I remembered him shoving Takahiro out of the way of one of the bullet storms. But Takahiro still hadn't caught up with us.

Arnie knelt, and peeled up his shirt . . . and four sleepy bunnies tumbled out, thought about it a moment, righted themselves, and hopped away. Jill, who had taken bunny duty over from me, set down the fifth, and it hopped after the others. Mongo, visibly tired for perhaps the first time in his entire life, sat down with a gigantic sigh, his tongue hanging out. I meant to sit down, but I pretty much fell, and Mongo immediately curled up against me, and I put my arms around him. "The best dog in the universe," I said, and he licked my face. (Mongo would never be too tired to lick someone's face.) I wondered how Jamal and Paolo were.

I wondered where Takahiro was.

I woke up enough to climb through the fence—completely cold now, although the edges of the hole were crumbly, like burned string—and then Arnie was carrying me piggyback after all. Somebody's belt was holding me loosely against him while he held my legs. I wanted to tell him to put me down, but I was too tired. I kept seeing a shining silver wolf with blood rivering down his body. "Taks," I murmured. "Takahiro."

"Hey, hon," said Arnie. "Just a little farther."

He let me down gently, finally, with my head on my knapsack as a pillow. Some pillow. I had pulled myself up on my elbows to see if there was something I could do about the fact that apparently someone had filled up my harmless knapsack with blunt knives and old broken bits of storm drain when Jill knelt beside me with a wet plastic bottle. "We only had one bottle of water," she said. "This is Goat Creek, but the guys say it's safe to drink." I drank most of it, not having been aware of being thirsty. It made me aware that I was hungry, but I didn't care. Nobody died of hunger on the first day anyway.

Takahiro . . .

I wasn't going to be able to sleep with my head on pieces of broken drain. But here was Mongo, settling down against my chest, and someone else—Athena—at my back. I could hear everyone else making themselves as comfortable as they could.

Takahiro . . .

But I was warm now. And I was so tired even the jagged chunks of whatever weren't going to keep me awake.

I don't know how long I had slept when I sensed something looming over me. I didn't have time to be frightened, because Mongo was awake, and I felt his tail thumping, and heard his little moan of welcome. Athena gave a squeak of surprise or courtesy, got up, and lay down again next to Mongo. And then something huge and warm and furry was lying down behind me. A head bent over me, and a tongue about the size of our kitchen table licked my face. I threw myself over on my other side to face him. *"Takahiro."*

As I turned around I felt something falling over, away from the leg it had been leaning against. I sat up long enough to reach down and pick up my algebra book. I had a crick in my neck already that was so painful my head would probably never stand properly upright on the end of my neck again. The algebra book couldn't possibly make it any worse. I put it under my knobbly knapsack and lay down again, facing Takahiro. Mongo laid his head in the little soft place between my last rib and my pelvis, and I wrapped an arm around as much of Taks' ruff as I could reach. Sleeping with my boyfriend, I thought, and almost laughed. We'd only kissed for the first time yesterday.

CHAPTER 14

I WOKE UP SURPRISINGLY WARM AND COMFORT-able and . . . peaceful. I thought I could smell coffee. And I had the oddest sensation that Mom was nearby. I had a vague recollection that something really dreadful had been happening, but I shied away from remembering and concentrated on feeling—safe? What was that about? Why did I want to think about being *safe*? But I shied away from whatever it was again.

That *was* coffee I was smelling. I didn't mean to speak out loud—and spoil everything—but the feeling that Mom was standing by my bed holding a mug of coffee was so strong: "Mom?" Except this wasn't my bed I was lying on.

Something, or rather someone, stirred. And I snapped back into reality. The reality of lying on cold hard bumpy ground with a pillow made of corners. The reality of being curled up against someone's chest. Um. Someone's *naked* chest. Takahiro was human again. Oh . . .

I raised my head cautiously. Takahiro's eyes were blinking open.

He saw me and smiled. There was something like a blanket draped over us but I was still, um, rather intensely aware of the full length of Takahiro's body pressed against mine, although I was still in all my (filthy) clothes from the day before. I had one hand curled up under my chin and the other over Taks' shoulder. I went to touch his chest and . . . *oh.* I didn't mean to move away from him, and I didn't move very far, but far enough to see what my hand was touching: he had the most *awful* scar: three ugly, grotesque starbursts of raggedly healed flesh: one just above his left nipple, one just below his sternum, and one over his right ribs. "Oh, *Taks* . . ."

"Yeah," he said. "I guess I have a problem, next time the doc tells me to take my shirt off to listen to my chest."

I stroked the starburst over his heart and realized I'd started to cry. "Oh, hey," he said, "don't cry. I'm fine—*genki desu.*" He started to struggle up to one elbow, and winced. "Well, almost fine. It still kind of hurts, but only a little. Really. And Mongo is the best. If he hadn't got me out of the way of that second . . . Hey. Maggie. Please don't cry."

I gulped and nodded and gulped again and got the hiccups. How dreeping romantic is that. He patted me on the back and said, "We're alive, we're fine, we're free, and you're a hero."

"*You're* a hero," I said, still staring at his chest.

"*Jā,* okay, we're both heroes," said Takahiro. "And Mongo. Live heroes. Those are the best kind."

There was the crunch of approaching feet. I looked up. Even having (mostly) remembered where we were and (some of) what was happening and that (presumably) we weren't safe yet and there were (probably) some very-pissed-off cobey units chasing us, I was still expecting it to be Mom. It wasn't. It was Val. But he was carrying two big plastic cups of steaming coffee.

He sat down beside us, and as we both sat up I realized it wasn't a real blanket over us, it was one of those crinkly plastic emergency blankets over two sweatshirts and a jacket. Both of us were moving cautiously for our different reasons, but my algebra book had been good for the crick in my neck, or maybe that was having Taks back. I almost started to cry again as I said to Val, "Look—"

Val was already looking. "Hurt?"

Takahiro gave a half nod. "A little."

"Even for a werewolf that is a great deal of damage. You are very brave. And very foolish."

Takahiro raised one shoulder in a careful shrug. "There wasn't like a lot of time to think. And Mongo helped. It got us out of there. All of us."

"It did indeed," said Val. "I thank you. All of us thank you."

"*So desu,*" said Takahiro. "S'okay. You'd've done the same." And he grinned.

Val laughed. "I would perhaps like to think so."

I drank half a pint of coffee in one gulp. I could feel my brain trying to plug itself back into its sockets. I was probably imagining the short-circuit noises and the burning smell. "Val, Mom's not here, is she? I know. It's crazy. I just keep feeling as if she's right behind me or something."

Val nodded, and this dopey smile spread over his face. They've been married two months, I told myself, trying not to think about my boyfriend's naked body one sweatshirt and a plastic blanket away from me. Taks shifted a little so he could sit up better. He picked up his coffee with one hand, and his free hand settled itself to hang over my shoulder. "She and her sisters have given us their protection," said Val.

"Protection?" I said, looking around. We were in a kind of glade with the sun striking through the leaves. There wasn't anything to see but trees, but I was pretty sure I could hear traffic noises not too far away. I had no idea what was out this way, beyond Goat Creek and the barrens. There were roads out here? With cars and stuff on them? It was like coming to the end of the world and discovering a shopping mall.

"*Sindurak*," said Val. "A—something like what the *gruuaa*—and the dogs—do, only more complete. Less flexible, less adaptable, but if we stay here, where they have cast it, we are effectively invisible. They are coming for us."

"*Coming* for us?"

Val nodded, and his smile got sharper, and he suddenly looked like someone I wouldn't want mad at me. "There has been, in the last eighteen hours, the most unholy row in this end of Newworld, and your three aunts, who seem to be curiously placed to cause maximum official havoc, have been doing so."

"Blanchefleur?" I said. "Blanchefleur too?"

"Yes," said Val. "All four sisters. While your aunts make generals weep and cause nervous breakdowns in senior civil servants, your mother is chiefly responsible for our protection—that is why you feel her presence so strongly."

Takahiro's stomach gave a growl like a whole pack of wolves, and Val said, "The rest of the story can wait. It will take Elaine a little while to arrive and meanwhile Casimir has brought us all breakfast.

"Takahiro, you will find most of your clothes—the ones, I gather, you managed to get out of before you 'changed—"

"I'm learning," said Taks. "I did get out of most of them first. But I was in kind of a hurry."

"Yes, I ascertained that," said Val. He stood up. Not like an old guy who had just spent a really uncomfortable night on the ground. Some day—soon—I was going to ask him about all the weird stuff his old life had taught him. "You did extremely well," said Val. "Most of your clothes are intact, and there beside you. Maggie, if you will come with me, and leave him to his ablutions." But instead of standing there glaring at me till I shrugged off my naked boyfriend and meekly got up and followed him, my not-so-wicked stepfather, two months married, turned his back and strolled slowly away, and Taks and I threw ourselves at each other and kissed as if our entire lives had been leading to this moment. Maybe they had. It was the most gorgeous thing that had ever, ever, ever happened to me and it was—terrifying. It was probably just as well that Val—still not turning around—paused and called, as if idly, "Maggie."

I kissed Takahiro's mouth one last time—I kissed the starburst over his nipple one last time—and tore myself away. When I caught up with Val he was smiling.

"Bacon," I said disbelievingly. "I smell *bacon*."

Val and I had come through a little grove and there was an insanely tidy campfire with a very bent grate that looked like it had once been a shelf in a refrigerator propped up over it, and half a dozen bacon rashers, and four slices of bread-becoming-toast lying on it. There was also what looked like a bucket with a plank across it sitting cozily at, or in, the edge of the fire, but that smelled like a coffeepot. Casimir was carefully and neatly turning the bacon over with another stick with a sharpened end. He was being watched by six dogs and one cat, but Arnie, eating an apple, was watching them and—possibly excepting Majid—I'd bet on Arnie. There was even a (large, mostly empty) bag of dog food being held closed by a small pile of firewood.

Casimir looked up and smiled his smile, and I immediately remembered that I was unbelievably filthy and tear-stained and disgusting, and I didn't want to think about what my hair looked like—and at the same time, with my mouth full of Takahiro and my body still burning with the touch of his hands, I wasn't too bothered. I smiled back.

Jill held out a paper plate and Casimir slid the toast and bacon onto it. There was also butter, jam, and a plastic knife. "Oh my," I said between mouthfuls. "*Sugoi.* Oh *wow.*" Casimir had already loaded up his grate again. Takahiro would take a lot of feeding. Mongo changed sides and lay down at my feet, giving me the full force of the big-puppy eyes. Not a hope, friend, I thought at him.

Jill settled down next to me and said, "*Daijōbu ka?* You okay?"

I thought about Taks' mouth on mine and a kind of explosive thrill went through me. I could feel my (uncombed) hair standing on end and the lightning zapping out of my eyes. It made my hand shake, and I nearly hit myself in the face with my slice of (heavily buttered and jammed) toast. Not quite. I bit it off and chewed. "Yeah," I said. "Pretty much."

Jill was smiling at me. I looked at Casimir and back at her and her smile got ever so slightly wider. "He's a lot better-looking than Eddie," I said very quietly. "He is, isn't he?" said Jill, just as quietly.

"So," I said in a normal voice. "What happened to you?"

They'd left me alone by the barrier as I'd asked them to but, Jill said, they hadn't gone two steps when Takahiro started stripping out of his clothes. "I didn't have a clue," Jill said, "but Caz figured it out instantly and was like whipping his socks off and I'm all whoa, I'm fine for skinny-dipping but where's the lake, but then Taks started growing fur and I finally got it." She paused and an expression I couldn't read crossed her face. "It's, um, pretty weird, watching," she said. "Caz said he'd never actually *seen* anyone change before, but it didn't seem to faze him any. I was pretty fazed."

I nodded. I didn't know but I could maybe guess. I hadn't seen much when Taks'd changed back to human out in Val's shed, but it had been disturbing. Whatever had happened last night after Taks-as-wolf caught up with us finally . . . I guess I slept right through.

But as Taks finished the change into wolf the dogs freaked and that's when Jill lost her grip on Mongo's collar—but she saw the two of them stampeding back toward where they'd left me. "It had gone all foggy where you were," she said. "And not a good fog. Like what the armydar might look like if you could see it. I . . . hoped for the best. Since there wasn't anything else I *could* do. The *gruuaa* network had other plans for me, you know?

"Caz really calmly, like he does this all the time for his were-wolf friends, folded up Taks' clothing and put it in his knapsack—

even his shoes, which are *gigantic.* When they're on Taks' feet you don't realize they're the size of backhoe buckets. Then Caz said that magic always takes longer than you think it's taking and we probably had some time. Did you see him poking around in the trunk of the Mammoth? Arnie is obsessive about some weird stuff—although I guess I'll never think about *weird* in the same way again—so all our vehicles have rope, matches, a first-aid kit, water purification tablets, a little hatchet, and an emergency blanket as well as a flashlight and extra fuel cells in the well with the spare tire. Caz had already put the rest of this in his knapsack and I'd been standing there thinking either this boy is totally anal or I'm a dead battery. I guess we know which it is.

"So after Taks and Mongo went back to join you—we hoped—the rest of us kept on toward what you'd thought was the front of the building. I'd been having this really *squashing* sense of doom, but it's been *so* bad the last few days I'm like, so? Big ugly sense of doom with a side of fries and an extra-large coffee, you know? I was also kind of distracted by Whilp, who was so totally trying to talk to me and I had no idea what she was saying. And then Caz says like idly, When will they get here? and I heard myself answering just as idly, About an hour, and then I stopped and looked at him—What? Sorry, he said, that's something else my mom taught me, and I know you're picking them up better than I am. Picking *what* up, I said. The army, he said. They're coming, aren't they?

"And then something like straightened out in my head and I thought, Yeah. They're coming. A *lot* of them are coming—I mean, a lot? For just Val and Arnie? Why a lot? What?

"I don't know, Caz said, but if we've got an hour we can prepare a welcome for them. Do you want the hatchet or my penknife? and he pulled this folding knife out of his pocket. I took the hatchet since I've split way too much kindling in my life—"

In spite of the circumstances I grinned. Arnie, Jill's mom and her four brothers all loved camping. Jill did not love camping. Occasionally she got to stay home with me.

"—and we started dropping brush across the track, and Caz untwisted the rope to make more rope and started weaving it through the brush—and muttering while he did it. I didn't ask him what he was muttering, but it wasn't English, and his mom taught him kind of a lot, didn't she? Sometimes it seemed to me that the rope kind of wriggled for a while after he let go of it.

"The *gruuaa* network you sent with us—they were all over what we were doing. It's a good thing Caz was so calm and focused because I kept kind of losing it—I'd start worrying about what was going on with you guys and I'd jerk myself back to what I was doing, preferably before there was any serious blood loss, and I'd discover that the jiggly woven thing that Caz and the *gruuaa* were making had gone way more complicated since the last time I looked. Then pieces of Caz started *disappearing* as the *gruuaa* moved around. It made me really dizzy, and Caz took the hatchet away and gave me some of his untwisted rope strands instead, and that worked because the *gruuaa* showed me where to wind them through.

"That's—that's when Whilp finally figured out how to tell me about hooking—pinning—I don't know what to call it—some of the *gruuaa* around us and the dogs. I'd let the dogs off lead when we were dragging the brush around—I didn't like the idea of them being helpless if something went wrong, you know? And Whilp needed me to help, uh . . . it wasn't just guarding, it was *invisibling*, like what was happening to Caz. Like Taks in the school yard yesterday, only more so."

"Wow," I said admiringly. "I don't know about invisibling."

"But stuff did happen faster than we were ready for . . ." Jill's eyes got huge and we stared at each other, and I knew we were both remembering wolf-Takahiro with the blood streaming down his chest.

Takahiro appeared through the trees and for a moment the world stopped as I looked at him. He didn't look like a boy who thought he was too tall any more. He looked like a hero. A live hero. The best kind. He looked back at me and smiled. That hot distracting thrill ran through me again.

Casimir was turning more bacon. "This is not ready yet, and I gave the last to Maggie. There are apples, and potatoes in the ashes, which might be done by now."

"You are a miracle, son," said Arnie, eating another apple.

"I serve the *mgdaga*," said Casimir calmly.

Ugh. "Where did all the food come from?" I said through another mouthful, and before anyone said anything about what Casimir had just said. Takahiro was rolling out black wrinkly-skinned potatoes with what I guessed was Casimir's jackknife and his fingers. "Ow," he said, and sucked his fingers. Werewolves when human still burn their fingers. He finished rolling them onto another paper plate, picked up a couple of apples too, and settled down beside me to eat.

"Caz," said Jill smugly. "He's the only one of us who saw *any* of this coming—"

"I saw *none* of it," said Casimir, glancing up from his fire and looking for the first time not merely drop-dead gorgeous but also young, young like Jill and Taks and I were young, and vulnerable, and *not* knowing a lot—but then knowing a lot hadn't done Val and Arnie much good. I suddenly wondered what it had really cost Mom to let us all go last night—and had to stop myself from looking over my shoulder again, to check she wasn't standing right there watching us. She felt so close I almost reached up to stroke the air, having got kind of accustomed to stroking invisible companions recently.

I hadn't noticed when Hix reclaimed my neck as her personal space, but I could feel her there now, and there were trailing *gru-uaa* ends more or less visible over both my shoulders and Taks', and a faint sweet smell in spite of the bacon. I noticed a shadow curled up on Jill's knee. She had a hand near that knee and was wiggling a couple of fingers in a petting sort of way. I grinned again. Whilp.

"But you saw that something was," said Jill. "The rest of us were all, oh, it's a cobey, it's several cobeys, who cares about deep lines, that's what the army is for—and you got all your money out of the bank and bought a first-aid kit and two emergency blankets and some chocolate and peanuts and a water bottle with a safe-water thingy and matches and kindling starter.

"So we all had blankets last night, you know?" she said to me, and the Casimir smile came and went on her face, and I was counting: the blanket from the car, that's one, and I was guessing Arnie and Val would have shared one, which left one for Casimir and Jill. "And this morning he was up before any of the rest of us and got the fire started, and then left it with Val while he went foraging."

"That was only sensible," said Casimir. "No one is searching for me."

"And by the time he got back—the second time, with the dog food—your mom had done her security-lockdown trick and . . . here we are."

I lied. When I thought none of the others was looking I gave Mongo half my last slice of bacon. Taks got through his first plateful in approximately one gulp, and his second almost that fast . . . his third . . . I began to lose count. "Maybe you should finish off the dog food," I said.

"Ha ha ha," he said.

Jill said, "She'll be here soon."

I think we all heard a car turning out of the general traffic noise and coming toward us, and then stopping. Nobody else moved as Val got up and went toward the sound of the hand brake going on. I had a chance to think, What in all the worlds is she *driving*? as I tucked my hand through Takahiro's arm—he was eating another apple with his other hand—and then there was a *bang* like a storm-drain cover being dropped, which was maybe the driver's door closing.

They came back pretty quickly, and Mom could have been a little flushed from the general circumstances, although they had their arms around each other's waists. I got up and ran to her, and I would have managed not to cry—I think—except that she started crying, and then I had to cry too to keep her company.

She was driving the biggest double pickup van thing you have ever seen in your life: the kind of truck that really wanted to be a stretch limo except it's on these like bulldozer wheels, and it had two seats like an ordinary four-door car and then an ordinary pickup cap over about two-thirds of the gigantic rear, like trying to put double-bed sheets on a king-sized bed. We were all going ooh and aah in a stunned kind of way—a lot had happened in the last twenty-four hours but the Super-Plus Mammothmobile was still startling—and Mom said, "It belongs to one of Gwenda's clients, of course. We didn't know how many of you there were but I remembered what you looked like leaving last night" —and her voice got all wobbly and she gave a gigantic sniff before she went on—"and Gwenda got on the phone to some construction boss whose daughter she'd defended, and this, this *thing*," she said, gesturing at it, "was delivered to our door about an hour later. It's like driving a *house* but we'd asked for large.

"Arnie," she said, "I've talked to Danielle"—Jill's mom—"and she's going to meet us at Haven. And the same construction boss sent his daughter and another driver down to Goat Creek to pick up the car Jill was driving last night. The army seemed to think it belonged to an escaped detainee and had impounded it, but the daughter convinced them that it was one of her dad's fleet of vehicles and is bringing it back. She said to tell you it wasn't a big deal, that the division at Goat Creek is still pretty confused."

"There are so many of us," said Arnie.

Casimir laughed.

There were quite a few of us to fit in even Mom's Super-Mammoth . . . especially when it turned out, to Val's horror, to include an ugly, raggedy sheep, which had somehow climbed through that hole in the Goat Creek fence and Mom's safety net. Mom, who was maybe feeling a little light-headed, laughed and laughed. "I am sorry," said Val about three dozen times. "I used a spell I only imperfectly remembered—"

"—and that *worked*," Jill said, "under pretty ghastly circumstances. Shut up, Val—I mean, sorry, Mr. Crudon, but shut *up*. We're all here, we're all alive, we're all *great*."

So because Mom said and Val very reluctantly agreed that if the spell was that strong it might injure the sheep to break it by leaving it behind, Arnie and Casimir blocked off a little of Super-Mammoth's gigantic rear so if any of the other animals noticed that one of their number was *prey* we'd have enough warning to stop and sort things out. The sheep, I guess demented with love, didn't object to this at all. Casimir somehow found time to pull up some grass for it, and it lay down and munched its grass and then chewed its cud like hanging out with dogs (and a small swirly-striped tiger, who, to my enormous amazement and relief, jumped into the Super-Mammoth with the rest of the livestock) was something it always did. Maybe it thought other sheep were boring and that it had finally found its spiritual home.

We were on the road for hours—hours and hours—but I was still so tired I slept through most of it, tangled up with Takahiro (and quite a few *gruuaa* and my algebra book), while Jill and Caz curled up from the other end of the luxuriously long back seat of Super-Mammoth, and the three grown-ups sat in front. Since we left the window to the rear open, there were critter heads sticking through and looking for opportunities most of the time, but there wasn't really space even for Majid at his most spaghetti-like between Casimir's back and Taks' long legs. So I'm not sure how I got squashed in with Mongo too, but I did. It's very hard to do submission well when you've wedged yourself in like a doorstop under a door, but when I opened my eyes long enough to discover Mongo jammed up under my chin and against my chest, he tried. I couldn't laugh either, my ribs didn't have room, but Hix patted my face as if she got the joke.

But Taks and I were mostly *out,* like hibernating bears, and the critters must have behaved themselves because no one woke me up to be Critter Master. We stopped at a highway service area at least twice. I remember Mom trying to get me to eat something. But all I wanted was sleep—and to know that Takahiro was still there. I could hardly bear to be away from him long enough to go to the ladies' to have a pee. Sure, I was a seventeen-year-old girl in love, but last night had been a little too epic.

It was dark again by the time we got to Haven. I recognized the smell of the pine trees in my sleep and for a moment I was four years old again and coming here for the first time, and frightened, and wishing I was at home in my own bed . . . the fear was too familiar, and for a moment, as I struggled back toward wakefulness, I remembered Dad intensely—remembered him more clearly than I had in years, his face, his laugh, his hazel eyes (that Mom said were *my* hazel eyes), his favorite tie, or the one he claimed was his favorite, because I'd given it to him, which had (surprise) dogs and cats all over it. He had been wearing it the night he died.

I was still tired, tired almost to death, and too much had happened in the last twenty-four hours, the last forty-eight hours. I was someone else than I had been two days ago—before the cobey in the park, before I tried to cradle a timber wolf in my lap, before my algebra book started following me around, before I knew what the sound of bullets fired at *you* sound like—before I'd kissed Takahiro. Before Mom took her magic back so she could protect us. Before . . .

For a moment I couldn't bear it—couldn't bear any of it. Couldn't bear that Dad had died, couldn't bear that he wasn't seeing Ran and me grow up, couldn't bear that he never met Takahiro—or Mongo . . .

But there was so much, recently, that was unbearable. Like that the world was nothing like I'd thought it was. That *I* wasn't what I thought I was. And that what I was might matter in this suddenly strange world.

For a moment it hurt. It hurt a lot, like it had right after Dad had died, when the world that Mom and Ran and I lived in shattered into millions of sharp little pieces, and we were walking around on the slivers, so every step cut into us, and all we saw around us was empty and broken. When we found out that people die when they shouldn't. That stuff happens, and sometimes it happens to you.

That the world was nothing like I'd thought it was.

It hurt like bullets ripping into my chest, or like being head-onned by some bugsucking assface at eighty miles an hour. For a moment it hurt so much I thought it would kill me. But—maybe because of the last two days, maybe because I was tired almost to death—I couldn't refuse to let it in either, like I'd been refusing for almost eight years.

At first I held on, held on hard, like the hurt and the grief and the fear were a piece of paper I was trying to fold, like I had to fold them up to make the cobey that was trying to eat me go away. But I couldn't fold them up, any more than I could fold *gruuaa*. I realized, hanging in my half-sleep and half-despair, that Hix was patting my face and humming again, and her sweet smell was stronger, like she was blowing it over me, like your mom tucks an extra blanket around you if it turns chilly. Mongo shifted fractionally (fractionally was all that was possible) and I had a familiar cold wet nose buried in the too-small gap between my neck and the curve of my collarbone. Taks, still asleep, let his arm slip down a little farther when Mongo moved, and tucked his hand between my belt and the waistband of my jeans, like making sure I couldn't escape without his noticing.

Now. This was what now was.

Mongo was snoring.

Slowly, painfully, I let go. It was like prying my own fingers off the edge of the cliff. And that hurt too—particularly the falling part, and not being sure what was at the bottom.

But I did know. *Now* was what was at the bottom. I was already there. With Mom and Ran and Mongo. And Jill and Takahiro. And cobeys, and the fact that the world(s) were so much different than I thought.

There are so many of us.

Arnie. And Casimir.

Hix. All the *gruuaa*.

And Val.

I woke up taking the deepest breath I'd maybe taken in eight years (in spite of Mongo). The car had stopped, and the front doors were opening. Jill murmured something, and then her door opened. I felt around for a door latch and just about managed not to fall out when I found it and our door opened too. Even Mongo looked a little stiff as he poured himself out onto the ground. I reached down for my algebra book: it was nearly full up with pages again. I patted it, but I patted it clumsily, and managed to get my hand caught between the top cover and the first page . . . and had the really odd feeling that it briefly *held* my hand, like some dogs will do, gently, with their mouths, as a way of saying hi. I stuffed it under my arm and slid out of the car. Takahiro followed me, yawning and stumbling like any sleepy boy, not like a hero or a werewolf. He put an arm around me and I leaned against him. The algebra book, of course, was in the way.

I finished waking up faster than I might've when my brother hit me like one of his own racing cars. Ran and I hadn't *hugged* each other in years—he wouldn't even let Mom hug him—but we hugged each other now till I think we left bruises, and then he let me go and stood there a moment like he wasn't sure what to do next. Eventually he said, "Hey, there's coffee and food indoors. Hey," he added to Taks, seemingly no more than mildly surprised at Taks' arm having replaced itself around me. And then left at a trot like he was leaving the scene of a crime.

The front door of Haven was open, just like it had been when I was four, and Mom had had to hold me up because I was too sleepy and too frightened to stand on my own. I thought I remembered that the light had spilled down the steps to the driveway like a golden river that long-ago night too, but this time it looked warm and welcoming, and I was standing on my own feet and (more or less) awake. I slid my hand under Taks' arm—he'd grabbed my algebra book with his other hand when Ran had thudded into me. Gwenda was coming down the steps at a very undignified speed, and hugged me almost as hard as Ran had. "My amazing niece," she said. "I *knew* your mom was wrong about you." There were two more figures on the steps up to the house. One of them was Rhonwyn. I was guessing the other was Blanchefleur: I was going to meet her at last.

Gwenda went on holding my hand for a moment when she let go of me, and there was a little buzzy sensation against my palm, like when Mom had kissed me before she let us go after Val. Like the human version of Hix tickling my neck. I was still thinking about this when Gwenda moved away from Taks and me to address all of us, like we were a jury she wanted to sway in an unpopular direction. "We are so glad you are here. We have an enormous amount to talk about—and then to do. Our world is changing—has already changed—whether any of us likes it or not—whether those who decide Newworld policy like it or not, whether General Kleinzweig likes it or not. For now you are safe here. For now. And we will *make* it safe for you in this new future that has begun." She held out her hands in a gesture that might have been threatening or it might have peacemaking or it might have been both, and I saw Gwenda, the courtroom crocodile, shine through my aunt in a way that was both scary and comforting.

"But we also need your help. We need your help urgently!" She laughed a little, and it was a real laugh, but it was also determined and impatient.

Rhonwyn and Blanchefleur, if it was Blanchefleur, had come down the steps as Gwenda was talking and Rhonwyn came up beside Gwenda and put an arm around her shoulders, but less like a hug and more like grabbing your over-enthusiastic dog before he scares off your visitors. "Gwen," she said. "Let them come in and sit down. They've had a long day."

I realized Jill was standing beside me, and Casimir looking uncertain on her other side. I took her hand with my free hand. She smiled at me and then reached out and grabbed Casimir's hand and drew him to stand next to her. He glanced across the other three of us and smiled—shyly, his dimple barely showing. "Welcome to Newworld," I said, mostly to him, but really to the four of us. The grown-ups would have their ideas, but we'd have ours too. "Welcome to the *new* Newworld. It's going to be . . ." and I paused. None of the words I could think of really fitted, and "insane" would probably be bad for morale. Mongo was sitting on my feet, Hix was humming in my ear, and I could see *gruuaa* wrapped around both Taks and Jill and—there was one or three scampering up the golden river toward Haven's open door. If my knowledge of ordinary critter body language was anything to go by, they were happy and excited. I looked up, and found Blanchefleur looking at me. She had to be Blanchefleur, she looked so much like the other three sisters. She smiled. I smiled back.

I looked around for Mom—and Val. They were standing with their arms around each other (of course). I smiled at them too. Mom's smile was one of the things I loved best in the whole world. My eyes moved to Val. There was, I thought, some irony in his smile—but maybe I couldn't see him clearly where they were standing at the edge of the light. Not seeing clearly was a good thing with that shirt. Although jail, escape over the barrens, and a night sleeping on the ground had subdued it somewhat. *I'm your apprentice now, you know,* I thought at him. *In the new Newworld.*

"Interesting," said Takahiro. "It's going to be interesting."